Foundling
by John Eklofe

Chapter 1

- You go here again! You vile bastard! - a stone flashed in the air and hit Ned in the shoulder blade. It hurts, it hurts, but most importantly, because of this, he stumbled and dropped the stinking puddle left by the cow, his entire lunch. He's dinner. He's breakfast. He's ... in general, all the food he was given for the whole day - a crumb of bread, an onion, a couple of hard-boiled eggs and a pinch of salt. The knot, made from a piece of old linen, was wet and soaked with a brown liquid.

"Everything - you can forget about bread!" - Ned thought bitterly - "At least the boiled eggs are intact, and that's okay!" And then he almost groaned in disappointment - a foot in an elegant boot stepped on the bundle, crushing it into a cake.

"And I didn't regret new boots!" Ned thought, looking up at Sally's smiling face. And as it often happened - his breathing was interrupted when he looked into this beautiful face framed by golden curls. Sally was lovely. So beautiful that he could not speak normally in front of her, stuttered and blushed, becoming a complete idiot.

She laughed with a melodious laugh, like the ringing of bells and derisively asked:

- What did you have there, Foundling? Hidden treasures? Or the poison that you decided to sprinkle on our cows?

"That was my lunch," he remarked bitterly, "and now I'll be hungry all day.

- Oh-oh - mockingly held out the girl, and screwing up her eyes angrily, she said - you don't need to be fed at all! Bad creature!

- How did I not please you? - Trying to speak calmly, Ned replied, keeping an eye on a group of five guys walking around him from the side.

- You?! You ... you ... you vile offspring of the Ards! You killed my brother! You robbed, you killed! Beasts! Hateful critters! - the girl choked with hatred, and with a swing hit Ned in the face. He only closed his eyes, and when he opened, the guys were already too close.

The first blow fell in the ear, which caused it to ring and go deaf. The second - in the eye, so that sparks fell and colored circles appeared.

Ned didn't resist. For his age, the guy was quite large and tall, but he was constantly aware of his worthlessness, driven into his head from childhood. His "family" - those people who took in and fed the Foundling - kept saying that he had to atone for the guilt of his ancestors, that he was insignificant, worthless, suitable only for grazing cows and doing dirty work. You stupid goof!

He was not dumb. But tell me if you please - who will be highly developed if no one has taught him anything before - except how to deal with household chores. And this would not be taught, but otherwise he will not be able to do his dirty work.

These seventeen years of life would be hell for anyone who knew another life. Ned - knew no other life. A cage in the barn where he lived, next to the cattle, wake up at dawn, housework - bring water, milk goats, cows. And when he grew up, he began to graze a public herd. His family received money for that, he also worked for food, and for not getting beatings - once again.

No - that is how he got slapped on the head, all the time, but is it really a whipping? Thrashing is when you cannot sit up and lie down from the pain in the body excised by the belt. His adoptive father did not like him. They did not have their own children - the gods did not give, and they had to "bring up" someone else's, and even someone! Arda. A pirate, a robber, a bastard of a hated tribe that has kept the entire coast in fear for a long time.

Seventeen years ago, an Ard ship crashed on the rocks near the Black Ravine village. The entire crew of this ship perished, whipped by the violent waves against the sharp reefs, and only by some miracle did a child survive, an infant whom the waves threw on a rocky shore.

On the morning after the disaster, the villagers gathered on the shore to see what happened to the ship and to profit from the remnants of its cargo, which had not been eaten by the voracious sea, and then someone found a baby goggling blue eyes at the world. He did not cry, but only made quiet sounds, as if muttering something under his breath in an unknown language.

Ned never cried at all. Even if the "father" whipped him with a rawhide belt, leaving red stripes with protruding blood drops on his body. Nor did he cry when the local kids caught him and beat him with mortal combat.

Children are small animals that, entering into life, win their place under the sun like all animals - with teeth and fangs. And if a creature weaker than them comes across on their way, they will certainly assert themselves, wiping their feet on it. So they wiped it off. Fortunately, there were no hindrances to this. If Ned tried to resist, the parents of the beaten children sliked his father and complained, after which Ned could not sit on his whipped ass for a week. After all, he has no right to harm the children of the Sansa tribe, the people that his fellow tribesmen have been robbing for many centuries.

Sometimes, climbing into his nook and lying in the pitch darkness, Ned listened to the clatter of cow hooves and dreamed that someday a ship with ards, his fellow tribesmen, would come and take him out of here, take him far over the sea, to where he would always have a piece of bread and no one will kick him in the rib at dawn. His understanding was enough to understand - this is all fantasy. This is all nonsense. Not real. The real one - here it is - a litter, a dog, huddled against it and smelling of a wet, warm dog. The only creature that loved him. Except for the cows, of course. And the old slave Silan.

Ned grew up. From a little man, he waved a hefty fellow two santas tall, and the more he became, the more the villagers did not like him.

It would seem - well, what did he do to them? And what does the arda have to do with the little man who miraculously escaped the storm waves? But the son of the wolf is the wolf himself. If he grows up, he will cut, beat, kill! Isn't it time to beat him up until he got into someone's house and raped his daughter, killed his wife, burned down the house - after all, the Ards are all like that - bandits, robbers, pirates. And this one will be a robber.

If not for the fact that his "father" needed an employee - Ned might have been killed long ago. However - when he began to graze a public flock - the voices demanding his death quieted down - who wants to wander the hills all day, watching the rebellious herd, in the rain and wind, without rest and holidays.

Only the children, who became teenagers from children, and then boys and girls, did not calm down, but did not change their rule - to poison this idiot Foundling, who so cheerfully flees away, without trying to give back. And these were not only the children of the free - Ned got a lot from the children of the slaves - even they were higher on the social ladder.

Why were they so angry? Who knows ... perhaps in their blood at the genetic level was laid - ard - the enemy! Kill Arda! Ard - danger, death, fear!

A dog that has never seen a wolf, even a hunting dog - if you draw a line in front of it with a wolf's paw, the dog will never cross it. He will curl his tail, whine, and throw himself under the feet of the owner. And how are people different from animals? Sometimes it seems - nothing.

Ned dodged the next blow with his fist to meet the knee of the enemy - the guy broke his cheekbone, and now Ned's face will look even more robber than before. He jumped out of the encirclement, rolled over his head and started running as fast as he could, to the hooting of the youth. Someone launched a stone after him, someone put his fingers in his mouth and whistled loudly, but now they could not reach him - Ned was running fast, everyone knew that.

Narda ran alongside, rejoicing - the silly dog thought it was such a game. People push, toss and turn, and then run - why not entertainment?

The herd was already climbing to the top of the hill, knocking down the morning dew. Ned caught up with the straggling cow, shouted loudly, adding a couple of expressions that he heard from "father" - for some reason the cows were better controlled if they were yelled at. He had noticed this a long time ago. The backgammon barked, which caused the cow to step up, squinting at the vicious dog, pretending that it was now biting the lazy mullein by the hind legs, kicked up, trying to hit the noisy dog and trotted to the main herd, driven by a hefty bull named Hurk.

Ned followed, sadly thinking that today he will have to eat what he needs from naughty cows. That was how it was punishable - the cows are not his, what right does he have to suck milk from them? But try, follow when he's in the hills.

And I was terribly hungry. His growing body demanded nutrition, so demanded that sometimes he wanted to howl like a wolf. Ned was thin, wiry like an old elm. His childish body, accustomed to hardship and hard work, strong, growing, demanded food, like a sprout languishing with thirst in a dry season. Alas, there was nothing to pamper the body with.

Ned sighed, and decided that while Narda would hold the cows, preventing them from scattering, he would float into the sea under the Cape of Hope. There shells are wonderful tasty meat. It is a pity that there is no salt, but nothing - there is a shell, there are hands, it will find dry moss, the pot is hidden under a dry oak tree, it will break branches - eh, and hot shell meat will crack!

Ned's mouth filled with saliva, and he spat it on the ground, into the dust, noting to himself that the saliva turned pink. Smashed lips, creatures. So you want to give back, but then what? And then ... then there's nowhere to go. And after he gives a beat to these scoundrels, he will have to not only walk, but run - wherever his eyes look. However - someday it will still happen ...

Sally's face was as beautiful as carved from white stone before Ned's eyes. Last year, when he began to grow up (and especially when he gorged on the belly of shells that gave off delicious white juice!), Sally dreamed of him every time he fell asleep. Beautiful, desirable ... and inaccessible. The headman's daughter, and he, a rootless foundling, is below the lowest, below even the slaves, who felt quite well in their collars and lived in the house, unlike him, the despicable ard. What are his chances of having this woman? It's even funny to think ...

Sometimes he dreamed that one day, a ship would land on the shore, people in shiny steel would come down from it, with sharp swords in their hands, and shout: "Ned! Ned, where are you! We sailed for you! We are your kin! Hurry to us, more quickly! " - and he will run to them, bury his nose in the armor, embracing his broad, mighty shoulders. And they will ask - "Who hurt you here ?!" And then ... then it will be bad. It is bad for everyone who beat him, pursued him, humiliated him. And No will sail away on a ship with striped sails, leaving behind a burning village, which he hated with all his soul. And Sally will be standing next to her, crying, desired. And then ... then he will bring her down, and she will understand that there is no one better than Ned in the world, and will love him.

He once shared his fantasies with the old slave Silan, who laughed for a long time, and then became sad and said:

"Don't tell this to anyone else. They will report to the owner, he will decide that you want to run ... and they will disfigure you so that you can hardly walk, and never think about running away. They'll smash your legs and you'll be a freak. I also once thought that everything would end well in the end, and where am I now? In the same place as fifty years ago. Leave your fantasies and live in the present. You didn't get the best owner, yes. But what can you do? Perhaps this is a punishment for your ancestors, who brought a lot of grief and suffering to this people. For many generations, hatred of your people has been cultivated here. Ards are demons, ards are the scourge of the gods. As soon as spring comes and the winds blow from the sea - wait for the raids of the Ards. Lost ships, plundered villages - that is what ards are. And now - their offspring fell into the hands. And now you atone for the guilt of your ancestors. Alas, life is often unfair. I, too, was once kidnapped by slave owners, brought to the market in the capital, sold, and here I am. No family, no children. Did I deserve it? I think no. But the gods think differently.

- And you never thought about running? Ned asked incredulously.

- Where to run? - the old slave answered sadly - look, how can I mix with the crowd of locals? Even you, if you get a haircut, shave, can pass for a local, and I? Look at me! That's the same ... - and Silan turned his swarthy, almost brown face away from Ned. He was once brought from the neighboring southern continent, and he was sharply different from the fair-haired and red-haired local residents.

- But you could walk through the forests, eat game, try to hire a ship - you yourself said that they always need sailors! Ned kept up.

"I ran twice," Silan answered sadly. They beat me severely, and in the end they knocked out the desire to run. The last time I was beaten so badly that I could not get up for a month. After that, something died in me. But what can I say ... here I am, in general, well fed, I have other slaves under my command, a roof over my head, the owner, one might say, respects me - as a good dog, which is useful, is respected. What more could I want? A woman? I had women. There were no children. Apparently they beat me off everything ... I can't have children. But it's also for the best - to see how your children are sold to other owners, or beaten, and you cannot interfere? This is scary. Until I was ten, I lived free, and I managed to find out what freedom is like. Everywhere there are pluses and minuses - I did not always eat my fill when I was free. And here - I'm full, shod, dressed. Yes, I can't always do what what I want - but did I always do what I want when free? You do not understand? But where do you understand ... you are a slave since infancy. I remember my childhood. Father hunted, mother did the housework. I, foolishly, ran to the seashore, so I caught the eye of the team, who was filling the barrels with water. They beckoned ... and now I am on the ship. Happy, stupid ... okay - that's enough. You don't need it. Go to your room, sleep. Otherwise the owner will get angry and beat him. He doesn't love you. You remind him too much of those who killed his father, right in front of him. Then the Ards made a raid on the village, his father defended his family ... Mother was raped - right above him, he sat under the bed and listened to her screaming. So why should he love you? Sometimes I think he took you on purpose to avenge his murdered father. As if he hopes that you are the son of the one who cut his father's skull with the heavy sword. What do I want? You do not understand? But where do you understand ... you are a slave since infancy. I remember my childhood. Father hunted, mother did the housework. I, foolishly, ran to the seashore, so I caught the eye of the team, who was filling the barrels with water. They beckoned ... and now I am on the ship. Happy, stupid ... okay - that's enough. You don't need it. Go to your room, sleep. Otherwise the owner will get angry and beat him. He doesn't love you. You remind him too much of those who killed his father, right in front of him. Then the Ards made a raid on the village, his father defended his family ... Mother was raped - right above him, he sat under the bed and listened to her screaming. So why should he love you? Sometimes I think he took you on purpose to avenge his murdered father. As if he hopes that you are the son of the one who opened his father's skull with a heavy sword. What do I want? You do not understand? But where do you understand ... you are a slave since infancy. I remember my childhood. Father hunted, mother did the housework. I, foolishly, ran to the seashore, so I caught the eye of the team, who was filling the barrels with water. They beckoned ... and now I am on the ship. Happy, stupid ... okay - that's enough. You don't need it. Go to your room, sleep. Otherwise the owner will get angry and beat him. He doesn't love you. You remind him too much of those who killed his father, right in front of him. Then the Ards made a raid on the village, his father defended his family ... Mother was raped - right above him, he sat under the bed and listened to her screaming. So why should he love you? Sometimes I think he took you on purpose to avenge his murdered father. As if he hopes that you are the son of the one who cut his father's skull with the heavy sword. I fled to the seashore, and so I caught the eye of the team that was filling the barrels with water. They beckoned ... and now I am on the ship. Happy, stupid ... okay - that's enough. You don't need it. Go to your room, sleep. Otherwise the owner will get angry and beat him. He doesn't love you. You remind him too much of those who killed his father, right in front of him. Then the Ards made a raid on the village, his father defended his family ... Mother was raped - right above him, he sat under the bed and listened to her screaming. So why should he love you? Sometimes I think he took you on purpose to avenge his murdered father. As if he hopes that you are the son of the one who cut his father's skull with the heavy sword. I fled to the seashore, so I caught the eye of the team, who was filling the barrels with water. They beckoned ... and now I am on the ship. Happy, stupid ... okay - that's enough. You don't need it. Go to your room, sleep. Otherwise the owner will get angry and beat him. He doesn't love you. You remind him too much of those who killed his father, right in front of him. Then the Ards made a raid on the village, his father defended his family ... Mother was raped - right above him, he sat under the bed and listened to her screaming. So why should he love you? Sometimes I think he took you on purpose to avenge his murdered father. As if he hopes that you are the son of the one who opened his father's skull with a heavy sword. You remind him too much of those who killed his father, right in front of him. Then the Ards made a raid on the village, his father defended his family ...

Mother was raped - right above him, he sat under the bed and listened to her screaming. So why should he love you? Sometimes I think he took you on purpose to avenge his murdered father. As if he hopes that you are the son of the one who opened his father's skull with a heavy sword. You remind him too much of those who killed his father, right in front of him. Then the Ards made a raid on the village, his father defended his family ... Mother was raped - right above him, he sat under the bed and listened to her screaming. So why should he love you? Sometimes I think he took you on purpose to avenge his murdered father. As if he hopes that you are the son of the one who cut his father's skull with the heavy sword.

- Tell us, Silan, who are the Ards? Why are they so hated? And in general - how does the world work?

- Oooh ... sonny - Silan laughed, almost extinguishing the greasy candle smoking on the table - you want to know what no one in the world knows!

Silan's wrinkled face, covered with small scars, wrinkled in a smile, then he spat through his thin teeth into the garbage can, put the chewing mixture behind his cheek, and said with a laugh:

- Nobody knows how the world works. None. I understand what you wanted to ask. It just became funny - how the world works! Okay, listen ... although I don't know how you can use it. We live in the kingdom of Zamar, where King Iunacor now rules. This is the Middle Continent. There is the South, and there is the North. And this is the Middle. Well, full of all sorts of islands. When the creator god threw stones, and of which a firmament was formed, part of it split and islands were formed from them. How many of them - no one knows. And then people appeared, after the creator god created them from pieces of flesh. Other gods were against the creation of people, but he did not listen to them and made great-people. The whole human race went from them. Only now he scattered them on different continents, and gave each tribe its own language, from which other languages came ... and then everything got mixed up, new languages turned out ... and how it happened - no one knows. The demons seem to have mixed everything up. So - the Ards, your relatives, live on the Northern continent. They come to us in spring, late spring, when their ice melts. It is so cold there that the ocean freezes and becomes hard as stone. Ice is called. Did you see mountains in white caps on the horizon? This is ice, it lies on the tops of the mountains, and does not melt, because it is very cold there. So it is very cold among the Ards. It is difficult to live with them, cold, hungry, everything is covered with snow and ice, that's why they try every spring to come to us and take away what we created. We are warm, there is no snow, and therefore everything is growing, everything is multiplying, we have fat herds and good fields - if only there is no drought. But drought rarely happens - after all, the sea is nearby, rains are not uncommon. And they would live comfortably - if not for the Arda. Huge, strong clad in steel armor, they arrive in late spring and take what they want. In addition to the captured valuables, they also take away slaves. Usually they take young, strong and beautiful boys and girls. The girls, of course, are concubines. Young men - into workers. The rest - if they resist - are killed. If they do not resist ... they also sometimes kill. Sometimes not. As you like. And also - they rob merchant ships at sea. Everyone who goes to sea should realize that it is possible not to return. Even if you are a simple fisherman. And also - they rob merchant ships at sea. Everyone who goes to sea should realize that it is possible not to return. Even if you are a simple fisherman. And also - they rob merchant ships at sea. Everyone who goes to sea should realize that it is possible not to return. Even if you are a simple fisherman.

- Tell us about our kingdom! Is this a good kingdom? Are there still such? Why doesn't the king beat the Ards if they come here to plunder?

- What an impatient you are - Silan grinned - you went to your place, huh? Otherwise, if you sleep in the morning, the owner will beat you up. It's getting late - see the red moon already high? And the black moon has already appeared, there, the edge sticks out! And we are all chatting!

- Please, Silan, I'm so interested! Well, tell me, eh? Tell me!

- Okay. But not for long. And then smear your back with ointment ... the owner is waiting to flog you. Iehhh ... a miserable fate. Others live in mansions, and you ... Okay. Listen further. So - our kingdom. It occupies a third of the Middle mainland, and borders on the kingdom of Isfir, where the king is now Sholokar the Third, and beyond Isfir - the kingdom of Harad, where is king Esson. It is said that all the kingdoms used to be one kingdom, but the three brother-princes fought and tore the kingdom of Zamar into three parts. And their descendants now rule that way. I don't know what the names of these brothers were, so you don't have to ask. However - don't we give a damn what their names were? The main thing is what is now, not what is in the distant, gray past. Zamar stretched out for a long time, and we are one and a half thousand li from the capital of Zamar - Genela. To imagine how far it is - if you ride a horse, riding fifty li a day, you will arrive in the capital in thirty days! But fifty a day is still a lot. Usually thirty or forty li, so the journey will take a very long time. On the ship, faster. But you still have to go thirty or thirty to the neighboring city, where there is a port - this is Shusard - pay for a place on the ship there, if at that time there is a ship going to the capital, and then sail on it. And it's very expensive. and then already sail on it. And it's very expensive. and then already sail on it. And it's very expensive.

- Is Shusard a big city?

"Hmm… there will be more of our village, that's for sure. Many people live. There is a port through which merchants transport their goods to our lands. There they unload, buy horses or bulls, and then deliver goods to villages, towns and villages. Probably a big city. To compare - you need to know more precisely. What do I know? Nothing. What I have picked up in fifty years of my life, that's what I'm telling. Many people from our village also serve in Shusard - children, fathers. Some disappeared into the sea along with the ships - this is also attributed to the Ardam. Maybe he really killed Arda, or maybe swallowed up by the greedy sea - who knows? It seems to me that the same ards are credited with more than they actually do.

- And when you killed the owner's father?

- No. I haven't been here yet. And there have been no forays for fifty years, since the father of the current king sent a large army to invade the Northern mainland. Then the ards got hard, and they, like, concluded a non-aggression pact with Isfir. Since then, they have not landed on the coast. But what they do in the sea - here no one knows. As I say, all the disappearances of the courts are attributed to the Ardam. You knocked me out of my mind, I'm already confused - I forgot what I'm talking about! In general - and so - arda - evil. That means the rear. And what else - go to sleep! And you yourself do not sleep, and you do not give me!

- Well, a little more, please! Tell us about the gods! Where did that come from?

- Again? I told you that nobody knows where it all came from. And there are eight gods, main gods. The god-creator Dinas, the goddess-creator Auda - his wife, the god of war Kualtuk, the goddess of love Selera, and the four gods of the elements - water - Pryon, air - Shashan, earth - Gina, fire - Zhadar. And yet - small gods who patronize crafts. They are worshiped by those who are handicraft zarats - the zarath of shoemakers worships their god, merchants - another, and so on. There are many of them, you still can't remember. I don't remember all of them myself. Those who want to receive the blessings of the gods bring offerings to the temple of the god they want to turn to. Sailors carry offerings to Pryon, and also - if they are on a merchant ship - to the merchant god Geres. Naval sailors - Praion and Kualtuk. Well and someone else for example, the goddess of love - so that she would give them attractiveness and women would hang on them. Everywhere in the cities there are temples, and in each there are statues of those gods who are worshiped by their worshipers. The temples in neighboring states and in ours are the same. At least that's what they say - I haven't seen it myself. But on the Northern and Southern continents there are different gods and different temples. In my opinion there are no temples at all. Or maybe there is - I won't lie. All sleep! Go to your place. The owner doesn't like it when you stay in the house. The last time I got so bad because of you, when someone reported that you slept in my room. Shouted - I almost went deaf. And to top it off, I went to the ear. Well, chew before bed - Silan got a piece of stale flatbread with a slice of meat from somewhere and gave it to Ned - you need to eat a lot. Look what shoulders have grown, but there is no meat on them. Skeleton, a living skeleton! Get out of here!

Silan died a year ago. I got caught in the rain, caught a cold and died. He was buried in the cemetery where the slaves were buried. Quickly. Without speeches and commemoration. Ned was not called. After the funeral, he crept onto the mound, under which lay his only human friend, and sat beside him, saying goodbye. His eyes burned, but Ned did not cry. I couldn't. * * *

Ned looked up at the sky, figured the sun was already high. The cows were busily grazing on a green hill surrounded by patches of thorny bushes, and Ned decided:

- Backgammon, guard! I'll go diving! I'll give you seashells too! What, got drunk already? Oh, bad! Can I get it? Caught a rat, right? Okay, okay ... clever. Guard.

He turned and walked towards the sea. The shore near the place where Ned wanted to dive was rather flat, but huge stones stuck out in the water, on which excellent shells grew, the largest and most delicious in the area. No one knew about his "field," and Ned had been harvesting a magnificent harvest here for two years. Shells with half a palm, fresh, hearty - if not for them ... in general - these were his bins that fed the guy all year round.

Having thrown off his clothes, he neatly laid them on a stone away from the water - suddenly the tide would carry away to the hellish demons. Then what to wear?

For half an hour, Ned dived into the clear, calm water, until an impressive heap of shells formed on the hem of the shirt in which he decided to carry shells. Then, pulling on his trousers and broken boots, Ned ran to the place where he hid the bowler hat, his only treasure.

It was a copper cauldron that had come from nowhere on the shore - apparently, storm waves threw out. The pot was rumpled, but Ned straightened out his purchase, and now he often used it for his culinary exercises - baking shells in it, boiling a stew of rabbits and birds caught by Narda, boiling herbal infusion, which quenches thirst well in the hot season. There were some letters engraved on the bowler hat, and Ned often looked at them, cleaning off the soot with sand, wondering what the unknown masters had written. So this time, he dug a cauldron out of sand, near a dry oak tree standing on the bank of a brook formed in a hollow above, between the hills, sat down and began to carefully examine the whimsical hieroglyphs and pictures skillfully engraved on the steep sides of the vessel. Human figures, recognizable in whimsical drawings, some dots, round pieces,

After observing the drawings, Ned sighed, and shaking the sand out of the pot, went to the stream - you need to wash it properly, otherwise the sand will creak on your teeth. He rinsed in ice water, scored up to half, carried it back, put it on the grass, and began to build a fire. Well - this is not difficult. Small dry twigs, dried up moss, a few blows with a krestal (a gift from Silan), sparks smoldered into the moss, blew ... and then a joyful smoke hit my nostrils - the smell of fire, the smell of food, the smell of life.

The fire was built between two stones, which he had rolled for a long time for this very purpose. It is so convenient to put the bowler on them, despite the fact that its bottom was absolutely round, like a half of a ball. He poured the shells into the vessel to the top and set it on the fire. Now just wait until it boils, sit a little next to the shells to cook, and then you can stuff your stomach. Sometimes he would cook seashells without water - just stirring in a thick pot. Then they secrete white juice, which he liked to drink. But after Ned noticed the effect of the juice, he began to boil it in water. After the juice, he really wanted Sally ... intolerably, painfully. Silane attributed this to the stimulating effect of shell juice, which doctors prescribed to men suffering from weakness in bed. And in general - to everyone who wanted to show themselves as a real man. Ned didn't want to show himself that way he already had enough potency ... but there was no woman. And it is unlikely that such a nonentity will have what kind of women? So I had to do it on my own ...

Finally, the dish was ready, and Ned, dumping the shells on the spread wide burdock leaves - to cool them faster - began to tear apart the doors of the desired amrias. This was the name of these shells, in which pearls were sometimes found.

Ned once found a hefty pearl in a shell, the size of his fingernail. The owner noticed how he looked at it in the yard, took it away from the guy, asked for a long time where he took the precious pink drop, the size of a pinky fingernail, but ... Ned said that he found it on the beach near the village. After that, they left him behind, and he no longer began to carry the pearls he found home, folding them into a rag and burying them next to the cauldron.

Now he did not get a single pearl, to which he did not take offense at all. His belly was full of hearty, hot meat. And all that remained was to wash down what he had eaten so that the dinner would be a success. To do this, you need to wash the boiler, take water, and throw in the fragrant grass from the slope of the hollow. The bitter broth quenched thirst perfectly. A little honey ... or sugar to it. but sweets rarely fell on Ned, and after Silan's death he had forgotten what sugar was. Or maybe that is why he had magnificent white teeth, capable, it seemed, of a steel knife? His magnificent teeth were secretly envied by all those women who saw his smile. However - he rarely smiled. Life is not about smiling and giggling and laughing like the children of the free.

- Hey, you seem to be full? - he gently pushed the "smiling" Narda, who rushed to the bunch of open shells he had prepared and greedily began to devour the pulp, slyly looking at her friend. Her teeth cracked open the shells, gnawing at the sweet flesh.

Ned patted her on the withers, got up, and went back to the stream. He lowered the cauldron into clear water and watched for a while how muddy stripes stretched from it, wriggling over the sandy bottom. Some kind of insect appeared from the sand, quickly burrowing back, and again there was peace and quiet. Flies buzzed, a huge dung beetle flew by with a roar - spring, everything is blooming. The rainy season is gone, with its puddles, mud and dampness. At such a time, you want to live, even if you are a miserable foundling, useless and persecuted by anyone.

Ned sighed and rubbed the cauldron with the sand scooped up from the bottom. If you do not clean it properly, the broth will give off like sea and meat, therefore it is necessary to scrub until it shines. Hands - large, with swollen veins and long, strong fingers, gently rubbing a precious object, always shining in the sun, like new.

Ned admired - he straightened him well, tapped the bottom and sides with smooth cobblestone. Smooth, round, like ... like ... a hat! Here. Like a hat. I wonder how it would look on the head? Ned grabbed his long hair, which he usually cut off with a kitchen knife, pushed it back, and carefully placed the bowler hat on his head. He tapped it with his finger, hearing a thick ringing, and proudly straightened up:

- I am the captain of the Ards! Fear, you bastards!

The sun, coming out from behind a cloud, brightly illuminated the guy in the shiny bowler hat, and suddenly, this bowler hat flickered, made a piercing sound, as if a string of iron had broken, and Ned screamed ... and lost consciousness.

How long he lay on the shore is unknown. I woke up from the sensation of something wet and cold, stubbornly poking into the eyes, nose, lips. Ned waved his hand and landed in a soft, warm, hairy ...

- Backgammon ... oh, what is it with me ... brrr ... well enough, enough slobbering! Yes - you love, you love, I know! Ned chuckled, got up and patted the dog's head affectionately. She devotedly looked into his eyes and said:

- Love ... master ... good! Good! Drink! Drink!

Narda stepped aside and began to lap the water noisily, and Ned looked at her in surprise:

- What are you doing? Are you talking or what? Like this?

Narda looked around, waved her tail twice and busily ran along the stream, saying:

- Search! Rat! Play, eat. Master, love!

Ned watched the dog, puzzled, and knelt down, picking up his shiny yellow bowler hat. He, as for the first time, looked at his sides, covered with a fine, fine mesh of scratches left by the sand with which Ned was cleaning the cauldron, and lifting it up, put it down on his head again, holding his breath. And ... nothing happened.

After standing, Ned removed the cauldron and carried it to bury it under the oak. He was already sick of drinking the broth, so he had to confine himself to ice water from the stream. However - and the fire has long gone out, leaving behind a barely warm gray coals. Ned wondered again - how long had he been if the fire he had left with its cheerfully cracking branches had long gone out? He looked at the sun, and with a sinking heart found that it was already leaning towards evening. He quickly buried the cauldron in the sand, jumped up, and with a heavy heart rushed to look for the herd. If at least one cow is lost, he will be beaten!

Ned rushed up the slope of the ravine, and jumping out onto the hillock, was relieved to find the herd calmly sprawling on the green lawn. He began to count the cows, and it all came together - one hundred fifty-three cows and a bull. Ned picked up a stick and went to the herd, feeling sincere gratitude to Narda - if not for her, the obstinate cows would surely have scattered, especially the two heifers of the headman and the blacksmith's cow, distinguished by a particularly vile, malicious disposition. Approaching the bull, Ned shouted:

- Get up! Home! Take me home!

The bull looked at him blankly with bulging eyes and said:

- Get up. I have no desire. Man with a stick. Displeasure. I want a female. I want a female.

- Everyone wants! - Ned said completely without realizing his words, and suddenly giggled - it all looked so funny. He's talking to a bull! To whom you tell - they will laugh! Who will he tell? Silan is not there, he is in the ground. And he doesn't communicate with anyone else. Only if on business ...

- Get up, you goof! - Ned shouted and imagined how he would now hit the side of the bull with a stick. I didn't cut it, but a bright picture flashed in his brain, he seemed to say to the bull - now you won't get up, this is what will happen to you! The bull roared dully, jumped to his feet, and shook his head, said:

- I don't want pain. I do not like a person. A man with a stick is pain. Pry on the horns!

- I'll screw you up now, you horned brute! - Ned was indignant - you will wait for your gratitude, your mug is stupid! Go home! Home! You will eat, drink (picture of bran poured into warm water).

The bull nodded, and walked towards the side of the house, roaring long and long. The cows quietly reached after him, urged on by the barking of the omnipresent Backgammon.

- Aha! - Ned laughed happily - you love bran, creature! How did you hear me, eh? What a miracle, so a miracle ... I should tell Silan ... ehhh ...

Throwing aside unnecessary thoughts, Ned drove the herd to the village - until they got there, it would be evening. We must hurry.

Narda, as if hearing his thoughts, rushed forward, and began to busily bite the cows by the legs, urging them on, accelerating the movement. The herd accelerated and grabbing the grass on the way, headed for the house.

Chapter 2

He got home by dusk. The villagers were waiting for the cows near the outskirts and immediately drove them home - well-fed, contented, full of hot fat milk.

Ned drove the three cows of their family into a stall, near which two young slaves, recently bought by the owner at the market in Shusard, were already waiting, then went to the well, took some water and poured it on his head splitting from pain with pleasure. He could not understand his discomfort - either his head was baked, or there was some kind of poison in the shells - Silan never warned him that this could be - they say, you need to be careful with unfamiliar shells. So he did not eat strangers ...

The mistress, a woman of about thirty (the owner's third wife - the previous ones died for some reason), always frightened, a kind of gray mouse, called him to dinner with other slaves.

Ned had a strange social position - he didn't seem to be a slave - he didn't wear a collar, and it was difficult to sell it - officially he is actually the adopted son of Branck, the owner of the estate, but Ned's actual position was lower than that of slaves. And even the slaves constantly reminded him of this. And now, the kitchen slave Antur, plopped a bowl of porridge for him so that it almost fell into the mud, under the feet of the slaves. Everyone giggled, and Ned calmly sat down at the end of the table, taking the due piece of bread and a mug of beer. What's the use of fighting? Try to start a fight, and you will definitely fall under Branck's belt.

Ned ate, and listened with interest to what was happening around him. As soon as he entered the village, he felt that everything had changed. He began to hear the thoughts of people and other living beings!

Cows thought stupidly, simply, dogs are smarter, people - oh people! And what had he not heard enough when he walked to his house! What dirty secrets I have not learned! For example, a quiet hostess runs to a neighbor's boyfriend when, allegedly, she goes to her friend to talk about this and that, and when she called him for dinner, pictures of love meetings floated in his brain, but in such details, from such angles that Ned was a little did not blush, hiding his eyes.

Two young slaves, apparently having heard about Ned, thought that if he had not been a damned ard, any girl would not refuse to tumble with him in the hay - look what grabbing hands, how she will press ... and how tall! With such a height, you see, he has a decent "tool" ... more than that of the owner, who can not be made to burn up properly!

Antur, it turns out, prefers men over women, and today he is going on a date with the fisherman Inuk, who lives on the edge of the village. So, these very relationships between men in Zamara were not persecuted, but they were not considered the norm - something like a harmless perversion, you never know who is fond of what? But the fact is that Antur has always boasted of his victories over women, so the opening was quite spicy.

Someone else's secrets poured into Ned's brain so that most likely all these thoughts gave him a headache.

Thoughts muttered, flew in the air, and he was seriously concerned about what had happened to him, began to think - how did it happen? How is it that he hears thoughts?

After some deliberation, I realized - this is a bowler hat. It looks like he got some ancient magic item, and he foolishly put it on his head. No - who could have known? How could he know that this demon cauldron has magical properties? He was all crumpled, as if he had been crushed between hefty blocks. However - it probably was. And Ned still managed to straighten it without even breaking it apart. The metal of the boiler is thick, heavy, how is it so easy to process? And why is he so shiny all the time? And when Ned found it on the beach, and when he used it for a long time, there was no trace of the greenery that formed on the copper. I should ask Silan ... alas, there is no old man.

- Hey, why are you seated, you moron ?! It is for you! Eat and get away! Antur leaned across the table and spat into Ned's cup, ruining the half-eaten porridge. So Ned was already full, but it was not in his habit to leave food - tomorrow it may not be.

Ned silently looked at the green-yellow slime in his bowl, and a fire of hatred flared in his soul. He spoke three words aloud quietly and made a gesture with his right hand. Anthur suddenly stopped laughing and grabbed his stomach:

- Oh, oh, it hurts! How painful!

The slave doubled over and collapsed to the floor, writhing in pain, pale as a sheet. Everyone froze, not understanding what to do, then one of the slaves rushed to the exit and a couple of minutes later appeared with Branck, wiping his oily mouth. It looks like he was torn away from dinner.

- Whats up? What's happening? - He asked with displeasure, looking at the writhing guy - what, ate something, or what?

- Nnnet ... - Antur managed with difficulty, wriggling on the floor - suddenly it hurt, and that's it! I do not know what happened! They stabbed me like a stake in my stomach!

- We'll have to call a doctor - said Branc dejectedly, and ordered - Ned, run after the doctor! Tell him how it turned out. Let him go faster, otherwise this moron will die yet, while the old fool trudges through the village. But let him not hope for a generous payment! One rip off from him, every powder sprinkles like gold, you bastard!

- Good. I'll tell you everything - Ned said indifferently, and slipped into the gap between the owner's sloping shoulders and the doorframe, managing not to touch Branca even with his clothes. I had to wipe the joint with my back, but the joint is better than this hated mug. "Dad"! - his mother is so ...

Ned walked through the village, which had sunk into the nightfall, and looking at his shadow cast by the red moon, he thought about this: WHAT was it? After all, he sent a curse on Anthur, it's clear! He said some words, the meaning of which he does not know, made a strange gesture with his hand, and now - a hefty fellow is lying on the floor, writhing in pain! Interesting, very interesting. Today is truly amazing.

Bowler hat! That's it. Bowler hat. We need to be careful with this matter - the villagers are very negative about the manifestation of any magic, especially the magic of curse. If the magic of healing is perceived very positively, then the magic of the curse, as they say, came from across the sea, from the same Ards, evil sorcerers, and if someone finds out, he will not be in good luck.

It was quite far to go, through the whole village, stretching for two or two along the coast of the sea, on a hill. The village was cut by a small river, from which, in fact, almost all of its inhabitants were drinking. Water was taken in buckets, transported in barrels, and the most efficient diverted water from the river to their homes by canals in order to water the gardens. Wells were not in all houses, only in the most affluent, such as Branck, who kept a shop with everyday goods - from cereals to needles, from flour to shovels.

A stone bridge, built in such ancient times, led across the river that no one remembered when it was built. They said that the bridge was left from the times when other gods ruled the world, not the present ones. Ned didn't believe it, although looking at the bridge one might think that this was the case - the bridge was so mossy and old that it left the feeling of incredible antiquity. Even the stones from which it was composed had a bizarre shape and did not hold anything together - they just lay on top of each other, and that's it. And besides, it was impossible to pull out a single stone from the bridge, they were so tightly held in it. They said that they held on with the help of ancient magic, now lost.

The bad thing was that young people always gathered near the bridge. There was a playground near the water, thirty to forty sants, where the boys and girls of the village usually walked. Here they played musical instruments, here they ran into the bushes to kiss or something more serious ...

Ned had never been there, it's not a place for slaves, much less for him, but he often spied on what was happening there, sneaking up to the site from the darkness. He lay in the bushes and listened to conversations, painfully dreaming that someday he would be able to embrace a girl like this, bite into her full lips and undress in the bushes, seeing her full breasts and slender hips flash in the dark. Dreams Dreams…

It was dangerous for him to pass by the site - to appear in front of the heated youth meant immediate aggression against him. Therefore, Ned accelerated, and keeping to the dark side of the street, not lit by the lanterns sticking out in the windows of the houses, rushed to the bridge. To immediately run into five of his haters, as if on purpose waiting for him by the river.

The main one - the innkeeper's son, Shisor, at that moment with satisfaction recalled Sally's elastic breasts, which he pawed last night, another guy, his friend Evor, thought how jealous Shisor had persuaded Sally, the third ... in general - all the small sins right there pounced on Ned, who braked in front of them, and prepared to beat. And she did not keep herself waiting.

- This is a gift! Look who came to us! - Shisor said mockingly - in the morning you ran away from us, and now you came yourself! What, did you like my fist? Or Evora's knee? Listen - maybe you love men at all? Guys, he's a man, for sure! This thought had never occurred to me before, but I saw it and understood - for sure! Is he! Listen, Ned, I have a proposal for you - serve us, and go wherever you want. We will not touch you. And also - we will protect from other guys. Really guys? Shall we?

- We will - Évor laughed enough - only if we serve well. By the way - I've heard that men serve men better than women! They seem to know how best to please. So you have to compare!

- Have you already tried it with women? - Nart asked incredulously, the son of a blacksmith, hefty, with Ned's height, but one and a half times thicker guy - you're lying!

- Fool! - Evor said contemptuously - you need to know who to persuade! It's a very pleasant thing, I'll tell you. More pleasant than the usual somersaults.

- You know better - Ned said unexpectedly - how it is with men. Your uncle trapped you in the barn when you were twelve years old and made you a woman - in every way. Did you like it?

There was a silence - such silence happens before a thunderstorm, when thunder is about to strike and lightning will tear the space with a crash and hiss. Evor opened his mouth like a fish trying to gasp for air, then coughed, and with difficulty squeezed out of himself, said:

- What are you talking about, creature? Oh, you creature! Shame the free ?! Damned slave! I'll kill you, bastard!

Ned unexpectedly deftly dodged the blow, knocked Evora down with a trip, and ran into the gap between the guys.

Everything went well, and Ned would have slipped past the stunned guys, but the blacksmith's son had not only strength and quick reactions, but also a lack of imagination. as if he hit the fence. Then he grabbed the guy across the body, so that Ned's ribs crackled, and in an unexpectedly thin voice for such a massive guy yelled:

- I keep it, guys, I keep it!

Ned, without thinking twice, hit Nat in the big toe of his right foot with the heel of his foot, he gasped, loosening his grip. Immediately followed by a blow from the back of the head directly to the lips, turning them into two bloody dumplings, and then, when Nart threw up his hands to his face - a seizure, and a throw over himself, right under the bridge, into a babbling river that responded with a big - BULK!

The road is clear! - and Ned ran to the doctor with all his might, on the way pondering how he would go back. The fact that it is now impossible to walk across the bridge is self-evident. The guys will be waiting for him, and perhaps not with bare hands.

Ned was stunned by his behavior - he had never fought a freeman before, he almost never fought at all. And all the more strange was the fact that he did it with such knowledge, as if it was a common thing for him to run a Stosusan guy into the river. His body by itself did what he could not, what he was never taught. And again a thought is a cauldron! Is it a boiler at all ?!

The lantern in the window did not burn - the doctor had already gone to bed. But Ned didn't care - he, or the doctor - who is more expensive? There is no need to receive punishment for failure to comply with an order.

And then Ned wondered if it really was time to run? Well, what kind of demon is he sitting in this remote corner, enduring humiliation and beatings, when there, outside the outskirts, the whole world?

This thought stirred him so that the guy stood for five minutes, pondering, sucking it from all sides. Without coming to any conclusion, he punched several times with his fist on the window frame, assembled from small pieces of glass. Only the rich had enough money for large glasses. A doctor in a remote village could not be considered rich - the villagers turned to him only at their last gasp, and then they strove to receive medical treatment on credit, and if they had money, they bargained for every copper like crazy.

- Who's there? - the doctor shouted in a hip from sleep voice, and Ned heard his thoughts: "Someone has brought, the demons would have taken you ... again, I suppose someone is dying, damned rogue! They climb, but you can't wait for money. Soon there will be nothing to eat, greedy creatures! "

"This is Ned, from Branck. There the slave fell ill with his stomach, and the master sent me for you. He just told you to go faster, otherwise if Antur dies, you won't get a copper. And he also said that in order not to count on a generous payment, your powders seem to be sprinkled with gold.

- Beasts! So that you all die! Are my powders gold? Yes, I take at the lowest rate, almost at a loss! Damned rogues!

The doctor's voice was dry and boring, and only after a few seconds Ned realized that these were not words, but the thoughts of a man.

Actually, Ned was already slowly beginning to distinguish between what people think and what they say - the thoughts were dry, boring, despite the fervor with which they were "spoken." That is, it was clear that the author of thoughts was experiencing that he was speaking with his heart, but these "words" were heard as dry, colorless phrases. Words aloud, on the contrary, were colored with shades of pronunciation, in addition, their tone was higher or lower, while thoughts were heard with the same loudness - like the speech of a person speaking in a full voice almost at the ear. Loud, in general.

Yes - besides - Ned found that he could listen to the thoughts of everyone around him for five cents, but if he concentrated, he could hear one person at a much greater distance. But only one. The rest immediately become silent, even those who are standing nearby. He found this out when he walked through the village to the house and, having nothing to do, experimented with his new abilities.

The doctor came out shaggy from his sleep, like a yard dog. His eyes, which had seen everything and everyone, looked gloomily and bored from the height of their fifty-odd years. No one knew how this man ended up in a remote village at the end of the world - he came, said that he was a doctor, and began to heal. By and large, no one was interested in why a person with such abilities suddenly settled in the village - they live, so what's the big deal? However - even if they were interested - they did not show their interest - it heals, and okay. Other villages cannot boast of a real doctor, and even laying hands on the patient. Powders are powders, but good healing magic is best. Powders cannot cure everything, especially if they are not spellbound. And a good magician-doctor speaks of his powders, and not just pounds in a mortar.

- Well, what am I doing here, in this backwater? - the doctor's thought was dry and boring, but then it struck Ned - and it was me, the court doctor, running to the silly merchant to treat his no less silly slave! For coppers, for beggarly wages! Why did I agree to make poison for this bitch then? If I hadn't prepared the poison, if she hadn't handed me over during interrogation ... now I would be sitting in a white-stone palace and drinking good wine with a beautiful woman ... ehhh ... Why is this moron staring at me like that? Hmm ... he has an interesting aura ... the guy is a potential magician. Only if the local assholes find out, they will beat him. His magic is black! The aura is red with black veins. But he is still too much, at most if he can - send diarrhea. Hmmm ... I wonder ... I have to ask.

- Hey, boy, what about this slave?
- Something with a stomach ... kind of hurts.

- With a belly ... very interesting ... did he send? And what - unconsciously, he is untrained. A black magician ... a rarity, however. Battle Mage. The kingdom knocked off its feet, looking for potential magicians, and he is here, sitting in a remote village, grazing cows! And who is a black magician, one in a hundred magicians! Isn't it a paradox? Maybe send a letter to the city? The mayor there? After all, the reward is ten gold for the message about a potential magician. They don't lie on the road. I'll send it tomorrow. In the meantime, you have to go - this creature may really not pay anything if the slave grunts. He will say - he walked for a long time. I wonder if they stopped looking for me, or not? Still, ten years have passed. Return to the capital ... ehh. Or maybe they will give more for a black magician, not ten gold? It seems that there was such an order - more for the black magician. I'll fill in the feast, I'll drink for three days without drying out!

- Come on, drive faster! - and the doctor hobbled so quickly along the road that Ned could hardly keep up with this man. He wanted to ask him a lot, but of course he hesitated. How will he explain that he hears thoughts? He will either be considered insane, or ... simply killed. Who wants to know that whatever you think becomes known to some idiot?

Ned lagged slightly behind the doctor, painfully wondering how he could cross the bridge, where the guys offended by him were waiting? If you try to wade across the river ... only the banks are steep, and it will be smeared in full. He will tear his clothes. There will be a scandal. And if you stay close to the doctor? Maybe they will be afraid to touch in front of him?

Increasing his pace, Ned caught up with the doctor and took his bag.

- Let me help you! It will be easier for you.

- Hmm ... well, take it - the doctor, with relief, put the bag over the guy's shoulder - just don't fall! There are valuable powders, flasks - you will beat them - they will cost me such a pretty penny that I will simply tear you apart! Damn it!

- No matter how he cursed himself - the doctor chuckled to himself - such a diarrhea will let loose that I'll go for a month, I'll go all over with shit! We need to be more careful with black. Then, fifteen years ago, one black magician cursed the entire advancing regiment, one and a half thousand people - they went on the attack, throwing shit out of their trousers! There was a picture. And the smell! The fighters of them after that became completely useless. This, of course, is far from a professional, but at the peak of effort - in irritation or despair, he can cast a very powerful spell. Such that the sent diarrhea will be just flowers. There were examples. I wonder how his abilities manifested themselves at that age? Usually magicians give themselves away at ten years old, or even earlier, and he ... he ... how old? Twenty years old? More? Hmmm ... no ... only looks older, but maybe sixteen or seventeen. Big-eyed guy. He would have to increase the meat - the slaughter machine will be ... The lantern would not be broken - damn stones! And so a decent guy - see how, he volunteered to help. The youth of today is one hamlo, creatures! And what am I surprised - the same creatures and bring them up. Cattle. Iehhh ... where is the capital, where the avenues are lit with lanterns, where the crowds of people walking at the Autumn Harvest Fair ... rocks, sea, wind ... and rednecks, which do not bother to retreat into the bushes in order to defecate, shit right on the path! Yesterday I got into a mess, you bastards! The impression is that someone deliberately did something to get me into trouble. And that - nothing surprising. How can you expect gratitude from this people? Here again - they are standing by the bridge and chatting! They have nothing to do, they hang out and talk! The youth of today is one hamlo, creatures! And what am I surprised - the same creatures and bring them up. Cattle. Iehhh ... where is the capital, where the avenues are lit by lanterns, where the crowds of people walking at the Autumn Harvest Fair ... rocks, sea, wind ... and rednecks, which do not bother to retreat into the bushes in order to defecate, shit right on the path! Yesterday I got into a mess, you bastards! The impression is that someone deliberately did something to get me into trouble. And that - nothing surprising. Can you expect gratitude from this people? Here again - they stand by the bridge and chat! They have nothing to do, they hang out and talk! The youth of today is one hamlo, creatures! And what am I surprised - the same creatures and bring them up. Cattle. Iehhh ... where is the capital, where the avenues are lit with lanterns, where the crowds of people walking at the Autumn Harvest Fair ... rocks, sea, wind ... and rednecks, which do not bother to retreat into the bushes in order to defecate, shit right on the path! Yesterday I got into a mess, you bastards! The impression is that someone deliberately did something to get me into trouble. And that - nothing surprising. How can you expect gratitude from this people? Here again - they are standing by the bridge and chatting! They have nothing to do, they hang out and talk! to retreat into the bushes in order to defecate, shits right on the path! Yesterday I got into a mess, you bastards! The impression is that someone deliberately did something to get me into trouble. And that - nothing surprising. Can you expect gratitude from this people? Here again - they stand by the bridge and chat! They have nothing to do, they hang out and talk! to retreat into the bushes in order to defecate, shits right on the path! Yesterday I got into a mess, you bastards! The impression is that someone deliberately did something to get me into trouble. And that - nothing surprising. Can you expect gratitude from this people? Here again - they stand by the bridge and chat! They have nothing to do, they hang out and talk!

The guys were waiting for Ned at the bridge, blocking it like a cork closes off a bottle of wine. In the hands of a stick - they are very determined.

Ned leaned closer to the doctor, and he, belligerently lifting his beard twisted in a spiral, went straight into the crowd, threateningly waving his cane, at the end of which there was a silver head in the shape of a dragon. The doctor was very proud of his cane and always walked only with it, although he clearly did not need support - he was a smart and energetic man.

- Well away! Loafers! If only to chat and spit seeds! The villagers are unwashed! Get out, said! Now, as I let the spoilage go, you will wear a month without breathing! Silly creatures!

The boys stepped aside cautiously, Ned slipped after the doctor, and after him flashed:

- Nothing, we'll meet again. Tomorrow. Where are you driving your cows there?

Ned felt a chill - that was not enough! Previously, they did not touch him outside the village ... they limited themselves to mockery in crowded places. And now ... it is not known what will happen now.

They were expected at home. Antur was lying on a mat that was put under him. His face was pale, and a heavy spirit emanated from under him, indicating that the guy had done the right thing. The owner cautiously looked at the patient from around the corner, and when the doctor entered the house, rushed to him and asked excitedly:

- What about him?! Not a pestilence? Otherwise, we'll all take a break here!

- Now I'll take a look - the doctor grumbled - just for the examination, the money ahead. Silver pool. And give water. Soap. Am I going to climb in powders with my hands dirty ?!

- On! Bloodsucker ... - Branc growled quietly, holding out a silver coin to the doctor. He hid it with a satisfied look, then said:

- Cost of powders separately. Hand treatment is also separate. Do you think everything is cheap? As in your shop, you don't give away painfully cheaply, but here you are all hungry! I suppose I hid a hundred thousand gold in hiding places, but you can't raise your hand to feed the slaves properly ?! That's why they are tossing with your stomach!

- Don't talk about what you don't know - Branc muttered and mentally added - one hundred not one hundred, but sixty thousand is available. It will be necessary to check in the cellar, no matter how anyone finds it, to bury it deeper! "The picture is a barrel with mushrooms, under it there is a wooden floor, in the floor there is a hatch, under it is a box with gold."

- Stop talking, Senerad! Do your thing! How much I have is all mine. You can make money, and then count someone else's good.

- With you you will earn - the doctor thought - damned little minions! Heh heh - and indeed the damned! It will be funny if the boy curses them! Alas, most likely he does not know how to deliberately cause a curse. Only in a fit of anger. Why, alas? If he could, the whole village would lie in layers. And even worse. Better not to know how. It is necessary to control it, otherwise there will be trouble. And so I want to leave him here - if only he would put things in order in this mess. They would have brought me just a bunch of money! Stop! Stop! And this is a thought. What am I missing? I will always have time to hand over to the authorities. And if, at my behest, he put on spoilage ... oh, and I would have had money! It is easy to remove, no powders are needed - a release spell, and that's it. His level is in the area of the first one, there is no need for great strength. And I still have the eighth medicinal one. Not so hot, but against him - like a dog against a chicken. Only one thing - how to make him start spoiling on my orders, and also - how to make him keep silent about it? Didn't you blab? And how do you take it away from this jerk? Now I'll think, I'll think ... No. It looks like you still have to surrender him to power. It would be too difficult a task. This Branc is such a creature - the bottom that will not give the guy to me as an assistant. Better to have money right away than to make problems. Ooooh! Exactly - he let loose a curse. The fool does not know that every magic leaves an individual trace, a trace of his aura. Launched the curse - now everyone knows that he did it. If it was impossible to distinguish spells - black magicians would do whatever they wanted. Although ... they said that especially malicious magicians know how to expose a blende aura instead of their own. Change shades. But it seems to me - these are idle tales. Wow ... yes, he's level four, no less! How is it that mass plagues and diseases did not arise here before? So, so ... why am I making up all sorts of nonsense? We must leave the guy alone for a while and see what happens! Let him cause damage as it should, I will treat the sick, and when the time comes, I will send him to the city. Like - I discovered an elemental black magician. And I will receive a reward. There is no need to force him, to force him, and no one will know anything. Everything is clean and elegant. Wow, well done, wow - head! And I will receive a reward. There is no need to force him, to force him, and no one will know anything. Everything is clean and elegant. Wow, well done, wow - head! And I will receive a reward. There is no need to force him, to force him, and no one will know anything. Everything is clean and elegant. Wow, well done, wow - head!

- Everything, your slave is ready. Healthy - the doctor disgustedly rinsed his hands in warm water, lathered them with soap, and grimaced - stingy Branc even saves on soap - smelly, for slaves.

- What happened to him? - the owner was worried.

- Three silversmiths! - the doctor eloquently stretched out his hand and wiggled his fingers. Branc put the coins in his palm, Seenerad put them in a purse tied at his belt and explained contentedly:

- You need to feed better than your slaves. Ate something stale. I wonder how the rest of the slaves did not fall ill. Judging by where they live and what they eat, it's high time to sleep. That's all I'm going to bed. If you need something - where I live - you know.

- He's definitely not a pestilence? - Branc inquired incredulously, looking at Antur, who had turned pink from the floor.

- I told you - no! Let the ass wash, and it will be as good as new - the doctor smiled, and knocking on the floor with an elegant cane went out into the corridor. There was a rumble from there, curses - apparently he touched a copper bowl for making jam and dumped it on the floor, then the door slammed, and everything was quiet.

- Dispersed to their places! Everyone, everyone dispersed! What are you staring at? - Branc glared at Ned and swung the rag in his hand at him. Ned did not bend as usual, did not flinch, and the owner wrinkled his forehead in thought - what would that mean? But the foundling has already turned and left. Branc did not think for a long time about his strange behavior - it was night, he wanted to sleep. Not to lousy assholes.

In the morning, as usual, Ned got up at dawn, barely tearing his eyes - it was necessary to lead the herd to the pasture. I went to the well, trying not to rattle, dropped a wooden tub on a hemp rope into it, splashed icy water in my face and shuddering from the morning breeze, went into the kitchen to grab something for breakfast.

Today he was lucky - the cook was in a good mood (all her thoughts were fiddling around the night games with a neighbor, and this time he did his best!), Gave Ned ham scraps, a fresh flatbread just baked in the oven, and he almost rumbling with delight, swept everything away in the blink of an eye.

Then he was presented with a lunch bundle, also quite voluminous. Whistling under his breath a melody that he had heard at a youth gathering one evening, Ned went to the outskirts to gather the herd.

It was there that his mood was spoiled - there was also the son of a blacksmith with a swollen face - as if a wild beast had walked over it (Ned remembered - under the bridge there was a wonderful blackthorn!) his twisted dreams. Sally stood there, glancing with some interest now at the blacksmith's son, now at Ned, and recalling how she squeezed with Shisor yesterday - her pictures were so clear, so bright, juicy that Ned almost blushed.

All this company was clearly waiting for him, and when Ned appeared on the horizon, they started up and came closer. The boys' faces were serious, and Ned could see that Shisor and Evora had sharp knives in their pocket, with which they were going to ... no, not to kill. Maim Ned. Cut well. Scare. Not here - later.

They said nothing, just stared silently, then Shisor grinned wryly and nodded promisingly to Ned - they say, soon, soon ... see you.

Ned also did not say anything, gathered the cows, and urging on the last one - the lazy cattle belonging to the fisherman Nustar with twigs, drove the herd into the hills, away from the cultivated fields, to which the villagers were already dragging - no one canceled the weeding and hilling.

Ned's main task was not even to make sure that the cows did not disappear - this very rarely happened here - but to see that the cows did not climb into the gardens, into the fields, and did not harm. Then he would have suffered hard from the headman, and his "father" would have paid a fine - he also receives money for the shepherd, and he should be paid. Well, Ned, of course, answer with his own skin.

The day started off well, and how it continues ... it's how the gods want it.

So Ned wasn't particularly religious — well — gods. Yes, they must sometimes make offerings. So what kind of offerings might an actual slave have? If he has nothing at all? Therefore - bear with the gods, there will be money - there will be offerings.

On reflection, Ned decided to drive the herd to distant meadows - to the sea bend. I have not been there for a long time - the grass has grown, and the watering hole is good ... and further from the village. That he would be in trouble tonight, Ned had no doubt. But he was not going to let himself be beaten anymore. What will he do? Who knows what he will do. Don't give a damn about them! He will do what he wants!

Ned watched his thoughts in surprise - why did such a fearless rebel suddenly wake up in him? Was it just because he put on the "cauldron"? Or maybe the time has come, and the blood of his pirate ancestors awoke in him? In any case, he liked his current state. As well as the fact that the belly was stuffed with delicious ham, the knapsack with lunch pleasantly pulled back the shoulders, the sun warmed, the breeze cooled, the sea rustled and smelled of fish and something bitter, fresh - why not life? Can you wait until the escape? So I began to live quite well. What was this doctor thinking about diseases and curses? As Ned realized, this demon old man was going to use Ned as some kind of walking disease. Ned curses someone, and the doctor heals and collects money for it. But for some reason it didn't occur to the old fool to ask - does Ned agree to this? The doctor didn't even think that he should somehow interest the guy, somehow oil him. We got used to using the labor of a slave without giving anything in return, it seems so normal. But it's not even normal at all!

Ned wondered again - where did he get these thoughts? He had never been able to think so coherently, and so ... reasonably, perhaps. Nobody taught him to think, build logical chains. And now ... now everything has changed. And again - he liked it!

Whistling and chasing the herd, frightenedly squinting at the shepherd, Ned reached the Lone Oak Hill, which is three from the outskirts of the village. It took a lot of time and the sun was already quite high above the sea, shining on the horizon.

The lone oak tree for which the hill was named stood in its place, its roots digging into the ground in such a way that it would probably hold the entire Imperial fleet without even swaying. He was in several girths - gnarled, knobby, like a hero in old age, strong but ugly. Ned liked to dine under it - a good shade, and you can see from here on all sides. If the cow decides to go where it is not necessary, it can be immediately noticed and returned, with the help of a mat and a stick. There were springs in the lowland, feeding a brook flowing down to the sea - an ideal place for rest and pasture.

Having settled down by the trunk of an oak tree, Ned sat cross-legged in tattered boots, sewn a hundred times over, and closed his eyes contentedly - Narda was watching the herd, he could take a break. I slept nothing at all - four hours, no more. Ned closed his tired eyelids, and sleep immediately pounced on the tired body, covering Ned with a soft patchwork quilt.

Ned woke up from Narda's barking - she almost wheezed, barked at someone else, and Ned immediately jumped to his feet, preparing for the worst. And for sure! They.

Ned almost groaned in frustration - why, why does it never happen that everything is good? Why do the gods send more and more tests to his tormented body? Why did they send these assholes?

- Hey, don't touch the dog! Do not touch! - he cried desperately, seeing how Shisor attaches an arrow to a hunting bow. Stupid Narda continued to throw herself at the enemy, protecting Ned, as if she sensed the danger coming from these people. She had never done that before. Why did you decide to rush at people today?

- Shisor, don't! - Sally shouted uncertainly - sorry for the dog!

- Shees, this is Branca's dog, a herding dog, he gave money for her - Nart intervened - look, there will be a scandal. It costs money. They say - the best shepherd dog in our village. Branck will drag you to the headman to the court, and dad will beat your head in. It is worth at least five gold pieces.

- Yes, what demon then he dissolves it ?! - Shisor was furious - maybe she is mad, mad! Yes, she's definitely pissed off - and then you will confirm! Look, she barely snatched me, grabbed my pants!

Shisor lowered his bowstring, and the arrow, singing its funeral song, almost pinned Narda to the ground. She drew a bloody line under the dog's belly and thrust herself into the ground, trembling as if from disappointment. Narda yelped and rushed to Ned, seeking his protection.

The foundling stood with clenched fists, panting with hatred. Then he squatted down, not taking his eyes off the enemies and hugging the dog, trembling with excitement. She bared her teeth, growling at the aliens, and all the time flashed in her head:

- Enemies! Painfully! Master, love! Painfully! Tear enemies! Bad people!

- Bad, bad, Narodushka - said Ned affectionately, and carefully felt the dog's wound. There was nothing serious - a scratch. It has been worse - it will heal. Once she ran into a sharp branch in a ravine, chasing a rabbit. The bitch stuck in her chest and it was thought that everything would die. No - I got out. Ned then carried her in his arms for several weeks, and nursed her in his cubbyhole for two weeks.

- Give me! - he heard the voice of Evora, and saw how he took from Shisor's hands a whimsically curved expensive weapon - I will now pin both of them like insects!

- You're crazy, Évor! Sally said firmly - our games are going too far! It's one thing to stuff him in the face, laugh at him, it's another to kill him! Can you imagine what it will be?

- Yes, nothing will happen - Évor was pale and determined - let's say that he pounced on us, set a dog, wanted to kill with a stone - there and the stone lies. I had to shoot him! He's not really a slave - that means he's not worth the money, and we won't have to compensate for him. We will not touch the dog - she is dear, why do we need problems, and he is a worthless, useless creature. And let him die. Sally, stay out! You'll get it in the head!

- Hey Hey! This is my girlfriend, why are you uncommanded! - Shisor was indignant - and for the "head-on" you yourself get a head-on! Get your girlfriend, then hit her in the head!

- Why are you soaring? - Evor was confused - well, he ruined the whole mood!

He lowered his bow and looked at Ned, who was calmly observing what had happened.

- Lucky those be, dirt from the sole - live. But we will beat off your insides! To pee with blood! And so that he never looked at the girls! Let's castrate him guys? What? He can work, but there are no girls to spoil! Funny, huh?

- Sally, how can you walk with such scum? - suddenly asked Ned - you know why he is mad? I revealed his dirty secret - after all, he tumbled with a man. And he pretends to be a normal guy. But this is all nonsense. He's just a creature, a filthy mean creature! And your friend? Do you know that he tells all the guys that you have a mole between your legs in this very place, and that you agreed yesterday to what he persuaded you for two months? He's as chatty as a woman! And these two bastards consider Nart to be a stupid cattle that runs around on a leash, and they release him when they need to beat someone. Do you need such friends? And after he was lying on you in the hayloft yesterday, he went and squeezed his younger cousin and told her dirty nasty things, telling her how he had you in all forms. They giggled and shared their impressions - she is also good, lying around with all the guys. Whore. You are all filthy creatures! Scum! How I hate you, you would know! Damn you, creatures!

The air suddenly smelled of rose petals, the smell was replaced by the disgusting smell of a corpse, or dead fish - stinking, unbearable, turning inside out. Then the smell of pine needles, and again the stench, already sweetish, as if manure and honey were mixed.

Ned said a few words quietly, with increasing height, petrified like a statue - only his hands moved, weaving a fancy ligature, leaving incomprehensible glowing signs in the air.

Then everything calmed down, and Ned looked in bewilderment at his hands, which had done something against his will, and at the four young people, frozen on the ground in different positions, with open eyes and trickles of saliva streaming from the corner of his mouth.

Ned rushed to the lying ones, felt them - they were alive. Their hearts beat evenly, measuredly. Young people seemed to be sleeping, or were in oblivion.

Then they stirred and began to rise to their feet. Ned bristled, preparing to attack - now they will begin to take revenge on him for those hurtful words that he, for some reason, uttered, having fished information from their heads. But they stood in silence, and as if they did not recognize either each other or the place where they were now.

Ned walked around the boys and girls, but they stood the same way as they had stood five minutes ago and stared blankly into space with glazed eyes. Ned whistled in shock, stood by and quietly began to walk away from the oak tree, picking up his cherished bundle on the way. He didn't know what to do. Leave them here? And what's next? They will definitely connect with him ... and expect no mercy.

Suddenly it dawned on:

- Go home and tell me you hit your head! And don't remember anything! Pick up your bow and arrow!

Why he said so - he himself did not know. Why on earth should they have obeyed him? But they obeyed.

Shisor picked up his bow, pulled an arrow out of the ground and limply wandered towards the village, like a dead man who came to life. The others followed, dragging their feet and drooling from their mouths.

Ned rushed in the opposite direction, at the barking of Backgammon, gathering cows in a heap - an urgent need to change the place. No matter how anyone came to see what kind of stone the four idiots hit....

Chapter 3

More this day did not bring any surprises. Except, perhaps, one - had to look for a cow, hiding behind the thorn bushes at the crevice leading somewhere up the mountain. This creature decided to lie down and chew its gum in quiet solitude - as it usually did. This cow already got Ned, and he dreamed that she would sooner be in the stew. Alas, it was not within his capabilities to resolve this issue. However ... no - I did not dare. Yes, and sorry for the stupid creature. She didn't do anything bad to him, unlike people. And the fact that she climbed into the jungle is what a shepherd is for, so as not to yawn.

In the evening in the village he was greeted by the news of an unusual incident - three guys and a girl suddenly lost their memory, and came home drooling like idiots. They ran after the doctor, but he threw up his hands - not in his, they say, strength! We need a doctor of the highest rank, but he will not cope. Now they are thinking - what to do? Where to take the unfortunate idiots? According to the villagers, this young growth climbed downhill, into caves, where it is absolutely impossible to climb. Because underground inhabitants live there, depriving unwary people of memory and taking their soul.

Ned carefully asked the cook who told the village news - where is this entrance to the dungeon, and received a vague answer - somewhere, in the hills. There, judging by the wave of the cook's hand, it occupied half the world.

After supper, Ned went to his room, begging for some honey and marmot fat from the cook. Mixing them, I got something like an ointment, which I rubbed into Narda's scratch. She gently squealed when her hands touched a painful deep groove, and then earnestly licked this ointment, at the end of the action, merrily poking her cold nose into Ned's cheek and happily thinking:

- The owner is good! Love! Tasty! Tasty! Kind!

Ned laughed, grabbed the dog in an armful and they rolled a little on the straw, fingering each other and mocking growls, as if they were about to gnaw each other's throats. Backgammon was still very young, so she adored games terribly.

After playing, they stretched out next to each other, Narda immediately fell asleep - in the evening she got a good, hearty dinner, and she ran into it during the day. Ned began to consider his future life. And the further he thought, the more he came to the idea that he needed to talk to the doctor. About what? Of course - about how to live on.

Ned carefully got up from his couch, pulled on his boots, and quietly left the barn, looking to see if anyone noticed him leaving the house? Night fell, and it was dark as in a cellar - the red moon was hidden by thick clouds and rain began to drip, still weak, but by the middle of the night it should have dispersed as it should - according to Ned's estimates. But this is good - the young people hid in their homes, the elders have been sleeping for a long time, so no one will see him wandering around the village.

And so it happened - there was not a single person in the village or on the bridge. The lanterns that illuminated the interior of the houses were also extinguished - it was as if a rainy winter had come again, when everyone was huddled in their houses and sat listening to the sound of rain. Only occasionally did the dogs shuffle when Ned crept silently along the fences, and even then sluggishly, more out of duty than willing. Do you need to somehow work out the piece that the owner gives?

The doctor was also asleep - his house was quiet and lifeless, as if no one had lived in it. The garden at the house was neglected and miserable - they did not follow it, the doctor did not care if there were weeds or flowers worthy of being presented to a beautiful girl.

After knocking on the window, after a while Senerad's hoarse, displeased voice was heard, and then the owner of the voice himself appeared, having time to throw a short fur coat over his shoulders. The doctor was not surprised to see Ned, and immediately, grinning to himself, thought:

- Looks like someone has cursed again. Come on, come on, my boy, try hard! Only not as with these pentyuh - easier! Uncle Seenerad needs a job, and more. Indeed, not work - money!

- What did you come for? - he said aloud - is someone sick?

- No. Yes. Maybe he was ill - Ned was confused - but nobody sent me. I came myself.

- Himself? - the doctor was surprised - why?

- You need to talk.

- You are crazy? What kind of conversations can I have with you, a rootless slave, and even at night? Go away. In the afternoon, come and talk. Everything, everything, walk!

- And if I curse now? Ned asked with a calm grin.

- What? - the doctor was taken aback, and thought:

- What a demon! How does he know ?! He knows?! Oh Gods! Well, well, we need to talk to him ...

- Come in ... - Seenerad replied calmly, and dived back out the door - just pretend it is tighter, the door is seizing. Lock on the hook. If it's completely dry, then you can't close it, or it opens up with the wind. It is necessary to repair, but there is no money. The villagers are stingy to the point of impossibility ... well, sit here. What were you talking about curses there? Tell me.

- Let's come to an agreement right away - I will speak frankly, and you speak frankly, without lies. I will feel when you are lying, do not hesitate. Well, shall we agree?

- A promising beginning of a conversation - Seenerad chuckled in surprise - I heard that you are a kind of village idiot, unrequited and harmless, and rather stupid, but how did you speak? Okay, let's be honest. Only you came to me, not me to you, so let's you start first. What brings you to me?

"I want you to teach me how to use my magic! - exhaled Ned - I want to be able to control my magic and be able to call it when I want, and not when I am angry, or in anger. This is the main thing.

- What does he know ?! O-ball-do! These are the requests! What a fool! I wonder how he'll feel like I'm lying? Empath? Well, I'll try ...

- Why did you come to me? I am a humble provincial doctor, and you came to me with some strange questions. How can I teach you something if I can't do it myself? And in general - what kind of magic do you have? Until I heard anything useful from you.

- And I am from you. All of you are lying. You know that I am a black magician, you know that I release curses, you know that I have bewitched Anthur. And I know about you - that you were a court doctor, that you poisoned someone there and were looking for you in order to punish, that's why you are sitting here in the backwoods. I know that you see when my curse falls on people and you can lift it. Maybe it's enough to lie?

- Gods! What else does he know ?! Where from? Who said? Damn it!

"Don't worry — I won't harm you. I haven't told anyone anything about you. And what I know - I saw in a dream.

- Seer ?! Is the black magician a seer ?! How can it be? Gods, how are you kidding a tired man! And your jokes are more and more sophisticated!

- So what do you want from me? - clearing his throat, continued Seenerad in a hoarse voice - if you already know everything?

- Well, stop it! - Ned said irritably - if you will make me angry, I will not resist and curse you! And from yourself, perhaps you will not remove the spell!

- And you will not impose on me - the doctor said automatically - I protected myself with protective spells. Your level is weak for me. I'm not a goof from the Black Ravine village. No matter how else your own spell has struck you - so I will put a reflection spell on myself, you will know then how to offend a peaceful doctor!

- First of all, don't lie - you are not that peaceful. Secondly, I'm not going to harm you, because all your complex spells are useless. And third, are you sure you can hide from me with spells? Not sure? Yeah. Then stop talking nonsense and let's talk like two reasonable people?

- Let's-talk-how - two-reasonable-people! - echoed, with an arrangement, repeated the doctor, and thought:

- Not a damn thing going on! If tomorrow a cow speaks to me and says that she owns fire magic, I will not be surprised. After this meeting, it seems that I will not be surprised at anything else in my life.

"I want to master my magic, and I want you to help me with this. Can you?

- No I can not. Don't look at me like that - it's not about me. The fact is that you have to learn, and not from me, but from those teachers who know how to teach. As regrettable as I may admit, I am not as strong a magician as I would like. Yes, I am a good doctor, but nothing more. To get a job in the palace as one of the court doctors, I had to give a bribe to the major domo. Five hundred gold. And this despite the fact that we are distant relatives - his grandmother is my grandmother's cousin. And this guy ripped off my money so that I became one of the five healers serving the court servants. Well, yes, I also practiced secretly, made love potions and something else, on which I got burned. But it's not about me, it's about you. If you want to master magic, you must study in magic agar. Moreover - in the one that deals with martial, black magicians. And I'm a white magician. I am a doctor. Everything, what I can do is aimed at removing the effects of spells cast by people like you. Do you understand? Do I explain it in an accessible way? You must understand - I am not against teaching you something, but how can I teach you something if I myself am not able to?

- You're not entirely honest. The training of magicians at first should be similar. Is that so?

- So ... but ... okay - how do you imagine it? Well - I came to your master and said - give me your slave - or your son, as he presents it there - I will teach him magic! And then everyone will connect your education with cases of unexplained diseases in the village. These four will be especially remembered! By the way, what did you do with them?

- Wow! And I thought YOU would tell me what I did with them! Stop! How do you know that I did this to them? AND! I say nonsense - in the footsteps of the aura, right? And why didn't you cure them?

- Yes. In the footsteps of the aura. And what you have done is beyond my reach. I cannot understand what you did. The impact was. There are traces of your magic. But the disease itself is incomprehensible to me. I can't take it off. Outwardly they are completely healthy, that's just ... idiots. They will be told, they do, nothing more. We need to read the literature on black magicians, but I have very little of it. To be honest, while studying at the agara healing faculty, I was not particularly interested in black magicians. However - if only a pretty girl did not act as black magicians. Although this was not particularly a reason for getting to know her - when you are with her, the thought is always in my head that - she won't like how I behaved in bed, she - rrraz! - and impose a curse. And you will become after no male part. Or none at all. Or you can do it right in bed. Honestly, this is not conducive to violent love games. Here's something spinning in my head - as if I heard somewhere, or read about such a curse that you imposed, but nothing comes to mind. Well, okay - maybe I'll remember later. So - what suggestion do you have on how I can work with you the beginnings of magic? And here's another thing - do you at least know how to read and write? No? I knew it ... It was stupid to ask.

- Yes, I have a suggestion on how to arrange all this. Listen ...

It didn't take long to present the notion. Cenerad listened in disbelief, raising his eyebrows, then, curling his lips, said:

- Stupid somehow. But it might work. But how will you go out into the street later? Once you left, then you got cured? If you are cured, then go back and work. You know what, you may not come up with anything new, but simply declare the authorities about you, and go to study in agar? I will get my money, and you ... you will get out of your slavery. By the way, maybe we should just rush to the capital? Much time has passed, my sins could have already been forgotten ... of course, the way to the palace has been ordered for me, but who prevents me from opening my own business somewhere in the merchant quarter?

- Who will let you pick me up? Why did you decide that Branc would take it so easily and give me to you - take it, they say, and go wherever you want with him?

- Also true ... - the doctor was slightly confused - so, so ... you need to think ... that's what! Invented. Do you know how to do it? Tomorrow the pearl buyer arrives on his ship. I'll wait for him to go back. Today is the second day of the week? He sails on the third day - so I will go with him to the city. There I will find the mayor, I will demand that they let me in on an important state matter. He will have to accept me. And I will inform him that I know about the whereabouts of the black magician, I will take the paper that I will take you to him. I will take from him two city guards and a ship, I will take you from Branck, I will bring you to the city.

- So? What's next with me?

- Here's how it will be - you will be examined by a special magician, the head of the local zarata of magicians, will give the conclusion that you are indeed a magician, and even black. I will be given a reward. And you ... you will have to go to agar for training. The nearest one is in the capital. I will volunteer to take you there, and accordingly, I will save on transport. They have to pay for travel to the capital, either by ship or by postal vans. Most likely they will be sent on some passing vessel. Those will be happy to receive passengers - why not? Money is never superfluous. In general, like this: your task is to hold out until I return from the city with the paper to escort you to the mayor, and try not to kill anyone during this time. Even if you really want to. By the way - describe how you feel? Your character has changed a lot since then how did you begin to notice magical abilities in yourself? What do you think - what happened to you? And when?

"I don't know what happened," Ned lied — suddenly became who I am. Yes, the character has changed. I stopped calmly accepting what seemed normal to me yesterday and the day before yesterday. I have become irritable and easily enraged. What else...

- More - sharply wiser, huh? - the doctor grinned.

- How can I know - have grown wiser, or not? - Ned answered in bewilderment - so you, can you say, have grown wiser or stupid in a few days? What to compare with?

- Hmm ... just got smarter - the doctor drawled thoughtfully - but where have I met such, where did I read? I can't remember ... have you come across any magic item? Didn't touch? However - where are the magical objects from here, in this hole ... But why guess - tomorrow I'll go to the library of zarada, read on your problem. It will be so soon.

- When will you arrive? When will you get the paper?

- Well, when ... look how everything will be - tomorrow the buyer arrives, usually he arrives at noon. He will buy it until the evening, rest the night, and in the morning he will go to the city. In the city by noon, then I start to go to the authorities. I will definitely not manage one day, which means I will have to stay for another day. And after this day, in the morning - I sail here, and for dinner here. So - in three days, on the fourth. Can you hold out?

"I held out for seventeen years, I'll hold out for four days," Ned chuckled wryly.

Back Ned flew as if on wings. My head was beating - that's it! At last! Really ?! He seemed to be freed from a heavy stupor, in which his soul was for seventeen long, difficult, terrible years. And Ned was very much afraid that everything would fall apart. What if the doctor will be hit and he will die on the way? What if the robbers kill him, and the doctor does not get to the city? Suddenly ... yes, a lot of things - suddenly! Who would have thought that his life would depend on a wicked, unfriendly old man living on the edge of the village ...

Ned made his way into his cage, lay down on a mattress full of straw, and closed his eyes, soothing his breathing. Before his inner gaze floated pictures of the future, which he had never seen - huge ships under white sails, smart women (they were dressed as villagers dress, only in bright, very bright - red and gold clothes), crowds of people - h a thousand, or two thousand people at once!

Ned could not have imagined more people than a thousand or two. In the entire village of Cherny Ravine, two thousand people lived, and he had never been in any other village. Silan's stories about crowds of tens of thousands of people were nonsense to him. Silan once said that at the market in the capital of Zamar there were going to be both twenty and thirty thousand people! He was there himself when the slavers sold him. So he knew what he was talking about.

Narda pushed in the side and her thoughts began to hum like small drums:

- Master! Warmly! Be in love. The owner is good! Be in love!

Ned grimaced slightly - no, he certainly loved his dog, but this incessant mumbling ... should you sleep sometime? And then there are the cows mumbling ... it feels like you are standing in a crowd of noisy people, and they - boo-boo-boo, boo-boo-boo!

Ned wondered how to isolate himself from other people's thoughts? How to plug invisible ears? I lay awake for a long time, trying to somehow drown out the rumble. Then a thought suddenly surfaced:

- You have to imagine that I plug my ears with plugs! Here! I take a cork, one! In one ear. Another cork - oops! In the other ear. Iii ... there is! There is! Happened!

The murmur around Ned died away, there was silence, and such that rang in his ears. It seemed that it had become incredibly quiet - despite the fact that the cows sighed, shifted from foot to foot and let gas.

Worried - maybe he lost the magical ability to hear thoughts? That would be bad. He is already accustomed to knowing the secret secrets of others. A person quickly gets used to everything, especially if it is something good.

Ned imagined that he raised his hands to invisible ears hearing thoughts, bang! The plugs are removed. And then with relief I heard the muttering of cows, and saw the picture that Narda saw - a running rabbit, high grass rushing towards him.

Narda squealed in her sleep and fingered her paws. Ned grinned and stroked the dog's large head, which immediately woke up and looked at his friend with a questioning glance - what, they say, master?

- Sleep. And I will sleep - Ned grinned, and with relief stuck the "plugs" in the "ears", closed his eyes, falling into sleep.

Morning was no different from all ordinary days. The people, driving the cows to the outskirts, cows, thoughtfully and stupidly looking at the owners and squinting at the shepherd. But there were no four young people, instead of them the workers drove the cattle.

By the way - Ned always wondered why it was his tormentors who drive the cows into the herd themselves, why the workers did not do it? And only then, listening to their thoughts, I learned that they were trying to get out of the house and free - to hunt, swim in the sea, laze around under a plausible pretext. Whether the parents of the boys and girls knew about it, or not, Ned was not interested. Maybe they knew. Most likely they knew.

The herd rushed out of the village, thundering with botals, and Ned looked at the backs of the cows with the air of a warlord. Sometimes he imagined that he was not leading a herd, but a military mob to conquer foreign lands, and here he, the leader, stood behind everyone and, with a wave of his hand, sent his soldiers forward to conquer foreigners.

Thank the gods - the mumbling, which he removed at night, did not appear. The "traffic jams" were holding tight and now he could not listen to this demonic herd, pestering him with their thoughts. However - like the human herd, with their dirty secrets and vile little thoughts. By the way, after several days and nights of wiretapping, he was sure that animals are much more decent and honest than people. Although, in truth, he was always sure of this.

- Wait ... how are you? Ned! Wait! - Hearing a voice behind him, Ned looked around, and immediately recognized a man of about forty-five, with a thick blond beard, arranged with a "shovel" for solidity. Headman. Sally's father.

- I am listening to you, mister headman - Ned answered gloomily, out of the corner of his eye watching the leaving cows - only I need to follow the cows, otherwise my skin will be spoiled if at least one is lost.

- You will have time - the headman said harshly, glaring at the guy - tell me, what did you have with Sally? I mean, what did you talk to her about? And with the guys? They all showed that they all hated you and always beat you whenever the opportunity presented itself. So tell me - when was the last time you saw them? What do you know about their strange behavior? Why did they get sick? The doctor could not cure them.

- You are laughing at the miserable shepherd - Ned chuckled wryly - you are such educated, important people, and could not understand what happened to the sick? Why are you asking me, poor man?

- Something I don't like how you answer me - the headman curled his lips - for a shepherd slave you are too impudent! And the speech is too correct ... who taught you to speak?

- Slave Silan. Only I am not a slave, if not forgotten. I'm Branca's adopted son. And I have never been a slave. As for your daughter and guys, I don't know anything about them, and I don't want to know. Sorry, I have to work.

Ned bowed to the headman, and walked briskly after the cows, accompanied by the headman's thoughts:

- He's lying, bitch! The guys kept poking him around, all the guys in the village showed it! They all hated him! And I hate you too, creature! Ardovskiy bastard! Cursed robber people! Hiding something, that's for sure. We need to look after him - where he goes, what he does, if there were any strange events near him. Can he immediately take it, try it well - will he tell you something? You could ... just don't want to spoil relations with Branck - he gets good money for a shepherd, a greedy creature. His brother works in the city, in the department of land relations, he can shit when I register land for fields in the magistracy. We need hard proof that the Ards bastard is involved in the trouble with the guys. Maybe he gave them something? Poison, or some other nasty thing? But how did he do it? We need to think it over ... * * *

The day dragged on and on. The cows chewed gum, rested in the shade of the trees, and Ned watched them and wondered where this road would take him. What will happen to him? Previously, he knew exactly what to do and what not to do, but now what? Stupid, animal life does not suit him now. Stop! Why not? I did it before, but now? What happened? What, he really got smarter? Hmmm ... probably yes. He began to formulate his thoughts more clearly, began to understand things that he had never even thought about before. For example - why on earth is he in such a humiliated position in relation to other people? Why on earth? How did he deserve it? By your birth? Previously, he was supported by the idea that in the next reincarnation, perhaps he will become a rich and respected person, having atoned for his guilt in this incarnation. That's just who said it was, will this incarnation be? Who has seen those reincarnated? If they don't remember their former life, who said that they incarnated? Maybe there is nothing like that - he died, and that's it, turned to dust? Maybe rebirth is a fairy tale for the likes of Ned so that they don't riot, regularly working for those who are lucky in life? Unknown. But the new Ned, wiser, was inclined towards this version of events.

His thoughts were interrupted by someone's voices, Ned shuddered, waking up from the half-sleep of the midday heat and jumped to his feet, finding himself in front of several strong men with clubs and lassos in their hands. He immediately recognized them as the headman's workers - pearl divers, fishermen, carpenters. The men stood silently behind their master, waiting for the command, and she immediately followed:

- Take him! Grab it!

The men moved forward, surrounding Ned on all sides. He jerked to one side, the other - ten men surrounded him in a ring, and there was no way out.

Ned thought with annoyance that if he hadn't shut up his mental "ears", he would have heard the guys approaching in advance, and would have had time to prepare, but he did not have more time to think.

The lasso that flew through the air nearly swept over his neck. Ned dodged, grabbed the rope, and pulled hard. The man flew up to the guy, losing his balance, and he hit his opponent's Adam's apple with a short jab. The man grunted and sagged as if he had been hacked.

The blow from the stick burned his shoulder, and it went numb. The next enemy was hit in the groin so hard that he passed out.

Further events were not deposited in Ned's head - he beat, tore, gouged out his eyes, tore open his mouths - blood splattered, bones crunched, people moaned. A dog screeched - Narda rushed into the center of the fight to help a friend, slashing enemies with sharp teeth, and someone stabbed her with a knife. The dog collapsed, twitching and bleeding through its teeth clicking in agony.

And then Ned, whose body acted already without his participation, became brutal. Previously, he hit like a mechanical doll, dodging, fighting back and striking as if he were hitting soulless dolls, wanting only to be left alone. Now - he was killing. Each of his blows crippled, and the next was the finishing one. He drank in the blood of battle, and deep in his soul was pain: Narda! Poor dog! She died loving him. The last creature in this world who loved him and to whom he was dear. So why should these creatures live? Why should they live when the one who is dear to him died?

The headman was the last to die. Ned broke his neck, and before that he broke his spine with a blow to the back when he tried to escape.

When it was over, Ned stood silently over the disfigured corpses for several minutes. How much he stood - he did not remember. And in general - everything seemed so distant, so strange and unreal, as if it were a dream. Then he woke up - Narda!

Ned rushed to the dog, pressed his ear to its side - useless. She was dead. Ned knelt down before her, closed his eyes and stood as he had once stood before Silan's grave. Then he got up and looked over to where the corpses of his enemies lay. It took only a second to watch - after he realized what he had done - he vomited in a violent fountain, knocking out of his stomach that simple food that he had thrown an hour ago. The urge to vomit did not stop for a long time - maybe it was a nervous overload, or maybe a physical one ... it's not every day that you kill ten people with your bare hands.

Ned, as if in disbelief, raised his thick hands and began to examine them as if for the first time. Hands are like hands. The knuckles were knocked down, a bruise - the club of one of the attackers got here. Here is a small cut - knocking a knife out of the hand of a hefty carpenter. Blood, abrasions. Nothing else. How did he manage to defeat a whole crowd of people, and even with his bare hands? Is he, a simple boy, a shepherd? And what struck him the most was that when he killed, he experienced acute pleasure. It was as if ... as if ... with a woman was. Yes! As if he was with a woman. And only when the obsession subsided did the mind refuse to perceive what had happened. Refused to believe my eyes.

Ned sat down on a rock and stared blankly at the corpses. What to do? What should I do? He wanted to cry - after all, in essence, he was a simple boy, offended by fate. What could he oppose to circumstances other than reason? And the mind told him: run. Get out of here, and as fast as possible! This is death! What else can be, what is the punishment for the murder of the head of the village? For killing ten people? Especially if you are a rootless outcast!

Turning, Ned walked over to the dog's corpse. He lifted Narda in his arms, carried her to the gully and began to dig a grave for her - right with his hands, helping himself with a piece of dry branch picked up under a large tree. It was easy to dig - the ground in the lowlands was loose and slightly damp, and smelled sweetly of sweetness and mushrooms.

Having dug a hole down to his knee, Ned stroked the dog one last time on the large, forehead head and, carefully, as if afraid of causing pain, laid Narda on the bottom of the grave. Biting his lip painfully, he looked down, and turning away, resolutely moved the pile of earth he had taken out with his strong hands. A few minutes later, a small mound stood on the site of the grave, which after the first rain will be level with the ground. Ned could do nothing more for his friend.

The guy looked at the sun - it was already high. Noon. He had a few hours before sunset to get as far out of here as possible. Until they understand that Ned and the herd did not come at the appointed time, while they set out on a search - and there he will already go so far that it will be difficult to find. If only with dogs ... But it will most likely be in the morning. So he has a long way to go. Where to? To the city, of course, where else?

After thinking for about three minutes, Ned decisively approached the corpses, and began to rummage through his pockets and belts. The catch was not very rich - who in the village carries a lot of money with him? So, for a glass of beer ... and even then rarely. During the day, only loafers drink. There are evenings and holidays for drinking.

In total, from the pockets of the deceased, Ned fished ten coppers, five silver pools, and ... that's it. No rings, no chains, nothing of value. Rednecks! The grumpy doctor would say.

Two good knives as long as Ned's forearms, sharp enough to shave. In this way, from time to time, trimming and cursing, Ned scraped off his youthful growth, which was still not completely strong, but thick as swamp reeds.

Having estimated it on his hand, Ned chose one that looked more expensive and more comfortable in his hand. It can be seen that it is not an ordinary blade. These usually had pearl divers with them - suddenly they would get entangled in old nets, and you can fight off the sea monster. Sharks rarely, but swam to these shores.

Choosing one guy, similar in height to himself, undressed him, taking off his good, sturdy clothes and strong, almost never worn soft boots. The clothes were slightly stained with blood, but Ned carried them to the stream and neatly rubbed off those brown stains.

He looked, and clucked his tongue in satisfaction - it was well washed. He threw off his clothes and threw them on the spot, not hiding. What's the use of hiding? Any hunter versed in the tracks, having examined the scene of the incident, can easily establish what happened here. What is the time to waste then?

He put the coins in a purse taken from the elder's belt. By the way - the silver pools were from there, from this purse.

With annoyance I thought that there was no time to return for the pot and a bunch of pearls hidden near it - there were fifteen of them - even, pink, each with a fingernail the size of. Silan said that for each one you can get at least ten gold pieces, or even more.

In the Black Ravine, everyone knew about pearls, even the last of the last slaves, or rootless foundlings. Pearls were the main bread of the villagers. Everything else - fishing, fields sown with rye and oats, cows with their milk - it was all secondary, to maintain the pants, as the old slave said. The main thing is pearl plantations, which were plundered by the villagers for hundreds, maybe thousands of years.

In terms of shells, they were robbed. And from the point of view of people, it was quite a decent thing. With luck, the pearl diver could immediately earn his own house by lifting several large pearls from a depth of fifteen Santas. However - such good luck had not been heard here for a long time, and in general - the shells became less and less. The catchers mercilessly destroyed the pearl mussel plantations without thinking about the consequences.

According to the stories of old people, as Silan said, in the old days it was possible to get shells with pearls literally from the depths of Santa. But for some time now everything began to change - the shells went deeper and deeper, and now only strong, prepared men and women could reach the bottom with the coveted shells. Divers after several years of such work fell into disrepair - they became deaf, fell ill with a disease from which their legs and arms were twisted. They said that the infection passes from the shells, taking revenge on the divers for their death. But as Silan said, he does not believe in this mysticism. Everything is simpler - daily being in cold water, at great depths, led to illness. He explained the reason for the disappearance of the shells by the fact that: firstly, the water really became colder than before - and no one knew why - and secondly, people so barbarously knocked out pearl plantations, that the shells simply did not have time to multiply. Only those that lived at great depth have survived. But in the cold depths, they did not want to reproduce normally. It was already said that if this continues, the village will soon end - people will scatter to other villages and leave for the city.

With regret abandoning the thought of returning for his treasures, Ned pulled on the last boot, stood up, stamped his feet on the ground and noted with satisfaction that the boots fell exactly on the leg, as they were sewn on him. I felt the fabric of a shirt and a light twist - of excellent quality! Discreet, but strong and not easily soiled. Just right for him. Ned had never had such high-quality clothes, and with pleasure he felt that for the first time in his life he was dressed decently and even well. So what, what about the corpses? They don't care, but he needs to live! Big, of course, but just right in the shoulders. But it does not press.

He collected his old duffel bag - a chair, tinder, dry moss, wrapped in an impenetrable, oiled piece of leather, threw the bag behind his back and, looking back at Narda's grave, walked along the path up the hill. He did not look back at the people he had killed. What for? Let them roll around. He did not ask them to come and pounce on him with clubs and ropes. Have you come to torture him? Let them rot now. He did not have the slightest feeling of remorse or concern about killing people.

Chapter 4

Step by step, step by step ... tum-tum-tum-tum ...

Ned's legs carried him further and further away from where he had lived his entire life. After a few hours of rapid stride, almost running, he went beyond the territory where he had been, where there were cows. He did not go along the main road - along it, by paths, and sometimes just across the grass. It's good that there is no rain - it's dry, clean, the sun is sparkling, the breeze blows - it's a pleasure to walk. Legs work, and the head thinks, ponders.

Ned had no idea what he would do when he got to town. Maybe try to track down Senerad? And what will it look like? He walks in a crowd of people and asks: "Have you seen Seenerad? Where can I find Senerad? " Stupid. Besides, where did he get the idea that after the murder of ten fellow villagers they would take him somewhere there? In the evening they will discover the absence of a shepherd, in the morning they will send a chase. Or maybe at night - Branca has money, so why not hire hunters? And this is already dangerous. Hunters are not village bumps. They also have dogs, those that follow the trail. Therefore, we must hurry. How many hours does it pass? Is it four? Five? If you take the smallest thing, he can walk without stopping for eight hours. He will get to the city in time for the morning. Only Silan said that the city gates were closed at night. Where is he to hang out all this time? And if the hunters arrive in time? Questions, questions ... but he still has nowhere to go. We must go.

So, for the sake of safety, you need to cut off all contact with your old life. No Cenerad - no training. The ships remain - the sailor. Or a loader at the port. And that - he is strong, carrying sacks and rolling barrels - no getting used to. The main thing is not to get caught ... * * *

Shivering, Ned crawled out from under an old launch lying on the seashore by the city wall. Before getting there, he prudently entered the water at a distance from the city and walked through the shallow water to the very city walls, hissing and swearing to himself, like a loader from a salted barge - pebbles pricked his feet, and in the dark it was impossible to make out where you were stepping. The red moon had already set, but the black one, of course, did not give any light.

In the light of the stars, he saw a longboat lying upside down, buried in the shore like a mossy stone, and finding a gap between its side and the coastal pebbles, he carefully pulled his long body under the boat. Now I could take a break. Throughout the night without stopping, he almost ran, escaping pursuit.

Ned did not see his pursuers, they were somewhere far away, but he felt them, felt them with all his skin. They were sure to follow the trail - or he did not know his fellow villagers.

The legs ached from the load and the muscles were like cotton. So the load for him was not prohibitive, but ... more than thirty without rest and food, at night - it's not a joke.

It dawned early in summer, so it would not be long before dawn. And Ned fell asleep.

He was awakened by bright, hot rays, breaking through the cracked boards of the launch. The arrows of the sun shot in his eyes, and Ned woke up willy-nilly, feeling terrible hunger - he had not eaten since yesterday. And that there was food, then ... well, just to satisfy your hunger.

Rustling round white pebbles, Ned climbed out from under the launch and looked around. Before him shone the sea - calm, calm, beautiful, like the smile of God. The gates to the city were already open - from here, from the blank wall extending into the sea, you could see numerous carts entering and leaving and people entering, waiting to be launched or released. It was necessary to hurry to enter in order to get lost among the crowd, otherwise the pursuers might grab him near the gate.

Ned pulled on his boots, grimacing with pain in his strained legs, splashed sea water in his face, driving off the sleepy stupor, smoothed his hair, which had become thick as thick strands, and walked quickly towards the gate.

Here a surprise awaited him. After a short time, he became poorer by two coppers. It turns out that the entrance to the city was paid. This upset Ned greatly. With his finances, he could not distribute money at such a speed. He needed something else to eat until he found a job and got out of Shusard.

The city greeted Ned with noise, screams, the smell of burning coals of braziers and the rumble of iron-bound cart wheels on the cobbled pavement. People were running around everywhere - the guy was pushed, swore that he stood on the road. Everyone ran somewhere, as if they were stabbed in the ass with an awl and lashed with a leather whip.

After a quiet village life, Ned thought that he fell into the demons. The guy was confused, and a crowd of people hurrying somewhere caught him up, and like a stormy stream playing with a pine chip, he dragged him along the gateway square, pushing him into the main street of the city passing through its center. Only ten minutes later he came to his senses when he almost fell under the wheels of a huge carriage with lacquered black sides and a gold monogram on its side - the coachman, with a shout and whistle, slapped the whip so that its tip flew dangerously close to Nedova's cheek. After that, Ned woke up from his stupor, then, pushing the passers-by with his shoulder, squeezed into the stall of pies, spreading the delicious smell of ovens throughout the area.

- With what pies? - He asked a broken guy a little younger than himself, standing at the brazier and turning over the ruddy pies on the wire rack.

- With a liver! - he immediately responded - two copper pools apiece! Will you take? Hot! Big! Leaver is fresh, not rotten, I guarantee!

Ned sadly estimated his cash reserves - at such a rate he would be out of money in a couple of days, but there was nothing to do - there was something hunting. And in a minute he was already eating a pie, washing it down with warm water from a wooden mug with bitten edges. Well, at least the water is free, otherwise it would be completely ruinous. After swallowing the pies in the blink of an eye, Ned asked:

- Listen, can you tell me how to get to the port?

- Do you want to hire a ship? - the guy figured, smiling knowingly - why not. They take everyone there. Just look, you run into a slave trader - they will quickly fasten a slave collar. They love to catch vagrants. So it is forbidden here to turn citizens of the kingdom into slaves without a court decision, but ... anything can happen. Prove later that you are not a slave, but a free citizen. By the way, what are you, ard? Come on, okay - I don't care. People like you are not uncommon in our area. You are from somewhere in the village, right? The villagers got it from the Ards during the raids. They really don't like yours. Arda fucked everything that moves, because we have a lot of their offspring.

- So you tell me how to get to the port? - began to get angry Ned, trying to insert at least a word into the stormy speech of the talkative boy.

- Yes, how ... you walk along this street, it is called Korolevskaya street, you reach the temple of Dinas, and turn right. You go all the way until you fall off the dock. This will be the port! - the guy laughed, and began to shout loudly, offering pies.

Ned stood there, digesting the information, and walked on to where the guy said.

Entering the city, Ned turned off his "ears", suspecting that he could not stand the murmur of the thoughts of so many people. Now, moving away from the guy, he decided to try to listen to what others think about. I turned on my "ears" and ... I almost fainted! He had never heard such a number of thoughts beating into the cranium, even when he was standing in the middle of a one-and-a-half herd of cattle. What cows - they quietly mumbled to themselves simple thought phrases concerning their simple desires - to eat, drink and so on, but people, people it was something! Their thoughts merged into a continuous roar, loud, in different keys, so merged that among these thoughts it was difficult to distinguish individual words. Ned lasted about five minutes and then, relieved, turned off his supersensible hearing. The mumbling immediately disappeared, and it seemed to him that the street was completely quiet, so quiet,

Thinking about the village where he suffered for seventeen years, Ned hurried, skirting passers-by and trying to get to his destination as soon as possible. He had the feeling that he was about to hear the barking of dogs following his trail.

The port opened twenty minutes later, when Ned was already beginning to doubt whether he was going there. The sea was not visible behind the tall buildings, especially since the street was on the rise at first. However, soon the road sharply headed down, and through the gaps between the spreading mulberry trees appeared the sea and ships that were at the berths and in the roadstead.

Ned bounced off to the docks, almost breaking into a run, and fifteen minutes later he walked out onto the harbor square.

What was going on here! Crowds of loaders scurried about, horses, straining, pulled huge carts with sacks and barrels, peddlers with snacks and drinks walked, sailors waddled, dressed in various bright clothes, and girls flirted with them, dressed so frankly and defiantly that in the village of Neda they would have been whipped for such behavior long ago.

Silan told Ned about the cities, but it was one thing to listen to, and another to see it all with your own eyes.

Ned again got a little confused, and decided to stand aside for now and watch what was happening in order to decide - where should he go after all? Previously, everything seemed so simple - the ship was standing - came up - offered his services. From the ship, joyfully - Yes! Yes! We need a sailor! Get on board, of course! And Ned swam to the distant lands, where his eyes were looking ...

The reality turned out to be more complicated. What if he really gets a slave collar instead of the position of a sailor? Here's how to identify the ship that he needs among these floating "houses"? What are the signs?

Ned scrutinized the ships at the dock.

Whoever was there - huge pot-bellied merchant ships with three, and even four masts, towering above the rest, like mountains above green hills, nimble boats of pearl buyers, slender ships of long voyage, distinguished by high-speed contours and suitable both for trade and for military operations.

The ships lay along the long quay, and a number of ships were lost somewhere around the bend of the port. But what Ned saw was enough to inspire him with respect for what he saw. Ships, coveted ships! How he would like these handsome men to carry him away from his former life ...

Ned sighed and focused on contemplating the ship's suitability for his purposes. For myself, I decided that the slave trader's ship should have some distinctive features, and most likely, these will be those long-distance ships that can cross the distance from mainland to mainland. After all, they need to swim faster, until the slaves died in the holds, existing in inhuman conditions.

According to the old slave, after such a ship docks at the pier, only seven out of ten slaves captured somewhere in distant lands leave it. The rest die on the way from poor conditions of detention.

So, you need a merchant ship carrying goods. There, like that big man, with three masts drawing the clouds.

Ned got up, pulling a skinny duffel with him, and walked towards the "merchant" who was standing five hundred paces away from him. He walked past a group of loaders, vividly discussing something very important to them, past a small booth in which a man in uniform was sitting - such as Ned had seen in public from the royal ships that entered the village, passed a flock of girls who looked at the guy with an attentive glance, and suddenly stopped, rooted to the spot. Then he leaned back, reaching the booth with a man in uniform, stood beside it and gazed at the pier where the "merchant" was standing. Exactly! They. The people from the village are three hunters and Branc.

Ned lowered his head, trying not to be recognized by anyone, took a step behind the booth and looked back at the dock. Branck was saying something to a short, fat man with a haughty face, apparently the owner of the ship. He nodded his head, and Branc with the men accompanying him went along the pier further, to the next ship.

Ned realized with annoyance what was happening. This is to be expected. Where will the fugitive go first? To the city, of course. And where in the city will he rush to get out of these places? To the port, or to where the merchant caravans gather. Ned was sure that now Branca's people were walking around the caravaneers, too, and they warned that the caravaneers did not take the crazy killer who fled their village.

Branc was approaching, and Ned turned his back to prevent him from accidentally revealing the whereabouts of the fugitive. With his back to the dock, he found himself face to face with a man in uniform.

- What, boy, do you want to enlist? - he asked cheerfully - our king needs strong guys! Come on, come on - you will immediately receive two gold coins, and then - one gold per week! Plus food, shape! You will travel around the world, you will see distant lands, you will fight for your king, punishing the adversaries who dare to claim the Masurian Islands! Marines - what could be more honorable, what could be cooler? You were nothing! And you will become - a black demon, which all enemies fear! And we don't care if a tail of problems, or even crimes, lasts behind you - by joining the army, you become part of our big family, and no one can offend you! You yourself will offend everyone! Well, have you thought of it? You just need to put your fingerprint here, and drink a mug of "waste" beer, and you are already a Marine, a storm of seas and shores!

- And exactly, that everyone will not care where I am from and who I am?

- Does not matter! - the recruiter gasped happily - what is your name?

"Ned ... just Ned," the guy replied, confused.

- And the middle name?

- Ned ... Black. Yep - Black Ned.

- Good! Sumptuously! So we will write - "Ned Black". Put a print here. aha, dip your finger. soooo ... right here. There is! Well done! Take a mug! Drink!

Ned carefully sniffed the malt-smelling liquid from the mug and carefully poured the contents into himself. Beer, like beer ... And then he decided to turn on the "ears". He winced slightly at the impact of a cacophony of thoughts, and not without difficulty caught the recruiter's thoughts. He looked at Ned with a grin, and thought:

- I wonder how long this goof will stand on his feet? The guy is tough, he can hold out for about five minutes ... you will have to lock him up while he is here and go for the corporal. One, perhaps, to strain? The guy is young, but he is so big and big. Mosles - they weigh more than fat. Here's another gold bonus in my pocket. Worked well this week. But not the best week this year ... yeah. began!

Ned's eyes suddenly dimmed and his legs refused to hold him. He softly fell into the arms of the seizing sergeant, and looked in bewilderment at his face with glazed eyes.

- Sorry, recruit, such rules - he said apologetically - are supposed to jam you until we lift you aboard the ship. And then what are you in the habit of - take two gold, and on the run! And who will die for the health of our king? Who will fight if everyone scatters? Now you are ours. And your gold coins won't go anywhere, don't hesitate! Everything will be good. So I put them in your wallet. Sleep, tomorrow you will wake up cheerful, as you were born again. Already a soldier. And then - you will not have to sleep ... sleep now.

Ned's eyelids slammed shut and he passed out.

- ABOUT! Our dead man has woken up! - the voice thundered in his ears, and Ned with difficulty opened his eyes, trying to figure out where this voice was coming from. His head ached terribly, red and white spots were spinning before his eyes, and Ned barely focused his gaze on what he saw.

Huge room. It's just enormous. If you drive the entire population of the Black Ravine village here, there will still be a place. And everywhere - people. They lie, walk, sit, and mumble, mumble, mumble ...

Voices fly from everywhere, swarm in the air, merging into noise and roar, similar to the sound of sea waves. It took Ned a moment to realize that he was hearing both the thoughts and the living voices of men. Yes - everyone who was here was men. Hundreds, maybe thousands of men.

I had to turn off the perception of other people's thoughts, otherwise it is simply impossible to distinguish thoughts from words, and Ned did not feel at all the desire to betray his abilities. Why would he need extra problems? He intends to pretend to be a simple guy for as long as possible, until he gets far, far away, where no one will ever reach him. No - not to the next world. Ned categorically did not want to let himself be killed, and intended to hold out in this world for as long as possible. And see the death of your enemies. Well - he gave himself such a vow. What kind of enemies? Hmm ... Branca, I guess. Why did he beat Ned, humiliate him? Whom else? Those guys who wanted to cripple him ... but they are already punished. There is no worse punishment than losing your mind, becoming a vegetable. Better death. Who else?

Ned never figured out who his enemies were, and deciding to postpone this important decision until later, he turned his attention to his neighbors.

The one who was surprised at his awakening sat next to him with his legs crossed at the heels and his hands on his knees. His eyes were closed and he seemed to be praying.

- Hey, what are you doing? Are you sleeping, is that so? Ned inquired cautiously.

- Don't bother. I gain strength tsu through my kankry - the guy replied quietly, without opening his eyes and without changing his body position.

- Where do you get it from, this very tsu - and what kind of kankry are they? Ned kept up. He was terribly curious about what was happening around and Ned was going to find out everything thoroughly. He remembered that he was recruited into the army, he remembered drinking beer from the recruiter's mug, he remembered that the recruiter said something to him ... and then he did not remember anything. And I did not understand where it was either. House? Ship? Most likely a ship. You can hear the waves hitting the side and shaking slightly. It's just strange - the pitching was weak. Are they standing still? Ned was on the boats that came to their village. So they jerked from every breath of the wind, but here it was as if they had tied this ship. So big that it won't rock? "Ned's breath caught in the imagination of HOW size this ship should be.

- Redneck! - The guy answered grumpily - you fool! Don't you know that you can't interrupt a watsu master when he connects to the universe? Idiot!

- Whose master ?! - Ned did not understand - what are you doing there? And for an idiot, you can actually get it in the forehead!

- From whom, from you, or what? - the guy chuckled cheerfully - I have a tark in uatsu! You would have held your tongue until I pulled it out!

- Hey, you wouldn't be catching Oidar. He really can fuck you up - the guy to the left of Ned said loudly, rummaging in his bag - he has already smashed two faces, and, moreover, both at once. Uatsu is such an art of fighting. People have been learning this for years. And then they become invincible. They seem to gain strength from the space of the universe, and then put it into their body through the holes, making themselves invincible. I don't know what kind of holes and where, only they are called kankars, or something ...

- Kankry, you fool! - snorted Oidar - and everything else is correct.

- And why are you all fools and idiots calling? - Ned was indignant - himself, smart, or what?

- Smarter than you, rednecks! - the guy answered contemptuously, and closed his eyes again.

- Don't mess - the neighbor whispered again, and Ned saw a grin on Oidar's lips - well, his to the demons. He is bad, he will cripple more. Impudent guy. Will end badly, that's for sure.

"You'll end up badly! - hoisted Oidar - now I have eyes like you, you dumb-headed dumbass!

- Hey, you moron - Ned said coldly - don't touch him! You are the same as the rest of us, and do not make yourself an important person! And I do not see the clever in front of me. In my opinion, you are an arrogant fool. Dumb as a sheep. A smart person would not rush at everyone and boast of his strength. Especially in front of strangers.

- Oh, you creature! - Oidar got up from his place, moving like a snake and looming over Ned - get up, redneck! I don't want to hit the lying one! But you need to be taught a lesson, insolent peasant!

- Now - Ned nodded his head, and deliberately grunting, got to his feet - just wait, I'll pump myself up through the hole. I have one, and from there it only comes out, but does not enter, but what if? There is a hole, and the power can fit into it! How are you doing there? Do you close your eyes and puff? I want to do the same. Strength.

Ha ha ha - suddenly there was laughter, Ned looked up and found that there were dozens of guys and men around, watching with curiosity what was happening between Ned and the young insolent. Apparently the interlocutors were talking very loudly, so those around them became interested. There is nothing to do anyway, so why not take a look?

- Laugh at me?! - Oidar blushed, and bit his lip from restrained anger - damn redneck! And you dullheads! None of you will stand in battle with me for ten heartbeats! We fight, redneck! I will cripple you, creature, for taunting the uatsu master!

- I wonder - Ned drawled thoughtfully - why you were kicked out of the battle school - was it because you could not restrain your feelings?

Oydar shuddered and looked at Ned with wide eyes, and then ... then attacked him. Instantly, mercilessly, striking the most vulnerable and painful points. It seems that he decided not to stand on ceremony with the impudent redneck. Rather, Oidar wanted not to stand on ceremony, he wanted to strike, but ...

Ned gently passed his right hand with a fiercely clenched fist past him, meeting her with a feline paw movement, instantly grabbed the guy by the neck, turning him along the axis and dropping on his knee bent him so that make another movement, and Oidar's neck would crack, break, like a dry branch. And at the same time, the guy's right hand was blocked by Ned's right hand, and his head, with an arched neck, lay in the armpit of the "redneck".

Ned acted completely unconsciously, as then - killing his fellow villagers. It was only when there was only a split second before the dry crunch of vertebrae was heard that Ned struggled to control himself and stopped, looking at the crowd eagerly watching the fight.

After this difficult feint of Ned, they made a noise, began to giggle and point fingers at the guys who merged in a single rush, like a couple in love. They began to whistle and say nasty things, happily slapping themselves on the thighs.

Ned looked into Oidar's tense, wide-eyed face and said clearly, looking back at the audience:

- Dispersed. Dispersed, I said! There is nothing interesting.

His voice was dry, harsh, and his eyes radiated such power that people stopped short and, while talking quietly, began to disperse to their places. Ned looked into Oidar's face again and said in a low voice:

- I'll let you go now, but promise that you will no longer offend anyone and behave so arrogantly. Good? Did you agree?

Oydar shook his head shallowly in agreement, and Ned carefully laid him on the floor next to his mattress. Then again Ned lay down in his seat and stared at the ceiling, throwing his hand behind his head and not paying attention to the neighbors.

He felt very strange after these events. Again - as if some kind of force was controlling his body. Apart from his will, apart from consciousness. As if someone looked through his eyes, and took control of the body at the moment when it became necessary. And Ned really, really didn't like it. And who likes to feel like a limp toy? Only not to someone who has been such for seventeen years in a row.

- Hello, you him! - the neighbor whispered - call me Arnot. Let's stick together? Where are you from? Well ... you don't have to answer - he continued slightly frightened - we are all here for different reasons, and many do not want to give out their names and where they come from. What's your name?

- Ned - the guy answered reluctantly, and turning his head examined the interlocutor. He was an ordinary village guy, there are dozens and hundreds of them in any village. Tired hands, strong shoulders, worn out shoes and neatly darned clothes are just a regular guy. What kind of demon is he doing here? What is he, Ned, doing here? Hear his thoughts? What for? What can he learn from him, or from these guys? Their dirty secrets? Their hidden desires? What for? What will it give? "Absolutely useless skill," Ned sighed softly. "I wish I could conjure food for myself. I ate for a long time, and only two pies. "

As if in response to his thoughts, the stomach emitted such a loud gurgle that was probably heard from side to side. Arnot chuckled when he heard this sound, and, rustling his bag, handed Ned a piece of flatbread, on which lay a piece of smoked meat:

- Eat. Eat, eat - I still have. We will be fed when we arrive at the infantry base, but for now we have to make do with what we have. I stocked up some food on the beach in advance. A neighbor, a disabled soldier, told me everything about how it would be, so I prepared myself properly. The water is over there in the tank. And the mug is there. Just do not advise drinking from a common mug. You never know who came from where - you'll pick up the infection. My family died like that - my father brought the infection from somewhere, sailed with the merchant. We all got infected. My sister died, then my mother ... my father ... and somehow I survived. They say there was a pestilence. The house was burned down, things were burned. He remained naked. Don't be afraid - it was long ago. About five years ago. I roamed, roamed ... begged ... worked ... and then decided - what have I got to lose? I will go to the soldiers. Here they feed, dress, and shoe. You will serve five years - and go for a walk. You can put together capital.

- And it is possible and ... what did your disabled neighbor lose? Here's something to lose - a familiar voice rang out on the right, slightly husky after Ned squeezed its owner's throat.

"I lost my leg," Arnot answered reluctantly, and turned away from Oidar.

- In-in - Oidar nodded his head - and we will be ugly, if at all. They will bury it somewhere on the Masurian Islands, and the worms will eat it. The disabled person is even alive ...

- Why then did you go to the soldier - asked Ned, swallowing the last piece of cake, and carefully collecting the crumbs, threw them into his mouth under the gaze of Oidar, wincing at such a clear manifestation of village origin - you seem to know everything - what lured you here ?

"Everyone has their own problems," Oidar explained reluctantly, and with a sigh, he made up his mind — you were right when you said that all my problems were due to my lack of restraint. And there is no need to smile like that, Arnot!

He hesitated for a minute, and continued:

- Yes, I am a watsu master. Almost from infancy they taught. There is a good school in Shusard. My father always believed that I should be able to stand up for myself. He was a guard. They killed. Nobody knows who. Apparently those whom he interfered with. I went home at night - they shot an arrow from a bow. Outright. I was ten then. After his death, everything went haywire ... no money, they ate the last thing that happened. Mother began to sew for the rich, but not very much. I was doing well in martial arts school, I am talented. The master noticed this and allowed him to study for free when I told him that there was no more money for the school. And then - I began to help him train others. Everything would be fine ... but my character ... And to it add the ability to kill ... They themselves got to the bottom of me, themselves! - Oidar fiercely hit his knee with his fist - I would have left without answering, but I ... In general - one died, and the other two will lie in bed for a long time. Everything would be fine - but the one who died is a relative of the mayor. And his friends are from the most respected families in the city. The guards who were investigating the case warned my mother that I quickly wash away - and I will not live to see the trial if they put me in prison. Here I am. Now - I am nobody. The army will not give me offense. The army itself will offend me. Is your name Ned? Yeah. Tell me, Ned - Oidar looked closely at the guy - how did you get me to bed? What is this fighting style called? I've never met him live. And more - thank you. The army will not give me offense. The army itself will offend me. Is your name Ned? Yeah. Tell me, Ned - Oidar looked closely at the guy - how did you get me to bed? What is this fighting style called? I've never met him live. And also - thank you. The army will not give me offense. The army itself will offend me. Is your name Ned? Yeah. Tell me, Ned - Oidar looked closely at the guy - how did you get me to bed? What is this fighting style called? I've never met him live. And also - thank you.

- For what? - Ned raised his eyebrows in bewilderment.

- For not having killed - Oydar sighed heavily - I am a master after all, I know that I was on the verge of death. You could kill me with one move of your hand. Bastard! And that's all. The end. But he didn't. And I would kill. I could not stand it. So thanks.

- I would have killed - I would have killed myself - gloomily threw Arnot - for the murder of his comrade, if it was not committed in defense of his life, or by order of the commander - death. Hang, and that's it. Or beaten to death with sticks. It's fast here. For stealing from comrades - sticks. For disobeying an order - sticks. For everything, sticks, or death.

- How do you know that? - Oidar shook his head incredulously.

- I told you - I had a neighbor, an invalid. He told me everything - what to expect from the army, what to fear. What to do and what not to do. So I know everything.

- Yes? So can you tell me what and how? Oidar curled his lips into a mocking smile, but Ned could feel his curiosity. The guy was the same age as he was, so what to expect from the boy?

- Maybe I'll tell you - Arnot replied solidly, and after a pause, for the sake of importance, began:

"We'll be brought to the Marine Corps base. Then...

- What will they bring? - Ned interrupted - where are we now? I do not know anything. As he grabbed the damned beer, he ended up here. And that's all. Were you drunk?

- Someone was intoxicated, someone was not - the guy shrugged his shoulders - I - no. And we are on a Marine Corps ship called "Sword of Vengeance", which can accommodate one and a half thousand infantrymen. A whole regiment. So, they caught recruits all over the country, and they are taking them to the base, where they will make heroes of us. They will teach for six months and then ... then they will be sent to where the king wants. We are the main striking force in the fight against those who want to chop off the Masurian Islands. Well, the rest that belongs to the king. That, in general, is all.

- And that's all - Oidar held out sadly - and - that's it.

- Well, what are you whining? - said Ned coldly - you are alive, well, a skilled fighter. Arnot and I need to worry, but why are you so worried? And for that matter - you knew where you were going. Not quite as redneck as Arnott and I!

- Do you need to worry? - snorted Oidar - to you, who laid the master uatsu, like a child? You never said - what is your fighting style? I read an ancient treatise - the lost art of ancient combat, it was called somehow ... hmmm ... now I remember ... Ah! Here! Shanzo. It was called Shantso. And the fighters of the Shirduan sect - black magicians, moreover, demonology owned it. They kept the traditions of this struggle and did not give out their secrets to anyone. They searched all over the world for children who had the abilities of a demonologist, and took them to themselves - negotiated with their parents, stole or bought. Children disappeared and never returned to their parents. Never. But these fighters were invincible. They never used any weapon, except for a staff and their body, but no one could defeat them alone. However - and the crowd too. They killed them all - Oidar finished unexpectedly,yak lay down next to Ned, staring at the ceiling.

- It's like this, interrupted ?! - snorted Arnot - if they were invincible? Fairy tales. Read all sorts of crap, and tell stories.

- Well, you do ... in general - it's not a fairy tale! - Oidar glanced sideways at the imperturbable Ned, lying on his back and looking at the ceiling boards - they were interrupted by bows, crushed by a mass. Burned, again. The mages were let loose on them. And a lot of people died in the process. For each demonologist - at least fifty people were killed until they were all put in. Historical fact, you need to read books! And do not talk nonsense! - Oidar got angry - they even put a dozen magicians down, until they were simply burned by "black fire" from the battle fiery tubes! They blocked their temple and burned it down! No one survived! And they say that they took out the treasures - just a bunch - they were transported by ships! Only a part of them perished, these ships with gold. The gods sent a storm, and the ships sank somewhere off our coast. I wish I could find the place where they lie ... I would really find a use for these treasures.

- Hmm ... held out Arnot - and I would find a use for them. I would build a big house, hire servants, workers. I would get married. I would take a beautiful wife. I would have had children. A family ... I so wish that I had many, many children! So that they run, make noise, and I will never scold them. Let them run. Let them make noise. It's so bad when the house is quiet, quiet, quiet, quiet ... like in a grave.

Arnot turned away, and the guys saw his shoulders shake with suppressed sobs. Then he calmed down, and Oidar continued, in a slightly changed, cracked voice:

- In general, the ships sank, and the treasures were taken to the king's treasury. That's all. The martial art of black magicians is lost, there are no demonologists. And the place where their temple stood was razed to the ground. And already no one remembers where it was, this damned place. And it has passed since then ... I calculated ... about a thousand years. It was a long time ago. So how do you know this martial art?

- Father taught - Ned answered reluctantly - and forbade me to talk about it.

- Father? You ard, what, do ards have ancient art left? - Oidar asked perplexedly - strange. They somehow did not have developed the art of fighting with bare hands of this kind. More fistfights, and the possession of various weapons. They are specialists in fighting with heavy swords and axes. I'm a watsu master after all, so I know a lot about fighting.

- I told you I don't want to talk about it. Once and for all I tell you - never ask me about it. And let's finish right away - don't ask to teach. I won't. Better tell me who the demonologists are, what they did and why the king took up arms against them. I have never heard of such cases.

- Never? Are you sure? - Oidar grunted incredulously, following Ned's imperturbable, like a fixed mask - well, as you know. If you don't want to talk, don't talk. Okay. Let's count - you don't know. Demonologists are such black magicians who can summon demons from the place where they live. Rather, they knew how. The art of summoning demons has been lost.

- Real demons ?! - perked up - Arnot - with wings. With teeth and claws? That would be to have a look!

- I do not advise. After that, you would have turned into minced meat - Oidar giggled - no, not such demons. Nobody sees these demons. They are invisible. But they move into a person, and he gets sick with some kind of disease. But you can't cure it. Rather, it is possible - but only if the demonologist himself expels the demon. Or other demonologists. It was like this - the doctor will come, the person seems to have been cured, but a week or two passes - and he gets even worse, so bad that he dies in agony. The curses of the demonologists were not healed by anything other than their spells. Here!

- It's good that they were burned - Arnot shuddered - as I imagine that some creature is digging into me from the inside, gnawing out my heart, liver ...

"Okay…" Ned drawled vaguely. Before his eyes was a picture: the doctor Senerad, informing Anthur that he was completely healthy. The guy's stomach went cold when he heard Oidar's story that it was impossible to cure the damned demonologist. Really ?! No, it can not be. Never!

- Ugh! I even got a stomach ache - Oydar feigned oyknul - well, you, painted a picture! So that's why they were killed. They took orders for murder, blackmailed the rich and the poor, behaved disgustingly - arranged sacrifices, orgies, got rich and accumulated huge treasures. They allegedly possessed ancient knowledge, and seemed to have discovered the secret of making gold from other metals. It seems to me - that's why they were banged. Not for all sorts of magic secrets, but they became too rich. What king will tolerate such rich people by his side? When the treasury is exhausted by wars and revelry ... Our kings have never been known for their ability to spend money carefully. And the current, they say, loves to arrange endless drinking and orgies.

- By the way, but it is impossible in more detail about the orgies that the demonologists arranged ... well, what did they do there, why and why ... it is possible about the royal orgies too ... - Arnot could not resist and burst out laughing. Oidar started laughing after him, Ned, and who smiled rarely, unexpectedly for himself joined the guys, and began to giggle more and more, until his quiet giggle turned into laughter. And now all three guys were laughing, holding their bellies and blowing tears from their eyes.

What was it? Hysterics? Maybe. Or maybe just young, healthy organisms were looking for an excuse for relaxation, release of psychic energy. And they found it.

- Hey, you horses! - Someone next to the guys shouted benignly - let me sleep! They laugh, scoundrels ... already enviable.

- Young, why should they - someone grunted from the opposite side of the hold - they were also once so bad. However - and now they are not smarter. If you were smart, you wouldn't get into this shit. For two gold coins and a mug of beer.

- Yeah ... supported by someone from afar - a bitch recruiter! Have a drink, you won't get poisoned! And he put his finger on it! Creature. They will bring us to the islands, and they will finish us there. And bury us in the damp earth. And why the hell is the king of these islands ?! If only the gods drowned them fuck, all at once, and until the end of the universe!

- Fool! On the islands there is both gold and silver. Black oil for pipes of fire. Forest. Aborigines are hardy and strong. Everything is there! That's why three kingdoms have been dogging for them for a hundred years. It's not for nothing.

- Not for nothing? And if...

Ned listened with the edge of his ear to the recruits' conversation, and thought about how hard he hit - from all sides hit. Like a rabbit in a snare. And now he needs to keep his eye out - not to show any signs of magic, not to give anyone any reason to suspect that he is reading people's minds. It would be good to give up fighting skills - but how can he do this if the body itself does what it needs? Well at least he didn't kill Oidar today. And I must admit - with great difficulty he stopped the murder. He just felt the urge to wring the guy's neck, barely stopped. Control, and control again - he said to himself, and was surprised - he never said such words, and what to think?

Oidar talked about life, about martial arts, but Ned didn't listen anymore. The story of the demonologists startled him. It is clear that he understood what he was talking about. It is not surprising to understand - if you are the one he was talking about. And it was scary. Ned really didn't want to go to the fire.

Chapter 5

The ship took two days to get there. Two days locked up, in the stale air of a living hold.

From time to time, hatches were opened, letting in fresh sea air and people grabbed it with open mouths, enjoying every gulp. By the end of the second day, many began to be indignant - they were not slaves, after all, sailing without feeding for so many days, and even it was not clear where!

Then boxes with thin breads, petrified from long storage, were lowered into the hatches, and everyone could eat, soaking them in warm, musty water smelling of rotten meat.

The ship's crew practically did not communicate with the recruits - either they considered it beneath their dignity to conduct conversations with such a rabble, or they were ordered not to communicate - in any case, they got off with only "yes" and "no" when they loaded boxes into the hold, and poured "fresh" water into barrels.

Ned took hardship quite easily - his survival school was more abrupt than two days of sitting in a half-dark hold, lit through barred hatches. Oidar and Arnot did not moan either; they behaved quite decently.

During these two days, the three guys became friends. It turned out somehow imperceptibly - in a day they ate together, slept next to them. No one climbed to them - they were afraid of the reputation of Oidar and Ned, already famous as strong fighters. If not for them, Arnot would have taken away his bag of groceries long ago, leaving no crumb for the owner. This happened all the time - fights, swearing, indignant screams.

The three guys did not pay attention to what was happening - they were fighting, and the demons were with them. The main thing is that they are not touched. And if touched, they will suffer. They did not touch.

For two days, two nights, the ship rolled on the waves, causing seasickness in its living contents, which surprised Ned very much - he did not experience any unpleasant sensations. And why? On such a hefty thing, but to make you feel sick? This is not a nimble little boat dancing on the waves.

However, his friends also felt fine. Oydar was always telling something, Arnot complemented him, or told something of his own - also interesting, and Nedmolcha absorbed information, like a dry sponge absorbs water.

He enjoyed himself. Than? Everyone! You can sleep as long as you want, lie as long as you want - no one kicks you, demanding to go to work, no one will offend you - simply because he is in a bad mood. He is among equals, he is respected.

But there is not enough fresh air. But not forever. Someday they will come to the place anyway.

And this hour has come. In the morning, when the recruits were still tearing their eyes after a sweltering, hot night, the ship trembled perceptibly - it moored to the pier. For another hour or so, nothing happened, then the thick wooden grates covering the hatches opened, falling to the side with a crash, and a loud commanding voice shouted:

- Recruits, out! Quickly! With things!

The people in the hold rushed up the wide wooden stairs. A crush was formed, several fights and scandals broke out. People were eager for fresh air, the taste of which had almost been forgotten after two days of imprisonment.

Ned stopped his comrades, who were trying to succumb to the general hysteria, and now they watched with pleasure as people forced their way into freedom. It would seem - what would it be if they had waited a while - they would all be released, they would not go anywhere! No - you have to break, you have to fight for a place on the stairs, pushing your comrades from it.

- Such is human nature - said Oydar thoughtfully, looking as one big man pushed a thin man with a village knapsack down the stairs - the stronger ones always try to climb the top step, crawling over the heads of their comrades. So my master spoke, and as usual - he was right.

- Why didn't he buy you off? - asked Arnot with interest - he seems to be rich enough?

- Well, how can I tell you ... who needs other people's problems. Moreover, there was no longer any talk of money. If the victims were ordinary people, like you and me, it would be another matter, and so ... That's it, let's go too, otherwise we risk hitting the ridge with a stick for not leaving on time.

The guys walked to the nearest exit and lined up at the back of the line of the last recruits leaving the hold.

Ten steps, polished by the feet of thousands of people, and here it is - freedom! The sea air fills the lungs, the sun shines in the eyes so that they water and close, as if covered with sand.

Ned lingers on deck, trying to see where he is, but they won't let him stand - a blow with a stick on his back burns like boiling water and a disgusting, torn voice screams loudly:

- Forward! Forward, hornless brute! Run, run, to the shore! Stop messing around! This is not your ancestral home - here is the army, misbegotten ones!

Swearing under their breath and rubbing the bruised places, the recruits run in a row down the ladder to the shore, and crash into the crowd of those who got off earlier. There are many of them, so many that the coast is teeming with people. Around are soldiers in full combat gear, chain mail, helmets, spears, swords and rectangular shields on their backs. They watch the crowd with a smile, talk, and drive away with shafts those who try to approach them in order to exchange a few words. It can be seen that the recruits for them are below the lowest, at the level of worms or toads.

- Stand up! We got up straight! Yes, straighten up, you bastards! - yelled the same voice - but what kind of creatures are you so brainless! If only a semblance of a formation was created! Why are you smiling, idiots? - the man shouted to the soldiers who were watching the formation - they themselves left not far from them, morons! All got up, got up! Have pulled up!

A not very tall, but strong, broad-shouldered man in a shabby uniform ran along the ranks of recruits, lined up by several people in the same uniforms, hitting particularly dull guys with a stick several times in the stomachs, and finally - something like a square made up of breathing in the back of each other's future comrades in arms. Conversations subsided, and silence reigned over the pier, which was interrupted by the clatter of the horseshoes of the boots worn by a man in an expensive uniform decorated with silver embroidery. He walked accompanied by several people similar to him, dressed poorer, but also distinguished by a military bearing - chest forward, shoulders back - as if he had swallowed a stake.

- Mr. Colonel! A regiment of recruits has been unloaded on the dock and is preparing to move to the waiting barracks! In the presence of one thousand two hundred thirty three people! There are no sick or wounded!

"Thank you, Lieutenant.

The colonel carefully examined the silent formation, and grinning, said loudly:

- Recruits! Tomorrow you will take the oath of allegiance to the army and the king. Tomorrow you will be one of those who will bring glory to Zamar! Our king trusts in us, and we will not shame him! Isn't that so, recruits? I can't hear you! Louder!

- Let's not shame ... - the unfortunate recruits roared dimly, shifting from foot to foot, and the only thing thinking about - not how not to shame - but about much more mundane, so to speak, matters. The rotten water acted as a good laxative, and a lot of the guys were holding their bellies, trying not to shit in their pants and on the dock.

Finally, the speech of the colonel, admiring himself and flaunting in front of his subordinates, ended, he imperiously waved the white leather gloves clutched in his hand and the lieutenant and sergeants screamed again, urging the human herd into his corral. * * *

Senerad almost jumped in impatience, watching the sailors at the dock strapping the boat to hefty wooden posts. The gangplank thundered along the side, and helping himself with a dandy stick, the doctor quickly climbed onto the dock. Then he looked back and waved to the two faded guards.

- Let's hurry up! Time is precious! In the evening they are waiting for us in agar!

They looked at each other, sighing, as people, resigned to a difficult fate, climbed over the side. The last thing they wanted was to roam the backwater villages at the edge of the world. And the fact that this is the end of the world could be seen without leaving the ship - wretched houses on the slope, trampled earth covered with cow cakes, stupid faces of the villagers meeting the ship.

Well, of course - not every day a guard ship appears! Something completely out of the ordinary must happen for the guards to appear here. However, didn't it happen?

- How did you know? - asked Branc in surprise, meeting the guards and the doctor on the way up the hill.

- What have you learned? - Senerad was unpleasantly surprised, and his heart pounded as if it wanted to fly out of his chest.

- Well, about Ned? Did you come for him?

- Behind him - the doctor answered with wide eyes - and how do you know what's behind him?

- That's what - intervened one of the guards, a man of about forty-five, battered, and not going to stand in the sun longer than required by the service regulations - take us to where this same Ned lives, and we'll talk there.

Branc nodded his head and took the whole party to his home. The doctor went last. He was very puzzled by the meeting and forbade himself to draw conclusions, although deep down he understood that something irreparable had happened, and it was connected with Ned. The only thing he said to himself was: "If only I was alive! If only to be in time! "

The large room was empty, although the curious eyes of Branca's servants peeped out from the kitchen, from around the corner. He signaled with his hand, and soon on the table stood a jug of cold milk, straight from the cellar, fragrant fresh cakes and salt in a dark clay salt shaker, cracked from time to time. The guards took off their helmets with pleasure, lowered them with a crash on the bench, sat down next to them on the wide board of the bench, and poured milk, forgetting for a while about the purpose of their arrival. However - they were not allowed to completely forget.

- So how did you know about Ned? - Branc began again, looking at the puffing healer, perched next to the soldiers.

- What did you learn? - Spitting bitter saliva right on the floor, asked the doctor. He had a sore throat, and Serenade noted with regret that he most likely caught a cold on deck.

"Well, did Ned kill ten people?"

- What did he do ?! - Senerad even got up from his place, and the guard choked, coughed, and doused himself with milk to his pants. He swore, and taking a rag from the table, began to wipe the chain mail.

- Tell from the beginning - said the guard - everything in detail. I see - you live here cheerfully in a quiet village.

- It was quiet - Branc muttered, while this bastard ... In general - it began with the fact that my slave suddenly fell ill. He - Branc pointed to Seenerad - allegedly cured him. By the way - return my silver pieces! Antur curls up. Over there, in the room. Bloody diarrhea - as if someone was eating it from the inside. I generally want to sue you! Cheater!

- Get to the point! - grunted the guard - then you will drag each other through the courts. What about the murder?

- Well, so - like he cured him. Only the next day another strange incident happened. Three guys and a girl went hunting in the hills, and returned insane. Well - absolutely! They are walking, and drooling from the mouth. They will be told to do something - eat, drink - they eat and drink. But you will not say - they will die of hunger.

- Alive? Interrupted Seenerad.

- Alive - Branc grimaced - only now they have become even worse! They scream, rage, beat their heads. The girl tore off all her clothes and ran naked into the street - they barely caught her. She bit, screeched ...

- Did you try to interrogate them? They asked how it turned out? - inquired another guard, refilling the mug with milk.

- What's the point of interrogating? They're insane! - chuckled Branc. When all this happened, the girl's father came to us. He was the headman here ... was.

- Was it? The doctor asked quickly.

- I was. Ned killed him - the man nodded his head - well, let me finish it in order, huh? What are you interrupting all the time?

- Mister doctor - shut up. - the guard nodded his head - and we, dear, are supposed to ask questions! You are having a good time here, stacking piles of people! Soon the king will have no one to take taxes from! We will find out what is going on here, and who should answer for it!

Branc was slightly obscured, and already half a tone lower, in a slightly ingratiating voice, continued:

- Well, I'm telling you - the headman came to me and said: "Have you had anything happening lately? Nobody was sick? " Well, I told you about the slave. He asked him around - then the slave was still in order, it seemed like he was healthy ...

- You see - healthy! Have you heard, gentlemen ?! And he is here trying to hang up a claim! I suppose he poisoned him himself, and now he's talking nonsense! - Senerad could not resist. And with a gesture he showed - I am silent, I am silent!

- He talked to the slave, then in my presence he interrogated the servants. The girl alone, a slave, showed that Ned, when Antur got sick, muttered something and made some movements. Like throwing something. The headman left, and before leaving he said that his daughter was delirious and shouted: "Ned! Ned! " So he came to find out what Ned was about.

- Did you find out? The guard asked calmly, glaring at Branck's rough face.

- Looks - I recognized - the man shrugged his shoulders - after a while I looked - the headman, and his guys go towards the hills, where Ned went. Nobody saw them again alive. So did Neda.

- What, he's dead ?! - jumped up Seenerad - he was killed ?!

- He killed everyone. And where it is now is unknown. I tell you further. In the evening - no cows and no, the herd is gone. The people waited, waited, dispersed. In the morning we gathered in search. Moreover, the headman and the guys were gone, and Ned was gone. Found. All ten people lay dead, disfigured as if they had fallen off a cliff onto stones. Broken arms, legs, ribs, broken necks and spines. And all around are the footprints of Ned. And the dogs. By the way, it was a good dog. Was, yes! They killed her. The hunters have restored the whole picture. It turned out like this: the headman with the guys came to Ned, and began to talk to him. What happened there is unknown, only Narda stood up for Ned, began to tear them up. They killed her. And Ned got mad and killed the guys. That's all. I've always said that these ards are insane! What if he had gone nuts earlier? Yes, he would have killed everyone in the house! Me first!

- And you say that the guy at the age of seventeen killed ten adult men? - the guard asked incredulously - what are you doing here, all went crazy?

"He's not just a kid," said another guard. "One can expect everything from him. Maybe he turned into some kind of demon!

- Demon ?! - the healer got up from his place - oh gods! What a fool I am ... ah, a fool ... the ends came together. It all came together. Oh, you ...

- No, no demons! What does the demons have to do with it? - confusedly explained Branc - there are only traces of Ned! He escaped, stripping one of the guys. Most likely - he went to the city and got lost somewhere there. We went after him at night - the hunters and me. But they didn't manage to open the gate. And in the city they were no longer found. Perhaps at dawn he hired one of the merchant ships, and sailed out of the city. The smart guy turned out to be, never thought that he was so smart. He looks like a real moron. And he behaved as if he was mentally retarded. Everybody thought he was half-dumb. But you see what ... The headman was certainly wrong - why kill my dog? But Ned avenged her ... I even had a little respect for this Ard cattle - Branc finished unexpectedly.

- Did you talk to his household? I mean the headmen, of course. What are they saying?

"His wife said the headman went to deal with Ned. It seems like he's to blame for what happened to their daughter and the three guys. The guys were going to find Nedai to teach a lesson during the day. Everyone in the village thinks Ned cursed them. Here. And he cursed my servant. Before the slave got sick, he spat into Ned's cup. So after all - why did you come here? Seenerad, why did you go to town? Did you bring the guards?

- I - the doctor answered lost - only now it does not matter in the least. Since Ned is gone. Here, read it! - the doctor took out a tightly rolled scroll from his bag and threw it on the table - I went to the city for this. And the guard ensures the execution of the order.

Branc unrolled the scroll, read for a long time, moving his lips, then his eyes widened in surprise, and he, stuttering slightly, asked:

- What, really? Is Ned a black magician?

- There is nowhere blacker - the doctor answered gloomily - be glad that bloody diarrhea has not gone away. Everyone who offended him in the near future would have to pay heavily for it. Here is the moral for you - no need to humiliate anyone, offend, mix with dirt - suddenly tomorrow this person turns out to be a black magician and your meanness will return to you many times stronger, and kill you! You, and you alone, are to blame for what happened to Ned. And your fucking village. That's it, guys, there is nothing to do here. Ned is not here - the doctor sighed, and got to his feet - I'll go and pack my things. I'll go to the city. I'll look for him there.

- Stop! What will happen to my slave? - Branc cried indignantly - what should he do?

- To die, of course - Seenerad replied indifferently, lingering at the door - now a demon sits in it, and eats away the insides. There was nothing for the black magician to cough into a cup.

- So heal him! You took the money for the treatment! Swindler!

- Shut up, bitch! You drove Ned to murder! If not for your village ... ehhh ... - the doctor waved his hand and went outside, then returned, and added - you can all be sued, idiots!

- And what is it for? Branc asked belligerently.

- For stupidity! - Senerad grinned, turned, and decisively walked to the house in which he spent the last ten years of his life. He was sorry that it had ended this way, but at the same time pipes were playing in his soul - that's enough! It's time to get back to town! Get out of this village with stupid, insensitive inhabitants! Away from the scolding and elders, away from this backwater, which makes a man an insensitive beast, having fun only with the suffering of his neighbor. In the evening he will be in the city, he will find himself shelter - fortunately, that he had a stash, he saved up for ten years. Get settled and start looking for Ned. It cannot be that he did not leave any trace. The guy has never been in the city, so he had to get confused and inherit. There is always some trace, always. * * *

- Keep your leg, keep your leg! What kind of brainless creatures ?! Rrraz! Rrraz! Rrraz - two! Turn! Beasts! When you hear this signal, you need to turn over your shoulder, without stopping walking! The legs are slightly bent, the spear is lowered and looks at the enemy! Why did you let him down, you damned moron? Where is the end of your spear looking? Is this your end ?! How are you going to prick, where? In a cow cake ?! Uuuuu ... morons! Every year the recruits are getting more and more debility! Soon absolutely idiots will be recruited! I would not let you get close to the weapon, and look at your neighbor, you will be stabbed like a beetle! Keep, keep the step! Rrraz! Rrraz!

- I hate him - groaned Oidar, stumbling and with difficulty lifting a hefty pole, here called a spear - my hands are already falling off this rubbish!

- Here - Ned chuckled - the Dragon will see, he will give you hot! Remember yesterday's boyfriend?

Oidar nodded with a martyr's grimace, and tightening his grip on the shaft, began to march on, diligently directing the blunt tip of the spear towards the "enemy", Sergeant Dracon, whom, of course, everyone called the Dragon. Yesterday, on the parade ground, he whipped a negligent recruit with a stick - personally, so much so that blood spattered from his broken back. Fifteen strikes with a stick is not a joke. The guy was stupid and did not know where and when to turn. And also - he dared to argue with the commander.

Now the recruits finally realized where they were - as the Dragon said - "This is not your home here! You are all meat! And by the end of the training, I will either make a soldier out of you, or you will die on the punishment bench, idiots! If you thought you came here to wallow in the grass and get gold, you are wrong! Every gold one will be washed with your sweat and blood, you idiots! But those who come out safe and sound from the gate of the training camp have a chance to survive when they get to the battlefield! Then remember old Drankon with a kind word! "

"I will remember him every time I go to the toilet - imagine that I am doing it on top of his head!" - Oidar whispered to his friends, and they giggled for a minute, biting their lips and wrying so that the Dragon would not notice their smile.

There were precedents - one guy who smiled in the ranks and caught the eye of the Dragon, received five sticks, and now stood pale and concentrated, without smiles or grimaces. Sergeant Dracon's methods were incredibly effective, and also very, very painful - all the recruits noticed it.

- Stop! Recruits! Now we are all going to the canteen! Keep your foot! Show that our company is the best! And who will not show - I will pour a boiling stew on his head, no doubt, assholes! Paaa ... let's go! Rrraz! Rrraz! Rrraz-ddtwo !! We pull the leg, donkey-headed, pull! Why are you limping there, you damned lump? Rubbed the leg? And you didn't rub your fat ass, pimply toad ?! Step straight, you bastard, shame on your fucking village! Rrraz! Rrraz!

"I wonder why he hasn't been killed yet?" - gasping from the heat and dust raised by the feet of his colleagues, asked Arnot - the disabled person told me that there were cases when soldiers quietly killed especially evil commanders as soon as they got on the battlefield!

- And what, did not find the killers? - asked Oidar with interest, looking thoughtfully at the stocky figure of the Dragon.

- Found. Always - Arnot sighed regretfully, and also watched the hated sergeant, who had been torturing them for a week as if he had set himself the goal of poisoning the life of the recruits as much as possible.

- What are you thinking there - Ned smiled slightly, holding on his shoulder the same pole as his comrades - let him live. We just didn't have enough problems. And how, I wonder, did they find out who killed him, this officer?

- And you there too? - giggled Arnot - magicians were summoned. They picked up the corpse and questioned.

- This is how it was raised? - Ned stumbled, and immediately straightened, cautiously looking sideways at the Dragon, patting on the polished bootleg with a wooden cane.

"Well… some black magicians have mastered the art of necromancy. They can breathe a soul into a dead body - for a while, of course. And the corpses themselves are stories .... ay! ah!

- Conversations in the ranks, you moron! Keep in line, donkey face!

Tears of pain flowed from Arnot's eyes - the Dragon punched him right on the top of the head. The guy stretched out and walked stupidly looking in front of him, and the Dragon nodded in satisfaction, looking at Arnot's neighbors before that - they say, did you see? And it will be the same with you!

- Spears into the pyramid! Fast, fast, brutes! Run! To take places in the dining room without hustle and bustle, but quickly! Whoever arranges a dump will be left without lunch! March!

The recruits ran up to a special rack in a chain and made up "shafts" there, which they carried in their hands all day.

Throughout the week, the sergeant trained the reinforcements, ensuring that the soldiers clearly kept the line, understood the signals of the trumpeter and carried out commands without delay. By the end of the week, the recruits moved quite clearly, understanding their place in the ranks, and also learned a lot about their origins, sexual addictions and mental abilities. Sergeant Drankon was inexhaustible in writing colorful definitions of the physical and mental condition of soldiers.

The recruits had a hard time. Even Ned, who was used to hard work and hardship. It is not so easy to learn not to stray from a step in a close formation, and even holding a hefty spear in your hands.

The spears were of different sizes - the third row dragged three-meter spears, the ends of which protruded beyond the first row, the second row had shorter spears, in front there were already soldiers with very short spears. This achieved the fact that when the enemy went to the line of spearmen, in front of him he would see a continuous forest of arrowheads. Interaction with slingers, archers and swordsmen has not yet been worked out. It will come next.

The bad news is - as Arnot said - that the spearmen are the real meat that perishes in the first minutes of the battle. They always stand in front and take on the entire blow of the enemy, raising the foe to the spears. And they retreat last, covering the retreat of the main group.

- Let's run, don't sleep! - whispered Oidar, and rushed after the others into the dining room door, slapping the thoughtful Ned on the shoulder. He woke up from his thoughts and also dived under a long canopy, where there were tables dug into the ground with narrow benches on the sides. Carts were already rolling between the rows, from which the soldier distributors poured and poured food into the bowls of the recruits. Everything happened pretty quickly, clearly and smoothly. And also - the food was quite decent, and for the unspoiled Ned - very tasty. Meat, cereal boiled in broth, thick soup with a piece of flatbread - eat as much as you want, but only at the time allotted for lunch. I didn't have time - I stayed hungry. I managed to eat it and if you want more - even eat it.

The army did not skimp on food for the soldiers. The more food - the more can be attributed to what the soldiers ate. And you get big sums for the command. In the total mass of the product stream, it is easy to steal a little from a large one. And if they were saving, the portions would be small - you can't steal anything from zero. In addition, you will not feed this "meat", they will not live to see the battlefield. A good master feeds his dogs.

Separately on the tables were vegetables and fruits - no one needs soldiers with loose and falling teeth, swollen from scurvy.

A few minutes later, in the dining room, there was only the sound of wooden spoons on wooden bowls, and a chomp, reminiscent of the squelching of boots in swamp slurry. Most of the soldiers were not well-mannered. Oydar always winced as he watched the opposite neighbor grind food, opening his mouth like a trash can. He constantly complained to Ned and Antor that the sight of the chewed food in the throat of this pimply bumpkin took away all his appetite. However, it was not true - the appetite of these guys could not beat off anything in the world - the food was swept away in the blink of an eye, and soon many recruits raised their hand, demanding more from the feedmen.

At lunchtime, in addition to food, there was another good point - after lunch there would be the longed-for two hours of rest, when the soldiers could take a nap in the shade, go to the toilet, dry their footcloths soaked in pungent sweat and unbutton their annoying uniform rubbing their neck. After the rest there will be new trainings, until dusk, but for now - these two hours belong to the soldiers.

- Oh, how I filled up! - Arnot plopped down on the bench of the fence, and leaned back, blissfully closing his eyes - this is how they feed well here ... if not for this drill, and not for the Dragon ...

- Quiet you! - shouted one of the soldiers sitting and lying nearby - there he is, walking around like a chain dog! Uuuu ... I hate! So I would have driven a knife in his back!

- Do not talk, what is not necessary - the older soldier, with a lush drooping mustache, frowned - they will report, you will find out how it is - when the skin on the back hangs in tatters! Why did he surrender to you? Walk right, but hold the spear right, and everything will be fine.

- Oh! - Arnot shuddered and looked back to the place where the old-time soldiers used to drill the fence - what is it?

Click! Click! - hard peas with clicks on the bench, and the recruits jumped up from their seats to the friendly laughter of the soldiers behind the fence - they stuck out cane pipes into the cracks and subjected the guys to brutal shelling.

- What don't you like, chicks ?! - the soldiers behind the fence laughed, continuing to shoot the recruits in quarantine.

- Assholes! - Oidar got furious - now I'll make you head off!

He jumped onto the bench, jumped, clutching the upper crossbar with his hands, and let go of the curse, falling down - his hands were torn to blood. On the tall abor, plus everything, there were small hammered nails, apparently the organizers of the military camp were well aware of the addictions of soldiers to roam where they did not need to. All contacts with the outside world among the recruits were kept to a minimum.

- Go to the doctor - Arnot shrugged his shoulders - you need to cover the wounds with ointment. If you do not smear it, inflammation may begin and your hands will be cut off. You will be disabled. But you will receive a pension - a whole gold a month, and tax breaks.

- Ugh at you! - Oidar spat furiously, and under the laughter of his comrades hurried to the white building behind the parade ground. There was a doctor on duty serving the regiment.

After the recruits arrived at their duty station, he had a lot of work to do - he had to treat a bunch of people - from commonplace diarrhea and scabies, to broken fingers and cracked jaws. Despite the fact that the soldiers with their feet came out of the hold of the ship that delivered them, thirty percent of them turned out to be sick to one degree or another. These were illnesses received in civilian life, and injuries, illnesses received during, albeit a short, but unpleasant journey. The doctor had enough work.

- Hey, assholes! - heard a voice on the right, and Ned, lying in the shadow of the fence next to the bench, opened his eyes. He was swimming half asleep, and he had just dreamed about Narda poking him with a cold nose on the cheek, which made his soul warm and comfortable. And then - some moron pulls him out of the embrace of sleep.

- They say you have two fighters here? - continued the voice, mercilessly and finally pulling Ned out of the embrace of the god of sleep - we propose to put yours against ours!

The lad, tall and wiry, was staring at the group of third company of spearmen, which included Ned and his friends. Next to the guy there were about ten of the same wiry, strong guys - they were immediately selected as swordsmen, who were chosen on an incomprehensible basis for Ned - why did they end up in spearmen, and these in swordsmen? Arnod suggested that the swordsmen were taken to be more intelligent in appearance, and those who were more pity to immediately let go for meat, than evoked a storm of indignation from the proud Oidar.

Ned only laughed at his words, and suggested that perhaps those who looked more nimble and skillful than the rest were really taken as swordsmen. Invisible, country-style and outwardly slightly inhibited, Ned and his friends did not in any way fall into the category of nimble and skillful. So there was a reason in Arnod's words.

Ned didn't want to move, so with a clear conscience, he closed his eyes, spitting on the proposals of the unfamiliar guy. He had not seen him before - the guy was not on the ship, this guy arrived with another batch of recruits of the annual draft.

- And what is the stake? What will we put on? One of the guys in the third company asked lazily.

- As usual - silver pool against silver pool, copper against copper. And if you want to put it more abruptly - you can shake it with a little gold! - the guy grinned - and the winning fighter will receive a gold one! Let's throw off him, from everyone on a copper - that's gold! But there will be something to see, huh, guys? Or did it out of fear? I heard - all of you in the third company are stupid rednecks, spear meat, but they say you have two fighters. So let's have some fun?

- You yourself are stupid ... sword meat! - a man with a mustache on the bench lazily broke off - and one fighter - there he is! See, it comes from the doctor? I just tore my hands to pieces, I wanted to punish the punks behind the fence. Do you know how evil he is? Give him free rein, he will drive you all with kicks! He is a watsu master!

- Hrenatsu! - the swordsman chuckled - all these pirouettes and jumps are one thing, and a real fight is another! We also have prize fighters, those who actually played in the arena!

- And why did your prize money end up here? - the man yawned - they beat him in the face all the time, or what?

- And this is not your business - the swordsman got angry - so will you put your fighters out of the company, or not?

- You ask them ... Oidar, they came here, they offer to fight, for money! Want to try?

- How? With these hands, or what? - the guy showed his hands tied with cloth ribbons - they smeared me with ointment, pinching everything fuck! What kind of fighter am I now ?! Let Ned get off. Hey Ned! Ned or what ?! Well, stop sleeping! Look - he sleeps like a dead man! Ned, go beat those assholes!

- The morons themselves! Is this redneck a fighter? Oh Gods! One freak of some kind, the other a redneck - I'd better go to the crossbowmen. With morons like you - what to talk about?

- And what is the rate, you say? Ned opened his eye.

- Gold - the guy stopped - and nothing to the loser. However, I can give you two coppers if you just five heartbeats!

- And if longer?

- If you stand a hundred heart beats, you will get five silver pools!

- And if a thousand heartbeats?

- If you stand for more than a thousand heartbeats, or - what the demons are not joking - you win - we will throw off your whole company for gold, and even crawl on our knees across the whole square! - the guy laughed - agree! Only if you lose, your whole company will give us gold pieces! And crawls across the parade ground! I agree?

- I may agree, but here's the company - Ned shrugged his shoulders doubtfully, getting up from the ground and looking at his colleagues - what if they disagree? And yet - how will the commanders look at this? The dragon will kill us by the light if we start a fight.

- Stop doing that! It can be seen that you are newbies! Command encourages competition between companies, which is believed to keep morale and comradely support. Our sergeant is in the know and has given permission.

- What are the rules? - inquired Oidar, excitedly glittering eyes - are there any rules?

"One thing is not to kill if possible. But if something like that happens, no one will persecute. Some of the recruits always die in training, this is normal. So are you ready?

- Wait, you need to ask the Dragon, you need to talk to your comrades - after all, a whole gold, this is not a copper for you! Come back a little later, we'll consult for a while, right guys?

- Yes, we must consult! - voices were heard from behind. Ned looked around and saw that a crowd had gathered around - the whole company, without exception, was catching the guys' conversation. People from other companies - the second spear, the first sword, two companies of crossbowmen - had already gathered a whole crowd.

- Guys, what are you doing, out of fear, or what? - shouted someone from the crowd, and another voice picked up - these spearmen are just assholes! Will recruit a redneck! Swordsmen are the strongest! Swordsmen! Crossbowmen! The most powerful crossbowmen! Swordsmen! Crossbowmen! Swordsmen! Crossbowmen!

There was a noise - everyone yelled, laughed - to Drankon, who shouted: "Silence!" - with difficulty managed to block the discordant chorus of voices. He pushed his way into a circle formed by a crowd of people and gloomily asked, waiting for the screams to subside:

- What's going on here? Who is disturbing the order?

- Mr. Sergeant! We are from the first sword company, we propose to put up a prize fighter in the third spear company. If we lose, the whole company throws off the gold, and crawls on all fours across the parade ground, shouting: The third company of spearmen is the coolest! And if they lose, then they pay gold and crawl across the parade ground, shouting: The first company of swordsmen is the coolest! How do you allow? In our personal time, without sacrificing service!

- Hmmm ... - the face of the Dragon, riddled with wrinkles, with a scar on his left cheek and broken ears smoothed out, he seemed to light up from the inside and kinder - interesting. It would be possible and not at the expense of personal time. The colonel is very fond of fights, he makes bets. I propose this: if the third company agrees to put up a combatant, I go to the colonel and ask permission to arrange a duel during official hours. At the same time, he will come up, look, and other officers too. Martial arts are useful for soldiers, they discipline, raise morale (the swordsman smiled rather and proudly looked at his comrades, they say, what did I say?). So the third company is ready to fight? Why are you silent? Ugh ... shame, but not the company I got! - The dragon grimaced and shook his head - not soldiers, but some kind of shit!

- Yes, we are agree! What's the shit at once ?! - picked up several voices, and they were echoed by the uncertain voices of comrades who did not want to risk gold, but did not even dream of being mistaken for cowards and goons. Sometimes it's worse than losing all your money ...

- If we agree, I went to the colonel. Wait here - the Dragon nodded his head contentedly, and quickly walked across the parade ground to the headquarters.

Ned again lay down in his place by the fence on the grass trimmed with sickles and closed his eyes, not paying attention to the excitedly gurgling soldiers from all the companies who had gathered at the place of conversation. The news that a duel is planned spread around the quarantine territory like lightning. In a cramped world, without an influx of any information from the outside, in the absence of any way to have fun, the offer of the swordsmen fell like a sprouting grain into manured, greasy soil. Everyone was just shaking with excitement, wanting to see this sight. The guys were looking forward to how they would place bets, and besides, if everything goes on during office hours, they won't be stupidly driving their feet into the trampled ground of the parade ground all this time! The rest will last! It was just gorgeous, and a lot of people clasped their index fingers together to bring good luck to the venture - it would just burn out! Only,

The dragon appeared after about twenty minutes. No one left, they were waiting for him, jumping up and down with impatience. The entire parade ground next to the third company of spearmen was covered with seated and standing soldiers, impatiently and heatedly discussing what had happened.

The sergeant was pleased. He paused for importance, curled his thin lips in a smile, and clearing his throat, said:

- The Colonel gave permission.

- Glory! Thank the gods! Glory to the colonel! The crowd roared. And when the sergeant raised his hand, calling for silence, they fell silent, eagerly catching his words:

- Immediately after the end of personal time, on the parade ground for physical training. Two fighters - one from the first company of swordsmen, the second from the third company of spearmen. I will judge the fight. What are the conditions, what have you agreed on?

The satisfied swordsman stepped forward and said:

- We agreed that if a fighter of the third company will stand against our fighter for more than a thousand heartbeats, then we will crawl across the entire parade ground on all fours, shouting - The third company of spearmen is the coolest! And we'll throw in a gold one to the winner. If their fighter does not hold out, they will do the same for us.

- And if both can not continue the fight? - specified the sergeant.

- Then no one will get anything - the guy chuckled.

- Good. I understood. Then this is what - the third and first companies run to the barracks for the money, give it to me, and I will keep the bail. The winning company will get everything. And one more thing - Mr. Colonel said that the company that wins will be released to the city for one day, under the supervision of its corporals, in order to sit in a tavern.

- Hooray! Glory to the colonel! Thank the gods! - screamed the recruits, and hurried to the barracks - some for money to ensure the duel, others - for money that will be bet.

Chapter 6

- Have you decided who will be the fighter? - The dragon looked anxiously into the faces of his soldiers who surrounded him in a half-ring - I don't know something, or have you got a strong fighter? Do you know who they are exhibiting? No? I will tell you. There's a real prize fighter there. It is said that he joined the army because he killed someone in a tavern brawl. Or somewhere else. Have you already been told that all your crimes are nullified when you get into the army? Yeah, they said ... there are so many street rabble among you! So who will fight?

The crowd parted and the Dragon saw the guy snoring carelessly by the fence. He covered his face with a rag, which lifted slightly in time with his breathing.

- Is he?! This goof? - the Dragon was amazed - oh gods! Now I know who to bet on ... here you are fools ... They were ashamed to refuse, right? Now the whole company will be disgraced! Nuya you ... hold on! Didn't find the courage to refuse in time - you will run on the parade ground until you die! I'll arrange a fun life for you!

Frustrated, Drankon walked away to the physical training ground. He was annoyed and disgusted. The army turned into some kind of garbage dump due to the fact that a stream of criminals and idiots poured into it. The king not only allowed to take criminals into soldiers, but by a special decree, five years ago, he ordered that everyone who served in the army for a certain period of time would be exempted from responsibility for the crimes committed.

This decree shook the society, there were many protesters, but after two severed heads of disgruntled people appeared on the city wall, the chorus of protest subsided. The king needed new soldiers. These internecine wars between the three kingdoms took up a lot of forces and manpower. So why not send criminals to fight and solve two problems at once? The problem of the lack of the required number of soldiers, and the problem of crime. Since these thieves and murderers do not hang out in the streets, does it mean that there are fewer crimes committed on the city streets?

Only one thing did not understand, or did not want to understand, King Yunakor - the army trained and educated fighters who would become bandits - when they served. If earlier they were inept, poorly armed robbers, then after going through training camps, willy-nilly, they became real killers. The Dragon and others like him knew how to train something. However - not everyone lived to the end of the service. It's good if half. Most of them died in the very first battles. Moreover, no one spared this mass of soldiers. And why pity these stupid boobies? Right now - they got involved in a knowingly losing business, well, what was worth giving up? Laughed at them, and calmed down. And now they will laugh at Drankon, who trains such idiots ...

- Mister Drankon! Monsieur Drankon! - the sergeant heard from behind him - wait! I have something important to say!

The boy with his palms tied caught up with him from the back, and the sergeant looked at his hands with displeasure:

- What, donkey-headed - jumped on the fence? What a moron! Everything is itching for you! Each call at least a dozen morons strives to get over the fence! Well, what do you want there? The same parade ground, the same morons! Only a little more fortunate, since they were able to survive a couple of last year's fights with Isfir! What are you, you idiot ?! Don't tell me you can't hold the spear! However - I already see it. Tell me why you got up?

- I just wanted to tell you - put on Ned. He is my friend and I know what I'm talking about. I am a watsu master, I have a tark. So - Ned laid me down in two heartbeats and nearly killed me. Bet - you won't be mistaken!

- Yes? Hmmm ... I'll think - Drankon grunted, puzzled - okay, get out of here. Let them come to the gym. They are already preparing everything for the battle.

Drankon turned, and wiping a drop of acrid sweat from his forehead, walked to the place of the duel. His mood improved a little, and he even began to doubt - is it really wrong to recruit any punks into the army? Indeed, the streets will be cleaner, and after going through the army, many of the guys will become smarter, quit their criminal business. Some will die (Good too! The prisons are free!), Some will remain in service, and as practice has shown, the robbers made excellent soldiers, brave, initiative, skillful and not afraid of blood.

Honestly - Drankon himself was one of this street punks. Twenty-five years of the army made him what he was now - a tough, absolutely not sentimental warrior, pedant and serviceman to the bone. The army was his family. The family is not without idiots, of course, but in general, Zamar's army, it should be admitted, was very efficient.

To begin with, they shut up the Ards - and it's not easy to fight with Ards. Each of them will kill almost any warrior of Zamar one on one. But Zamar's army is all about discipline and teamwork. Zamar's regiments used to defeat a much more outnumbered enemy - due to the organization of the battle, correct tactics and the most modern structure of the army.

Behind his thoughts, Drankon did not notice as he walked to the exercise site at the very end of the range. It was good here - colder than anywhere else in the camp. The shadow of the huge Black Mountain sheltered from the scorching sun, which, although it began to tilt towards the horizon, was roasting as if it wanted to turn people on the trampled square of the parade ground into ruddy steaks.

Drankon sighed, took off his cylindrical cap with the emblem of the king and the insignia of the Marine Corps, wiped off the sweat, smoothed his hair, put on his cap again and walked almost ceremonially to the table, at which the colonel and the other senior officers sat comfortably.

- Mr. Colonel! On the third company side, there will be a fighter named Ned. Sergeant Drankon reporting!

- Come on, Drankon ... - the colonel brushed aside good-naturedly - there is no need for such officialdom. Thank you, Sergeant.

- I serve the king and fatherland! - Drankon clearly raised his hand in salute with a clenched fist, and quietly added - and for what thanks?

- For the opportunity to at least a little distract from the routine of service - the colonel laughed, being in a great mood - when you can still watch the prize fight, and even for a decent amount, as far as I heard. By the way - I would like to see how the company will crawl on all fours across the parade ground, screaming glory to the winners in bad voices! Did you come up with this, Drankon? You have always had a peculiar sense of humor, haven't you, gentlemen? - he turned to the other officers - remember how last year he made one recruit run around the parade ground naked and yell - "Glory to Sergeant Drankon, the kindest of all sergeants in the world!" Imagine - it has reached the capital! One lady in Mrs. Maubor's salon asks me: "Was the soldier completely naked? And what - were the ladies there? And is he naked? Quite quite?!

- Drankon, sit down at the officer's table! - the colonel cordially suggested - pour wine, cold water. do not be shy!

- I won't wine, but I'll drink water with pleasure - the sergeant nodded gratefully - it's hot today, very hot.

- Hmm ... no matter how thunderstorm there was - the colonel nodded in agreement, and immediately switched to the subject for which everyone had gathered - tell me, Drankon, what kind of fighters will fight now? Could you describe them Aty? At least - your fighter from the third company? Is he strong? Fast?

- Honestly, Colonel - I don't know the first company fighter at all, I saw a couple of times on the parade ground, that's all. They say - the beast is the beast. Assassin. As for our fighter - what can you learn in a week? They showed me to him as a strong fighter. The company put it out on its own. I personally did not see anything strong in him. A boy of eighteen or twenty years old, thin, wiry - tall, really ... What else ... Yes, he gives off a feeling of strength, and his colleagues seem to respect and fear him a lot. But this is purely my observation. And so - a redneck, a redneck, which comes to us in hundreds and thousands. Nothing special.

- Yeah? - slightly disappointed colonel stretched out - this way the battle will end in two heartbeats ... he cannot resist the prize fighter. Sorry. I was hoping for a long and beautiful performance.

- Maybe the boy will last longer? - suggested Major Nivor, the commander of the first battalion - can you talk to this prize-winning soldier, let him play with the guy? Well, what would be interesting if he put him down in two heartbeats! We were going to look longer!

- No, gentlemen - Colonel Heverad resolutely dismissed - it will not be military, it is a deception. Only a real fight. And nothing else. Who will be accepting bets? Drankon, will you?

- Sorry, I can't - the sergeant shook his head - I will judge the duel, in addition, I keep the cash register - three hundred gold pieces. So, alas ... Excuse me, gentlemen! - Drankon got up from his chair - it's time for me to provide a duel. Enjoy your sight!

- Thank you, Drankon - one of the lieutenants shouted, pecking a bunch of grapes with a flatbread on both cheeks as if he had been starving for a whole week - we are waiting!

Drankon quickly walked away from the table with the officers and walked towards the crowd of fighters standing near the battlefield a hundred paces from the commanders.

The swordsman, who started the duel, stood with a bag in his hands, talking with Sergeant Dufar, the commander of the first company of swordsmen, next to Arnot, with a similar bag into which the soldiers threw their hard-earned gold.

Finally, the last coin clinked, gobbled up by the neck of the bag and the guy carefully tied the heavy purse.

- Everything! Done! I thought they put everything down. One hundred and fifty gold! Tough sum! Ned, how are you going to beat this guy's spirit - you get a beer for all the guys, and I get two!

- For what two? - someone from the crowd shouted.

- For the experience! I don't have that kind of money, but he will! I might get upset about it!

- Chatterbox! - Dufar laughed - you still win. You have not seen our fighter, otherwise you would have described yourself with fear. Your hulk is still asleep - well, spearmen, well, sleepyheads! He came - he sleeps, left - sleeps, came again - sleeps again! These are your soldiers, Drankon! Soon they will crawl across the parade ground, glorifying our company!

- It is important for a soldier to eat on time and how he will have a free minute - to sleep, otherwise he may not have to - one veteran taught me - Arnot answered edifyingly - Mr. Sergeant Drankon, right I say?

- Right - Drankon grinned - give your money. Yes, a good jackpot - the sergeant weighed a bag on his hand - weighs no less than a zusan. By the way, who doesn't know, you can donate extra money for storage to the regiment's office. The service is free of charge. It is not recommended to carry large amounts of money with you, just as it is not recommended to leave money in plain sight in the barracks. I do not want to hang those who would be tempted by other people's coins later. But you have to. If we catch. Okay, guys, let's go. Time. Raise this sleepyhead.

- I'm not sleeping anymore - Ned smiled slightly - I'm here. Ready. How are we going to fight - in clothes, or should we take off our shirt? I saw how the fighters were fighting at the festival in the village. Naked to the waist - should I undress too?

- In the village ... - the sergeant sighed - naked to the waist, yes. You can be barefoot, or you can wear boots - no difference. And there your opponent is coming. Look who you're going to fight with.

- Now it's too late to refuse! - Dufard hastened - if you refuse now, all your money goes to us - it is considered a loss!

"And no one is going to refuse, Mr. Sergeant," Ned said calmly, looking at the guy coming up to them.

He was twenty-five years old. Until he took off his uniform - nothing remarkable - a guy like a guy - long-armed, with strong, well-developed leg muscles, covered with uniform pants, broad-shouldered. The only thing that attracted attention was very wide, thick wrists and blue-veined hands, large, capable of breaking a horseshoe. Ned had the same - only the Nedovs were more muscular and clawed, thinner. The guy seemed slightly, as it were ... tight, or something. Why - it became clear when he took off his uniform.

A mountain of muscles. But not loose, like the loaders, lifting heavy bags and then, after work, pumping themselves with beer under fatty pork and scrambled eggs sizzling in fat, but twisted from knots, elastic steel muscles, developed by special training to the limit of the body's capabilities. This guy looked like a deadly machine, like a catapult, throwing stones the size of a cow at a distance of five hundred paces. Even Oidar, always so cheerful and self-confident, whistled and said dimly:

- Yes, his mother ... Where do such monsters come from? He will beat a man in the ground up to his throat! Maybe you will refuse? The demon is with them, with the money! And what will our beloved colleagues shove at you - will we fight back somehow? He will kill! Look at your wrists - this beast will break a horseshoe in one heartbeat!

- What will be, will be - Ned answered, and also took off his shirt.

No, he did not impress with the power of the prize fighter, did not amaze with the width of his chest and inflated muscles - a strong guy, thin, but wiry, with large arms and broad shoulders - an ordinary developed guy of about twenty. Maybe younger. He seemed older because of his unsmiling and harsh, piercing gaze.

Despite his not particularly impressive dimensions, the guy left a feeling of confidence, strength and a kind of aura of danger hovered around him ... he moved like an animal - carefully, sparingly, exactly. And most importantly, I was confident in myself, like an old, experienced fighter.

Drankon carefully examined both fighters, and smiled slightly - and the guy from his company is not easy, oh, not easy ... And as if the smile from his opponent's face very soon did not evaporate, like rainwater on a stone under the scorching rays of the sun.

- Ready? Follow me! - Drankon commanded, and the two fighters, followed by the whole crowd of recruits, went to the place where the battle will take place.

It was a playground for hand-to-hand combat and wrestling.

Slightly loose soil - sand in half with small pebbles, compacted by numerous rains and strong legs of guys. Before her stood a table of officers, looking at the soldiers with pleasure, whose torsos were blown by a fresh breeze from the mountains, carrying the coolness of distant glaciers.

The edges of the white tablecloth that covered the table with drinks swayed, slightly drunken officers were excitedly talking, anticipating the spectacle, the soldiers who gathered in a half-ring around the battlefield were laughing happily, from behind the fence, old servicemen were peeping into holes and cracks in order to have a peek at the interesting battle. They heard everything when the swordsmen came with their proposal, and their interest in the fight was not less than that of the recruits. Boring. Everyone is bored here. And such a fight is just a holiday.

Drankon motioned for the soldiers to come out to the battlefield, but the colonel waved, canceling his order and called the sergeant over to him:

- Wait! They also wanted to see Colonel Zayd, and Colonel Évor! And a few more officers ... or rather - all who could! Wait. And one more thing, Drankon - are you going to bet? Lieutenant Sirdon accepts. How much are you going to bet, if not a secret? And to whom? I understand - this is a bit unethical on my part, but still?

- It's okay. I'll bet ten. no - twenty gold for ... for ... Ned! - suddenly concluded Drankon.

- Patriotic, no words - the colonel drawled with a grin, don't you think that it would be ... hmm ... impractical? No? Wow ... you are an old warrior, there is no reason not to believe you. Hmm. maybe you should bet on Ned too? It accepts bets one to twenty. Do you have any information about him? Who is he and where is he from? What is he like a fighter? Or just the flair of an old warrior?

- Rather - all the same, flair - Drankon smiled slightly - okay, we are waiting for the officers. I'll go and tell the fighters, otherwise they're probably already worried.

- Something not to see - the colonel smiled - so that they were worried. And your face looks like it was carved out of granite. At least one emotion would be reflected. The statue is a statue. And the second smiles - a cheerful killer. Do you know who reminds me, gentlemen? The wolfhound dog! I saw this one - kind of cheerful, cheerful, and then - rrrrr! And shreds flew from the wolf! Dangerous people. Both. Very, very interesting! Let's raise a toast to our Drankon - he knows how to bring joy to colleagues! But he doesn't like feasts - his element is battle, war!

- For Dracona! - the officers raised their glasses, and together drank to the slightly bowed sergeant.

The wait was slightly prolonged, but soon a group of people appeared on the parade ground - about twenty people, leaving the gate, guarded by watchtowers. Officers from all over the military base, with the exception of those who were supposed to be on duty.

They went to the table, greeted their colleagues, then the wait began when more tables and chairs would be brought from the officers' mess.

The soldiers spoke quietly, glancing at the commanders and grudging under their breath, calling the officers the most offensive curses they knew.

Ned sat in the pose of a flower - as Oydar had taught him - and tried to absorb this very tsu, which fighters fill through some holes there. What - he did not understand, although Oydar several times began to explain this. Ned simply didn't have enough data to understand. After all, his interests all his life revolved in a completely different plane ...

He sat with his eyes closed and listened to the thoughts of those around him. From all the cacophony of thought sounds, he tried to catch those that were needed - for example, the thoughts of the one with whom he would soon have to fight. After several attempts, he managed to suppress the noise coming from all directions, muffle it, focusing on the thoughts of the enemy.

- Dead guy. I'll break it in five heart beats. A two in the puff and in the jaw - and ready. Maybe play with him? Look how many people have gathered! I will be the hero of this year! Maybe the sergeant will be given? They have a bigger fee, and they will not force them to climb into the heat. However, it would be better to stay at the base and manage the canteen. Getting closer to food is always more reliable. And why is he smiling like that? An idiotic smile! Redneck! You will smile at me! You will be the fifth person I killed. In the arena. Well, I'm sorry, boy. That is life. Someone hits and someone dies. If you furnish it more beautifully, everyone will be happy. Ehh, now I would be lying on clean sheets with Elra ... Well, what demon did her husband come so early? Why did he climb on me to fight? Demon ... shouldn't have beaten him. It would be better if he punched me - it would not disappear. What is his pitiful jab to me? See how bad it turned out. five years now with these assholes, five long years! So, Hart, stop crying! Being a corpse is much more disgusting than hammering a village guy for the amusement of an officer. And here, at the base, you can settle down if you think. I'm a smart guy, strong - and then I'll make my way. Well, finally, they are coming ... I wonder - is there a brothel in this town? With one hundred and fifty coins you can have a good time with the girls! Why is he smiling like that, this moron?

Ned smiled one last time and got to his feet, following Dracon's gesture. He was fresh, the body was rested and satisfied, and every corner of it was sending signals to the brain - I'm ready! Master, I will do whatever you ask!

And Ned stepped into the middle of the battlefield - to the enthusiastic howl of the crowd and the applause of the officers.

Ned himself did not know why he got involved in this business. Why did he need this fight, why did he need this money ... He did not know the price of money - whether it was a copper or a gold - for him everything was the same. He was indifferent to his salary. If a person in his entire life has never paid for a single thing in the shop, how can he realize the value of money? Well, yes, nice circles, clear and beautiful. The man is knocked out on them. So what? What can you do with them? Why are they to him? He is fed here, given clothing, shelter, and is not forced to work more than he used to do at home. Everything according to the order, everything according to the sound of the bell - in comparison with the previous life - the palaces of the gods!

Ambition? What ambitions can he have? He, lower than the lowest, mud under the feet of people - what are his ambitions? Do the comrades hope for him? Afraid that they will take offense at him and will not respect him? He lived for seventeen years in a state of war with the whole world! The whole world was constantly trying to offend him, offend, hurt him - can he be afraid of disrespect for his comrades?

Then why does he need all this? He didn't know himself. Something inside him was pushing Ned forward. Pushed to perform actions that he personally, by himself, would never have done. Something dark, strong, squeezing his will into a fist made him: "Go! Go! Punish this asshole! Show how strong you are! Make the crowd howl with delight, so that they carry you in their arms! Isn't that the way of a man? Isn't that right? Be calm - you are strong. You are the strongest! Nobody can resist you! Do not be afraid of anything, give free rein to your subconscious, and everything will be fine! "

And Ned was not afraid. He was in a strange state of elation and at the same time calm, as if he went out not to mortal battles, but to a fun game, such as he saw on the youth playground in the village - round dances, dances, "streams". There was a certainty in his soul that everything would be just wonderful, and he could not separate his own thoughts from the strange, new ones that were not inherent in him.

Ned's opponent began a warm-up - he twisted, waved his arms, jumped up, delivered instant crushing blows to the air, glancing sideways at Ned - does he see how terrible he is? Did a cruel fear awaken in him, gnawing at the insides and depriving him of will? And he was convinced, to his displeasure, he did not wake up. Smiles like a suifari flower. Silly type ...

Ned stood for a second, looking at the manipulation of his opponent, then suddenly began to slowly make circular movements, bending so that joints and vertebrae cracked. His hands moved on their own, forming figures in the air so bizarre and exotic that everyone around him fell silent - what is this guy doing? Even his rival froze, opening his mouth in surprise - this is a performance!

Oidar, standing next to Arnot, squeaked, and painfully squeezed his friend's hand, glaring at Ned, shimmering in the air like a flexible blade of grass in a stormy wind.

- What is he doing? - asked Arnot quietly, curling his lips in bewilderment - why is that?

- What is he doing? - Oidar repeated stifled - he, he ... beast! Refused to teach me! This is the Shantso Master! He pumps into himself the energy of tsu with special exercises, like a pump! I feel the energy hitting him - don't you feel the movement of subtle matters? Don't you have goosebumps running down your skin? I will never forgive him. Deny me! Pig! The reptile! I dreamed, all my life I dreamed of finding a chantzo teacher, and now - a village boy, a goof - a chantzo master ?! And he refuses to teach me ?! I want to cry ... I feel so small, so humiliated ... such a gray mouse ...

- Eck you fucked up! Have you smoked some Mazis? - Arnot goggled in bewilderment - all I see and feel is that Ned wriggles like a snake and waves his arms like a windmill, and you look at him, sweat so that you stink like a goat! What's so strange about that?

- You fool ... - said Oidar with regret - look what will happen now! I don't envy that guy!

A surge of Force swept over Ned. It was like a full sack bursting at the seams, imbued with strength, bursting out like a bottle of sparkling sparkling wine. His hearing, sight, all sensations sharpened and he saw far, far away, on the ridge of the headquarters building, a small bird holding a grasshopper in its beak, whose legs dangled from both sides of a thin beak.

He heard subtle whispers in the crowd of guys: "What is he doing? Look, look what he's doing! "

I heard the quiet voices of the officers, admiringly examining what was happening and dressing up about the rates - one of them, during the "performance", immediately put on Ned, fascinated by the movements that he made.

I could feel the subtle smells coming from the heated, dusty ground, and the smells brought by the wind from the mountains - the smells of mountain meadows, melted snow and eternal, gray glaciers.

He has become different, and it seems - forever. The thought struck him in the very heart, so that Ned shuddered, realizing the truth, and tried to resist it with fear ... for which he almost paid.

The enemy struck an instant blow, darting for Ned's jaw, deciding to end the strange guy in a split second - who knows what to expect from this abnormal? A good fighter will not play with his victim. He knows that no matter how strong he is, there are always too many surprises in the world that can lead to failure, accidents from which no one is immune. And the best path to victory is the shortest - a direct blow to the jaw, crushing it into small pieces.

Missed. The abnormal guy with a slight movement of his hand took the blow to the side, passing it at such a distance from the cheek that it was blown off by the wind from the flying fist. From the side it seemed as if Ned lazily raised his left hand and waved away from the enemy, like from an annoying fly - with a bored expression on his face and eyes, looking hazy into the distance.

The crowd roared, screamed, and the fighter flew into a rage, blushing like a feshang fruit. But then he pulled himself together, realizing that everything is not so simple, and you need to be as careful as possible.

A series of three blows aimed at the liver and head of the enemy also ended in nothing - the guy somehow turned, easily touched the hands of the fighter and they only thrashed the air senselessly. It was like a bizarre dance in which the prize-winning fighter played the comic role of a clown bustling around a goody, ridiculously easy to beat off a stupid and awkward character.

The blows whistled one after another, the fighter increased his speed to the maximum limit, and more than that - but his opponent stood as if bewitched, paying no more attention to him than a bull driving away an annoying gadfly with its tail. And the best part is that Ned hasn't struck a single blow yet! A minute has passed since the start of the fight, no less, dozens of blows whizzed through the air, but not a single blow reached the goal and not a single blow followed in response.

Ned was in a daze. He watched what was happening from his eye sockets, as if from windows opened after a dark night. This was not happening to him.

The one who sat in it enjoyed what was happening. He played with the guy, watching the enemy blush, turn pale, breathe heavily and get furious with such bullying.

Ned wanted to end the fight as soon as possible, it was unpleasant for him to pay such heightened attention to his modest person, but he, inside, did not let him do it.

A strange thought flashed through my head: "Don't rush. Remember the terms of the agreement. On them you must stand a thousand heartbeats. If you lay him down now, they may find fault and give you only one gold piece. And you should get EVERYTHING! When time is up, you will kill him. "

"But I don't want to kill him!" - thought Ned and immediately received the answer: "You must kill him. Must! He talked nasty things about you, thought nasty things about you, besides - he WANTED to kill you! Isn't that enough? Doesn't the one who wants to kill you deserve to die? After all, he wanted to kill you only because it would be more profitable to end the fight so that everyone could see what a great fighter he is and give him a good position so that he would live better than others. Doesn't THAT deserve to be punished? Of death? You must kill him, and so that the others shudder with horror! So that they know - jokes are bad with you! So that no one else dares to offend you, never! Never! Never! If you are so unbearable - roll him around a little. Just be careful, do not damage until the right moment ... "

Hot sweat splashed from the guy, scattering like raindrops. He was breathing heavily, giving all his best, already with all his soul hated this cold, haughty statue named Ned.

Suddenly, when the next series of blows was supposed to overthrow this man, he grabbed the fighter by the hand, twisted it in an unthinkable way, and ... the prize fighter, like a doll made for a village child, flew into the air and rotated around the axis crashed onto the site. It was unexpected and rather painful - air flew out of the guy's chest with a hack, and snot popped out of his nostril, sticking to his lip.

For a second, all the spectators were silent, and then they shouted, made noise, laughed:

- Brat! Hey freak, get up and choke on your nozzle! Hey, your snot gets in the way, it gets tangled in your legs!

The fighter jumped up from the ground in one jump. His trained, strong body surpassed itself in a furious impulse to kill, tear, trample the enemy! Hands, legs, flashed in the air, merging into hazy ghostly shadows, and every time a fighter rushed at Ned, he flew head over heels, covered with bruises, dust and blood.

After five minutes of such felting, the prize fighter who killed five opponents in the arena, a proud, strong and mocking person who cherished and cherished his ambitions, was a piece of meat covered with dirty streaks and blood streaks.

The spectators screamed, raged, screamed so that flakes of foam flew out of the mouths of some especially zealous ones, like race horses after a long run. The officers at the table got up from their seats, hooted, knocked, forgetting about the honor of the uniform, about the fact that they are in front of their subordinates - all merged in one, single impulse of the viewer, who was immersed in the spectacle.

Colonel Heverad enthusiastically clenched a white tablecloth in his well-trimmed fist, decorated with precious pearls, and exhaling, said:

- Great! Best fight I've seen!

"Enough!" The thought flashed through Ned's head that it was time to end the game. Once again, when the staggering and sweaty fighter stepped towards him to deliver a series of powerful, but completely meaningless blows, Ned with a fluid movement screwed himself into the space next to the enemy's body, and putting into the blow all the accumulated Force, all the power of his young, powerful body punching the guy's Adam's apple, aiming at a point behind him.

The effect was amazing. The hand, like a damask blade of a sword, passed through the opponent's flesh, tearing, flattening, crumbling soft tissues and hard bone. Ned felt nothing but a slap and resilient resistance, as if he had slapped a wave of the sea.

The man's head came off, and, flying into the air, made an arc, falling with a thud right in front of the officers' table. The body stood for a second, gushing from the broken veins and arteries, then softly settled on the platform, shuddering several times in the last impulse - to live! Live at all costs!

You could hear the bees buzzing, rushing about their bee business, how somewhere far away, on the slope of the mountain, in the thickets of thorns, an unknown bird cried out - drink and weed! Drink - weed! A bell rang in the city, gathering people for evening prayer to the creator god, and his priest, in a thin, piercing voice, began to chant mantras befitting the solemn sacrament of divine services. Only at the exercise site of the Marine Corps base was everyone silent, frozen like marble statues.

And then - the silence exploded with screams, screams - an excited crowd rushed to Ned and, picking him up in their arms, carried him around the site, trampling the remains of a soldier who gave his life for the amusement of the audience.

Ned seemed to wake up from an obsession - he looked in bewilderment at those who threw and fiddled with his body, turned his head, as if for the first time he saw the site and the audience, enthusiastically showing him signs of love and respect. The officers joined the general celebration clapping their hands, and Colonel Heverad took a wallet with several coins from his pocket and shouted:

- Additional prize from the command! Ten gold! (I must say that the colonel, in general, did not risk anything, giving away the coins. Then he spent this prize as a reward for the service, writing out fifty gold pieces. Total - forty gold pieces).

The crowd roared, and brought Ned, who was lying on his back like a dead man - with his arms crossed on his chest - right to the command table.

Following the colonel's example, each of the officers took a certain amount of money out of his pocket and put it on the table, where a decent pile of coins formed (Try not to put it when the commander did it! Consider disrespectful. It can harm your career.).

Sergeant Drankon tucked them neatly into the bag of money to be paid to the winner and stepped aside to watch Ned being honored. Then, when he was released, he went up to the guy and handed the bag, said dryly:

- It was interesting. Was it just worth killing the guy? This is not a real fight with the enemy, this is just a competition! Why did you do that? Didn't expect this from you ...

- Come on, Drankon! - Colonel Heverad laughed cheerfully, who approached from the side - this battle will be told in all units of the royal army! These are the kind of fighters we train! Let the enemy be afraid! He took it - and tore off the guy's head with his bare hands! Well done! Here's a corporal ready for you, sergeant! You haven't appointed corporals yet, have you? No? Here's your ready! I will order to prepare an order today! Now, boy, you're going to get 1.5 gold a week instead of one gold! That would have been more, but the length of service is small, and he did not participate in hostilities. Are you literate? No? Sergeant is an omission. Teach him to read and write. Let's prepare an officer from him! He will make a great sergeant!

- It is unlikely - just as dryly replied Drankon - the task of the officer is to make sure that the task of the command is fulfilled, and the soldiers are saved as much as possible. In the tasks of the officer, there is nothing about the senseless killing of his soldiers.

- Yes, stop that you are like a virgin - murder, murder! Better order the first company to fulfill the terms of the contract - let them crawl across the parade ground on all fours, and we'll see! Gentlemen! - the colonel shouted to his colleagues - now there will be a most curious sight! Pour glasses, it will be impossible to look at it without laughing!

Chapter 7

They got to the city only three weeks later. The quarantine was reduced - everyone who could get sick and get sick, were cured or removed from the recruits camp, the rest continued to be subjected to the most severe drill from morning to evening.

It was rumored that the quick release from quarantine was the result of the activity of Isfir's army, plotting around the islands, and that the kingdom urgently needed new "meat" for the war, but as always - the rumors were only half true. Now it was not about the islands, but about a strip eighty long and twenty wide along the border with Isfir. The army of this country captured this piece of Zamara land, and urgently dug in for retaliatory actions. Therefore, the exhausting, old, like decrepit pants of a beggar, the war continued and continued, taking more and more souls of people into the furnace of battles.

Generation after generation, people were born and died in a state of sluggish war, and no one remembered that it could be otherwise. Each king, ascending the throne after his predecessor, solemnly promised that he would end the war, that his people would live happily and richly. And each king, dying, passed on to his successor a country in a state of war with three neighboring, kindred states.

We must pay tribute to the current king Zamar, despite the fact that during his reign no progress towards reconciliation was made, he managed to eliminate one of the biggest troubles that annoyed all three states - he put the Ards, the northern people of pirates, robbers ... and travelers in line ... It was difficult to do this, but oddly enough, Iunakor was able to do it, creating a powerful Marine Corps, into which he poured huge money. And this corps gave a return - after the raid on the islands of the Ards, a peace treaty was signed, which the Ards strictly observed.

However, they were not respected because they experienced sacred horror before the paper signed and decorated with royal seals, not at all. The five-thousandth corps of thugs, half-bandits, ready to do anything on the orders of the king, held back the rebellious sailors better than any papers and exhortations.

Zamara Marines. Each of the infantrymen wore a polished Marine Corps badge, the three initials of their unit, proudly on their ceremonial cap. They were proud of this sign. And they knew that not everyone would live to see demobilization. Well - if every second. And since life does not shine ahead - why not live on the money that the king generously poured?

And when the recruits, who received their "mortal" gold, were released into the city - it burst at the seams. Wine flowed like a river, corrupt girls greedily rowed coins, robbing drunk visitors, innkeepers did not have time to cook, emptying their storerooms in one day of soldier's dismissal.

Once upon a time, when there was one small garrison of one hundred people, the city was quiet, patriarchal, although quite large - ten thousand inhabitants, this is not a joke. After the construction of the Marine Corps base, the population of the city increased threefold, practically switching to serving the needs of the corps. Someone supplied groceries, someone to a merchant, someone sewed and adjusted boots for the army - everything was done nearby, in the town. It was simply stupid to bring uniforms and boots here from the capital.

And all this stormy flow of supplies went through Colonel Heverad, the base commander, who generously pays for all purchases from the army treasury. Some of the money was immediately returned to him in the form of bribes, and then deposited in the imperial bank. However, not everything. The lion's share of this money went upstairs to the commander-in-chief of the army Zamara. But enough for everyone. The army, as it often happens, was corrupt to the last degree. Or rather, not the entire army, of course, the top leadership. The lower ranks, starting with the lieutenants, were content with salaries and dreamed of climbing higher in order to pinch off this sweet pie at least a little.

It is interesting that all the locals disliked the soldiers and treated them rather contemptuously, which did not prevent them from ripping off clients like sticky. They smiled in their faces, and behind their backs they called them stupid soldiers and "caps", not missing an opportunity to stick a knife in their backs. Therefore, when the command released the soldiers on leave, they strictly ordered: to walk only in groups, not to fight off the team, and also to obey the corporals supervising the process of pumping wine.

And that was the nastiest thing. For all. For soldiers - because some moron will hang over his shoulder and whine, interfering with enjoying freedom, and for corporals - who wants to catch a dozen soldiers crawling like lice on the crown of a beggar's head? And even those in a state of "drunkier than wine"? If you can't keep track of whether some freedom-loving or just a bad infantryman escapes, you will receive a cash deduction in the form of a week's salary (for each lost one), plus - you can rake up to five hot sticks if the outflow of military meat is too great. Therefore, the most authoritative, most powerful fighters were taken into corporals, and moreover those who themselves did not look to the side when going to run.

Usually the sergeant-trainer appointed corporals after a week or two of the recruits being in quarantine, when the guys cut their hair, rallied, and it became clear who is who.

However, the matter was not allowed to take its course. The unit had a special security service, closely monitoring the moral and psychological state of the units. Major Shentel was at the head, each regiment had its own security major, and all information about the soldiers flocked to them. How? In the usual way - denunciations.

Almost every soldier was dragged to the security guard, and demanded that he inform on his comrades. I was interested in everything - the mood in the unit, the attitude towards the king and the whole country, whether someone was inclined to escape and whether he was not going to engage in all sorts of criminal acts. Many refused to report, but many agreed - for the refusal they promised various vague and not very troubles, for the consent - they hinted about indulgences in the service and about future career growth, which will certainly be provided to loyal infantrymen.

Ned was also called to the security guard, and he refused to give information about his comrades. Not because he was a hero, and considered it impossible for himself. He just didn't want to do it, just as he didn't want to be a corporal. He was not interested in career growth, the benevolent attitude of his superiors was of no use to him - which he immediately announced. Everything suited him, and he had no complaints or requests. Which, however, was true.

His comrades - Oidar and Arnot did the same, both in words and in fact - he probed their thoughts, and they completely coincided with what was said.

Oidar, he was indignant at the offer to become an informer, and Arnot just pretended to be a village idiot, barely understanding what he was told.

As the cunning guy explained, one could agree for the sake of appearance, from time to time give evasive and deceitful reports about anything, but ... if colleagues, half of whom had a criminal past, find out about the denunciation, then you can actually get stabbed, or else get a crossbow bolt in the back of the head. And no one will find out, investigate how it happened. Not an officer. Prove later that you lied to the command, that they slandered you, calling you a snitch, but in fact you are a great guy - late, when the knife sticks out in your back.

However - Ned suspected that most of those who spoke so violently about informers themselves knocked. Rather, I didn't suspect - but I knew for sure, but I could not tell my comrades directly. Only in this way: "I suspect ...", or "I surrender ..."

The one who sat in it - or, as it seemed to him, was sitting in it - forbade him to give at least someone extra information that could harm Ned. Talk about anything, just not about your abilities, your skill and wait for an opportunity. Which one? Ned didn't know that yet. Opportunity ... by that one could mean anything. And wait forever.

Not much has changed in his life since the day he killed the guy in a duel. Contrary to expectations, Ned was not even elevated at all, well - except for the rank of corporal, of course. And who needed him - an illiterate redneck who only knows how to kill. Such a place in the war, where he will soon go.

The colonel several times tried to organize a fight between Ned and one of the soldiers, but they categorically refused to participate in suicide, disdaining all the threats and promises of generous rewards.

Oddly enough, the terrible death of Ned's opponent served as a good shield, protecting him from attempts to make a prize fighter out of the guy. Seeing the futility of his efforts, Heverad abandoned the venture and forgot about Ned - which pleased Ned a lot. There is no need for close attention to his person. While it was necessary to calm down and lie down on the bottom, like a flounder fleeing from a predatory fish. The danger will pass, and it will be possible to swim out into clean water.

But as much as Ned thought, he could not understand - what is the danger? Well, what threatens him? He is in the army - even if they find him now and be charged with the murder of ten people - he is clean according to the law.

Magicians. That's who worried him. As soon as he thought about what would be next to them, he shivered and wanted to hide away. Fortunately, there were no magicians at the Marine Corps base, not even magic healers. They lived in the city, as did almost all of the Corps officers. Right there, in the city, the magicians studied, trained, and when the Corps went overseas to fight, they appeared on the ship, and even then they lived in separate rooms and never communicated with "meat". Never.

This was the highest caste of the army, even with contempt for officers, let alone ordinary soldiers. There was a chance that Ned would face the mages. But it is very small. And it is unlikely that they would have begun to look out among the gray mass of soldiers for a magician, a black magician, a demonologist who was clinging to the ranks of spearmen.

Incidentally, this point was the most terrible. What will they do if they find out that Ned is not just a black magician, but also a demonologist, but also .... Ned was afraid to admit it even to himself - an OBSTIATED black magician ?! In their place, he would simply chop off this type's head ... if he could. Therefore - Ned has developed an action plan for the coming years:

1. Learn everything the army can give and get away from the village where they know him, as far as possible. Why? So as not to point the magicians at him.

2. Understand your abilities, and make sure that he can control them as much as possible. (This will help with survival).

3. The most important thing is to survive, survive under any circumstances. And for this - study, study, and study (Which does not contradict the first point).

The tasks are precise, army-like clear - and Ned followed them, guided by the instinct of a man who was used to surviving his whole life, and also ... listening to strange thoughts emerging from the depths of his mind. Until they contradicted three points of his program ...

- Drink! - Oidar plopped a full mug of wine in front of Ned, and he stared in disbelief at the dark, odorous liquid - what are you looking at, drink! Wine! Have you ever tried it? Good, red, only expensive, infection! And in general - everything is expensive for them! Hey, innkeeper, why is everything so expensive ?!

- Is it really expensive? Ned inquired in a whisper, leaning over to Arnott's ear.

- You know ... - he winced - one and a half times more expensive than we would give for the same thing in Shusard. Oydar, stop yelling - the innkeeper will call the guards, and Neda will burn for us. Better look after those two idiots - they seem to be trying to dump somewhere. It is clear that everything is more expensive - the city is livelier at the expense of the Marine Corps, and is drawing money from us. Ned, have you really never tasted wine?

- No ... not necessary - Ned once again leaned over the mug and cautiously took a small sip. He winced and stated with disgust:

- What disgusting! And how do they get drunk? It's bitter, disgusting! Yes, it even gives off with resin!

- With resin? Oh, he's a bitch! Exactly - with resin! - Oidar sipped - now I will go to this goat that slipped these slops to us instead of good wine, and I will say everything I think of him!

- Oyd, you got drunk - shook his head Arnot - I tell you for sure - it will end badly!

- Yes, we are this guard ... yes we are her ... hey, assholes! - he started - where are you going ?! The corporal is sitting here, and where are you going?

- What do you want most of all? - A guy of about thirty asked menacingly, with a predatory, narrow face - sit and do not rock the boat! We'll come back, don't put it in your pants with fear! And we will unfasten you a share!

- Guys, you will not go to the robbery - Ned said calmly, and clasped both hands in the castle - if you leave the inn now, I will catch up with you and break your bones. Do you believe?

- What are you ... corporal ?! - the guy asked sharply, and the second, similar to him with a wolfish expression of eyes, frowned his eyebrows, glaring into Ned's face - he imagined a lot about himself ?! What to do and what not to do? Remember - you will not always be on your feet. Someday you will have to fall asleep. And when you fall asleep, you may not wake up. And martial arts won't help you! Better let us go - calmly, without noise and fights, and we will unfasten your share, and you will live quietly and peacefully, as before. Good?

- No. Not good - said Ned quietly, barely drowning out the dashing music, to which two tipsy couples were dancing - guys, I already told you - you will not rob while I am a corporal. And you will not leave the inn without my permission. Ditas, do you understand?

- Got it. How do people change - did you guys see? Was a normal boy, and now? In essence, who are you? Redneck! Bastard! Like all of us! And as soon as you put on a patch - immediately became higher than everyone else ?! Well, nothing, nothing ... as long as you're a corporal, you say? - Ditas grinned promisingly, and a picture appeared in his mind - a dark barracks with rows of beds three stories high, and Ned, sleeping on the lower bed under his comrades. A hand with a knife stabbing into his heart ... Ditas was actually going to kill him, there was no doubt about that.

Ned got up, slowly, as if he was being dragged by force, walked over to the man, whose smile reluctantly slipped from his face, replaced by a grimace of fright, and then, without a swing, slapped the palm of his right hand, folded into a boat, on Ditas's chest.

The robber suddenly wheezed, fell to his knees, his eyes rolled back as if he had been hit on the head with a hefty log, and then fell silent, losing consciousness. His accomplice backed away, looking into Ned's terrible, black as a pool of eyes, fell, stumbling on a stool, and subtly screamed:

- Do not! Do not touch! You are welcome! We're not going anywhere! Dont kill!

A puddle spread under him - the guy got scared as if a red mountain bear attacked him, capable of tearing a man in half with one movement of his paw.

Ned exhaled, touched his sharply ill head, in which jerks were beating, and said hoarsely:

- Go to the toilet, put yourself in order. It stinks. Give this one wine. He's alive.

Ned leaned over to the reclining guy, goggling at meaningless eyes, and quietly said:

- Again you go against me - I won't leave you alive again. Got it?

The guy nodded his head shallowly and, choking, began to swallow wine from a mug that one of his colleagues gave him. All this time they stood around and watched as Ned dealt with the displeased. And everyone knew - Ned almost killed him. And he would have killed - but ... did not do it.

- What was it? - asked Arnot quietly, looking at the excited, biting lips Oidar - what did he do? He just slapped him on the chest!

- He stopped his heart - just as quietly answered the master uatsu - stopped it for a while. And if I wanted to, I would have stopped it forever. One touch. "The Palm of God" is called. Imagine a murderer who passes you by and by accident - quite by accident! - slaps you on the chest. Or over the head. Or on the shoulder. And you fall and die. And no one can understand why? How did it happen? Oh gods ... I am sometimes afraid of our Ned ...

"Is he a killer?" Arnot asked in a whisper.

- I do not know. He's not saying anything, damn fellow! How I would like to know - I would give everything for this knowledge! Maybe they have the last chanzo masters in a remote village? Maybe they are still taking students and I can learn secret knowledge from them ?! I'm just going crazy with ignorance and desire to know everything!

Ned walked over to his seat and sat down, ignoring his friends standing beside him. Oidar looked at his friend probingly, while Arnot pretended that nothing had happened and defiantly watched the two girls dancing so that their skirts were lifted to the waist and then it was clear that there were no underwear under them.

- Look, guys, what it does! - Arnot smacked his lips admiringly - Oid, how about women?

- Yes, they ... yes, I ... in general - I'm a specialist in seduction! I will persuade anyone - the boy boastfully answered - only that there would be more money ... For some reason, they do not like without money. I wonder how much it costs to buy a woman? What, guys, can we do it? I'll go and find out how much he wants. We still have a lot of time - we only get to the base two hours after dawn, so we can go all night!

Oidar jumped up from his chair and went to the counter, where one of the girls of a certain profession was bored. Arnot looked at him with envy, and said with regret:

"You know, I've never been with a woman. I don't even know how to negotiate with them.

"Do you think I know? - Ned smiled - and I have never been with a woman. I just saw ... and so ... peeped.

- And I too - sighed Arnot - peeped, and ... in general, peeped! There is no need to laugh! - Arnot could not resist, and giggled, and immediately whispered excitedly - look, look, he is leading her to us! Oh!

- Guys, this is Zelena, she agrees to be with each in turn. Two silversmiths per person. I am the first! We have a discount for wholesale, so there would be three pieces of silver. I went!

The woman was quite young, even younger than she seemed - she was aged by bright makeup, powder and specific clothes that emphasized the profession - a tight bodice with sagging breasts and colorful skirts, slightly faded from constant washing. She smiled, and through the smile was visible the absence of one tooth in the upper jaw. As she left, the girl blew a kiss, and Arnot fidgeted in place, shaking his silversmiths out of the purse:

- Finally, I will become a real man! Here it is!

- Do you think a real man is distinguished by whether he was with a woman or not? Ned inquired with interest, taking a bite of the pie on the wide plate in front of him. He ate a hefty pie that evening and he wanted more - it was very, very tasty. The local chef added some spices to the meat, which gave the filling a special flavor.

- Well ... yes! - giggled Arnot - if the gods gave us this tool - it's a sin not to use it, right?

"Hmm ... I guess," Ned shrugged as he watched his subordinates scattered around the hall, squeezing girls and pumping themselves with wine. Ditas had already moved away, and sadly sat by the window far from Ned, buried in his plate and listening to what the accomplice was saying to him. Ned tried to listen to their thoughts, but they were quite far away, and besides, in this noise of thoughts and voices it was very difficult to make out something. After a minute, Ned began to have a headache and turned off his supersensible perception.

- What are you so boring ?! - Arnot cried indignantly - now you will go to a woman, for the first time in your life - well, what doesn't make you happy? I've heard so much about it, and even seen ... hmmm ... but haven't tried it myself.

- What, there was not a single woman who would lie with you?

- And I would lie down and get up - not one. I'm young, not very handsome ... why are you smiling? It's easier for you! What are you! The mound is tall, the muzzle is cute, handsome! And I?! Plump, with a belly ... the truth is now the belly is gone - thanks to the Dragon - but you can't go anywhere! So, for women to love me, you need money. But with this I always had a problem.

- And where did you get the idea that I'm handsome? Ned wondered.

- Beauty - Arnot smiled - I would give everything for such a figure and a face like yours! The girls were supposed to hang on you! It is not clear how you have never been with a woman all this time! Darken, buddy ... Okay, okay - I know you never talk about yourself! That's it, I went. Quickly you shot something, Oid! Arnot said sarcastically and immediately received a slap on the head:

- What are you talking about! I tried for you! I wanted to quickly! Get out, asshole - second floor, third room, she's waiting for you. Or will you go, Ned? And then he?

- I'll go, I! - Arnot almost fell over the chair, rushing to the stairs - I'm already tuned in!

- He tuned in! - Oidar laughed - it was cool! Baba is fire! You will see! Raise the dead! Do you want me to tell you how it was?

- Something there is no desire - Ned confessed, and suddenly asked - tell, Oid, here you serve, what will you do? Where will you go? What will you be doing?

- I will open a school - without hesitation, answered a friend - I will teach people uatsu. I'm actually a master, don't think that since I'm such a freak, I don't know how to teach. I know the whole training system. You know what - let's work together, as soon as the deadline expires, we will work together? Shall we train people in martial arts? Just tell me - where did you learn Shanto?

- Again for your own? - Ned frowned - leave me alone! I will not tell you anything. Consider that I have a ban on this. Nobody. Nothing. Forgot!

- Okay, forgot - the guy sighed - and what were you going to do? What to do after the end of the service? Do you not always think of carrying a shaft with a point?

- Why not? Maybe I decided to stay in the military for the rest of my life - Ned shrugged his shoulders - out, the Dragon has served all his life, and nothing.

- Have you seen his face? Do you know that he has no family, no wife, no children? They say - once a month he gets drunk to shit, and rolls on the floor in his room. And then again for a month drills such idiots like us. And he gets drunk again. And so all my life. Is that what you want?

"I don't drink wine," Ned muttered in confusion.

- Start ... start drinking. From despair, from boredom, from longing, from the fact that there is nothing in life except this parade ground and our faces. To look at Arnot - you'll be sure to get drunk - he giggled, looking at a friend shining like a polished shield coming down the stairs. He said - I quickly shot, but myself? What is it yourself?

- All perfectly! - Arnot nodded blissfully, and plopped down on a chair, greedily sucking on a mug with exhausted beer - go, Ned, she's waiting! Oyd, she's sixteen, no more! And so hot! Wow, the beast-woman! Go Ned!

"No, guys... I'm not going," Ned said hesitantly.

- What are you? - Arnot did not understand - go, everything is all right! He's waiting!

- No. I do not want! After the entire Marine Corps had been on it ... no.

- Oooh! Look, Arnie, we are clean! Just look! He disdains! You must forget what disgust is, Ned! You are a soldier!

- I'm a soldier. But if I feel thirsty, I'm not going to do it from the first dirty puddle I come across! - snorted Ned - if you like that kind of love - come on, have a good trip. I won't. Everything.

- All the same, you have two silversmiths - Oidar got angry - I agreed on all, with a discount! Then I'll go instead of you!

- On! And shut up! - Ned slammed the coins on the table, his friend brushed them away with his palm and, expressing his complete displeasure with his entire back, went to the stairs.

- What are you mad about - Arnot asked incomprehensibly - the girl is really good. So young, elastic, boobs - in! - he showed himself - it smells a little bit, but it even adds piquancy.

- What does it give? - Ned did not understand, thoughtfully chewing on another piece of pie. During this month, he sounded strongly in the shoulders - a lot of meat grew from good, hearty food, and now his figure resembled that prize fighter whom he had killed on the court - muscular, powerful, only a little drier and his face became younger than it was. Gone is a kind of raid of ferocity, readiness for trouble. Ned even began to smile, which had rarely happened before.

- Piquancy ... you are a kind of redneck - Arnot waved his hand hopelessly - goodies, then.

- Did you eat it, or what? Ned squinted, and they both rolled with laughter, snorting and dropping crumbs of pie from their mouths.

We returned to the base in the morning, with the whole crowd. One half carried the other. Ned had to drag Oidan on him, who got drunk to the point of insanity and for some reason mistook his friend for a master of the uatsu school. He always tried to bow, and at the same time he fell, resting his forehead on the pavement and lifting up his skinny bottom. I had to put it on my shoulder, and grunt, carry it like a sack of grain.

Already before the base, he began to sing some warlike songs, beating the rhythm with his fist on the bottom of Ned, to which he threatened that he would throw his friend into a roadside puddle so that he sober up. To which he received a portion of sobs - Ned was informed that he was his own father, and no one loved Oidar, since all goats and creatures.

Arnot walked on his own, moving his legs as if they were made of wooden sticks - straight, earnestly driving his feet into the stone pavement of the city.

The rest of the squad soldiers were also in varying degrees of intoxication, but in general, the whole binge went without incident - except for the fight in the morning, when they began to find out who was cooler with the soldiers from the company of crossbowmen, who, unfortunately, had entered this tavern.

Ned did not participate in the fight - they were afraid to bully him, Oidar too - he just slept on the bench and could not participate in anything purely physically. Arnot waved his fists a couple of times and was immediately driven under the table, where he sat until the end of the action. At the end of the battle, the soldiers who smashed half of the inn paid double the price for the damage and fraternized, pouring cheap wine at a hefty price over their wounds and hugging like brothers after a long separation.

The road to the base was littered with the bodies of snoring, completely drunk soldiers, some of whom had already been robbed - their pockets were turned out, and instead of wallets, only laces remained on their belts. The returnees stepped over these "corpses", but Ned noticed how someone thievingly looked around, rummaged through the pockets of their comrades, hoping to snatch at least a copper left by the previous marauders.

The base met the returning soldiers calmly - they came and they came. Those lying along the road - then the patrol will gather in a special van. Those who did not return - they will still be found - will be betrayed by kind local residents, and then the reprisal will be inevitable and terrible. Whipping - sometimes to death.

The day after the dismissal, according to tradition, was a day off - for those who went on leave. What's the use of soldiers who roll around like logs, vomit and can barely make a run to the toilet? One disgrace. It's disgusting to look at them. Better to sit in the barracks.

Officially, the day after the dismissal was called "the soldier's personal day", when they had to fix their uniforms, go for a routine check-up with a doctor - they were supposed to visit a medicine house at least once every two weeks - for the sake of preventing infectious diseases like scabies or other skin diseases. However, as a rule, this schedule was not followed and the soldiers turned to doctors when it was necessary. For example, today ...

- Ned! Ned! - pale Oidar, swaying, stood by Ned's bed, holding on to the wooden posts of bunks, and pulled the guy by the shoulder - yes, wake up!

- What?! - Ned opened his eyes with displeasure, looking into the rumpled face of his friend.

- Hey guys, I'm in trouble! - Arnot came up to the side, sat down next to Ned and bit his lip, clutching the couch.

- You too? Oidar inquired gloomily, sitting down at Ned's feet.

- What do you have too? Ned asked blankly, looking at the gloomy friends.

- I went to the toilet - began Arnot - and this ... I can't! Painfully! Very painful!

- And I, too - Oidar nodded his head, and the accusing one asked - why didn't you stop us yesterday when we got on this girl ?! Ned, there you are!

- Contagion now - you, as I understand it - smirked Ned - and Arnot. In general - why are you sitting on my bed? Go to the same idiots! I suppose half of the company is now lining up to see the doctor. I told you - her entire base was visited, and you?

- We, we ... smart it hurts - Oidar grunted - escort us to the doctor! Something is not good for me ...

- Aha! Do you know why it's not good? There was less wine to eat. Okay, let's go!

Ned jumped out of bed, did a few exercises under the envious gaze of the trembling Oidar, then waited until the friends who were still not quite sober left the barracks, and followed them, making sure that the movable structure of two unfortunate hungover guys did not crash to the ground.

No, we got there normally, and joined a line of the same sufferers, buried in the white door of the medicine room, on which the sign of the doctors was roughly drawn - a man in a white cassock, stretching out his arms over the bedridden patient.

- I can't stand to stand here! - Oidar moaned, holding on to Ned - this is some kind of nightmare! Everything is itching for me, and also - I'm about to fall!

- Why the hell are you still sober? Ned frowned.

- So we took a little with us ... it was so bad, we added. It got worse! - Arnot spattered his lips - I'll vomit now ...

He ran around the corner, and then the door to the medicine suddenly opened. A physician emerged from her - a hefty man, as tall as Ned, only four times thicker and a beard an inch long. He silently examined the line, which immediately died down under his gaze, and growled loudly in a bass:

- Hey, donkey-headed rams, inadvertently wearing the emblem of the Marine Corps - those who had fun with the girl in the Red Stallion tavern yesterday - step aside, now let's go to the city, to the magician-doctor. I do not have the necessary powders for you, and you cannot wipe out such an infection with powders. You did a good job, you damned rotten! I would have burned this "Stallion" as a source of infection! And the girl, the girl ... uuuuu ... idiots! When you arrive - there will be a lecture - how to safely fuck a whore! And at least one bastard will evade - you won't come near me anymore! Rotting alive, idiots! Why are you laughing, shafts? And you got it, fucking winner?

- No, mister doctor - Ned calmed down, forced from his face an uninvited smile - I'm healthy, how ...

- This is good - the doctor interrupted - get out of here then, do not block the horizon! And you, donkey bogs, load into the cart behind the medicine, now the duty sergeant will come up and write out a pass. Hey stop! Stop, shafts! How are you there?

"Ned, Master Doctor," Ned turned.

- You will go with me. We must watch out for these nits, otherwise they will creep around the city like infectious lice! And do not make such a face as if you found that you had a knife stuck in your back - there was nothing to show up in the eyes of the authorities, you would not have any problems! Stand still and wait at the drug!

Ned sighed and trudged back. So it was not at all difficult for him to accompany a team of thirty guys, but he only really wanted to sleep in the barracks after a sleepless night, and so that no one lifted him, did not drive him, think, dream - now he had something to dream about. And yet - he was worried about one thought - they were going to the healers-magicians! God forbid him to catch the eye of any of these magicians. The village doctor immediately identified his aura. However, he thought, who knows that he can control demons? And then the thought came up: "Idiot! Don't try to catch their eye! They will send you to agar, start digging - they will immediately figure out the demonologist, and then, then it may end badly! "

The duty sergeant appeared half an hour later. He handed the doctor a small paper with a regimental seal, he beckoned Ned with his hand, and in a minute they were already rumbled across the parade ground towards the gates of the base in a long van resembling a ship under sail. He was dragged by two dirty, old nags with matted hair and withers worn out from old age. However - the cargo of the van was not much different from its draft power - pale, shaking, hungover faces.

The doctor looked back at the guys and winked at Ned and said:

- Look! It seems that this girl was sent to us by Isfir! To disable more than thirty soldiers at once - even you, a soldier, cannot! This is power, this is a weapon! Why didn't you climb on it? You were with them?

- Disgusting ... - Ned shrugged his shoulders - who was she with before me?

- As they say - you didn't find yourself in the trash, right? - the doctor laughed - right, well done. Smart kid. If you really want a woman, I'll tell you the address. There is a mother and daughter, they are not professionals, they earn extra money - well, here many earn extra money than they can - and so, they are clean, they look after themselves. Slightly more expensive, of course, but safe. And they'll also feed them. And in taverns only such idiots collect dirt.

- Should we go far? - asked Ned to get away from the sensitive topic.

- This is what you are - continued the doctor, not paying attention to the question - near the temple of Pryon, diagonally from his statue, there is a house with green shutters, so small, clean. Nelga and Osara live there, you go, say - from Geresard. They hide the fact that they are moonlighting, but they will accept it from me. If you want both, you want one. I guarantee both are clean, I check them regularly. Remember - at the temple of Praion, Nelga and Osara! House with green shutters!

- Thank you, remember - nodded his head slightly flushed Ned. He felt uneasy, and he again tried to turn the conversation to something else:

- And what, the magicians will immediately cure the guys?

- Immediately, that's what the magicians are - the doctor nodded - they are on duty, so they are obliged to heal. We, ordinary healers, treat minor wounds and injuries, but we take medium and heavy ones to them. At the base, you see, they don't want to work. White bone! Not like us black asses! - the doctor spat, roared in a bass at the icy horses and slammed the reins - hey, damned, step up! You are taking your relatives, donkey heads!

Geresard laughed and fell silent, looking ahead. Ned was silent too. He thought that lately so many things had fallen on him that his brain was splitting from new knowledge. Yesterday also taught him a lot. Especially the fact that behind a beautiful facade such filth can be hidden that it is impossible to imagine. You have to be very, very careful ...

Chapter 8

The ride was pleasant. Ned sat next to the hefty doctor, looked around and enjoyed the sun, the breeze from the mountains, the sight of lovely girls rushing past and squinting at the young corporal, examining the houses and shops, reading the signs by syllable. All this time, friends, on behalf of the sergeant, taught him to read and write, and he quickly grasped the essence, as if he had been studying for more than one year. He could already write - really slowly, and read, too slowly. His progress was so great that it surprised his friends. They reported that they themselves studied the art of writing and reading in elementary school for a whole year.

The doctor shouted loudly, demanding the way, and passers-by scattered from the pavement, skillfully mother of "damned martyrs", to which they received ornate phrases consisting practically of only swear words. The healer was a master abuser. Army service, Ned noted, was very helpful in developing these abilities.

To the place where the magicians lived and worked, the cart arrived in about an hour and a half, having driven through the entire city to the very outskirts, to the place where the families of officers and magicians - white and black - lived in houses built behind a high fence, healing and training in their combat skills. There was also agara - a school of magic. The corps crushed under itself including agar, putting training in the service of the army.

The wagon was not allowed inside, ordered to leave these nags outside. The soldiers were lined up in a column of two, and taken to the territory of the military town.

Ned stayed outside, with the horses, to wait for the first cured sufferer to appear in the field of love affairs. He hoped that Oidar and Arnot would be in the forefront of the cured - he was bored, and with them it was more fun to kill time on duty.

The horses, tied to a hitching post at the entrance to the town, stood calmly, their heads down and expressing with their whole appearance the hopelessness of existence. Ned listened to their thoughts - but apart from simple, stupid thoughts like "Gadfly! Bad! Hot. Stop "- I heard nothing. Boring!

The pavement, cleanly swept out in front of the military town, reminded him of how he once dived into the sea near the cape, and when he dived especially deeply, he noticed a cobbled road leading into the ocean. It was exactly like this street near the military town - like two drops of water. There was no one to ask where this underwater road came from and where it led - by that time Silan had already died, and he did not communicate with other people on such topics.

Turning away from the pavement, Ned lifted his head up and looked up at the sky, leaning against the van. The sky was clear, blue, as if washed with a cloth with a soldier's laundry soap - smelly, but wiping away both sweat and blood.

After a short time, the sky got tired of looking, all the more so, except for two flying birds, nothing interesting happened there. One of the birds flew by and launched a white stream, and Ned thought - if it hits the horse's head - everything will be fine. And if it doesn't, then ... it didn't. Then he began to persuade himself that he did not have time to guess to the end, which means that it does not count. On that and agreed with his conscience, chuckling to himself like a ten-year-old child.

Lowering his eyes, Ned noticed the sign: Predictions of the Master of Magic Sitara Saludskaya. I will predict your future by hand - inexpensively and accurately! "

Ned stood for a while, wondering if he needed this. Then he looked around, and leaving the tied horses, he strode resolutely across the street to the peeling white door, on which was painted a black robe.

Approaching the door, he hesitated - should he come in? So he heard from the guys that not all magicians are classified as magicians. That is, there are people who are not considered magicians, but have certain magical abilities - for example, the gift of prediction. However - half of them are real swindlers, pulling money from simpletons. And maybe more than half.

Ned was afraid that the fortuneteller would hand him over to the magicians. But I really wanted to know my fate! After all, he was still a young man, almost a boy, prone to rash acts. And Ned pushed open the door.

The bell rang softly, and Ned sank into an atmosphere of coolness, incense, the scent of antiquity from old scrolls lined up on a shelf behind a wide table lined with magical utensils.

Ned flinched at such a clear sign of the wizard in possession of these treasures, stepped back - but it was too late. The passage was blocked by a fat woman, thicker even than the physician Geresard. She looked at Ned affably, and thought:

- What an interesting, nice guy! Oh gods, where are my twenty years ?! I would not let you go, I would have dug into your ruddy lips, I would have saddled like an unbroken stallion and until I sucked you dry - you would not have left here! And how cute she blushes! I never would have thought that today's young men can blush like that. Infantryman, about Dinas! Unhappy boy. Of these, only a third survive. If not less. Probably came to find out - will he live to the end of the contract? Honey, you are cute ... how do I know? Aunt Sitara has gone through the best years, now her insights are too rare to have a lot of clients. But you have to live somehow!

- Well, chick, do you want to know your fate? - the fortuneteller said affably - sit down, now I'll tell you fortunes. I'll tell you everything as it is - Aunt Sitara is the best predictor in the whole district! (She was! - Sitara thought sadly - once she gave hope even for a white magician! But ... it didn't work out. She's weak.) Only three pieces of silver - and I'll tell you everything, everything is as it should be, as it will be. My eye sees for years to come! Do you see my eye? - she leaned forward, like a landing craft, and pulled back an eyelid, showing her discerning eye - here! He sees everything!

- I think I'll go - Ned tried to defend himself - I only have a silversmith. No more! Such an important lady is unlikely to guess for one silver pool!

(This damn important lady wondered cheaper - Sitara thought pejoratively - just right to go to work as prostitutes, there are no shit about the clients for predictions! Prostitutes need an old deck! Give me your silversmith and don't twist your brains - I'll lie down with bones, but I won't let you out! Another greengrocer needs to give five coppers, but the milkman seven - where can I get them for you ?!)

- Nothing, nothing, take a seat - a discount for you! If you are such a fine fellow, a soldier! Here, here, give me your silversmith ... yeah, well done. Sit down and relax. What are you looking out of the window for? - Sitara turned and looked over to where the sad army horses stood under the window - ah! You guard the wagon! Do not be afraid - no one in their right mind cramps this stupid medicine wagon - everyone knows it. I suppose, again Zherezard pinned the guys with a bad illness - like a leave of absence, so at once twenty people are dragged here the next day. They brought the disease from somewhere from the southern continent, so it has taken root here - if the boy just dunks his farm - in five hours he can't go to the toilet! They say that the organisms of us, Zamarians, are so susceptible. Blacks don't get so sick, they don't care about this dirty trick. Take into account - do not climb on anyone or fall, at least sniff. If it stinks, run from her like from fire! (Why am I telling him all this? The boy, I suppose, is half a year left to live, or even less - climb on whoever you want, my boy, try what you want - your life is so short that you may not be in time. listen to the old fool ...)

- Well, give me your hand. The service has been paid, get it.

The woman smelled of sweat, some kind of incense and cheap powder, with which she smeared her drooping cheeks. She was slightly out of breath, like all fat people, but her eyes looked young and cheerful.

Ned regretted at first that he had come here. No, not because he had to give the silver piece - he had money, and quite a lot by the standards of soldiers, but he did not want to feel like a fool, cheated by money. But when he listened to Sitara's thoughts, he did not feel sorry for this silversmith. She was a good woman. And also - she sincerely cared about him and worried about him. And there are so few people in this world who worry about it, and there is not a single woman among them. He so always wanted to have a mother ...

Ned held out his hand, Sitara took it with her seemingly plump hands, which turned out to be unexpectedly strong and rigid, closed her eyes and leaned back in her chair. For a while, nothing happened, then she began to chant:

- I see you standing on the battlefield, handsome, mighty and warlike, and enemies are falling around you ...

Suddenly she fell silent, twitched, and grabbed Ned's hand so hard that his palm twisted, then exhaled, opened her eyes and said in a strained voice:

- There are two of you. He's scary. Black as death! Fear him! He will try to take over your soul, destroy you! Don't give in! Think with your head! Feel with your heart! Trials, blood, fire, losses and gains await you ... and a great future. If you survive. Fear! Fear him!

The sitara shook, then froze, threw away Ned's hand and sat for a minute in silence, as if she were speechless. Ned tried to feel her thoughts - they were not there. The woman seemed to have died, or fell asleep deeply. Then she looked up and continued:

- A trip overseas awaits you. Don't touch the dagger!

- What dagger? - Ned could not resist, Sitara shuddered, and stared at him, as if she saw for the first time:

- What other dagger?

- Well - you said - don't touch the dagger - which dagger?

- I don't know - the fortuneteller was confused - it dawned on me. Honestly, this happens less and less often. The last time was six months ago, when I predicted to the city treasurer that his wife would cheat with the groom. He did not give me money for the prediction, and also scolded me - they say, such a nice girl like his Yusta cannot change! And when it happened, and everything was revealed, he accused me that I had bewitched her! Ungrateful creature! What did you hear?

- Well ... about some kind of dagger, about a trip overseas. What does that mean?

- And how do I know - Sitara threw up her hands guiltily - your prediction, you should understand. Here's the thing, son ... most of the predictions are such that until the event happens, you will not know how to prevent it. It seems to me that the gods do this on purpose so that people cannot change their destiny. What happens if everyone knows what they need to do and what not? After all, then they can avoid what God is preparing. And this is wrong.

- Whose side is it wrong? Ned asked unexpectedly.

"Hmm, that's right… well, yes, from the point of view of the gods - wrong. And from the side of people - everything is correct. You are a clever boy.

- So if all the same, all the predictions are incorrect, vague and suitable only for chatter - so why guess?

- And here is an interesting question! - Sitara perked up - not all predictions are vague. Sometimes it happens that the prediction comes in advance, long before the event, and it becomes clear what to do. Why is this happening? They say - the gods allow. They give the chosen one to understand what is in the prediction. And the rest - of course - empty chatter and chatter under a magical entourage. That's how I have - the woman smiled - but I have worked your silversmith in full. You got a prediction. And you have to go - I look, there your comrades with rumpled faces fall out of the gate. Run, son! And good luck to you! Survive!

- Thank you, Aunt Sitara - Ned chuckled, and added - I'm sure you were a wonderful beauty in your youth. It's a shame I was born late.

- Ha ha ha ... killed! Well done! A real man! Or here, I'll clip you - mmma! Erase the kiss, otherwise they will think of something ... and let them think - you guys, it is considered a valor - to seduce a beauty. You can think of something. Okay, let me wipe it off. Well, what a darling you are ... blushed from a kiss on the cheek. That's it, now clean! Run, son!

Sitara followed the boy with a moistened look, sighed, and wiping off an uninvited tear, began to get ready for the market. It was necessary to go to the niece on the way, pick up the turned dress from her - she traded in sewing. Then to the bazaar - to distribute debts. It's been a pretty good day today. * * *

- Where are you roaming? - Oidar was benevolent and contented, like a cat - come out, but you are not! That's it, the trouble is over! We are healthy and cheerful!

"I see," Ned chuckled, "I should have left you sick for a week. For memory, so to speak. To think ahead!

- Well, what are you, like an old grandfather? Thought, thought! I think! Arnot, do you think? You see - and he thinks. Where is the shop nearby ... to buy some Mazis, eh?

- Again? It wasn't enough for you to get drunk, do you still want to get stoned? Sit here and don't go anywhere - Ned frowned - just not enough problems! Better tell me how it was. What kind of magicians, what did they do ...

- Mages? Magicians as magicians ... haven't you seen magicians? Ordinary-looking people. Such a decent guy in a robe, began to drive with his hands and mutter something, and before that he gave him some nasty drink. By the way - very bitter. As he muttered - it was as if fire burned me! I gasped. And he, like you - "Be patient, you shouldn't have climbed anywhere without hitting!" Well, that's all - "Next!"

- I have the same thing - interjected Arnot, smoothing out the protruding vortices - and you know, we also have a hangover gone. It has become so good ... I will not get so drunk anymore. Fu, disgusting even to remember! After all, where did you go?

- I asked about the future. You see your aunt at the crossroads - she is a fortuneteller. For the silver piece she told me the future.

- And what did she say? - the eyes of friends sparkled with curiosity - well, don't sweat it, tell me!

- Nothing. Why are you making faces? She didn't say anything - she was carrying some kind of nonsense - don't take it, don't grab it, that's all. She said - soon I will go overseas.

- Tyuyu… yes, any fool knows! - disappointedly stretched Oidar - that's what the marines are to go overseas! The swindler is fucking! Your silversmith was crying!

- Crying - Ned agreed easily - so be it. I was interested, and helped her.

- He's a good-natured man - a friend chuckled - and you won't think that it was he who ripped off a man's head not so long ago! By the way, you never said - why did you do it? All gossip behind their backs, cannot understand. Why all of a sudden such atrocity? Well, I would hurt him, and that's it, Arnot?

- Truth. It was scary even to watch. You were so cold, and your eyes were like two black holes in the Underworld! Exactly, exactly! Even proteins were not visible - black holes, and that's it! I sat close, saw everything, so the blood from the severed neck got on me - I almost vomited! You were not you. I had bad dreams for a week - it seems like you got out of bed, walk through the dark barracks, and tear off the guys' heads. And then you come back and say: "You saw everything! Now you must die! "

Arnot shuddered and fell silent, looking at the sky and chewing on a blade of grass plucked somewhere along the road. Ned frowned, staring at the ground - he didn't know how to answer his friends. Then he turned and quietly climbed onto the van's beam, putting his hands on his knees and looking into the distance, down the street leading down to the sea.

- Are you offended? Do not worry so - Oidar said guiltily - we are always for you, no matter what. This is us in our own way ... you are such a mysterious person ... we told you everything about ourselves. And you about yourself - nothing. No, no, we love you anyway, you are like a brother to us. But ... okay, I won't talk about it. Do you want me to tell you how there, in the city of officers?

- Well, how is it? Ned perked up.

- Good. Well, why are you smiling? True, it's good - everywhere there are flower beds, clean, paths are sprinkled with fine gravel. Ladies walk with their daughters. Daughters - mmmmm! I would have given myself up! Five at once! No - ten! No - a hundred! So nice, so clean ... just a dream! And how they looked at us - with all their eyes! Probably such handsome men as we have not seen, they are kept locked up ...

- Here every dog knows that after the dismissal, a crowd of idiots is taken to the magicians-doctors for treatment - Ned winked - the fortuneteller told me. So don't be fancy. To them, you were a stupid soldier, plus a bad illness. Here.

- You're always like that! - Oidar answered with a mournful face and shook his head - not a drop of romance in you, and where only did you get brought up like that?

"In the country," Ned answered unexpectedly, with sticks, stones, kicks and cuffs. How it befits to bring up an orphan-Arda. The hated arda, pirate and robber.

- Did you study martial arts there? Or Ards? I am silent, I am silent! ABOUT! Another portion of healthy "meat of war"! Well, guys, let's repeat our run through the taverns sometime? No? Come on ... a week will pass and you will forget! I personally will definitely forget! * * *

After a trip to the mages, life in Ned's unit returned to normal. Wake up at dawn, wash, breakfast, workout before lunchtime, rest for two hours and workout again until you start to collapse with fatigue. However - now almost no one fell. The loose, untrained recruits turned out to be tough, like fighters carved from dry wood. The excess fat was gone, and those who did not have it had grown muscles that could easily carry huge spears and a pound of iron armor, which they put on their shoulders. Yes, the soldiers have already trained in steel armor - shoulder pads, chain mail, greaves, a heavy helmet that even covers the bridge of the nose and protrudes from the sides. So he covered better from impact, but he had to turn his head more - the field of view decreased at least twice.

The soldiers were trained to wield all the weapons that were in service with the infantry corps - from knives to crossbows, but at the same time, the main thing was distribution by specialization. Working out movements to automatism, to such a state when a person performs something without thinking, completely unconsciously. Signal! Turn. Signal! U-turn. And so endlessly, endlessly, to madness, to the boil of brains in the hot summer sun.

It was hotter here than in the Black Ravine - the proximity to the south affected. The soldiers, drenched in sweat, paced and paced on the parade ground, jogged to attack, stabbed, chopped, shot - endlessly, endlessly. For three weeks they were not allowed into the city - not because they had a strong sensation last time - all this is nonsense, there was nothing terrible. Strong - this is when they killed a dozen people and burned ten taverns (And this happened! Heverad then had to grease someone so that the stench did not reach the king, make expensive gifts and compensate for the damage in double the amount. The perpetrators then paid with their hide, otherwise and life ...). No. Not because. They said that in a couple of months they would have to sail to the border with Isfir and the command was in a hurry to drive as much knowledge as possible into their soldiers. And not because that Heverad loved his soldiers so much - the large loss of personnel will badly affect his image of a knowledgeable, efficient officer and some may think that he is not rightfully taking his, such a monetary position. And he was not going to retire yet. There was money, yes - mansions in the capital, a round account in the imperial bank, his own business, which was managed by brother Heverada, his own small fleet of merchant ships ... but the more you have, the more you want. Losing a stable source of income when money floats into your own hands would be just silly. your own small fleet of merchant ships ... but the more you have, the more you want. Losing a stable source of income when money floats into your own hands would be just silly. your own small fleet of merchant ships ... but the more you have, the more you want. Losing a stable source of income when money floats into your own hands would be just silly.

So the unfortunate recruits were screwed up to such an extent that the physician Geresard, on one of the last days of the week, made up his mind and went to see the colonel to express his opinion on this matter. And what has he to lose? No further than the medicinal booth and the ambulance van on the battlefield will not be sent. His salary will not be taken away. Will they be fired? But who will go to this position when you can just normally sell powders to sneezing townspeople, and not think about the fact that tomorrow a line of sick soldiers will line up for you, moreover, "for free."

"I ask permission to enter, Mr. Colonel! - the doctor boomed, squeezing the mighty body through the doorway, not intended for its size.

- Come on, Geresard! Come on in! What happened? - The colonel looked up from the pile of papers, which said about the latest deliveries of products for the needs of the corps. The colonel never left papers for the accountant - he personally checked each invoice and I must say - he was very successful in the merchant business of counting and accounting. It couldn't be otherwise - it's his bread and butter!

- I have to report, Colonel, that if the corps is not given rest in the near future, you risk being left without a part of the soldiers. Overwork is evident - the fighters for three weeks from morning to night perform heavy exercises, and the accumulated fatigue - physical and moral - will soon make itself felt. Trust me, I know from previous years' experience. If we are going to send healthy shelves to war, we must give them at least one day in the week to rest. It's my opinion. We just drive people, some will get sick, those who remain on their feet will not be able to perform their combat missions as they should, appearing in front of the enemy in the form of half-dead donkeys. In addition, the increase in the training time for the entire daylight hours, adopted by order of the corps headquarters, does not allow the soldiers to recover properly. They sleep five to six hours and this is after toil from dawn to dusk. It's impossible. Every day, there is a queue of patients in the medicine room who have to be given exemption from classes, and every day several people find themselves on the parade ground unconscious from overwork and overheating. We will lose the corps. It's my opinion.

- I see that this is your opinion, and not someone else's - the colonel chuckled, getting up from the table. He went to the open window, wiped his forehead covered with sweat with a white handkerchief, stood there, said into space:

- Yes ... hot. No breeze, no rain ... however - we don't need rain either.

Then he turned around, and carefully looking at the doctor, asked:
- Why so bad?

- Even worse - the doctor boomed - as if they didn't start dying. I am surprised that no one has thought of rebelling so far. There were no leaders to be found.

(It was found! - thought the colonel - how it was found! Only they are already in the next world ... you do not know much, my friend Geresard).

- What do you think you need to reduce stress?

- Yes. Certainly. To make classes ten hours long, as before, and every seventh day to recover - rest, leave for the distinguished guys. Not for everyone, of course. Let the efficient soldiers rest, those who are above all in terms of performance, and the rest strive to catch up with them. There are enough of them - for example, the same Ned Black! Remember this, mister colonel? Well, the winner who tore off his opponent's head? The guy is very smart, correct! He doesn't even drink wine. She doesn't run around dirty girls. He always does his job in silence, without groans and complaints, and his platoon is the most skillful and combatant. Well done, boy! I wanted to take him to my place, offered him, and more than once - as an assistant. Alas - he refuses. He says he is not going to become a doctor. Looks like he wants to make a military career. But it's not about him - the general condition of the fighters today leaves much to be desired. It is my duty to report to you on the state of affairs in our regiment. All the healers that I supervise are of the same opinion. All ten people. I finished.

The colonel sat down on his chair again, put his hands on his elbows, took his fingers into the lock and lowered his well-groomed head, with an impeccably combed parting, on the bottom. He was silent for a long time, then looked at the doctor, and said:

- Do you think it would be better if they were killed on the battlefield? Okay, let's say we turn down the intensity of our training. But we will sail in two months. What soldiers will we go there with? With dropouts? I don't care if they get killed - they knew what they were doing! But the king is counting on us, so what? We will not complete the task! What will they say about us then? Who will they call us?

(They'll call you, you brute! - Zherezard threw to himself - are you afraid for your ass? And to substitute the boys - no? You are not afraid to ruin them here, exhausting training? Well, what kind of idiot are you ?!)

The colonel was silent again, and looking at the gloomy doctor, added, in a softer voice:

- I understand your concern for the personnel of the regiment and the kopus as a whole, but understand that your task is to heal, and my task is to carry out combat missions. I don't understand why I'm discussing such things with you. Apparently, simply because I have known you for twenty years, and I know that you have always cared about your subordinates. Geresard, my friend - give up these stupid thoughts! Mind your own business, and do not go where you do not need!

- Nulan, I knew you as a lieutenant, once we were friends, don't you forget? - the doctor went all-in - don't be an idiot, you will ruin the boys, you will have no one to go out to fight with! Don't you understand that even a horse needs to rest, otherwise it will fall down dead ?! Is your head not working, or have you forgotten how you yourself fainted when Major Shetzel made you run through the mountains with your unit in the scorching heat? And you honestly ran with your soldiers until you fell off a cliff and broke your arm! And how many soldiers died then, because the tyrant decided to make superhumans out of them and did not believe that not everyone could afford it ?! What happened to you, Nulan? Where is the lieutenant who personally accompanied the soldier to the infirmary and quarreled with his superiors because your subordinates were unjustly offended? After you married the minister's daughter, you changed dramatically and became a merchant from the army, not a soldier! Think about it!

- What are you allowing yourself, you brute! - the colonel got up from the table, his face turned red, and his eyes almost rolled out of orbit - I will expel you from the army, with a yellow prescription, for non-observance of the command order and violation of command! Forgot who you are ?!

- You forgot who you are! - roared the doctor - you are a merchant from the army, and I am a doctor, without whom everything here will fall apart, and all the soldiers will rest like chickens from a careless peasant! Idiot! I do not hold on to this place, take it - the doctor tore off his white coat with the doctor's emblem and threw it on the table - put it on and heal! And I will go to the city, start a private practice and I spit your corps and you with it in one place! Heal, maim what you want to do, idiots! Only when the rabbit asks you - why is your Marine Corps taking a break, like a rabbitry from a pestilence - you tell them - I drove them in training! And I have no healers - I, out of my stupidity, dispersed everyone! Bring your precious magicians here - all three healing magicians, and let them dig in the soldiers' asses! They don't have to sit in their agar! That's it, I'm done with that!

Geresard turned, and ignoring the stunned colonel, with a quick step, shaking the floor with the weight of his mighty body, left the colonel's office. He walked past the clerks, pretending that they did not hear anything, past the adjutant, Lieutenant Sirtak, the nephew of the colonel's wife, went to the parade ground and walked to the medicinal room, beating the rhythm of the movement with a clenched fist. Everything inside him was boiling, and red circles swirled before his eyes. Either from the heat, or from rage - it was not in vain that he was once called Mad - with the same Lieutenant Heverad, many heads were hit in taverns. We walked merrily. They were friends. Until he became noble and important, marrying the daughter of a nobleman. And then the friendship ended. A nobleman cannot be friends with some kind of military doctor.

Geresard had almost reached the medicinal room when a breathless messenger caught up with him:

- Mister doctor, wait! Mister doctor! Mr. Colonel asks to return.

- What does he want? - Frowningly threw Geresard, looking at the young boy, the son of one of the staff officers.

- I can not know, mister doctor! - answered the messenger, and his boyish face lit up with a smile - he does not report to us! This is Mr. Colonel!

- Okay - the doctor grunted - I'll come right now. Run, tell your ... Mr. Colonel. The messenger nodded and dashed across the parade ground, kicking up the dust with his polished boots. Geresard sighed and walked slowly to headquarters.

The colonel was sitting at a table near the window, and in front of him was a bottle of wine, from which he had already drunk a good deal. There were also fruits, dried smoked fish, candied and salted nuts of all kinds - there are a lot of them on the market and they are a good snack for wine.

The colonel looked gloomily at Geresard who had tumbled in, paused, then said dully:

- Close the door more tightly and lock it with the latch.

- Will you kill? - the doctor chuckled - so I won't give up without a fight.

- Idiot! Cover up! It is not for me to drink with all the medicinal trash - Heverad smirked - take a clean glass. I won't drink from one glass with you - you mess around with all sorts of infectious martyrs. Drink! - he gurgled out of the bottle, and turning, poured for himself - come on, for the old days, for us young! Drink, don't act like a hymen! Like this!

The wine fell easily into the throats, and the colonel remarked with satisfaction:

- Collection, Isolskoe. There is a vineyard on the side of a mountain, nothing is harvested from it. And five barrels of wine are made. For the king. Well ... a barrel for me. What? I didn't deserve it, or what? Twenty years with faith and truth, twenty years in the shitiest places! And the corps always won, because always, tell me, my former ... old friend. I always knew how to fight! Yes, I make money, yes, I look everywhere for profit, but I don't forget the service! No one can blame me except an old ... former friend. You know, buddy. over the years you stop believing people. All the time it seems that they want something from you. Some kind of benefit. This is often the case. And you yourself already think - what can this person give me? Why do I need it? How can he benefit me? You are the only one left with me - you carry everything that comes into your head. There is no one else to talk to. With your wife? A pompous fool - he sits in the capital and makes tricks with young court guards. They report everything to me. Children? They don't need me - a daddy sitting in the backwoods, a soldier with provincial manners. But they are mannered, smelling of perfume ... disgusting! Disgusting, Gera! Money? Yes, I have so much money that you never dreamed of! And why, why are they to me ?! Honestly - I was happier when you and I fought together from a whole squad of swordsmen! Do you remember how you threw that big guy with a stool out the window? Ehh ... it was a fun time! And we were young. Today I imagined that you were not there - and my soul felt disgusting. No one else from those whom you believe next. Some sycophants, assholes, flattering and deceitful creatures. Pour wine ... for both. Come on - from the old days. Then the girls were more beautiful, and the sea was cleaner, and the friendship was stronger, and the soldiers were stronger.

Glasses of expensive blue crystal clinked, old friends drank, crunched nuts, then Geresard, smiling into his beard, hummed:

- You called me to cry on your vest? It was possible to go to his mistress for this, bury her nose in her smooth ass and complain about a hard life. Why are you telling me all this? I can't break the chain of command!

- Yes, stop, or something ... well, it happens, got excited. What kind of demon are you going to make faces like a little girl? You can understand me too - I need to get the job done. And in no time. Yes, I understand that the soldiers are exhausted, but this is bad for them now, and then, in battle, they will survive, having received training here! We have little time! The king sends dispatches demanding to send untrained soldiers into battle - it looks like the situation at the border is just shitty, and he needs to plug the hole with the Marine Corps, which - mind you! - has not lost a single war! Agree, this is my merit! For five years I have been in command of this corps, for fifteen years I have been going to this position, and I occupy it by right. No one can command this unit better than me, no one! We are the best! And now they are demanding from me that I put these boys into the heat - untrained, frail, untrained! How is this side of life for you? Or do you only see how they fall from exhaustion on the parade ground? And if they fall with a severed head, or with released guts - how's that for you? That's better? You, Chief Physician of the Corps, are an intelligent person - don't you understand that? Yes, I make money. But have you seen my soldiers starving? So they don't have clothes or shoes? So that they don't have enough chain mail or leggings? That's the same ... I can be blamed for anything, but not for lack of professionalism. to make my soldiers starve? So they don't have clothes or shoes? So that they don't have enough chain mail or leggings? That's the same ... I can be blamed for anything, but not for lack of professionalism. to make my soldiers starve? So they don't have clothes or shoes? So that they don't have enough chain mail or leggings? That's the same ... I can be blamed for anything, but not for lack of professionalism.

- Okay, I got excited too. I didn't know everything was so bad. But I'm telling you for sure - you need to reduce the tension a little, you need to give the guys a rest. I have been in medicine for over twenty years, I know what I am saying. A day of rest is needed - let them relax. Otherwise, there may be a riot.

- There will be no riot - the colonel dismissed - pour, yeah ... like this ... let's be healthy! May the enemies perish! Do you remember when we raised a toast at the Silver Horse? There was such a beauty then ... we had a fight with the crossbowmen, and then we made up, drank. Oh, I wish I could give up everything! Tired of it!

- After all, you will not give up - the doctor grinned, blotting his mustache with a handkerchief - this swamp has sucked you in. You can't get away from your money.

- Money, money ... by the way - you also have from the pie, you don't have to talk about money! Every week, neatly, in a bag. What a frown? So ... don't talk about money. Let's think about how to do better. Yes, you have to follow your lead, you old bastard, not observing the chain of command! By the way - you will still yell at the entire office - I will order you to whip with sticks! What are you, a fool, or what? Are you screaming at the whole neighborhood? I'm supposed to yell at you, you don't! Okay, they forgot ... but actually I could apologize to the higher authorities!

- Sorry, high-ranking - the doctor smiled - I'm sorry, I have such a voice. My mother said - go to study to be a singer, now I would stand in the temple of Dinas, and did not know any worries, he only wrote psalms, and that's it. And the demons carried me to these healers! Do you have more wine? Something it does not take me. And so tasty, you always knew a lot about wine.

- And the same! It was only you who strove to sip on beer, and pour some vileness into a mug. Taught you, taught you, to distinguish good wine, but never taught you.

- What's good there? Usually at the front you eat a triple distillation vinyl, which is for washing instruments. You grunt a glass, and your soul feels better. We have no time for frills.

- Okay, you don't need to be pity ... I suppose you have already saved up a decent amount. That's what you are talking about your practice. I'm also tired of running around on business trips. How is Elsa, healthy?

- Yes, thank Gods, everything is fine - the doctor softened - he is engaged in children. Swears - I disappear all day in the service, like a unmarried wife lives.

- Oh, what a beauty she was! - smacked the colonel - I was just grinding my teeth when she fell in love with you!

"She loved you at first," the doctor smiled sadly, "and when she realized that she needed you as a mistress, and not as a wife, she left for me. And you married your ...

- No need about that bitch - the colonel winced - here, everything is there - money, position, but there is no happiness. He's gone, buddy. I envy you. Beloved wife, loving children - what else is needed for life? Let's pour some more - for love!

- For this you need to drink - the doctor nodded - and you won't have enough? The sun is still high, the service ...

- Am I drunk, or what ?! Remember how much I could drink! Well, yes - no more than you, it's impossible to get drunk at all, but I was good too! After three bottles of wine, I could still fight five assholes! Where do the youth have such strength, such power now ?! Dead people, freaks ... faint from the heat! Although - out, that same Ned is a beast! How he tore off this soldier's head! Song! And you know - I offered him to become a prize fighter - he refused. Says - I don't want to kill people! You heard? He doesn't want to kill people! And he went to the army! It's just laughter! And I liked the boy. You say correct? So it seemed to me too. Listen, can we put the guy in the officer's school? Why waste his abilities? Although - he's illiterate ...

- Literate. Already literate. I learned it, and very quickly. The guy is smart, reasonable, the department is afraid and respects him. You know - how it looks - they already flinch. And after all, he does not hit, does not drive - he will say that quietly, calmly, and they run to perform. This is a real officer - if he lives.

- If he survives - the colonel echoed - we will return from the Isfir border, I will try to send him to the capital, to the officers' school. There is such a thing when rootless soldiers who especially stood out in military operations are accepted for training on the recommendation of the command. This is also the grandfather of the current king. There is always a shortage of good military personnel. I myself am not painfully well-born - impoverished nobles from a provincial town. My dad sold all the cattle to bribe the director of the officer's school, and they took me. And how much shit I sipped there - of course, no normal horse, no uniform. Everybody goes to the pubs on leave, and I sit in the room, studying tactics and strategy. I have nothing to wander about in taverns. Father did not live long afterwards. As he knew - when he sent me, he said: "Son, I could not give you what the descendants of the Heverads deserve. Forgive me. I give everything I can. Remember me with a good word, don't forget. Take yourself what you owe from life. I believe in you!" He died when I was on summer maneuvers, he didn't even manage to come to the funeral. His brother was burying him. They say - the heart has failed. When his mother died, he gave up badly, was ill. He left quickly, just burned out.

- I remember, Nul, you told. I have not forgotten anything - the doctor said softly, and looked pityingly at the colonel, who laid his head on his crossed arms - I must go. Now, I suppose there is already a crowd of suffering at the door, after a glorious sweatshop training.

- Yes, go - the colonel brushed the moisture from his eyes, rubbed his reddened face with his palms - we will reduce training to ten hours a day, every week will be a day off - only we will not let everyone out into the city. Only those who deserve it. And those who were not guilty last time in dismissal. Those who do not go - let them sit here, envy. An added incentive for good service. About the guy, well, this ... Ned - can you really take it with you? I will translate by order, that's all. They'll kill the demon girl!

- By force? I will not translate by force. You know - not everyone wants to pick in the mud, in the shit, like doctors. What's the use if you force it to do? Let him serve. That's just ...

- What? Speak ...

- Can he be promoted to sergeant? You can do it. Easily. For special services.

- And what are the merits? - the colonel chuckled - tearing off the enemy's head?

- Well ... some. I'll watch. By the way - you can just use the wording for blameless service. And that's all. Let everyone see how we elevate those who serve well, who are examples for other soldiers!

- Will it not be perceived by other sergeants as an upstart elevation? They got their ranks in military operations, and before that they had been ordinary soldiers and corporals for five years!

- Do you care about their opinion? Who are you, Colonel, or a sickly doctor?

- Heh heh ... you tell the truth ... a stale doctor! That's why I love you - I never greased myself, I didn't play on friendly feelings, I didn't want anything material from me, not like the others. What you think is what you say. I'll do it. For the cause. Not for the sake of friendship or for this guy himself, but for the sake of service. Such personnel must be protected, and as a sergeant he has a better chance of surviving. And now he will have more free time - let him study. You make him read, let him teach good manners - the officer will come in handy. The army needs good officers. Someone must actually fight, and not wipe the parquet flooring in palaces!

- That's for sure - the doctor nodded, and got up from the chair - I'll go, that's it. We had a good time.

- Yes OK. It immediately became easier for me, as I talked to you. And it was so disgusting in my soul, so disgusting that I couldn't even say it in words! I'll go now and sleep for an hour. I will give the commands according to the schedule, I will order to prepare documents for the guy, and sleep. The heat, something made me a little bit upset. Tell the clerical rats to come in here, I'll give orders! - the colonel unbuttoned the belt of his pants, loosened the collar of his uniform and happily leaned back in his chair. His head was noisy, the world was rocking, and he felt very good.

Chapter 9

- Rota - get on! We are listening to the order of the Corps Commander, Colonel Heverad! - Drankon scanned the frozen ranks of spearmen, shining with brushed steel armor - fifteen squads of those who came to school a few months ago from civilian life - men who had never held a spear before. Most are very young boys - recruited from the age of sixteen. However - who checked this age? If only the shoulders were wider, and the arms were stronger. And how old is he - what does it matter? Will die just like adults.

The ranks of the infantrymen froze, and seemed to hold their breath - has it really happened what they have been thinking about all these months? What they were trained for on hard days, from dawn to dusk - war? Is it time for them to go to war?

- Mr. Colonel Heverad, announces: for special successes in the service, Corporal Ned Black is promoted to sergeant! - The dragon looked around at the stunned soldiers, after a pause, he added - any soldier who honestly and conscientiously carries out the service, serves as an example to his comrades, can be promoted to sergeant, with a corresponding increase in salary and benefits. Sergeant Ned Black, out of line!

Ned, more dazed than his comrades, took three steps forward, turned clearly around his shoulder and made a military salute - his hand, clenched into a fist, thrown above his head, then returned to its place - on the short spear, with which he stood in the front row.

The dragon examined the new sergeant's equipment, nodded his head in satisfaction - everything was polished, everything glittered, not a speck anywhere, then commanded:

- Disperse for dinner! Collect on signal! - and added quietly - Ned, follow me. Let's talk.

Drankon walked forward, not looking to see if Ned was following. He walked after him, pulling a spear on his shoulder, and with his other hand holding a short sword on his belt.

As Ned walked - pondering the news all the time - what would that mean? And why on earth did he suddenly become a sergeant, consider it a junior officer in the army, the only officer who could be appointed a corps commander without any training. No — Ned didn't mind, but what would that mean? Suddenly - rrraz! And you're done! And he knows almost nothing about the service, where is he against such bison as Sergeant Drankon ?!

They went into the house where Drankon lived - the sergeant refused to live in the officers' town, his whole life passed at the base, so he lived right there. The rest of the sergeants lived in the city, some had their own families.

Drankon took off his high cap with relief and nodded to Ned.

- Take off your helmet and carapace, let your shoulders rest. You will also train iron.

Ned nodded, snapped off the carapace clasps, and pulled off the First Rider's heavy armor. He carefully folded everything on a wide bench against the wall and, remaining in special quilted clothes worn under the equipment, looked inquiringly at Drancon.

- Sit down - he nodded - drink - this is water with agura juice - sour, good thirst quencher. Probably questions are spinning in my head, right? - The dragon grinned out of the corner of his mouth - they are spinning themselves. I tried to find out - what was it? I couldn't. Don't you fuck the colonel's daughter there? Or maybe a relative of his mistress? Okay, don't frown. He was stunned himself today - a messenger brought a package, I read it - everything is for sure. You are a sergeant. I went for clarifications. Received an audience with the base commander. Exactly - no doubt about it. You've been promoted to sergeant. Probably for that fight, or something. Someone told me that the colonel won a lot of money in this fight. However - I too. Maybe for this, the recruit was awarded the rank of junior officer? We can only guess. Okay. Do you have any idea what you have to do? Usually a sergeant is given to us from old-timers, proven in combat. Those who have already completed at least one contract, and who know what to do in any circumstances. You are zero. If you are put in charge of a company now, you will ruin it. A sergeant is a field commander who is sensitive to how his company is beating and quickly closes gaps. Lieutenant - he is responsible for the two companies, for their interaction with other specialties. Tomorrow we will begin training with swordsmen and crossbowmen. Do you know how to interact with them? No. That's bad. Lieutenant - he is responsible for the two companies, for their interaction with other specialties. Tomorrow we will start training with swordsmen and crossbowmen. Do you know how to interact with them? No. That's bad. Lieutenant - he is responsible for the two companies, for their interaction with other specialties. Tomorrow we will start training with swordsmen and crossbowmen. Do you know how to interact with them? No. That's bad.

Drankon sighed, paused, and added gloomily:

- Will teach. Not only them, but you. Where to go? I was told to teach you to command a company of spearmen as soon as possible. So you will have a hundred and fifty people under your command. Glad? I see - not happy at all - Drankon laughed - but what can I do? The commander's orders are not negotiable. He knows better who to appoint, who to raise and who to execute. Come on! But now you have a better chance of surviving. The first rows usually fall first when faced with an enemy army. Then the rest of the spearmen. Then the turn of the swordsmen comes - they fight in the closest combat. We are the frontline unit, meeting the enemy with our chest. Come on, don't be sad — you now have "gingerbreads" that are inaccessible to ordinary soldiers. Your salary is now three gold a week. This is a lot of money for the villagers! You can even go to the officers' town, rent an apartment outside the base, leave and come to the base whenever you need it. No pass required. You have two days off a week, you can eat with the officers or with the soldiers - of your choice. What's more ... the shape is better quality and more beautiful. Here you can live in the barracks for junior officers. By the way - I strongly recommend moving there if you are not going to rent a room in the city. There will be less familiarity - this is not welcome. The soldier must be at a distance from the officer. Corporal - another matter, consider - he is a senior soldier. But the sergeant is already an officer. Taak ... what else? You hand over your ammunition to the warehouse, you get the sergeant's combat equipment. Which one? Chain mail, long sword, dagger, oval shield. Now you don't have to stand in line, you have to lead the soldiers, giving commands to signalmen. Any questions?

"Hmm... I'll figure it out... I'm stunned. No, not the right word - I ... ..

- And me too - ... ... What can you do? Service. I am no longer surprised at anything. I've seen a lot of things over the years. You will make a good sergeant, I'm sure you just need to be trained properly. Otherwise, you will spoil the business and ruin people. Who would you put in place of yourself as a corporal?

- You know better, Monsieur Drankon ...

"Hmmm... funny. I thought that you will now name one of your friends - Oidar, or Arnot. And how are you. By the way - you can call me by name - Lysard, and you. Now we are with you in the same rank. It is customary for us to call our fellow sergeants to "you". And by name - when addressing unofficially, of course. At the service - when how. So your friends are not suitable for the position of corporal? Honestly!

- No. If only Arnot, but he has no authority. Oydar is hot, can not cope. He himself needs supervision. You ... you know the people of the company better, put it yourself. By the way - I don't understand about the company. You're a sergeant here. This is your company.

"I'm a training sergeant, boy. When you go into battle, you will have another sergeant. And I'll stay to wait for the new recruits. After you go to war, your people will greatly diminish. So there will be a new set soon ... Before sailing, you were supposed to be handed over to the new sergeants, and you and him spend two weeks grinding to each other. I tell the sergeant about the company, he himself looks who is who, well, and ... like this. Traditionally, after the appointment, you have three days of rest, starting tomorrow. You arrange your life, think about where you will live, get uniforms, walk, get drunk, and then you come and start learning how to be a sergeant. Clear?

- Clear. Is it possible without drunkenness? Smiled Ned.

- Can. But not desirable. How is it - a soldier, and without drunkenness ?! Just kidding, just kidding ... I know you don't drink. It's strange, actually. Does some vow not allow you to drink? Your health seems to be fine. What's the matter? People who are somehow different from others are always suspicious. If you don't drink with the team, it means either you are sick, or you are going to snitch a security guard, passing on conversations at the table. So many will think, consider this.

- Why don't I drink wine? Ned asked, because he didn't like it. It's ... bitter!

For a while the Dragon sat silently, looking at Ned, his lips twitching, as if from the cold, then he could not stand it and began to laugh so that his eyes flowed from tears:

- Bitter ?! Oh, he died ... well ... I thought he was joking, but he really is. A child is a child ... Don't be offended, boy. I'm fit for your age as a father. I've seen everything, but such a ... pure soul, how did you come to us? - he asked sadly, having finished laughing - I cannot understand you. It is almost impossible to meet a more righteous person people. And at the same time - I close my eyes, and I see the head of that guy. You killed him like you swatted a fly. No emotion, no regret. Was that the first person you killed? Drankon asked unexpectedly, not expecting an answer.

- No.

- How many?

- Ten. They were bad people. They came to kill me, and they killed my friend. I didn't want to kill them, they ...

- Quiet, quiet! Everything! This is in the past, do not burden me with your problems. I am not your own mother and not your father. Killed - so they deserve. Knowing you, I'm sure - you can't kill flies just like that. Everything, boy, run away from here. Go to the officers' mess for lunch. You hand over the iron after lunch, anyway, there is no one in the warehouse now - everyone ran away to eat, damned swallows. What else can I say - good luck, Sergeant! Serve. Survive ...

There was no one in the barracks except the orderly. He looked at Ned with curiosity, nodding his head - of course, the news that the soldier was promoted to sergeant by the order of the colonel spread throughout the Corps like a hurricane wind.

This was, of course, an exceptional case. Usually, such appointments took place after hostilities, from those soldiers who actually showed themselves in the war, and not only by individual actions, but mainly in group military clashes. For example, a sergeant was killed, and a soldier (corporal) took over command of the company. And here - what? Well - I had a fight in a duel, yes. Nicely tore off the head of the enemy (why, one wonders?!). And what, now all the combatants are officers? These thoughts were written on the face of the orderly, and he was also thinking them.

Ned rarely now turned on supersensible perception, although he had learned to slightly muffle the background of general thoughts, intending to overhear the thoughts of a certain object. He was simply not interested. Listening to friends is what they think and what they say. Play the soldiers? What for? Learn about how they drank, how they did somersaults with a dirty aunt? What is the interest in this? No - well, so informative, yeah. Ned was not very enlightened about women, and at first he was very interested and amused by some of the details of physical love between men and women, described by the soldiers and represented by them in the form of pictures. But when you listen to it for the one hundred and thirtieth time, in all the details, the novelty is lost, and all this just gets boring. Yes, and unnecessary excitement ...

Ned was a healthy, mature guy, clever, and quick to grasp what was what. He, like all youths of this age, wanted a woman, dreamed of a woman, women dreamed of him - they beckoned, smiled, sparkled with their smooth, attractive body ... Waking up, he sometimes found that he had received relaxation in a dream, and while washing, avoiding his comrades, without embarrassment of those who discussed the process of self-gratification, went away to the side and washed in the shower, not wanting to expose their problems and dreams.

Honestly, that time when his friends called him to the girl in the "Red Stallion", he regretted that he refused. At first I regretted it. And his well-mannered speech about puddles was nothing more than a fear that someone, such as a girl, would find out how uneducated and inept he was.

With annoyance, Ned discovered this property of himself - a slight vanity. How does someone know that he is so uneducated, inept, not knowing simple things? And this after Ned became known throughout the corps as a skilled fighter?

After discovering this bad trait in himself, Ned began to resolutely suppress vanity and timidity. Shy to ask? He takes it and asks. Can not? He came up and asked someone who knows how. So it was during military exercises, and so it was during the study of reading and writing.

Oddly enough, people were happy to show and tell Ned whatever he asked. It's nice to realize that such a formidable fighter, dear Ned, doesn't know something! The person whom he asked, seemed to rise on himself, towered in his eyes and he was pleased. And since he felt pleased at the expense of Ned, it means that Ned was associated with pleasure, with a good mood. Because - Ned had an excellent relationship with most of the soldiers, of those with whom he communicated.

Yes, there were exceptions. Envious people, spiteful critics, and besides, those whom he forced to abide by the rules, to serve. The same Ditas, whom Ned put in the tavern, killing Edwana. The criminal got friends, the same as himself - including from other companies. But he did not touch Ned, did not touch him, trying not to even approach him, so Nedne probed his thoughts. And why probe? Lives for himself and lives, and the demon with him. Ned had no intention of befriending him, so ... don't give a damn?

Tucking his things into the sack, Ned looked around his bed, which had been made exactly as taught. Here he spent several months, and I must admit that this was the best time of his life. He even felt a little sad - his friends stay, but he leaves ... How will he be friends with Oidar and Arnot now? Will the guys look at him as an upstart, as someone with whom it is now impossible to communicate? The bosses, they say ... He, personally, was not going to end the friendship, but how will they look at everything?

Sighing, he threw two sacks - with armor and clothing - on his shoulders, and walked to the exit from the barracks. At the entrance, he grabbed his spear from the pyramid, which had been polished with palms to a shine for many months of training and headed to the military depot located behind the headquarters.

The arsenal building, made of large white stones, loomed over the headquarters like a huge landing ship would hang over a fishing boat. And it's no wonder being so big - everything was stored in the warehouse - from weapons and armor to laces and buttons. Everything a soldier needs to cheerfully lay his head on the altar of state power and go to the grave, praising the king's generosity.

On the back of the storage building there were food warehouses, half buried in the ground and filled with bags of cereals, dried meat, corned beef - in general, everything that can be stored for a long time and that you can eat here and take with you on a business trip. These products, perhaps, were not very tasty, but nutritious, and they were also stored for a long time even in a damp sea climate, for example, on ships.

Colonel Heverad strictly monitored the safety of the contents of the warehouses and once ordered to have cats, for the war with rats, which he hated with every fiber of his soul - real rats and office rats. He could not exterminate the latter, with all his desire, but for the former he ordered a gift - rat-catchers, once bred in Isfira.

War was war, and trade between states was proceeding regularly, without delays, and soon striped hefty cats reigned in the warehouses, ruthlessly cracking down on the tailed terrorists. After that, the soldiers stopped finding rat tails for the cutlets and mouse shit in the porridge.

Cats multiplied, and often walked on the parade ground even during drill exercises, glancing displeasedly at the stomping people, for some reason did not understand that it was time for a cat's walk, and disturbed their peace.

These striped robbers have become for some time the same symbol of the Marine Corps, like tall caps with three shiny letters KMP. They did not touch the cats, did not offend, and the soldiers also fed them, dragging the pieces left over from lunch to the snickering cats. The colonel even forbade feeding the cats at one time - on pain of reprisals, fearing that they would stop catching rats. But they still caught, leaving the corpses of the vile creatures under the doors of the headquarters, as if they knew to whom they owe their existence. The ban was lifted.

Cats served as something like an outlet for callous soldiers' souls, having no family, no normal life, and in the future - no life at all.

- Ahh! Newfound Sergeant! - the storekeeper on duty lazily stretched out, lying on a bench at the entrance and scratching his belly through his unbuttoned uniform - I actually have lunch! Come back in an hour - I'll take everything, give everything. You don't march for lunch, do you? Here I am, too - I don't work when lunch. Go, Sergeant, get out of here!

- Well, at least take it, or what? - Ned was agitated - am I going to carry sacks?

- What did you think when you walked here? What, you couldn't come after dinner? And now you stand here and spin your brains! Get out, get out of here! I don't care if you are a sergeant, or ... In general, the shop is closed!

The storekeeper got up from the bench, groaning, and began demonstratively closing the gate, not paying attention to Ned.

- Hey boy - Ned touched the storekeeper on the shoulder - take the junk. And nothing will happen to you. Except ... this one - he handed the storekeeper a silver pool, which he immediately dropped into his dimensionless pocket.

- This is another matter! - shone the storekeeper - there is beer! And then everyone is worried, and there is no one to take care of the unfortunate servant! And you will be a good officer, I know for sure! You understand the soul of a soldier, but why? Himself a soldier! I'm sure you'll go far. Follow me. Lay out the armor here ... yeah. Throw it on the floor, I'll take it apart later. You still need to have dinner, guess what? It's okay, it will lie down. So ... completeness ... yeah ... plates ... greaves ... come on, I'll give you new ones now, with better quality. And the shape is different. You are supposed to have three sets - two for every day, and one day off, ceremonial, in order to impress girls in the city. I have one batch of uniforms - by mistake they zababahali from Major's cloth - eh, and a cool thing came out! The cloth is thin, woolen, blown through - you can walk in the heat ... aha, thanks! Well done! (Ned took the hints and gave him another piece of silver. He already knew how important good equipment was, and it depended on this goat what it would be. So save yourself more. Drankon warned him.) Well, young man! Always come to Pernal - I'll pick the best for you! Here, look what a day off uniform - class! It is not gray, but bluish, like the top officers! And nothing against the charter - everything goes according to the requirements! Are we to blame for the fact that by mistake we sewed them from Major's cloth for the sergeants? Do not burn them? I keep it for my own, use it to your health! Such a handsome man like you must! All your girls will be, this is a copper against a hundred gold! Now the boots. So - two sandals, weekend boots and boots for the field. Look - here are the strong, bound with iron. Strong - like armor! You can kick them properly. I advise. And for a parade and a walk with a girl - these are these, soft. The leg does not get tired in them. Measure it. Fit? Good. You change right here, then I will write down the clothes on the list. And boots too. Put on your sandals for now, it's hot. Here there is. I'll give you a new one - two duffel bags, one for the armor, the other for the uniform. Teeeks ... a combat suit for armor. he is the same for everyone ... first-aid kit - bandages and ointment, harness, cap ... oh, handsome! The form sits on you, like a glove! Then it will drop a little, the wrinkles will disappear. Let's get you a weapon. Trust Pernal - I know a thing or two about dusting machines. Come here, to the corner. Well, look at this sword ... - the storekeeper pulled out from somewhere from under a pile of old swords, laid out on the rack, a long blade, dimly gleaming with a matte edge. It was dusty, completely invisible, and Ned looked a little disappointedly at this work of an unknown blacksmith. The storekeeper, apparently, noticed this,

- I don't understand, right? Come on, follow me!

They emerged from the dim warehouse, and Ned spent several seconds getting used to the bright light, blinking helplessly. The storekeeper managed to take a rag with him and lovingly wiped the blade, took it by the handle, weighed it:

- What is the balance, miracle! Actually, I wanted to give it to Sergeant Evos. He asked me for a long time to pick up something real, cool!

- What is cool? Ned shrugged.

- Look here! - the storekeeper threw in a rag, the sword whistled lightly, and the rag fell to the ground, divided into two parts - and yet - he cuts armor like paper! And don't be blunt! Look at the drawing of the blade! Do you see the pattern? Such swords were forged for months, then allowed to rest, and again forged. Do you see any signs on the blade? They say that these swords are enchanted, they have some kind of supernatural powers! Well, I don't guarantee it, but the fact that it's amazingly sharp and always keeps sharpening - I can say with complete confidence.

Ned carefully took the sword in his hands, and began to examine carefully, trying for sharpness and balance. He was lovely. An odd pattern of metal that Ned had never seen — steel gray, intertwined, wavy. The sharpest blade - it was worth touching, and the skin immediately began to feed, unraveling under the lightest pressure. On the blade, in the middle, along the groove, are small golden letters in a language Ned does not know. The handle is simple, straight, without any frills, wrapped in some kind of rough black material.

- Shark skin! - the storekeeper explained with the air of a connoisseur - they say a very old sword. It is several hundred years old. Where did it come from? Who knows? There is enough iron here. I did the tidying up and found it in the corner. I wanted to sell ... - the storekeeper stopped short and looked sideways at Ned - did you understand? He made sure that he didn't react and continued:

- Here I keep it for my own ... maybe someone's life will save ... Yeah, thanks! Well done! Here is a clever girl! So I earned an award! I'll pick up your scabbard now, and a dagger, and a boot knife, and two throwing knives with a sling! Three knives! Put your fingerprint here ... yeah. And sign, can you? Well done. Like this. Excellent. Come on, I'll find you everything. Leave it here, don't be afraid. Now everyone is at lunch, no one will resist. Take the shank with you. Stop carrying it around.

Loaded like a donkey of a pack, Ned walked to the sergeants' dorm. A certain chill lurked inside him - it's so easy to take it and come to the officer's dormitory - his heart sank and beat fast, like a bird in a cage. Until now, he had a kind of reverence inside him for sergeants, symbols of army service. Therefore, he walked slowly, as if delaying the moment of arrival at the place.

However - everything went calmly and routinely. He introduced himself to the orderly, asked to be shown an empty room, he took him to the corner, overlooking the mountains - which Ned really liked - and wishing a pleasant rest he retired to his table, where he again took a resting position, legs raised as high as possible.

Ned dropped the bags to the floor, stood in the middle of the room and laughed happily - his room! His first room and no one, no one can enter here without permission! He can lock her up and leave! Put things here the way he wants and no one will say that they are not the way they should!

A window covered with a thick grille, a simple table, three chairs - after all, a sergeant can receive guests, his comrades! The bed is narrow, not at all for sleeping with a girlfriend. What kind of girlfriend is there in the military camp?

Here was the most important thing, the most valuable thing that can be in the army - solitude. After all, a soldier has nowhere to hide - he sleeps with everyone, eats with everyone, washes with everyone, even in the toilet, and then with everyone! Like mountain eagles, in orderly rows ... Many swore - at least they would have put partitions or something, otherwise everything was in plain sight. But this has been the practice since ancient times and no one was going to change the state of affairs. Here, in the hostel, the toilet was in the corridor, as well as the shower room - the orderly immediately showed him where the "amenities" are - war is war, and the toilet, like lunch, is important.

Ned neatly laid his cap down on the bedside table, and, not making the bed, fell onto the mattress, throwing his hands behind his head. It is not known what was ahead, but now he was fine. Very good!

After lying down, he got up, put things on the shelves in the closet, armor and a sword in a special weapons cabinet, shoes in a shoe. I admired it, then caught myself - lunch! What demon did he not go to dinner ?! Immediately my stomach grumbled and I felt a terrible desire to eat. The body was accustomed to receiving food at the time strictly allotted for this and now violently resented the violence committed against it. I looked out the window - judging by the sun, lunch break was coming to an end. The soldiers ate a long time ago, but what about the officers' mess? Is it open?

He quickly put on his boots, pulled on his uniform, went out into the corridor, locking the door with a key, and past the orderly, who was watching him, went out into the sun's rays, which stuck into him, as if they wanted to turn him into a fried piece of meat. He thought for a second and resolutely headed for the officers' mess.

It was cooler here, thick stone walls sheltered from the heat. In contrast to the soldier's barracks-like dining room, the officer's is divided into small offices, fenced off with a net made of twigs, to which small wooden blocks with burnt drawings are attached. Basically - beautiful maidens with courageous young men on horseback or battle scenes with heaps of defeated enemies.

Probably an unknown artist believed that for a military man there is nothing sweeter than the sight of heaps of defeated enemies and images of half-naked women in their underwear near a weeping willow. As for the second - perhaps, and most likely it is. But the first one was already sick of the officers during their service in the coolest of the corps of the Zamar army, and they constantly grumbled that this bawdy-dismembered person had to be removed for a long time and defiantly burned on the parade ground, and then urinate on the ash. But, as always, nobody's hands reached these pictures, so they hung from time immemorial, and hang just as much, unless they are burnt by an accidental lightning bolt launched by the creator god.

The hall is empty, only a couple of lieutenants and a sergeant from the crossbowmen finished their dinner, hastily swallowing pieces of pie and filling them with water and half with juice - they stayed at the service, sorting out a fight that suddenly broke out right in the middle of the parade ground. One of the soldiers fell, struck by heatstroke, the next one plopped on him, the one who followed him kicked the fallen one, the friend of the kicked one drove into the face of the aggressor, the other in the opposite direction - everything a little turned into a mass slaughter. I had to resort to the help of a platoon of guards on duty, who dispersed everyone with batons and buckets of water, prudently prepared in the guards' room.

This was not the first fight that broke out out of nowhere - the heat and overwork did their job. The guilty were whipped, though not much - everyone was shitty, and even the executors find it difficult to raise and lower sticks on the backs of the adversaries through such hell.

- Look, the new sergeant has appeared! - muttered one of the lieutenants - I wonder how he got his rank? What did the colonel like so much?

- Do you care? - the second threw in bewilderment - what do you care? Well, I got it, and I got it! What are you running into?

- No, well, after all! - insisted the second, a young guy, a little older than Ned, who had just arrived at the unit from the officers' school - maybe he's a special guy, eh? Did well for the colonel, and here's your job! From a redneck to an officer! Commercials will go further, will command us, "silver lips"! See what plump, working lips he has! Damn upstart, man-lover!

The guy spoke deliberately loudly, probably so that Ned could hear and immediately understand his place in this world, where a cattle and a redneck like him have no place at the same table next to an impoverished, but glorious noble family.

Here it is necessary to clarify. "Manly love" in the Marine Corps, and in general in the army of Zamar, was considered the worst crime, along with fleeing the battlefield or attacking a superior officer. It was believed that this vice is inherent in corrupted civilians and slaves deprived of female society. And that those are engaged in this, who, in addition to this sins, also use the services of various types of cattle and small ruminants. In general - in fact, according to the army canons, Ned was inflicted with the most severe insult, washed away only by blood. Ned knew about it. The soldier could be called what you want, but the officers ... there was a code of honor, and no one could step over it. Caught red-handed "on the hottest" sodomite soldier was allowed through the ranks, beaten to death with sticks, while the officer was expelled, stripped of all ranks and given him ten hot sticks.

Where did it come from? Unknown. But only the army had a sharp, categorically negative attitude towards manifestations of sodomy (And this despite the fact that the top leadership, as always, did not deny themselves any "pleasures", even such!)

During his service, Ned encountered hidden sodomites - their thoughts were visible to him at a glance. But they never allowed themselves any actions either towards him or towards those around him, because he did not care what they were doing when no one saw them. Don't give a damn.

But in this case, it was not at all to give a damn. As he joins the team of officers, so the service will go on - this was explained to him by Drankon. And the old, shabby sergeant was right. "Upstart" will have to conquer their place in the sun.

Ned changed direction, and instead of going to serve food, he walked over to the table with two lieutenants. The one who insulted him looked into the guy's face with a cheerful smile and casually asked:

- What do you want? What do you want, redneck?

The second lieutenant, who knew Ned and saw his fight, quickly wiped his lips with a napkin and, without finishing the juice from the mug, got up from his place and walked aside, sideways watching what was happening. Of course - he was terribly interested in what would happen next, but he was not going to be in the center of the scandal, with the risk of getting a black eye.

The newly arrived lieutenant was a swordsman. Large, broad-shouldered, with strong muscular arms, accustomed to exercise. He is only five years older than Ned, but he has already participated in six duels, in which he won all six - due to the art of swordsmanship, natural animal speed and strength. So he was not quite such a lost guy, but a toad sat inside him, requiring him to constantly assert himself, and preferably at the expense of other, weaker people. An ordinary guy, of which there are many. The gods gave him excessive strength and agility, but did not give him intelligence and even a little indulgence towards those who are weaker than him. They make tyrants and murderers if they are not stopped on the road strewn with the bodies of their victims.

In addition, despite the fact that the guy was one of the impoverished nobles - otherwise he would not have ended up in such a corps - he had connections - an uncle, an assistant to the imperial treasurer, prepared for him a warm place in the capital. After Zasler has served in the Marine Corps for six months, it will not be difficult - what a hero! After all, the marines are always at the forefront of striking the enemy. The fact that he was recently going to transfer to the Security Service, under the wing of Major Shentel, did not matter - anyway, the documents will indicate that Zasler participated in the hostilities of the Corps. Even if he never went on the attack, and saw the enemy only in the form of a corpse, worked by other associates.

Lieutenant Zasler was very angry today. He had to deal with a fight, and then, in the sun, flog negligent soldiers - so that his mood was below the lowest. And then there's this cattle in its uncrumpled sergeant uniform! Well - uniform cattle, and more! The pun really amused Zasler, so he smiled in the face of this idiot.

- I need you to apologize - said Ned quietly, and closed his eyes for a second - such a wave of hatred, rage rose from the depths of his consciousness that he almost began to perform witchcraft.

- Before whom, in front of you, moron? The redneck is manly! - the guy grinned, and immediately followed by a deafening slap, from which the lieutenant flew from the chair. Ned's hand was very, very heavy. And during training at the base it did not get any easier.

- What's going on here? - There was a sharp commanding voice, Ned turned and saw Major Shentel - the head of the Corps security. Next to him are two captains and three lieutenants - his entire department. Apparently, this valiant detachment lingered on the interrogations of those who participated in the fight today and only now the officers were able to start dinner. And what do they see? In the dining room, where all the conversations were only in an undertone, in the holy of holies of the Corps - a fight! And who is the instigator? Sergeant! Yesterday's soldier! Beats an officer with a higher rank! Yes, Shentel was convinced - sedition took root in the Marine Corps too deeply. Colonel Heverad dismissed his subordinates. And here is the result - the sergeant appointed by him beats up the senior officers!

- Take him! - commanded Shentel - you are under arrest, sergeant! For violation of paragraph four of the Code of Ranks! Lieutenant Nitras, Lieutenant Darth - Deliver Sergeant Black to the Garrison Jail!

Ned's first thought was to rip off the heads of everyone who was there. Everyone! A fierce desire to kill distorted his face, turning him into a demon's mask, and the officers who stepped towards him froze in place, not daring to come closer. They remembered who Ned was and what he had done to the prize fighter.

Then Ned calmed down and allowed them to pull his arms. So, accompanied by two officers, he proceeded to the garrison prison - a low structure behind a grocery store, dug into the ground almost along the roof.

When Ned was taken away, Shentel, who was angry with Ned about his refusal to cooperate, asked the beaten lieutenant:

- So what happened here?

- A redneck came up and hit me in the face. I made a remark to him about the need to say hello when you enter the dining room. He hit me. That's all.

Zasler's face was serene and calm, as if he was sitting on the seashore and watching the sunset. His blue eyes and the innocent face of the "good guy" expressed complete innocence - except for the sergeant, who was sitting in the distance and busy with his bowl, and the lieutenant from his own battalion, there was no one else in the dining room, which meant that there was no one to turn him over. And he will somehow agree with the witnesses.

Shentel was pleased. He had long wanted to insert a hairpin Heverad, as it seemed to him - the collapse of the Corps. For a long time he reported about this upstairs, to the management, but the ministry did not draw any conclusions. Honestly, he wanted to take the place of the corps commander himself. He'd do better with the missions assigned to the Marine Corps. And most importantly, he will gain control over cash flows. He had enough length of service, he should have received a colonel's patent long ago, but the position that Shentel held was only a major. As they say, you can't jump higher than the major. Now, after the colonel's henchman in the first hours after the appointment started a fight, attacked an officer of higher rank, Heverad will not turn his back on trouble. Enough for him to sit in his place, it's time to resign!

The news that Ned had been arrested spread throughout the building in the blink of an eye. The lunch break had not yet ended when the whole hull began to hum like a hornet's nest. The soldiers gathered in groups, discussed what had happened and the picture acquired more and more new details.

After the twentieth transmission of information, it turned out that Ned entered the officers' mess drunk, urinated on the table where Major Shentel was sitting with his brothers and Lieutenant Zasler, and when they tried to twist Ned, he broke their arms and legs, and was stopped only by half a squad of swordsmen in full combat weapons. And then networks. The soldiers argued among themselves, made assumptions, swore until hoarse and agreed on only one thing - it would not end well. The offender is threatened at least with demotion and sticks, and as a maximum - death in a noose.

Geresard stomped through the office to the door of the colonel's office, and looking back at Heverad's adjutant, asked:

- In place? Not busy?

- Actually busy - the lieutenant shrugged his shoulders - he has suppliers of food and cloth. They've been sitting for two hours already. I don't know when it will be free. He ordered not to let anyone in. ABOUT! Your happiness. Like finished.

The office doors swung open, steaming red merchants emerged from them. The colonel once again squeezed money out of them, and after the fierce resistance of the merchants, he still managed to squeeze out a rollback for each item of goods. Not much, but the delivery for the entire body was quite acceptable. The merchants came out so shabby, as if they were knocked down by a mad mule, and then rolled on the floor by a chain dog. The colonel knew how to insist on his own when he needed it.

- Hey, Bonecrusher, why are you coming to me? I told you - tomorrow they will bring bandages and everything else! What happened? - Heverad looked attentively into the gloomy face, as a cloud of a doctor waved his hand - come in!

He closed the door and asked quietly:

- What? Is there something with Elsa? What happened? Children? Help?

- No, thank the gods! - Geresard boomed with feeling - trouble with Ned.

"Fuhh... scaring me. I was thinking ... sooo ... what about Ned? What's the trouble?

- Beat Lieutenant Zasler.

- This shit? This guy from the capital? The right word - I would have filled his face myself ... hmm. Poorly! - the colonel caught himself - he's a sergeant, and that lieutenant. And even with ties. How did it come about?

- According to Zasler's version: Ned came into the dining room, entering - did not say hello. Zasler reprimanded him, he gave him a muzzle. And what a sin - Shentel immediately formed behind his back! Ned was arrested and sent to the garrison prison. Wait - soon Shentel himself will appear. I came running to warn you.

- Did he resist arrest? Beat someone? Heverad asked anxiously.

- No, thank the gods! Everything is quiet.

- Although it's good - the colonel chuckled, feverishly pondering what had happened - you see, I told you - they don't like upstarts. It's unpleasant. Very unpleasant. Have you talked to Ned?

- No one is allowed to see him. Shentel walks proudly, as if he took the capital of Isfira by storm. It just glows about happiness.

- Still would! The bitch has long been aiming at my place - Heverad chuckled - now he has a reason to send a foul letter describing how I exalt violators of the charter, and how I disbanded the unit entrusted to me.

- Will you hold out?

- Hold on ... he went to ... ..! Not that goat meat to dump me! Only money will cost me ... big money! Oh, how wrong time, how wrong time! There is some kind of ferment in the capital, they say that there will be changes in the ministry, no matter how it turns out to me. And then there's this shitty story ...

- Mr. Colonel! Major Shentel to you! - knocked on the door, and after the answer came the adjutant - let him in?

- Will you stay?

"No... to see his oily face is beyond my strength. I don't believe Ned just kicked the bastard in the face. I heard something about this Zasler.

- And I heard ... - the colonel nodded thoughtfully and ordered the adjutant - let the major go. Let him come in.

Geresard went out, not paying attention to the major - in fact, he and Shentel were in the same rank. Although the doctor was a non-combatant, if necessary, he could be drafted into service, and then his rank would just be equal to that of Shentel. The doctor and the security guard have long disliked each other. Geresard could not stand the major for his duplicity, and the major did not love anyone at all. Except yourself. Geresard, on the other hand, did not like him for his independence of character and unwillingness to cooperate with the security service. For a long time, Shentel had a whole pile of denunciations against the doctor, from which it was clear that he had disapproved of the policies of the king, the state and the top leadership of the army. So far, the major did not give a course to the papers - he was waiting for a chance. It seemed that one would soon come. As soon as his patron disappears ...

- Greetings, Colonel! - Shentel was as benevolent as ever, calm and at the same time emphatically official - I will report to you. Allow me?

- Report, Major - Heverad answered dryly and sat down on his chair at the work table.

- Probably, you have already been informed about the unfortunate incident in the dining room? - the security guard continued calmly.

- Yes, I know - the colonel threw abruptly, sorting through the papers on the table and not looking at the major.

- Wonderful. On what day shall we appoint the court of officer's honor?

- Right for tonight and we will appoint. Six o'clock in the afternoon. What is the time to delay? Have you interviewed witnesses? Have you found out all the circumstances of the case?

- Yes of course. There were no witnesses. The word of the officer, against the word ... of the criminal.

- Until the court of honor recognized him as a criminal - Ned is not a criminal! You, the security man, should know this better than me, Shentel!

- Yes you are right. I apologize - easily, the major agreed with a smile - I'm very sorry that this happened to your protege, Mr. Colonel! Now let me leave your office - I must notify all available officers of the impending trial. And the most important thing is to warn the judges. You already know, it remains to inform Colonel Zayed and Colonel Evora.

Shentel clearly saluted and left the office. The colonel sat in silence for a minute, then violently grabbed some paper and tore it to shreds, growling with excitement. He calmed down and shook his head sadly:

- Well, what have you done, Ned? Your officers' school cried. It's good if we save your bad head. He looked at the snatches of the show and shook his head again.

Chapter 10

It was cool in the cell. We must pay tribute to the garrison prison - clean, swept, no rats or insects. However - can it be so only in the officer's cell? Of course, Ned was not shoved with the general, to the violators of the order of the soldiers. No, but an officer.

Ned was not afraid of the trial. The only thing that was bitter and insulting was that everything went well, and so it ends badly. He wouldn't let himself be killed - Ned knew that for sure. What will it do? Who knows what he will do! But he will not allow himself to be killed, and that's it. Let the demons go, for example. And then the question arose - what if friends were set against him? The same Oidar and Arnot? Well, for example, they will order them to attack him and twist him! Or just kill! What will he do? Will he let demons on them too, so that they eat them up from the inside? What should he do? On the one hand, they will try to kill Ned, and on the other, they are friends! But let them kill you? How so?

Confused in his reasoning, Ned did not come to any conclusion. Laying down on the bunk, he began to think, dream, looking at the small window under the roof, which barely let in the daylight.

If it had not been for this incident in the dining room, he would now be walking through the city. All so smart, handsome, in new clothes ... Maybe I would have met some girl ... she would have fallen in love with him, and invited him home, to meet her parents. After all, all girls who have serious intentions introduce them to their parents.

Ned had heard of this back in the village. I just could not understand - what is it to introduce, when they have lived side by side all their lives. However - in the city it is different, here, I suppose, people do not know the names of those who live on the next street. It's hard to believe, of course, but anything can happen. And so - she brings Ned home, and says: "This is my favorite, I want to get married!" And the father - he is always so tall, gray-haired - like Colonel Heverad, like - says importantly: "Mother, daughter brought my future husband! Good guy! I like him!" Mother: "Oh, how glad I am! Please pass! We were just about to have dinner (or lunch - no difference). "

And so, Ned walks into a room, such a large living room. And taaam ... on the table - soup with chicken giblets ... porridge with meat ... candied fruit (tried it once for a holiday, a drunken woman treated it), all sorts of smoked meats. Seashells - Many seashells with spicy grass. And Ned eats, eats, eats! Until the belly begins to swell from the eaten!

Ned's stomach gurgled wildly, reacting violently to gastronomic love dreams, and the guy involuntarily laughed - whatever he started dreaming about, all his dreams always go to lunch or dinner! Just - some kind of curse! I didn't have time to dine, but there was no fat layer. How to endure? Maybe they will bring at least some supper to the prisoner? Will they not judge him when he is hungry? Why not? Very much even will. So that it was discouraging to rot in the dining room!

Yes, I missed the canteen, of course. For some reason, I thought that he had the right to punch the lieutenant. The guards explained everything to him in an accessible form: yes, he is an officer. But if he is offended, he must submit a report to the commander of the unit in which he serves. He will consider the complaint and send the report on. Or he will punish the offender on his own - if the sin is minor. Major sins are considered by the Corps commander himself. He is the chief judge. But he also obeys the code of officer's honor. And if he deems it necessary, he will appoint a court of officer's honor, where they will consider the guilt of the violator. This is how it should have been done, and not throwing fists at a superior officer. If he had rushed at the sergeant, there would have been no such noise. Two sergeants fought, that's all. By the way, duels are prohibited by order of Colonel Heverad, as well as fights. But with the sergeant, it would have been a monetary deduction, the maximum Ned would get. But now ... things were pretty bad now.

Ned's thoughts were interrupted by a rumble outside the door, and the familiar bass roared:

- You fools, do not you see the seal and signature of the colonel ?! Cattle! Yes, I'll put you in trouble for not following the command's order! Open, immediately! Idiots! They took a lot of power with their Shentel! They sat on the neck, parasites! Well, bitches, in the first row of spearmen, you would be released in the attack, ass-heads!

Geresard's voice was so powerful that it pierced even through the oak doors, bound with iron, and it seemed that the doctor was standing somewhere nearby, in the cell.

The bolt rattled, and a red, battered doctor burst into the dungeon. He glanced back at the guard, stepped back, and pulled the door open with such force that it nearly pinched the curious guard's head. He barely had time to pull back, otherwise, instead of a head, a pancake could turn out:

- Get out, bitch! - Geresard shouted at the door, and quite hooting, remarked with satisfaction - it's good here with you! Cool! More beer, and lie down to sleep for three hours. How cold it is in the cellar! And it's hot outside! So every situation has its advantages. At least, you have to think so so as not to get upset. Really, son? So what have you done? Behind did you give this goat in the face? For the cause I suppose?

- For business - smiling, nodded Ned - I came to the dining room, he was sitting there. He saw me, began to say nasty things about me and the colonel. I walked over and demanded that he apologize. Then he repeated his abominations. I hit. Rather, he did not hit, but only gave a slap in the face. I didn't think he was so frail and would fall to the floor. Downright - like paper ... and in fact she was so healthy. Well, and then this very security officer appeared. I was twisted and taken away. The lieutenant immediately began to lie that ...

- I know, I know that he started lying! The doctor interrupted impatiently - I'm not interested in this. I'm interested in what he said about the colonel! Heverad is a real warrior, but he does not forgive insults, like some court intriguer. So ... You know what a thing ... you accidentally got into the center of intrigue ... I don't know if I can tell you ... in general - only for you, and no one! Do not talk! There is a struggle for the position of corps commander. Shentel has long been aiming for this place, digging under the colonel. But he has everything under control in the ministry (you don't need details). In general, he cannot do it. And here - you, with a crime for which a soldier is flogged to death. Or they can screw up the officer, but most likely they will demote him and put him in the most dangerous place - in the spearmen, in the first row. To death. That is, to where you safely left. Moreover - the colonel wanted to send you to the officer's school. And with military crimes, they won't take you to an officer's school - a rootless person who has no money. That is, your career will be broken for sure. And that's if you survive five years of service in the front row. What I started about ... about the colonel. So that's it. They will not be able to overthrow the colonel, but he will have to try hard to stay in place. And yet - a drop wears away the stone, and the next time it may no longer resist. Got it? I didn't understand a damn thing. You are a child, a child. The body is older than any adult, and in intrigue - a small child. But maybe it's for the best? Why do you need this dirt ... Now tell me what this kid was talking about. And that's if you survive five years of service in the front row. What I started about ... about the colonel. So that's it. They will not be able to overthrow the colonel, but he will have to try hard to stay in place. And yet - a drop wears away the stone, and the next time it may no longer resist. Got it? I didn't understand a damn thing. You are a child, a child. The body is older than any adult, and in intrigue - a small child. But maybe it's for the best? Why do you need this dirt ... Now tell me what this kid was talking about. And that's if you survive five years of service in the front row. What I started about ... about the colonel. So that's it. They will not be able to overthrow the colonel, but he will have to try hard to stay in place. And yet - a drop wears away the stone, and the next time it may no longer resist. Got it? I didn't understand a damn thing. You are a child, a child. The body is older than any adult, and in intrigue - a small child. But maybe it's for the best? Why do you need this dirt ... Now tell me what this kid was talking about. But maybe it's for the best? Why do you need this dirt ... Now tell me what this kid was talking about. But maybe it's for the best? Why do you need this dirt ... Now tell me what this kid was talking about.

Ned recited the lieutenant's speech in a few words, the doctor froze, thinking tensely, then exhaled.

- It attracts a crime. If we prove that he did so, we have a chance to fight off the accusation and give Shentel a penalty. To humiliate him so that he will not rise for a long time, or maybe never will. Zasler, after all, his protege, he took him under his wing, in safety. Let's think - were there any witnesses?

- There were - Ned nodded his head.

- HOW WERE? - the doctor jumped up from his seat - where from ?! Zasler claims that it was not. And Shentel too - they say, when he came, there was no one except you and Zasler! Well, the chefs are at the serving, but they don't count. Although ... they should also be interrogated. So who was there?

- Zasler was sitting at the table with a lieutenant from his company, as I understand it, and not so far away was a sergeant from crossbowmen - I don't remember his name - he was thin, his face was like an ax (Dert! - commented the doctor). Zasler spoke so loudly that they should have heard. You know, the impression was that he deliberately provoked me. And this very Shentel appeared like a toy demon from a box - have you seen such a toy? You open it - click! And he jumps out. I didn't think about it then, and then it occurred to me! (He lied! He immediately after the incident discovered that everything was set up, and the second lieutenant was also aware. Everything was thought out in advance. They were waiting for him. They knew that he would come. And if he had not come - the same option, only where- somewhere else, and everything was directed at the colonel. "That he knew too. Just how to tell the doctor? However, it doesn't matter now - he has figured it out anyway).

- What do you think - Dirt was in the know? The doctor asked tensely.

- I'm sure not. He happened to be there.

- So-so. that's good ... so, you say, there was a second lieutenant, and Shentel said he was looking for witnesses. and at the trial they suddenly appear. Why suddenly? And so as not to be processed as it should. Therefore, they were not allowed to see you either. Like - no one before the trial, not even the Corps commander! Donkeys! There is a code according to which, before being brought before the court, you must be examined for whether you can be before this very court! What's the use of judging a senseless log or a corpse ?! This is an old code, the colonel's splendid memory! They shouldn't have contacted him. Eh, and in vain. It's a pity that you got into such a mess, but you had to think before you let go! Although I understand you. I would have killed the goat myself. And now ... now - the alignment is completely different! We learn the lieutenant's name from Dert - he will not hide it. See how ... but here's what option is possible - we find this lieutenant, invite him to the court, he promises to tell everything as it happened, and then - once! And takes Shentel's side, as expected. That would be a number! Well, that's it, I'm going to the colonel to report that you are alive and well, not crazy, and you can take part in the trial. With what I congratulate you!

The doctor jumped off the bunk and took a step towards the door, but Ned stopped him:

- Wait! When is the trial?

- Soon. Today. Don't worry - we'll think of something. They will dance with us ... By the way - how could you repeat that fight? Well - where did you get your head off?

- Nuuu…. Could - hesitantly answered Ned - just would not want to.

- He would not like it! - barked the doctor - and on the bench for punishment you hunt? Fool - do what I tell you. What smart friends will tell you! Let's say - jump up, what should you ask?

- To what height, right? Smiled Ned.

- Here! You start to get smarter! - the doctor grinned and immediately drove a smile from his face - that's it, I'm running away. You need to be in time before six o'clock. Rest, gain strength.

- To devour! Ned shouted plaintively.

- Oh! Demons! I forgot! Nna! - the doctor threw a hefty bag at Ned, which he miraculously carried under his robe. Eat!

Ned grabbed the package and opened it to the creak of the closing door. With a rumbling rumbling into the circle of smoked sausage, he pushed the first pieces of fragrant juicy meat into the hungry for food sip, took a bite of the cake, washed down with water from a bottle ... and everything seemed not so bad!

Half an hour later, well-fed and blissful, Ned was already dozing on the bunk with folded hands under his head. When the guards came for him, he was as fresh as a flower after the rain - how much time does a young, strong body need to recover? * * *

- Sergeant Ned the Black is accused of ... legislation ... paragraph ... despite the fact that ... in spite of everything ... dared ... the officer's honor ... the honor of the Corps ... and this is on the eve of the march .... - Major Shentel's voice itched, itched, itched ... it resembled a fly rushing over a bucket of slops ... zhzhzhzh ... zzhzhzh ... Ned alternately closed and opened his eyes - now left, then right, examining those present, and Geresar sternly frowned, they say - stop! Serious business! Then Ned looked out the window. But there is nothing new - spearmen stomp on the parade ground, swordsmen run across the rows, changing places with the crossbowmen. Everything is as usual, everything is as usual. And only then - zhzhzhzh ... zzhzhzh ... evoking a dream ...

- Ned the Black! Why, he fell asleep, or what? - Colonel Zayd even got up from his place - hey, spearman! Push him or something!

- Ned! - roared the doctor - the guy guiltily blinking his eyes moved away from oblivion and looked around the hall, as if he had just seen him. He himself did not understand what had happened - as if he had failed somewhere and had dreams - white-sailing ships sailed, the sea rustled, smelled of some kind of incense - as if Ned was there - he touched, felt, smelled.

- Ned Black, what can you say in your defense. Was that how it was, or not?

- Is this about what Major Shentel told? Ned asked innocently.

- No! Demons take you! This is about the girl from the port brothel! - Zayd barked - gods, who are we judging ?! Geresard, is he normal? It seems to me - his brains are twisted in this prison!

- Normal, normal! - boomed Geresard - son, tell us how it really was. Tell me everything, don't hide it! Don't hide anything. And we will already decide whether to believe you or not.

- Good. Just don't be interrupted, okay? Ned chuckled.

- Let's not interrupt - Colonel Heverad smiled - come on, dump the truth ... whatever it may be.

- Good. So, I went to the dining room to have time to eat before the end of my lunch break. There were two lieutenants sitting in the dining room, one of them was Zasler - I later learned his name - and the second lieutenant - I don't know his name, he sits on a bench, the third one is from the edge. And also, a little further away - the sergeant was sitting, that one, on the third bench, the second from the edge. Entering the dining room, I headed for the distribution to get my lunch. When I passed Zasler ...

For about ten minutes Ned recounted the events of that hour in detail, under the deathly silence of the hall. And when he conveyed Zasler's words addressed to Ned, the audience gasped, and Zasler screamed from the place that it was a lie, and this villain deliberately wants to slander him.

Heverad stopped the lieutenant with a sweeping gesture, as if driving away an annoying fly. He shut up and Ned continued, pausing at the moment when he was arrested and taken to jail.

Silence lasted for several seconds, then Heverad spoke, and his heavy words fell into the hall like granite tombstones on fresh graves:

- Tell me, sergeant, your opinion - why did all this happen? How do you explain what happened? What do you think about this?

- Objection! - Shentel yelled - all this is a lie, attempts to evade responsibility! No need to listen to his nonsense!

- Be silent! - barked the colonel and hit the table with his fist - forgotten, Major Shentel ?! Who allowed you to shout from your seat ?! Who gave you their word! Personal reprimand! For breach of discipline during an important investigation! If someone else interferes with my investigation, they will be punished! Speak, Sergeant! (Well, boy, why did you goggle! Don't let me down! Come on, hit the goats! Don't be afraid! - Heverad thought) And Ned "hit"!

- I believe that this was a deeply and subtly conceived conspiracy against the commander of the Marine Corps, in order to defame him, cast a shadow on his authority as a commander - Ned said calmly and clearly.

The hall made a noise, the officers got up from their seats, but the colonel, nodding in satisfaction, ordered:

- Go on! Do not be afraid, say everything as it is, as it was!

- This conspiracy was organized by Major Shentel, with the help of his people - Zasler, and this lieutenant. They both knew. One insulted Colonel Heverad and me, the second covered him to create the appearance that he had nothing to do with, but he himself had to serve as a false witness. In my opinion, the sergeant who was in the hall has nothing to do with the provocation. Yes, I admit that I could not resist and hit Zasler. He insulted my commander, insulted me, which means he insulted the entire Marine Corps. I guessed about the conspiracy, pondering all sides of this case. For example - Zasler fell to the floor from my light blow, not even a blow, but a slap in the face, as if he were not a grown man, but a small child. The second lieutenant played his role unconvincingly, very weakly, without a soul. He was obviously lying - I also realized this after the end of the scandal. Major Shentel with his people appeared exactly at the moment when I entered the dining room and punched Zasler - as if I guessed what would happen now. Sitting in prison, I mentally imagined the location of the windows in the office of the Security Service, and I realized that the major was watching the passage to the dining room from the window. He saw me. And then he gathered the people and ran after him. Why did he do everything through me? Because I was elevated by Colonel Heverad, and Shentel needed to cast a shadow over him for some reason. After thinking, I understood this reason. That's, in general, that's all. I can't say anything else. And then he gathered the people and ran after him. Why did he do everything through me? Because I was elevated by Colonel Heverad, and Shentel needed to cast a shadow on him for some reason. After thinking, I understood this reason. That's, in general, that's all. I can't say anything else. And then he gathered the people and ran after him. Why did he do everything through me? Because I was elevated by Colonel Heverad, and Shentel needed to cast a shadow on him for some reason. After thinking, I understood this reason. That's, in general, that's all. I can't say anything else.

- Thank you, Sergeant - Heverad nodded his head - and thank you for protecting my honor! Honor of the Corps! An officer's honor. You can sit down. Major Shentel - what can you say in your defense?

- Lying! All lies! - said Shentel coldly and the colonel interrupted him:

- I agree - everything you said is a lie. Can you explain why you lied? For what purpose?

- No! I didn't lie! Your protege is lying, your ...

- Well, go on ... very interesting - Heverad nodded calmly - what is mine?

- I propose to interrogate the listed witnesses - Shentel said triumphantly - this will immediately clarify!

- Are you sure? - Heverad asked with a slight mockery, and thought: "And dick you didn't want to ?! Bitch! So sure, goat! You started competing with me early, you didn't gain strength, but there you go! "

"Lieutenant Brock, report to the officer's honor court what happened in the dining room?" - asked Heverad, and buried himself in the officer's face with a heavy, piercing gaze.

- Please forgive me, mister colonel! - Hoarsely, with difficulty pushing the words out of his parched throat, Brock replied - everything was as this sergeant said!

- Aaaaa! Cheating! They talked him into it! - Shentel jumped up and throwing slobbering splashes along with the words, continued yelling - this is a forgery! They intimidated him, so he said what they needed! I'll find a job! I will go to the ministry today and ...

- Sit down, creature - the doctor grabbed the major by the uniform and pulled him back so that he plopped down on a chair, throwing his legs up - he knew how to start conspiracies, be able to answer like a man! Be quiet, and listen, or I will now shut your mouth with my fist! - and Geresard demonstrated this construction of clenched fingers, the size of the head of a five-year-old child.

- Continue, Brock - the colonel nodded encouragingly and again turned his hard gaze on the lieutenant.

- I committed a misconduct in the service, and Major Shentel recruited me as his agent. He said that if I carry out his instructions, he will leave me alone. It was only necessary to put the upstart sergeant in his place, to knock off his arrogance. So it was said. They didn't tell me more. I didn't know that the attack was directed against Colonel Heverad. I have a lot of respect for him, and I would never go against him. When it turned out that it was under him, I decided not to be silent, even if I incur a well-deserved punishment. Everything is as the sergeant told me, and I apologize to Colonel Heverad and Sergeant Ned the Black for participating in this farce, and it took me a while to uncover the Shentel plot. Sorry gentlemen!

"Okay, Lieutenant Brock. We will consider your fate after the end of the investigation. Sergeant Dirt - can you explain?

- What can I explain? The guy told it exactly - Ned, I mean. I myself was going to come and tell how it was. At least I was sitting in the dining room and far away, but I heard everything - I have an exceptionally keen hearing, I beat the animal to the rustle! Everyone knows that. By the way - these are here! - he nodded at Zasler and Major Shentel - they drove up to me with an offer to pay for silence, and also with threats that if I tell someone how it was, they would kill me. I took their money, and promised to tell it as they demanded. Here's their damn money, Colonel, I don't need it! - Brock took out a bag with something heavy and deftly, as if, across the room, slammed it into Zasler's ear. He screamed and fell off his chair, not expecting such a blow. And when he got up, his ear was red like the setting sun.

- What, Zasler, fell again? You must be sick. You fall all the time - Heverad chuckled - you need to rest from the labors of the unrighteous.

- This is a slip of the tongue, Colonel! - hoarsely breathing, Shentel blurted out - I demand satisfaction! I do not believe your witnesses! And I do not believe your protege! This is a conspiracy against me, because I wrote dispatches to the Ministry, in which I exposed your criminal activities and the style of leadership of the Corps! You made these people say what they said! Lying! All lies!

- So you think that I am lying - the colonel said boredly, defiantly covering the yawn with his palm - then I propose this - a court of honor. Do you know what a court of honor is?

- What?! You can not! You yourself have forbidden duels! Duels are prohibited on the territory of the base! - Shentel shouted, and stopped short.

- Yes. On the territory of the base are prohibited. But the one who has banned may temporarily cancel the ban. Or move the duel outside the base. What's easier? Probably - after all, cancel the ban before the execution of the court of honor. So, Major Shentel - I inform you that for an indefinite time I have lifted the ban on duels in connection with the clarification of questions of honor. You claim that I made my subordinates lie, and I claim that you and your person are lying. Our votes are about equal ... well - almost equal, if you forget about the sergeant, so deftly threw a bag of damned money at your man.

By the way - Sergeant Brock, you should consider a professional ball game! I am sure you would have achieved great success! Great throw! Then show me the technique of your throw - the colonel grinned, and the whole audience laughed, rejoicing at the opportunity to relieve tension - so, Shentel, I challenge you to the court of honor, to a duel. The one who wins is right. And the one who lost - no. What's easier, right? If you win, I will retire as Marine Corps Commander. And if you lose, then in shame you will be dismissed from military service by decision of the officers' meeting. Everyone can choose their replacement - any fighter. The choice of weapon is yours as the called party. Do you agree? However - what is left for you - otherwise I will simply order to chase you with sticks - for cowardice. For refusing to accept the challenge.

"Are you playing dishonestly, Colonel? - Shentel snarled angrily - good. I accept the challenge. Zasler, sword fighting.

- Can I take a spear? Ned asked quietly, and the gazes of those present turned to him.

- And why did you decide that you will represent me? Heverad chuckled.

- Who else? - Ned shrugged his shoulders - I am in the center of this scandal, smeared in it up to my ears, and I must defend the honor of the Corps.

- Really - who else ?! - the colonel laughed, having come in a very good mood. Everything went as it should, and in any case - he will win.

- Why with a spear? - Heverad asked - not a dueling weapon. A sword is better, more comfortable.

- I was taught to attack the enemy with a spear, so I'm more comfortable with him.

- Shentel, do you agree that the spearman will go to a duel with a spear? - Raising his eyebrows, Heverad asked, and noticed how Zasler nodded his head in the affirmative and whispered something to the major. (Good! I will chop this moron with his stick into strips, do not hesitate! Swordsman against a redneck spearman, what could be funnier?

- We agree. Just no armor, and no more weapons. We will have a long sword and a dagger - it's legal, a sword is always paired with a dagger!

"How is Ned, is that okay with you?" - the colonel asked doubtfully - look, fight to death ...

"It's okay, Colonel," Ned replied, and his face blossomed into a smile that made the guy look very young and fresh.

The colonel sighed to himself: "Well, the gods didn't give me such a son, huh? Mine is mannered, languid, loose ... Iehhh ... maybe let Tyra give me a son? Maybe at least something decent will start from his mistress? Not as bad as my bitch?

The guy is sure of victory ... with a spear against a sword and dagger? Are you taking risks, boy? I hope you succeed. I'm not losing anything - if you lose, I'll leave the post of corps commander, and that's all. I have long wanted to, but did not dare. All the same, everyone knows perfectly well that it was the vile bitch who hoisted me and set you and me up. They will remember it forever. Officers don't like such villains. And I won't let him stand on the hull - there are connections, and there is money, I will poison his life until he dies. Or until I die. A fool after all, this Shentel. I decided to outplay! Dert would never have turned against me, he is the right warrior. And Brock - this one is a bastard! But he wants to live. He knows that I will kill him from the light. When everything was revealed, I did not dare to go against it. Especially when he was shown the gallows. There is a gallows - but we will find sins! He knows this is a bastard. Ceremony with people like him is impossible! As they are, so are we. But the boy, well done, how he kept himself! I did everything as it should, as if listening to my thoughts! Good girl. It's a pity if he dies. But such is life! You chose it yourself, boy ... "

- Well - the weapon is selected. The duel site is an exercise area. Fight to death - opponents are obliged to finish off the loser if he is still alive. Half an hour later on the site. The officers to dismiss the soldiers, let them sit in the barracks. They need not watch the duel of the commanders.

- What about me? Brock got up from his seat, and biting his lip looked at the colonel.

- With you? But nothing. Serve. Atone for guilt before the corps. There is military action ahead, try to distinguish yourself there (Better to die, bitch! Because I'll kill you anyway! - Heverad added to himself) We parted, gentlemen! Half an hour later at the square. Yes! I almost forgot! Close the exit from the base - FOR ALL. So, just in case. * * *

- Boy, are you nuts? - Colonel Zayd, a heavy, but fast-moving man of about forty-five, looked attentively at Ned, who stood at attention in front of him - relax, do not stretch, still no one sees. Do you realize that you have no chance with this shaft against a master swordsman? This Zasler is a famous duelist! Only those duels that were reported were six! And he won all six! His father was the winner of the Imperial Sword of Zamar Tournament! He tried to prepare his son properly! And if you add to this the strength and speed - this creature is a real killer machine! And here you are - a boy with a shaft!

The colonel turned to Heverad and said indignantly:

- Nulan, prepare documents for the transfer of the corps to one of us - Evora or me. Better than Evora. You know I was going to retire this year. Enough business trips, enough tents and bad water! And even more so with this scoundrel Shentel! I will resign today.

- Why am I stupider than you, or what? - snorted Evor - he will devour me in six months! You dump, and then I will disentangle? Clever guys! You have always been like that, and in the officer's school too! How to beat windows - all together, but how to fight off the guards - so you are not! Sly-ass!

- You had to learn to run. Always stuck with your belly and yell! It was necessary to eat less!

- Look at yourself - the belly is like a pregnant woman's on her nose! And generally speaking…

- Quiet! - Heverad interrupted - not with the boy! Remembered, your mother! What will be will be! It's not that simple, is it, Ned? Well, will you defeat this jerk or not?

- Must win, Colonel! - looking ahead and up, Ned answered clearly.

- Well, you see, gentlemen - and you said! - the colonel grinned - the guy is sure of victory. Everything is good. Listen, what kind of demon are you dogging ?! What will be will be! Well, resign - and let Shentel disentangle it! He will remain a senior officer, will automatically take over the corps. He will fail the expedition, that's for sure. He will be given a hat, and they will call us back - especially since I will try to arrange it. Well, they will not call - what, there is no money, or what? Everyone has so much that you can't live! What demon are you carrying here? And I followed you ... The guy - everything that we have said here - should not leave the walls of this office. Otherwise, I'll just trample you! Got it, Sergeant?

- Understood, mister colonel! Ned saluted.

- You see - he understood. By the way, will you tell three old warriors why the hell are you crazy and took a spear as a dueling weapon? It is clear to the idiot that the spearman is nothing against the swordsman! Come on, explain to us!

- And really - interesting - Evor chuckled - I understand something in sword fighting, as you know. And my eyes just went up to my forehead when I heard what I heard.

- And I - shook his head Zayd - with a sword, even a beginner has a chance. You never know what will happen - the enemy's sword will break. A pebble will fall under the foot. The sun will blind your eyes. The wasp will sting in the ass. Lots of accidents affect the fight. But with a clumsy three-meter shaft ?! I immediately decided that you were crazy. Well, enlighten the veterans!

"I have no chance of winning with a sword. I do not own it well.

- How bad? You were taught! Even though you are spearmen, each of you wields a sword - Zayd shrugged his shoulders - I don't understand!

- And I understand - Evor intervened - they are hardly taught to work in an individual fight, you think for yourself. In the ranks, from under the cover of shields, moreover, the movements are not chopping, but piercing. He never fought with a long sword and no one taught him how to do it. You forget - he became a sergeant a few hours ago! But they are taught to use a spear professionally - he is a spearman. The dragon trained them like good horses!

"Hmm… maybe. But I still don't understand! If I go out against any of the spearmen with a sword, and even more so with a sword and a dagger - the result is known! You chop off the tip, and you cut the spearman like meat for curing. Spearmen are strong in formation, when the enemy cannot come close, crossbowmen shoot from afar, and if the enemy approaches, swordsmen open their belly! If, nevertheless, a collision at a short distance happened - spears to the ground, swords in hand and away we go!

- Who are you telling this - to him? - Heverad grinned, pointing at the frozen Ned - or are you teaching us the basics of combat? Do not waste your time. There will be what will be. Everything, go, choose your spear. Time.

- Can you solve the question, Mr. Colonel? Ned asked unexpectedly.

- Well … come on - Heverad raised his eyebrows and looked at the guy with curiosity. For the first time in a long time, he was interested, and if you forget about the importance of what was happening, he was amused. Fights, fuss around intrigue, unpredictable results - all this tickled nerves and made people appreciate life more. After such shakes, life seems more juicy, tasty, full! Sumptuously! If only it weren't for the Corps ... sorry for him.

- Why duel to death? Do you have to kill the enemy? Do all duels end in murder?

- Have you seen, gentlemen, what a kind fighter we have? - Heverad chuckled, and turned serious - no, boy. Not all duels end in murder. But ETA - yes. Why? This duel concerns the honor of the officer. Honor is restored only by the blood and death of the one who inflicted a grievous offense. If it's just a duel - that's what they say - a duel. If a duel of honor is to death. Replacement for a combatant is admissible - which is what happened today. In which cases? This is strictly stipulated: if the caller or the summoned is sick, if they are on duty in the service of the state. Do you understand? We are senior officers who serve the king. If we now start poking each other with glands to death - what will happen? It will be bad. Therefore - a replacement for a combatant. Well, so that they think another time before being called by a combatant - fight to the death. Only to death. The loser can commit suicide - at his will - or retire into exile and never appear in public again. He has another way - to refuse the fight altogether. And then - he, too, will retire into exile, like a loser - forfeiting all privileges, titles and benefits. These rules apply only to the military. Civilians can behave however they want. Although I will note that since ancient times these rules have been transferred to civilians. Try to behave differently - they will stop greeting you and walk around as if spat upon. Willy-nilly, you will run away to your estate and you will sit there without leaving for the rest of your life. Not a single neighbor will come to you and ask how you live. Honor issues are very important and very subtle. Moreover, the shadow of dishonor will fall on your children. They will never make a career, they will not be accepted into the court, they will not be taken to a military school. Shentel is now at stake with everything he has - a career, life itself. If he does away with the failure after the loss, everyone will know that he acted like a man of honor, redeemed, even if he stumbled before. And the life of his children will not be spoiled by their father's actions. But I doubt he would do that. He's weak.

- And you? Don't you lose your honor if you lose?

- No, not at all - Heverad laughed - everyone understood perfectly what happened. And if I lose - you lose - I retire from my post with my head held high and a clear conscience. This loss is yours, not mine. And it is quite possible that the king will call me again when the time comes - well, for example, when Shentel completely destroys the Corpus, drowning it somewhere in the Harad swamps. Everything. Walk. Do you need anything to fight? Drink, eat? By the way - I do not recommend eating. The heaviness in the stomach will interfere with combat. In addition, with a wound in the stomach, if you did not eat, there is a chance to survive. The contents of the stomach and intestines will not spill out into the abdominal cavity. And don't drink too much - you will sweat a lot. Rinse your mouth, and a couple of sips of sour juice, no more. Go to the toilet, be sure to relieve yourself. Put on sandals instead of combat boots - easier to move around. Take off your uniform - it constrains your movements, and let your shirt loose - let it hide the outlines of the body, confuse the enemy. Tie your hair tighter in a ponytail - your eyes will go down, while you throw it back, you will already be chopped like a deer chop. No chain mail, no weapons - except this very spear. Otherwise, defeat will be recognized. And you will be killed anyway. Write to whom to transfer your salary and money stored in the Treasury of the Corps, leave a will - just in case. Well ... that's all. kept in the treasury of the Corps, leave a will - just in case. Well ... that's all. kept in the treasury of the Corps, leave a will - just in case. Well ... that's all.

- Listen to him, he won't say bad things, he knows what he says - Colonel Heverad was always in a duel by his youth - Zayd chuckled - he killed seven people in duels for sure.

- Eight - Heverad chuckled - but don't talk about it. Go boy. May the patronage of Kualthuk be with you!

- Glory! - all those present made a hand gesture, covering their face with a religious greeting. Ned hesitated for a split second, did the same, then, turning over his shoulder, left the office, typing a step.

The door closed behind the guy, and Évor sighed and asked:

- Zero, do you think he has a chance? Green is completely immature ...

- We were all once immature, until suddenly - rrraz! - and not overripe. Next to this boy, I feel so old, so weak ... Maybe I really should go to rest? - Heverad sighed, and suddenly announced - I put a thousand gold on him! Who is involved?

- You are in your repertoire! - Evor laughed - good! A thousand for the bastard Zasler! Come in, you?

"Hmmm... let's go to the meeting, let someone take the bids. Why not? There is so little entertainment here. We'll get at least some benefit from this disgrace. Sorry for the guy. But such is life!

Chapter 11

- Oooh! A friend of mine! Heard, heard ... - the storekeeper's thick face broke into a smile, then gave way to concern - you volunteered against the sword and dagger with a spear? Oh, how unreasonable! I gave you a sword, a sword to all swords! You will simply chop the enemy with it! Why a spear?

- Poor sword control, but good spear - serenely, for the twentieth or thirtieth time, Ned explained.

While walking to the warehouse, I had to explain the situation to everyone who wished. You can send well-wishers to a well-known address, but why spoil the relationship? They weren't asking out of spite, Ned knew it. You just have to be patient, and they will lag behind. Someday. And if they do not lag behind, then you can bark. However - Ned was about to bark. Got it!

Why did he choose the spear himself? Why was he so sure of the outcome of the battle? I was not sure! But inside there was a firm, clear understanding - only a spear! No swords! And then there will be a victory. Where does this understanding come from? Ned didn't know. Rather, I guessed it, but ... did not want to admit it to the end. It's more convenient that way. From time to time, Ned recalled the prophecy of the diviner - he remembered every word he said. And about his second essence, and about the dagger ... about the essence, it was clear - some thing possessed him and gave him special abilities. She, this dirty trick, makes him run away from magicians and demands not to give out magic skills. And Ned was convinced - until now everything that this entity made things happen - everything was right, everything was right. Everything for the cause. The Entity did not try to take control of the body, did nothing to harm him or those whom he respected, who was dear to him. So why not follow the directions from within your consciousness? Ned followed. And now, he was clearly told - a spear! Only a spear!

- Well, let's go and pick your spear. No, no - nothing is needed! Old Pernal has his own concept of honor and conscience! You are going to battle with a scoundrel, a scoundrel, and it is my sacred duty to help you with this! But if you insist. aha, put it here. What a clever girl you are, sergeant! Why are there only idiots around, and not enough fellows like you ?! Today's youth are becoming smaller - look how small - both in body and soul, some poor ones! And you are strong in body, beautiful, generous soul! And the hand ... Yeah, right here. No, don't look - there are pathetic pieces of iron. Take a look here! I will offer you this - look - a shaft made of seasoned iron wood, you won't cut it right away, a long one - as you wave it - will take down the foe! It's hard, yes. It is better for them to beat from the horse. And here! Look at what! What are you looking at there? Yes, there were several of them. Or similar ... Where did you come from? Fuck knows! This is from the southern continent, or something. It looks like they were captured on some of the expeditions. Like a trophy. Or maybe from somewhere here, in warehouses, they found it. Ancient. It is unsuitable for combat combat, and unsuitable for horse fighting. Hmmm ... well, yes ... the steel is great. Subscription - see the initials of the master? And the runes are here ... listen, but it's like a pair of that sword that I gave you. Interesting. Do you know how much junk is sketched? I bet you a copper against a gold one, that a lot has not been listed in any register for a long time. Like this spear, for example. It is not in any statements! I give! Take it! I see that it has sunk into your heart. Hmm ... let it sink into the heart of the idiot Zasler in the literal sense of the word. By the way - such a shit! I came to get some uniform, so at least I would say thank you! Arrogant creature ... It is unlikely that anyone will regret if you beat him. Not if! You will beat him definitely! Well, good luck, Ned! Come visit old Pernal - we'll sit and chat about this and that! I have no one here to talk to. Some idiots come ...

During the entire conversation, Ned could not get more than three words in. The storekeeper talked, talked, talked ... Ned nodded his head in time, and by the end of the "conversation" it seemed that he had turned into a toy, nodding his head, into a figurine on a spring, like the colonel on the table - she kept nodding her head in time to the owner's movements cabinet. The colonel had a habit of touching the dummy's nose during a conversation, and the idiot nodded, nodded, nodded ... * * *

The spear was great. Ned went through several dozen copies, but could not find the one he needed. But when he cleared away the rubble, covered with age-old dust, he saw Him! It stood forlornly behind the chipped halberd, between the second row spear and the equestrian spear with a triangular armor-piercing tip.

There was a click in Ned's head - it! This is it! A hand reached out and grabbed the smooth shaft, never letting go.

The long blade of the tip is exactly the blade, not just the tip. Leafy, double-edged, sword-like, about seventy sa long. Sharp like the sword Pernal gave, the narrow tip flared slightly towards the end. Familiar matte pattern, interlacing of lines. Set on a short shaft of unknown ebony, smooth and cold to the touch. The spear is about the length of Ned's eyes. Of course - what to do in the ranks with such a spear? It is almost twice as short as even the copies of the first row! Is this the sharpest blade? You wave - and the neighbors' heads are gone.

Ned once again felt, examined the spear ... There are no cracks on the shaft, no notches - a magnificent example of weapons creativity. Nowhere are there any decorations - an honest working spear that drank the blood of the enemy. Why did you decide that it was already in fights, that it had already drunk blood? Small, almost imperceptible - if you do not look closely - scratches on the shaft, probably left over from sanded impact marks.

Ned took the spear in his hands, closed his eyes and suddenly felt how it fluttered, twitched in his hands, as if it were not a spear shaft, but a huge hardened snake! Ned nearly dropped the strange weapon and stood it upright, leaning against the wall in his room, where he had gone to change for battle. And at once everything became as before - a dimly shining spear, a room neatly tidied up and not yet acquiring the individuality of its owner, a blushing sunset visible between two huge mountains covered with white snow caps. The glaciers of snow, illuminated by the evening sun, turned pink, recalling the flowers and the blood spilled by many people throughout the history of mankind.

Ned thought ... he really wanted to learn. Find out what these mountains are. Where did the human race come from. What is generally happening in the world and what will happen. He was torn by a desire to know the world, and a desire to hide, to hide under a snag, like that fish that is afraid of pikes. While he was lucky. So far, he emerged victorious from those situations in which any other person would have died long ago. But how long can this go on?

He shook his head, chasing away gloomy thoughts, got up, went to the armory and took out the sword he received from the warehouse. He took it in his hands - with his left hand for the scabbard, with his right hand for the handle - with a rustle he pulled out and closed his eyes. No, nothing happened. The sword is like a sword. Then he fully drew the sword, put his left hand on the blade, and concentrated again. There is nothing. An ordinary sword is expensive, high quality, very sharp. But ... none.

He left the sword on the bed and went to the spear, glistening in the twilight. He grabbed the handle ... blow! Some pictures, flashes, smells, people in strange robes and black loose robes with closed faces - they wave the same spears to the viscous, unusual music, falling to the beat of the drum with a thick, low sound. Nearby wriggle almost naked girls, women, slender and muscular, like real fighters. However - they are just that - swords sparkle in their hands - long, narrow, predatory. The girls then slowly, languidly bend, then instantly explode with a series of elusive movements, striking their partner-rival blows with such speed that they merge into a misty whirlwind.

Suddenly one of the girls falls. Across her chest, right between the beautiful hemispheres, a red stripe appears, the edges of which diverge and blood is thrown out in jerks. The girl's eyes glaze over, and a man in black rises from the throne, holding in his hands ... a spear! The same spear as the one Ned is holding now!

A man dips a spear in the blood of a girl still alive, shuddering in convulsions and utters heavy, terrible words:

Hesserannnakarr! Shshasar! Ishchusanar! Archhhh! Archhhh! Archhhh!

It darkens in the room, and the runes on the blade of the spear begin to glow. And... Ned saw it clearly, as if in reality! - the spear began to wriggle, and instead of the blade there was a terrible mask with glowing red eyes!

Ned screamed and dropped his spear, which rattled across the floor. The picture disappeared.

The spear was on the floor - a common tool for taking life. The room is simple and squalid after the chambers, decorated with gold and figurines of creatures with terrible faces, similar to the one that crawled out of the spear. The chambers of the man in black.

Ned clutched his head, rubbed his forehead, breathing heavily and trying to get his thoughts in order.

Why didn't the sword respond to touch, but the spear responded? Why did no one except him feel that there was a demon in the weapon? That it was a demon, Ned had no doubt. And also - what did this man say? What are the words? They reminded him of the words that Ned, in the heat of hatred, blurted out at his opponents in the village. Similar - but not quite.

Ned somehow knew that the words spoken were Call and Conclusion. I did not understand what an appeal and a conclusion are.

Fragments of information, fragments of memorable events flashed through Ned's head and tried to acquire a harmonious structure, nestle in his skull. He was aware of this, and subconsciously interfered with the process, without realizing it. Ned, as if from a huge warehouse with goods, took what he needed, not allowing memories to merge together. What he was afraid of - he did not know. But he knew that if he allowed himself to succumb, it could be very bad. Again I remembered the soothsayer with her "black man" - maybe it was He?

He softly touched the spear. It was silent. There were no pictures. The runes flickered faintly in the dark, and if you don't look closely, you won't see. Raised the spear, took it with both hands - nothing. Did a few exercises - dive! Hit! There is not enough space - he almost ripped open his new uniform. He exhaled and swore. He would have a training ground to work his full strength. But ... we have what we have.

Knock on the door:

- Mr. Sergeant! They are waiting for you at the exercise site! You are ready? All gathered!

I got up, put on military sandals woven from strong leather belts, stamped my feet - they hold well, comfortably. And the leg does not get tired, does not shrink, as in these boots, turning in the sun into oven ovens.

- I'm on my way! - opened the doors.

Two lieutenants and Sergeant Drankon. They look encouraging, Drankon imperceptibly winked - they say - hold on. I didn't read my thoughts, turned off my supersensible hearing - let it not distract, do not hit the brain. And it is so easy to guess who and how treats Ned and what he wants. Of course — the entire garrison — well, almost all — was for Ned. But that doesn't mean anything. The procedure must be followed. The fight must take place.

The evening chill has not yet descended on the base, quietly seething with anticipation of the upcoming events. The long shadow of the Black Mountain faded into the twilight, dispersed by the flames of torches that crackled in the evening breeze. Along the edges of the site there were dozens of oil lanterns, releasing black columns of soot from burnt oil and for some reason spreading the smell of cake and freshly crushed seeds.

Ned has always liked the smell. He sucked in the evening air with swollen nostrils, took a deep breath, and strode towards a group of officers dressed in ceremonial dress uniforms.

- Make yourself wait! - Colonel Zayd said condemningly, drilling Ned with a displeased look - a matter of honor! Are you ready for a deadly duel of honor?

- Ready - Ned nodded affirmatively, leaning on a black spear.

- Then - show your weapon. We must examine him for the presence of poison.

Ned stepped forward, took the spear in both hands and bowed his head, handed the spear to Zayd. He took up the weapon and raised his eyebrows in surprise:

- Is that a spear? Interesting! Something doesn't look like a spear! Where did you get this?

- This is my spear - Ned stubbornly furrowed his eyebrows - according to the terms of the duel, I fight with a spear. THIS is a spear. If someone can deny that this weapon is a spear - let him say.

- No ... - Zayd was slightly confused - by itself - a spear. Only something strange, I have not seen this. Look, gentlemen! Colonel, have you ever seen this?

Heverad examined Ned's weapon with interest, stroked the blade with the gesture of a military man who truly loves weapons, and said with satisfaction:

- A spear! The most real spear! - and quietly added - that's what he was counting on! Well done boy! It will be cooler than the sword. The same sword, but a spear!

- Present your fighter's weapon! - demanded Shentel and tried to grab hold of the spear - give it here!

- Look in my hands - Heverad said displeasedly - what, can't you see? There is no poison. There is no plaque on the blade. The weapon is clean.

- Is it a spear ?! - Shentel was indignant - a spear, this is what this sergeant is running around the parade ground with! And this is not a spear!

- A spear! - Heverad shook his head stubbornly - the length of the shaft is much longer than the length of the blade! In addition - the tip is set on the shaft, like a spear! Shentel, do not make a woman's tantrum! If an object bleats like a ram, looks like a ram - what is it?

- You insult me! - squeezed out Shentel - this is contrary to the officer's code!

- Actually, I was talking about the spear - Heverad remarked calmly, amid the laughter of the officers - and what are you talking about? Or about whom? Don't you think it's time to start? We were already late - instead of half an hour - an hour and a half! It's getting dark. Time to go into exile, Shentel.

- We'll see who will go into exile! The major exhaled furiously, turned to Ned, and his face contorted with hatred - a puppy! You will die, creature!

Ned said nothing. What are words for? And so everything is clear.

- The weapon has been examined. Opponents are ready for battle! I order you to get together in the middle of the marked area and wait for the steward's signal! The fight will begin after the white handkerchief is thrown onto the site. Forward!

Ned grabbed the spear and stepped out into a square with flaming lanterns at the corners and sides. The lighting was sufficient for the audience to see the fight, but not quite enough to properly monitor the particularly insidious blows. A fight is a fight, there is always the possibility of losing, even if you are a master of the highest class. The gods sometimes do strange tricks.

Zasler knew about it. Therefore, he was as focused and collected as possible. In his right hand was a dagger, his left hand was occupied by a long, thin sword, which was used by most of the officers of the kingdom. Depending on the length of the owner's arms, the sword could reach a length of up to a meter, was flexible, resilient and relatively light - up to one and a half zusans. In skillful hands, he was a terrible weapon. A strong fighter could cut a man without armor in half with one blow of such a sword, and if he was in chain mail, cut it like paper.

Zasler's dagger was a half-meter blade - a reduced copy of the sword, only thicker with steel. His task is to catch and beat off the spearhead in order to chop off the shaft with a sword, leaving the enemy with a mop instead of a military weapon. This was allowed by the rules, and no one made any substitution. The sword is broken - fight with the broken. It was necessary to take a good sword, or not allow the enemy to hit the flat part of it in order to prevent a fracture. A straight, double-edged dagger was almost as dangerous as a sword. In the hands of the master, of course. And Zasler was a master.

Opponents converged on the site, and stood a meter apart. It was quiet, and only in the pond behind the fence the frogs screamed loudly, singing their merry love songs. Torches crackled, casting false shadows, in which Ned dreamed of men in black making strange gestures that resembled a snake dance.

Ned didn't notice when Zayd's handkerchief flew into the middle of the court. The white piece of cloth had not yet touched the ground when Zasler rushed into the attack.

He was very, very fast, and his sword was even faster. The blade bent at impossible angles so that it seemed - this is not a blade of the strongest steel, but a flexible reed, which the stray wind amuses itself with.

Ned barely had time to parry the blows — with the back of his spear — a dagger, with the blade — a sword. Zasler all the time strove to get into close contact - at a long distance, of course, the spearman had a clear advantage.

In the first second, Ned received a cut wound in his forearm - shallow but unpleasant, bleeding profusely. Foolishly - he was confused, and missed a cutting blow with a dagger. A little later - the blade of the sword cut the skin on the side. The shirt in this place immediately got wet, and turned red like a sunset.

Ned began to retreat, amid the deathly silence of the audience, and Zasler intensified and intensified the onslaught, although it seemed that there was nowhere else to go. In a minute, Ned received six wounds - all shallow, but nasty, bleeding, and quite painful. And in his soul, slowly but surely, a panic began to arise.

The fact is that he knew how to handle an exotic spear - but! - he could not afford to relax and completely surrender to the black that sat in his soul. His brain subconsciously slowed down movements, did not accurately execute turns, strikes, feints. Resisted the commands given by Ned's subconscious. And here's the result - a slowly but surely losing battle. Lost to some pathetic Zasler - what is this pathetic boy with his two spears? No - Ned was losing to himself! Because I didn't want to obey. Because he did not want to accept what had settled in his head. And now he will die.

The thought struck Ned so much that his hair almost stood on end - how, he will die? Why? What for? And this after what he went through? After what he had? So all the torment is in vain? He, who did not have time to see anything, barely found friends, a good life, a future, who did not know a woman, will now lie down here and die, filling the ground trampled by the feet of thousands of soldiers with his blood ?! Not fair! This is unfair! You can not do it this way!

And Ned gave up. He released his soul - as when he killed a combatant, as when he killed ten fellow villagers.

Blackness flooded his brain, escaping from the depths of his soul and taking over the body, completely controlling the movements, to the very last particle of the body. Ned now seemed to be sitting by the window, watching what was happening outside, on the street. He was aware of his personality, but the body moved by itself, controlled by the subconscious.

Ned stopped at the very edge of the lanterns, which was not legally allowed to go beyond. Now his body easily caught and repulsed the blows of the swordsman, without feeling pain, falling into a combat trance, turning into a perfect combat weapon.

Ned's movements changed. Now he moved like a snake, bared his teeth, hissing through white teeth, flowing from pose to pose, and these poses were so strange, so bizarre that the audience moved, and buzzing like a swarm of bees, they began to point a finger at Ned.

Zasler noticed the change too. A triumphant smile left his face, and when the flexible blade of the spear first touched his skin, he shuddered and took a step back to the place where he was destined to meet the last minute of his life.

Ned hissed like a snake, looking at Zasler with black holes in which he saw the fire of hell. And Zasler was not far from the truth ...

The first wound was in the shoulder of the swordsman - the sharpest blade of a spear loosened a dandy silk shirt, trimmed with lace, and ripped the skin one and a half spans wide. The second blow completely cut off Zasler's ear along with a piece of scalp, leaving a hole in this place, from which blood was thrown out by jerks.

Ned smiled evilly in the face of his opponent, and Zasler realized with horror that he was going to die now. But no - his time has not come. Now Ned was playing with Zasler, inflicting wounds on him, as the lieutenant had done a few minutes ago. In a matter of seconds, Zasler's body was covered with long, painful cuts, as if Ned had cut the peel of an exotic fruit, trying to get at the delicious pulp. Finally - it's time to kill.

With a powerful blow, Ned knocked the dagger out of Zasler's hand, chopping off three fingers at once, which fell on the platform like bean pods. Zasler screamed, covered himself with a sword, but it was too late - the next blow cut off Zasler's left arm along with a piece of his shoulder, and the last, final one - from top to bottom - ripped open the lieutenant's chest and stomach, like a fisherman gutting a fish, preparing it for a dinner pot.

It was a terrible, terrible blow - from the bridge of the nose to the groin, almost tore Zasler in half. Those who saw the details of the battle conveyed it this way:

"- The guy soared up, grabbing his demonic spear almost at the very end and hit - like a lumberjack splitting a block of wood! This fellow, Zasler, was simply gutted like a shark! Only the blood spurted in all directions, and the guts fell under my feet! A beast, not a sergeant! "

Zasler's body fell forward and fell, shuddering in death throes. Ned walked over to the fallen man and thrust a spear into his back, fluttering in his hands. It seemed to him that a muzzle with red eyes protruded from the blade, and Ned clearly heard the joyful howl of the demon. The spear seemed to drink fresh, hot blood, enjoying its spicy taste.

And then something incredible happened! Ned's body was filled
with strength, freshness, the fatigue was gone, the wounds stopped
hurting and the blood oozing from the cuts stopped immediately.
Neda was just bursting with energy - he wanted to run, jump, laugh.
It felt as if he had smoked a mazisa - this is how those who were
fond of this business described the consequences of using this soft
drug. There were many such soldiers among the soldiers.

Pulling the spear from the body of the defeated enemy, Ned went
to the officers who stood silently outside the site. No one shouted, no
one greeted Ned - everyone was shocked by the transience and
cruelty of the reprisal against Zasler. However - after a while most of
the officers decided that it was fair and beautiful - after all, the
winner is always right? And there was applause.

Ned stopped in front of Zaid, who was acting as the duel master,
bowing, and said in a hoarse voice, as if ripped off from shouting:

- Completed. The enemy is dead.

Zayd looked probingly into the guy's face, stained with blood, and
said loudly:

- The duel of honor is over! The winner is Ned the Black!

And the audience burst into applause again. * * *

- Sit down! Sit up straight and there is no need to frown! Not a
woman! Sooo ... what have we got ... hmm ... quite acceptable. That
is, the wounds are clean, nothing dangerous. Strange ...

- What's weird?

- Yes, they look like they were applied a few hours ago. And the
scar tissue began to tighten ... Interesting. You, boy, have a frantic
recovery of the body! I haven't come across this before. Can you tell
me where you came from? It would be nice to show you to the
magicians ... Okay, okay, what are you ?! Sit down! Why are you
scared? Sit down! I will not lead to any magicians! I myself hate
them and only apply when I myself cannot cope. Or no time. They
are such pompous donkeys! Aha ... we'll wash this one out ... be
patient, your mother! Sissy! Ugh at you, donkey head! Why are you
twitching! I boiled these tools for half an hour, and you put the tray
on the floor!

- Why are you swearing here? I recognize old Geresard! If you
personally can sew your skin with threads and you won't even frown,
so are not everyone so insensitive? Sit down guy, don't get up. How
is he?

- Fine, Colonel. Now I'll put stitches on a couple of wounds, that's all. Healthy and nimble, even too nimble kid.
- We need nimble ones. How much does he need to recover?
- A week, no less. This Zasler shredded him well.
- But he did not remain in debt either. It's scary to look. What's going on in your head, boy? Now you are a good-natured person, which are few, just some kind of girl, then - a beast, like a chain dog! Well, why the fuck did you shred it to pieces? I would poke it in the heart, that's all. You could have!

"I don't know, Monsieur Geresard. Sometimes it rolls over me. I can't help myself. Apparently very angry.
- Hmm ... you let him out in front of the troops, Nul, he will get angry and crumble everyone! - Geresard - hooted like a wading bird and caught himself - I apologize, Mr. Colonel! Forgotten!
- Come on ... what does he not see, or what? In my opinion, even the cats in this gang know that you and I are old friends. In general, so - I give him ten days to recover and rest, this is together with the three days due after receiving the sergeant's rank. But that doesn't mean you just have to hang out in the barracks with your feet on the headboard! You will cram the guard duty, study everything that is supposed to be a sergeant. Then Drankon will take the exam. And look - you will not know - you will receive a penalty. Cash deduction. Incidentally, the colonel took out a heavy bag from his leather commander's bag - here's a prize for protecting the honor of the corps. And my honor. One hundred and fifty gold pieces. Heavy, infection, barely reported! I should have given him a promissory note, but I'm afraid the guy doesn't know how to handle them. You know what a bill is, boy?
- No, mister colonel, I do not know ...
- Who would have doubted ... well, be treated. Thank you for your service, Sergeant!
- Yes, demons take you with your service! Why are you jumping up, infection! I dropped the tray again! I'll kick them in the head now! They said - don't get up! * * *

- Be careful for now, otherwise the seams will disperse. No work, otherwise the whole uniform will be covered with blood. Even handle the girls more carefully - I suppose you will immediately rush into the city, huh? Haven't you visited the women I told you about yet? No? Why are you blushing as a girl? Uh ho ho ho ... boy, are you still a virgin? Oh Gods! What hole did you come here from? Get out of here. It's already night, and I need to go home. My Elsa already nags me for paying more attention to soldiers than to my family. Children grow up without a father. What do you think, maybe it's enough for me to stagger on business trips and look into the throats of donkey-headed soldiers? The wife thinks enough. Are you silent? Shut up. How can you understand me when I don't understand myself? So I look at you, and I think - what will come of you? The Colonel wants to put you in an officer's school - if you survive the Isfir confrontation, sure. How do you feel about this idea?

- Which one?

- Learn to be an officer. Do you want to devote yourself to military service? Or will you serve five years in the Corps - and let's go for a walk free?

- I dont know. Honestly, I don't know what I want yet. You see, Monsieur Geresard ... I am an orphan. And until then he lived very badly. Highly. And he himself did not understand this. I don't even know how to spend the money that Mr. Colonel gave me. What are they to me? I have uniforms, a roof over my head, they will always give me something to eat and drink. What else do I need? I can't imagine. I feel good here. I have friends here, they respect me. I'm talking with you, you ask me as an equal, but who am I? Nothing, a boy from a backwater village. What I want? Live! I want to live. And so that the fairy tale that I got into does not end.

- Fairy tale? Service in the corps is a fairy tale ?! Unhappy boy ... you had a hard time seeing - the doctor walked through the dark medicinal room, turned on the light in the lantern, and turned to Ned - listen - you are off tomorrow, come and visit us, huh? What? Why not! Have you never visited the townspeople? Here you come. At noon. I'll run here in the morning, give orders to my subordinates, and then go home. Let's sit and talk, I'll introduce you to your family. I have such a nice wife! She will be glad. And children - I have two guys and a daughter. They will also be interested - with whom their father is dealing. And then they all hear from me about the case, but they themselves have never been here. I try not to take them with me - dirt, blood - to nothing. They have a summer vacation now - classes at school will begin only in two months. It is not clear where the assholes are staggering. Let them at least see what kind of military there are. And then they are always loose, long-haired - how many times they flogged, they do not understand anything. Well, will you come?

Ned didn't answer right away. He looked into Geresard's face - the doctor looked expectantly at the sergeant. The eyes, surrounded by a net of wrinkles, smiled, and Ned suddenly sharply envied the children of Geresard - why, why does one get a beautiful, calm life, smart and kind parents, while others ... why, oh gods ?! His eyes stung, and Ned swallowed to chase away the lump in his throat.

- Yes ... of course I will. Where to?

- Didn't I say? Zelyonaya street, fifth building. If you ask where the military doctor Geresard lives here, they will tell you everything. Everyone knows me. How much I have treated them - the mind is incomprehensible. And he didn't take money. So come on, come on. Now go to the barracks. Sleep well. You did a good job. Stop, stop! I forgot my bag of money! Tomorrow, be sure to take it to the office, deposit it. Of course, the officers 'barracks are not like the soldiers' ones, every rabble does not hang out, but ... no need to tempt people. You never know.

Ned walked out of the medicine room, closing the door behind him. The wounds ached, itched, he knew that they would soon heal, leaving almost no trace. How did you know? I knew, and that's it.

The spear pulled back his arms, and Ned, completely unconsciously, stroked the shaft. The terrible weapon nestles comfortably in the bend of the elbow, capable of turning around at any moment and inflicting an instant blow on anyone who dares to attack its owner. The runes flickered softly in the groove of the dull blade, and Ned felt that the One who Was in the Blade was asleep, satisfied with the sacrifice he had made. Until next time.

Ned knew what had happened — this weapon somehow contained a demon summoned by ancient sorcery. And this demon, having drunk the soul of the enemy, transferred part of the vital energy, part of the soul to Ned. This was undoubtedly - at the moment of Zasler's death, a stormy stream of Power poured through the spear, such that Ned was swept over like a mountain river swollen from the rains. That is, if you think logically - Ned killed a man in order to feed the demon, and he shared with him part of the life force of the killed? And there is. And now what i can do? How to live with this knowledge?

Not deciding anything, Ned made his way to the barracks, took out the key to the room and burst into it, throwing off his sandals as he walked. However, he did not throw the spear on the floor - he carefully put it in the corner next to the bed. So that the hand can always reach and ... stroke him.

Ned was irresistibly drawn to the spear, and if it were not for the thought that it was indecent and stupid, he would have slept with him, putting him next to him in bed. So attracted to itself this seemingly simple weapon. Intellectually, Ned realized that such a craving was rather strange, and that it had a magical basis - a strong bond was established between him and the demon - but he could not help himself. Well, he wanted to touch this spear all the time, and that's it. Iron like a toy. Like ... a favorite dog.

Ned was saddened - remembered Nardu, the only creature besides the old slave who loved him. Now I would run, bark at the cows, cheerfully sticking out her tongue and smiling with a white-toothed smile. And now ... now her spirit hovers over the hills, knocking down blades of grass, free and happy, under the moonlight that illuminates the ancient hills ...

She died as a warrior, protecting a friend, and had to go to the halls of the gods. Ned rubbed his wet eyes, and began to wonder - and to which of the gods would she get? To the god of the earth, Guinea? Go to the goddess of love Selera? No, most likely, to the god of war, Kuultuk - she died in battle!

That she would go to heaven, Ned had no doubt. Such a glorious and brave dog must definitely get to the gods in their halls. And since she gets to Kuultuk, then if Ned continues to serve in the army, they will meet with her! Well - they will kill him, for example, or die in retirement as an old and decrepit colonel, or a general (which he did not believe in and did not hope to live) - all the same it will be in the halls of the god of war. And here - and Narda! And they will again run up and down the hills with her, as before sharing a piece of bread.

The thought made Ned feel good and calm. He closed his eyes, smiled and suddenly heard a dog's breath and a hot tongue licked him right on the lips.

- Fffu ... Backgammon! - he said indignantly, opened his eyes ...

The room was quiet, dark, and a huge red moon peeped out the window, and on its crimson disk, covered with night clouds, a smile seemed to spread.

Ned sighed - he was just dreaming. He closed his eyes again and now consciously fell into a deep sleep. The guy never dreamed of anything else that night.

In the morning Ned jumped up like a madman. Sleepily for a while I could not understand - where he was, what to do, then I realized, and sighing with relief, sat down on the bed. Today is a day off! Today he will visit! Today he is free and can do whatever he wants! Oh gods - thank you!

Ned slipped into the middle of the room, not dressing as he was - naked, began to perform special exercises that were stored in his memory. Of course, he realized that these exercises came to him from the outside, from the essence that sat in his brain. So what? Why not take everything he needs for life. And for his life, which he now firmly decided to devote to military affairs, he needs a healthy, trained body. Skillful body. Fast body. The body is a weapon, the body is the focus of strength. And he pumped up the strength as he could.

Ned felt the blood flow, felt the renewal of his body, felt the Force flow through invisible channels and renew every corner of his body. From within, from the subconscious, quiet approval came - yes, yes, you are doing the right thing! So-so! Turning ... stretching ... moving ... so ... so ...

For half an hour, Ned did all sorts of strange figures, not thinking about what he was doing, why he was doing, and when he finished, his body burned, reddened from the overflowing energy and the sweat that covered his skin glittered in the morning sun like morning dew.

Ned walked over to the closet, took a towel and wrapped it around his thighs. So it was possible to go into the shower and naked, here it was in the order of things, but ... Ned was shy. He and in the general soldier's soul was somehow uncomfortable. Probably because more often in my life I was alone. I'm not used to such frank public events.

He took his pants with him, put on sandals, and then frowned in annoyance - bandages! I forgot to take off the bandages! He's all in bandages!

He took out an army dagger from the closet, carefully pushed the knot on his forearm and cut it, began to unwind the tight bandage. Here, in this place, Zasler's sword reached the very muscles, almost chopping off his hand.

The bandage smelled harshly of healing ointment, and Ned winced at the foul smell. Rolling the stinking bandage into a ball, he threw it to the doorstep. He stroked the place where the wound was. Exactly, because now instead of a wound there was only a thin line of scar - overnight, while Ned slept, the wound healed completely. So when he twisted his rules in strange body movements, the wounds did not bother him! Ned had somehow forgotten that just a few hours ago he had been cut up like some kind of fruit. Or a vegetable.

In a few minutes all the bandages were stripped off, cut off, torn off, and Ned examined the body with satisfaction - scars, thin, almost imperceptible. And nothing more!

"Well," Ned noted with grim satisfaction, "demons are useful sometimes, too! Now wash, and ... wondering what time it is?

Ned grabbed the prepared clothes, soap, and a sponge to rub his body (Pernal gave him everything in good faith - according to the list, from knitted socks and footcloths to underwear), went out, closed the door and walked to the shower room - fortunately, she was only three rooms from here. When he was leaving, he caught a glance at the spear, and it seemed to him that it shuddered, as if alive, leaning behind him.

The corridor was quiet, there was not even an orderly. Apparently he went outside, or went to the toilet. Ned went into the shower room. The stone room was deserted, covered with wooden trellises. No wonder - someone is on duty, someone in the city or sitting in his room. The time for the morning wash has long passed - the sun is already quite high.

Ned turned on the tap that turned the water into the pipe and stepped into the stream of icy, refreshing water. He was burned with such cold that he almost screamed in surprise - apparently the contrast between the temperature of the skin heated up by the exercises and the temperature was too great.th water flowing down from the mountains along a long viaduct. The city was supplied with water through a system of viaducts, and the mountain glacial water was so cold that even in such heat it did not have time to warm up to a temperature acceptable to a bather. The soldiers always swore, jumping with squeals and laughter under the streams of icy water, accusing their superiors of unwillingness to create at least minimal comfort for their subordinates. They say - about livestock, and that is better taken care of than the soldiers of the Marine Corps. The used water then drained through the sewer system into the city sewer and then into the sea. For a long time already voices have sounded that, they say, it is time to stop pouring any dirty trick into the sea - there are fewer fish, the sea is dirtier, and if the discharge continues with the same intensity, then in a hundred years this coast will have nothing but shit. However - no one believed the predictors. The town has stood here for hundreds of years, and it will stand for as long. And sewage treatment plants cost money. Where to get it, this money ??

Ned, of course, did not know about these complexities of city life, he enjoyed the freshness of the water, the purity of the streams flowing around his body, health and youth, which were the only wealth given to him by fate. The water was rustling, drowning out sounds, and Ned turned off his supersensory perception yesterday so that it would not interfere with his rest. Therefore, he did not hear the light tread of the feet, shod with soft officer steps.

A strange event saved him. When he was washing, he suddenly felt as if someone pushed him in the thigh, as if someone's hairy head demanded attention and affection. Ned turned, bending down to look ... and the sword whizzed right next to his head, nearly removing a piece of scalp.

Then - blows rained down one after another, striking sparks, immediately extinguished in a stream of icy water.

Chapter 12

Colonel Heverad watched Ned, whom the doctor was taking to his medicine, and turned to Shentel, who stood in silence and pursed his thin, evil lips in a disdainful grin.

- Well, Major - served! How long do you need to turn in cases and collect personal belongings? Is the day enough? Or do you wish to commit suicide? I can provide a good blade!

- Don't wait! We'll also see who wins. Enough day - Shentel coldly answered, and straight, as if swallowed a stake, walked to the security service premises. No one followed him - neither the guards, his subordinates, nor the officers. Everyone looked after him and thought that they would never want to be in his place. Never.

Despite the outward calmness, Major Shentel was seething, no, not the right word - he erupted like a volcano, spewing out streams of hatred, red-hot, hissing like lava.

Who are these people that dared to cross his path? Who are these creatures? Heverad, a pathetic nonentity, unworthy to lead a corps, a drunkard and a thief, friends with a beggar doctor! Sergeant, nothing, no one at all - how dare he?

Shentel tried to find out who he was and where he came from - he could not. The guy himself was silent, did not talk about his origin, and it was impossible to find out something in the usual way - he did not drink, did not smoke drugs, did not sleep with corrupt girls - well, how would you order information to be extracted from him?

Shentel tried to take his friends, Oidar and Arnot into circulation - they refused to cooperate, even under the threat of reprisals. And Ned was no longer friends with anyone. Who is he, this guy who broke Shentel's life?

The major unlocked the outer lock of the room, entered, bolted it, walked down the corridor to his office, opened it, and stepping over the threshold immediately went to the safe with the personal files of his agents. He took out the papers, fastened with twine and went through for a long time, as if trying to peer at the yellowish denunciations. There was everything and everyone. Separately lay the files on the officers - from their petty dirty sins, to the crimes that Shentel learned about and which, for the time being, kept secret - as in the case of Brock. And all to dust. Everything! Everything that I have collected over the years, all the dossiers, all the precious leaflets of denunciations - revealing, revealing, illuminating.

Shentel reached into the safe and took in his hands a bottle of wine taken from one of the soldiers on the territory of the base, resolutely pulled out a soft cork from the bark of a shirr tree with his teeth, and, applying it to his lips, threw the bottle back, pouring the contents down his throat. A harsh stream flowed into the stomach, and my soul felt better. What should he do? How will he survive the exile? Now the news of his shame will spread throughout the capital. Don't care! There is money, he will sit out in his estate and try to start a career again. The connections have been developed, and he will take this precious material of denunciations with him. Compromising evidence will always come in handy. Colonel Heverad doesn't last forever ... especially with some effort.

Shentel himself was a little scared of his thoughts - to go for the murder? Why not? There is a problem - Colonel Heverad. He is a mortal man. There will be no him, there will be no problem! As with Ned ...

Shentel finished the bottle, and again put his hand into the safe, taking out another ...

He drank all night, and hardly drunk. It happens so - the nerves are tense, the body is working to the limit and does not allow itself to relax. When the wine ran out, Shentel switched to mazis.

A light drug - in general, it was no different from wine - excitement, relaxation (everyone has it differently), laughter, depression, a desire to do something, fussiness and loss of orientation - you can list all the symptoms that the ointment caused for a long time.

There was no particular harm from this herb. But he had one property that made him dangerous. You can not smoke ointment if you have drunk hard. A drug mixed with alcohol made a person insane. No - not as crazy as the real madmen, gnawing at the bars of the cage of a madhouse or convulsing in fear, seeing ghostly monsters that suddenly grew out of their household. No. The man walked, talked, did his usual business ... but he did not understand what he was doing. The drug completely liberated, releasing the desires that sat in the subconscious. And the smoker did not understand that he was doing something unrighteous, something contrary to logic. But at the same time, he built complex schemes that seemed completely natural and logical to him.

After the fifth pack of mazis ended, Shentel got up, looked out the window - the sun had already come into its own, driving the night away. The major - or now - the former major took his officer's sword and dagger in his hands, wrapped them in cloth so that they could not be seen, left the security office, leaving it open, and went to the officer's barracks, trying not to be seen by anyone ...

The head major was glazed, the pupils dilated, and if someone met him on the way, it would be easy to know that the major was under the influence of drugs. Probably even a child knew the symptoms of drug use in this city. But ... he was "lucky." Nobody met, nobody stopped, nobody noticed anything.

The day sergeant looked in surprise at the former commander, who narrowed his eyes as if from the light, and, just in case, getting up from his seat, asked:

- For what purpose did Mr. Major visit the barracks? What is looking for here?

"Is Ned Black in his room?"

- Yes - the orderly answered in bewilderment - did not come out.

- The rest?

- Everyone is on display - today Mr. Colonel arranged a review, they say - one of these days there will be maneuvers. Who are you looking for? Is there anything I can help you with?

- Yes you can. Look here! - The major put the day's package on the table and began to open it. Fumbling for the handle of the dagger, he squeezed it tightly with his right hand, and with a sharp pull of the blade from the package, thrust it into the heart of the guard.

The unfortunate man died almost instantly, losing consciousness, without making a sound, softly sinking into a chair and throwing his arms out to the sides. Shentel only slightly held his twitching body, looking into the dim eyes, in which the reproach froze - for what ?!

Shentel did not pull out the dagger so as not to splash blood, neatly grabbed onto the collar of the guy's uniform and dragged him down the corridor towards the shower room.

In fact, few people lived in the officer's barracks - everyone preferred either the officer's town or private apartments in the main city. Only such servicemen as Drankon lived here, or Ned, who was not yet going to rent an apartment, or maybe he just did not have time to do it.

Chentel left the corpse in one of the booths, leaning against the wall. There was no blood - the dagger plugged the hole in his chest. Now all that was left was to wait for Ned.

You could try to knock on the door and call him out of the room - but where is the guarantee that the major will not be disturbed by someone who accidentally returned to the barracks, and Ned could have time to prepare, take a weapon, and then Shentel will not be in good shape. Ned was an excellent weapon, proven. So - take him when he is naked. Shentel wanted to be sure.

And minutes of waiting flowed.

They had to wait relatively long - the door slammed, the lock rasped, and someone entered the shower room. Shentel didn't see who it was, but there's no one other than Ned. The water rustled, and the man snorted, splashing and spitting like a child.

The booth where Shentel sat was located quite far from the entrance, so from there it was impossible to notice that someone was in it.

The major broke away from the wall, which he had been supporting for the last half hour, took the sword at the ready with both hands, and quietly stepping in soft officer's boots, moved forward.

Yes, it was him, the hated puppy! Ned stood with his back to the exit, between the stone walls of the booth and snorted, throwing splashes and trickles of water with visible delight.

Shentel raised his sword high, brought it behind his head, aiming slightly obliquely at the top of the enemy's head, prepared himself ... and then the unexpected happened! At that very moment, when the sword had already gone down and to the right, the guy shuddered, bent down and stood half-turned to the major, looking at something near his leg! The sword, instead of demolishing half of the villain's skull, slipped past and, with a clang, crashed into the masonry of the shower room.

Shentel went mad - rage, hatred, a sleepless night, drunk alcohol coupled with a smoked drug - everything merged into a single impulse - to kill, to kill, by all means! The sword flew in the hands of the mad man, like a feather, but Ned somehow managed to dodge, and sometimes even with his bare hands beat off the blade, lightly hitting it in the flat side and redirecting the blow to the stone of the wall. Shentel did not feel tired, he had no thoughts left except one - Kill! Kill! Kill!

Suddenly, Shentel saw the incredible - his sword was stopped in the air, sandwiched between the palms of this strange guy, who was looking at the major with black holes in his eyes. The sword was motionless for only a fraction of a second, and then, twisted out of the man's hands, with a clang flying off to the shower wall. A second later, the major felt a terrible blow to the neck, tried to breathe, cough, but he issued only a gurgling chirp. And then he fell to the floor, twitching in the last convulsions.

Ned with disgust smashed his torn trachea on the floor, stretched out his bloody hand under a stream of cold water that could wash away everything in the world, and the red thick liquid that stained his fingers stained pink the transparent "blood" of glaciers that came running from the top of Mount Black along the stone gutters ...

Ned rinsed himself once more, then stepped out of the booth, stepping over the Major's corpse, dried himself with his towel and pulled on his pants, trying not to look at the corpse, under which a red stain was blurring. Going to my room, dressed in formal clothes, again went out into the corridor. Returning to the shower room and walking along the stalls to confirm his suspicions. Finding the corpse of the orderly, he nodded his head - he expected so, and walking along the corridor, left the barracks. His soul was rotten. Nothing ever happens just like that - happy, good morning - and as a counterbalance - a mad killer. Either Ned is so unlucky, or life is so difficult ...

On the parade ground, as always, spearmen marched in orderly rows, swordsmen and crossbowmen moved through these rows, only the volume of simultaneously maneuvering units was greater than usual. And on the sidelines he watched what was happening Heverad himself, and both colonels, commanders of the second and third regiments.

No, he figured out how best to proceed, and found no other way out but to head straight for Heverad. * * *

- Pathetic bastard ... - Heverad said quietly, watching as the body of the major was carried out on a stretcher - there would be no nice committing suicide, leaving with honor, so he also took the guy with him! For what? It will be necessary to give help to the family of the deceased, and assign a pension. He died on duty, so he deserves help from the state. Adjutant, did you hear? Arrange the office. And here's another thing - Major Serta to me. Let him take the affairs of Security. Someone has to deal with slander. You, Sergeant, will write a report describing how it all happened. Everything, down to. the smallest details. At the same time, you will practice in the letter, it will come in handy. One must be able to express thoughts in writing. Orally, you're good at it. If you don't write today, for example, tomorrow. Rest. How are the wounds, okay? Something I do not see Zherezard ... I took the day off, or something. Oh come on. Rest, sergeant. You did a good job today. Removed the problem. No man, no problem. He deserves it. However, you are strong - with your bare hands and against the sword! Of course, he was a joke - he smells like a barrel of oil scent - but still. The sword is a sword. I saw notches on the partitions - ten strokes, no less. It's amazing he didn't blow your head off.

- They helped me - Ned said thoughtfully, looking at the door of the barracks from which at that moment the body of the orderly was carried out.

- Who helped? - the colonel did not understand - you were alone there? Or not?

"The spirit of my dead dog helped me," Ned said calmly, and froze again, examining the corpse on the stretcher.

- The spirit of the dog? Hmmm ... (And the guy, a little of that ... moved out - thought Heverad - no wonder, with such and such events. However, each of us is a little crazy. Is there any normal? If you delve into the soul of any person, you will definitely find a bunch of different madness and abnormalities And he is no exception. The main thing is to direct the madness in the right direction. He is a magnificent, simply divine fighter! So let him kill for the good of the kingdom, for the good of the people. Someone has to do this so that the "grateful" townspeople sitting at their they snorted after him at a peaceful table. You always want someone else to do an unpleasant, dirty job. And that's when we, soldiers, despised by "clean" civilians, appear.)

- Rest, guy - the colonel said sympathetically - spirit, so spirit. As you wish. The main thing is not to let anyone sneak up from the back. From the front, they definitely won't beat you. Well done!* * *

The guard at the entrance base winked at Ned cheerfully, giving him a military salute. Ned threw up his hand, too, smiling slightly at the guy, then walked through the gate, freshly painted with oil paint. The paint had not yet fully hardened, and Ned walked sideways, trying not to touch his new uniform.

He was very pleased to put on a new, beautiful thing - after all, he never had new clothes, new shoes - only rags and rags. And now - here he is - walking like an inveterate dandy! He also had the white gloves he had for the parade, but Ned did not dare to put them on. It would be too much. It occurred to him - the villagers should have seen how cool he is! I suppose they would have stopped turning up their snouts at once! And would have died with envy! He felt funny - would they have died, or had they stopped turning their snouts? At first, they would have stopped turning up their snouts, and then they died!

Giggling quietly to himself, Ned walked into the city — from Base to the streets there was a single cobblestone road, clean swept and smooth. With a grin, Ned remembered how he and Oydar and Arnot had returned home from a drinking bout. The whole road was strewn with soldiers defeated with wine, moving listlessly, as if after grievous wounds. Since then, about four weeks have passed, and he no longer went out into the city. However - SO he never came out at all. Alone, without soldiers, without a whole crowd of guys striving to crawl around like cockroaches.

It was pleasant to walk. Beautiful stone houses, running around of people striving for their very important business. The shop signs were brightly colored and inscribed with simple and elaborate curlicues.

Suddenly the thought occurred to Ned: How can I come empty-handed? Isn't it supposed to bring something with you? Or is it just such a custom in the village?

Seeing a shop with a pretzel hanging from a chain, somehow painted with gold paint, Ned resolutely headed across the road and stepped onto the high porch with polished dark railings.

All the shops, and in general the entrances to the houses here were much higher than the level of the pavement - Ned noted this for himself right away, even on the first exit into the city. At first he was surprised - why so? But friends said that powerful showers happen here, after which the streets are flooded to a height literally to the waist of a person. Stormy streams descend from the mountains, trying to wash the city into the bay, which is why all the entrances were located so high.

The shop smelled of some kind of spice, the name of which Ned did not know. Pastries and sweets created a unique aroma, from which saliva collected in the mouth of the visitor. Behind the counter stood a short, beautiful girl of about eighteen, in a sundress that hugged her chest. She looked at Ned without surprise, and with a slight smile, asked:

- What does the officer want? Want some candy? Or a cake with whipped cream? Everything is fresh here, my parents are masters of making cakes and sweets. Two hundred years of experience, after all.

- And what, only sweets have been made for two hundred years? - For some reason asked Ned, whose gaze was drawn to the chest, visible in the low cut of the dress. When the saleswoman sighed, her chest lifted and protruded from the tight bodice. The girl followed Ned's gaze, smiled sweetly and asked slyly:

- Do you like our product? (A handsome boy. It is a pity that a warrior. Mom would not approve of such a groom. However - why not? This is a sergeant, and not some kind of soldier. And what lips, what lips! I would have dug ... Ugh, Sanda! sinful thoughts visit you! Goddess of love, why do you evoke carnal thoughts?

Ned blushed at the girl's thoughts and forced himself to look away from the seductive hemispheres.

- Uh ... I need it. needed ... in general - I'm going to visit, and I need to bring something with me. And I don't know what. Can you help me?

- Who are you going to? Hmmm ... I mean - a man, a woman, a girl, family or friends? Whom you are looking for a gift - the offering depends on it.

- Family. A man, two adult sons, a daughter and a wife.

- Well ... then let's get these cakes for women - they are very popular, as they are tasty, and do not spoil the waist - they are airy. There are also several kinds of sweets ... biscuits - salty and sweet. Salted to beer - there are spices. What else ... hmmm ... that's all! Add a bottle of wine - a shop across the street - and the guest set is ready. You have five pieces of silver. Yeah, your gold, no smaller? You are a rich young man! Be careful - pickpockets got divorced - how many horror. They'll cut off the wallet and don't even notice. Keep your change. All the best and a successful visit to you! (I would like to grab you, squeeze you with my hands and feet ... and not let go! What kind of demonic behavior ?! Am I cursed? Look - they look, but to invite you somewhere to a good tavern, dance, and then ... a century a virgin to walk, Thanks to my mother - I took care of myself, and now I stand like a fool at the counter! The men shy away! Look - all sorts of freaks, right there they find a peasant, they find no one, and sleep with them, and get married! And I, beautiful, cannot! Are they scared, or what? Are they afraid of the beautiful? Can you pluck your eyebrows more ugly, or ruin your hair ?! Maybe then the men will be bolder? That's disgusting!)

Sanda's smile faded as the door closed behind Ned, and she sank empty into a chair, resting her elbows on the counter and resting her head on them. Suddenly, the shop door swung open again and the former sergeant entered.

- Have you forgotten something? The girl asked in surprise.

- I forgot! - Ned smiled warmly - forgot to say that you are as beautiful as the sunset over the sea! And every man would be happy to marry you. And including me. But alas, I am only a military man, and my life is unpredictable.

Ned suddenly leaned over the counter and kissed the girl on the cheek. His cheek was smooth, and this sensation when his lips touched warm skin, smelling of spices and incense, he remembered for life.

The girl was numb with surprise and froze, looking at the guy with wide eyes.

Ned took his bag of brownies and quickly dashed out of the shop. He himself was surprised at his bold act - why did he do it? But he was terribly pleased to see delight, surprise and joy in the girl's eyes. And also - it was his first, very first kiss, and Ned felt it on his lips for a few more minutes, remembering the green eyes that were so close to his eyes.

He no longer saw how the girl rushed to the slammed door, grabbed the handle, changed her mind, returned behind the counter, sat for ten minutes, jumped up from her chair again and ran out onto the porch to turn her head, looking out for someone in the crowd of passers-by. Then, silently and sadly, she entered the shop, sat down, looking into space in front of her, and then burst into tears, like children cry, having lost something that was dear to them and without which their life is impossible. Having burst into tears, I decided: I will find it! I'll find it anyway! What would it not cost me! "

With this she calmed down, took a rag and began to rub the counter, polishing the already smooth varnished board. Gradually she began to hum, and when her mother entered, she was already spinning in a dance, and from the side it seemed that she was holding an invisible partner by the waist, surrendering herself to the dance all, without a trace. When she was asked in surprise what she was doing, the girl was silent and only smiled mysteriously ...

Ned walked, smiling slightly, remembering the girl's stunned shock. Then I noticed a sign with a bunch of grapes and a bottle - I went there. After five minutes of discussing the properties of wine, he became the owner of a bottle for a whole silver coin - it seemed wrong to him to buy wine cheaper. The seller claimed that it was wine of some year, that the very first people in the capital drink it, and in general it is not wine, but the blood of the earth! And that he sold this wine to the sergeant very cheaply, only because he himself was a military man and was trying to give a discount to the soldiers.

Ned had to believe, as he had absolutely no understanding of this issue and was guided only by price - expensive wine means good. However - the high cost was relative - in the shop there were bottles and gold. But this is too much - the guy considered.

The shopkeeper explained to him where Zelenaya Street was. It turned out - only three blocks from here, so he didn't have to hire a cab to get to the place - this option Ned considered in the first place, in case the foot was too far to go.

The very first passer-by he met on Zelena Street pointed out to Ned the two-story house in which, according to him, the doctor Zherezar lived. Everyone here really knew that.

A door painted green, a large ring with a lion's head. Ned wanted to knock with his fist, then he thought - why is this ring here? Gently pulled on it - an "anvil" was found under the ring. You grab the lion's head and knock on the "anvil"! - Ned realized, and glad that he had solved the "riddle" three times energetically struck the ring. A minute later, the door swung open - in the doorway stood Geresard, dressed differently than at the base - he was in knitted slippers, a loose shirt and the same loose pants.

- Oooh! At last! - the doctor boomed joyfully - come in quickly! Our pie is getting cold! We have been waiting for you for a long time! Why are you late?

- There were reasons - Ned nodded - I'll tell you later.

- Anything serious? - the doctor frowned.

- Well ... in general - yes. But it's already over.

- In a nutshell, come on, otherwise a piece will not crawl into my throat - the doctor muttered - what happened?

- Shentel. Tried to kill me - Ned answered shortly, stepping over the threshold of the house.

"Hmmm... here's a fool. Well, I conclude that since you are here, Shentel in the morgue?

- Yeah - Ned drawled thoughtfully, looking into the corridor behind the doctor's back. There was one of the most beautiful women he had ever seen in his life. She was already about forty, but she was so well preserved that it was impossible to give her more than twenty-five. Huge black eyes, a stately slender figure, beautiful hands - she simply stunned with her appearance. Ned froze, eyes widening to this revived goddess.

- What was dumbfounded? Heh heh heh ... this is my wife Elsa. Come on - don't be embarrassed. Everyone reacts like that the first time. Then they get used to it. Or they don't get used to it. I myself sometimes - I look, I think, why the hell did I get such beauty?

- Because you are a good person - the beauty answered in a melodious voice, and laughed, as if bells were ringing - and also - you have a good salary.

- Have you seen ?! Here's the main thing for you - your salary! - Zherezard said in a deliberately plaintive manner - and women don't need us without a salary!

- Do not listen to him, he is joking - the woman smiled - call you Ned, right? Don't be embarrassed, come in. Don't take off your shoes - you have clean boots. And in general - all so neat, clean - our oglamons would learn to look after themselves like that. Come in quickly, we'll have lunch now.

- I here grabbed on the road - Ned, embarrassed, handed the woman the package - take it!

- Oooh! My favorite cakes! What a fine fellow you are! Are all the soldiers in the Corps that smart? Go to the living room, Costa, escort him!

- Let's go, let's go quickly - the doctor beckoned Ned with his hand, and putting his arm around his shoulders, slightly pushed in the direction of the room from which his wife came out.

The living room was large, bright, and in general - the whole house was so cozy that Ned involuntarily relaxed, as if he was in his home. However, he relaxed in vain. When he entered the living room, he saw on the couch by the window a copy of Elsa, only young, and with such a haughty look that looked Ned from head to toe.

- This is my daughter, Delora, and these are the sons - Hagen and Nascar. Something has already been eaten! Why didn't you wait? - roared the doctor - I ordered not to eat without us!

- Well, there is a hunt, dad! - Bask threw a long-haired guy, hefty as a closet.

- Aha! There is a hunt! - echoed another - we are waiting for mom's pies in the morning!

- Okay - let's go to the table. And you sit down, Dela. Stop looking at the street. The prince will not come for the golden horse!

- But what if?! - the girl giggled - however, dad, you are right - in this backwater of the prince you will definitely not wait. Here some beggar soldiers wander! - the girl shot her eyes at Neda and imperceptibly wrinkled her nose, turning to the brothers so that her father could not see.

Ned sat down in the seat offered to him and froze like a wooden idol. He did not know how to behave in society. And I didn't even know in which hand to hold the fork, in which knife, and in general - how to hold them. No - in fact, he knew how to hold a knife, and even as best he could, but only for combat. But I didn't know how to behave at the table. Ned tried to access Black's memory, but received no response. It seems that the knowledge he gained through the artifact concerned only magic and martial arts. Then Ned turned on supersensible perception. He had an idea how to deal with his ignorance.

- Well, what a fool! Why did dad bring him into the house? Everyone knows that the soldiers of the corps are the most perfect loons and rabble! He doesn't know how to behave at the table! Now, I suppose, he will tear with his hands and poke his snout into the plate! - thought Delora.

- Well, let's start? - Elsa asked with a smile - we were expecting you early, so we got a little hungry. (Good boy. Shy. And Delora again behaves like a fool!) What are you going to do? Let me put a little bit of everything on you myself, okay? The woman smiled radiantly at Ned, and he felt his nerves ringing like strings relax a little. It was easier for him to fight with Shentel than to sit here now, at a common table with the Geresard family. There at least he knew what to do!

The soup was delicious. Ned watched as the others were doing - after them he took pieces of cake, carefully, trying not to make noise, sent the contents into his mouth and ate quietly, without chomping, remembering how Oidar swore at the rude soldiers in the dining room.

Delora silently commented on his behavior, expecting the failure of "this stupid soldier." Ned was calm, collected, but he just could not enjoy the delicious food to the fullest - this constant control over himself interfered.

Finally, we moved on to tea and cakes. The maid brought the unopened bottle, the one Ned had brought, and Geresard, grunted with satisfaction, looked at Ned in surprise:

- And you know about wines, as I can see! This is a very good year, glorious wine. Would you like a drink? Just a little so that you know the taste of good wine! And I'll give you a drink, loafers - purely for the company. Very little! Hey, where did you pull the bottle ?! What kind of children! By the way - why do you have a fingal under your eye? Played again? Well, what will grow out of you is completely incomprehensible! Here you are, Hagen, a hefty oryasina, what are you going to do? Or sit on your father's neck all your life?

- What is it on the neck? - the big man was offended - by the way, I asked you - get me into the Corps! What are you doing?

- And I asked! - grunted more puny Nascar - that's why Ned can, but we can not? Why are we worse?

- Hmmm ... - Geresard muttered puzzledly - Ned's circumstances are such that he had nowhere else to go, and everything in your life is in order, why expose your chest to enemy arrows?

- And what about Ned's circumstances? - Delora asked innocently - what, killed someone? Or robbed? Or robbed? They say there are only robbers and thieves in the Corps. And also - half-witted.

Silence fell in the room, then the doctor's voice boomed:

- Get out from the table! You fool!

The doctor threw a rolled napkin at his daughter, and she hit her right in the forehead. The girl pouted, and defiantly, without looking at anyone, left the table. After a couple of moments, her shoes were already knocking on the stairs leading up.

- Sorry, Ned - the doctor looked at the guy guiltily - well, a fool, and that's it! She took beauty from her mother, but the mind ... did not receive the mind.

- Sorry - Elsa nodded - well, what to do - her whole life is in rags, conversations about a profitable marriage, and metropolitan life. Her father has already flogged her - it's useless. Maybe he gets married - wiser? Although - hardly.

The woman sighed with a sad smile, and sipped the wine from the glass:

- Yes, good wine. Have a little drink. I know you don't drink, but for the sake of such an occasion ... no big deal.

- Soldier, and does not drink? - Hagen snorted - what is this? Why don't you drink? Some kind of vow? Go something else? Sick?

- Stop it, Hagen - stopped the doctor - the corps soldiers are never asked about their former life. That life is in the past. They started from scratch. Everything. You should have learned from Ned how to lead the right life! Who dragged home drunk last week like a dockman after work? Are you not? Start early!

- Dad, I want to go to the officer's school - Hagen said suddenly firmly - and he wants Us. Why are you against it? Praise Ned, but we always go bad! Ama do not want to become merchants or doctors! We are fighters! We are stronger and more agile than any of your soldiers! We are the same age as Ned, and we want to join the army!

- Fools! - Geresard muttered with annoyance - the army is hard work, the army is sweat, blood, this ... this is ... death! Mother will not forgive me if you die! No, no and NO! As for the fighters, you are puppies, compared to Ned! You are one and a half times wider than him, and you won't stand a second in battle against him!

- Stop it! - smiled Hagen - in life I will not believe. However - with a sword it may be so. Or what they are taught with ... And in hand-to-hand combat - they cost nothing. Nascar and I have been going to martial arts school for a year now! And we are the best students there!

- How are you walking? - the doctor frowned - how ?! Where did you get the money for the school? You gave! - he realized, looking at his downcast wife - and why? Why do you indulge their nonsense? Why didn't you ask me ?!

- Costa ... you're wrong - the wife frowned - I know my sons better than you. You are stuck in your building, and do not notice what is happening at home. They rave about the army, read scrolls and books about martial arts, dream of going to an officer's school and making a career like Nulan! My father was a military man, so what? Alive and healthy, sitting in his house and raising bees! Receives a good pension. You can, after all, help them to enter the school through Heverada, and find a good place. Why are you letting things go by themselves? What if they run away and enlist in a murderous place like your corps? And then what? Have you thought about it? Better to direct and control in the right direction than like this ...

"Why are you giving them wrong thoughts? What do you mean - run away ?! What is this? I'll run to them!

- Let's run away, we'll run away! - brothers nodded - we will definitely run away!

- Ned, I'm sorry to intervene in a family scandal - Elsa smiled - I wonder what do you think about the desire of my children to serve in the army? How do you see this army from the inside? You just recently entered it? How do you like there? Can you tell my kids? My husband fanatically loves his demon corps, but at the same time forbids others to love him! They asked a hundred times to go with him to the base, but he refused them the same number of times! So what do you think about the army?

Ned paused, looked sideways at the brothers, who were frozen with smiles on their faces, sighed, making up his mind, and said with regret:

- Sorry, but I think that both guys see only lacquer shine in the army. They believe that when they get into the army, they will become the coolest, famous fighters, and also that all the girls will run after such brilliant officers as they are. They think that now they are the coolest, that they can defeat anyone - due to strength and dexterity, due to knowledge of martial arts, and they want to rise even more in this regard. And they don't think about anything else. In my opinion, they should not yet be allowed close to the army. Their heads are full of duels and beautiful uniforms. Have listened to all sorts of nonsense, and that's what weird.

- Here! Exactly! - Geresard clapped his hands three times, and his clapping sounded as if someone had hit the table with a hefty stick - and I think so! The idiots have heard a lot of stories, read some books about the army, and imagined themselves to know what! They, they say, will beat any soldier with their shitty skill! Yes, you have never been in a real battle, and you do not know what it is! You don't know what death is! You don't know what the blood of the person you killed smells like! And there - to talk about the army. Doodles, one word. Grow up, then we'll talk. Better to learn how to take care of themselves - look - what a Ned - clean, ironed, ironed! The hair is clean, styled in a warrior's tail! What are you doing? Like vagabonds! Look disgusting!

- Well, why are you still poking us with Ned? - Hagen was indignant - he is as old as we are, he has recently been in the corps, and does he know how the blood of the person he has killed smells like? Completely dishonored! And I tell you - we are not worse, and better than many fighters! And we'll roll your Ned like a bunch of brushwood! We are the best students in the school! Stop belittling us! And you, Ned, would hold your tongue - a braggart and a talker! Daddy was on fire for you with paternal love, for some hell, and begged for the position of sergeant! I don't know, or what ?! I heard them talking to their mother - like, an orphan, I feel sorry for him, a clever boy, I asked Heverad, so he arranged ... blah blah blah. And now here you are talking about what you do not know. Upstart and braggart! (Damn idiot! I would break you on your knee, you pompous brute! You advise my parents something else, you moron!)

Silence reigned at the table again, broken only by the clinking of a spoon in Nascar's mug. Then there was such a roar that Ned almost flinched.

- Beast! How dare you insult a guest ?! Rubbish! I invited the guy to stay with friends, as if in his family, and what did you do ?! This little rubbish began to say nasty things, and you took up the same thing ?! I grew patly, don't you clean it up properly? I'll rip them out for you now! Oh, you brute!

A complete confusion and chaos began - Geresard jumped out from behind the table, tried to grab Hagen by the "patla", he dodged and hid behind his mother. Just in case, Nascar ran to the side, happily supporting his brother with shouts like "Comes in from the left! Hold on, body! " On the stairs, Delora was laughing as she came down to look at the scandal, and only Elsa sat quietly, smiling sadly. She watched Ned eat a piece of cake, ignoring the noise and screams, then said:

- You see, this is how we live. He will come, drive - it seems as if he fulfilled his fatherly duties, and then back to his Corps. Who do you think they are not hearing? So wild and stupid? After all, he was promised a career as a singer - do you know how he sings? Ask me to sing something sometime - just goosebumps. And he went to the doctor. And do not be offended by the guys ... so they are not spiteful. Forgive them - bad heads. We spoiled them a little to see. It seems to me that an officer's school would be useful. Only Costa doesn't want to hear anything about it, and that's it. Once again, forgive me for dragging you into this scandal - I did not think that everything would go wrong.

- Come on - Ned chuckled - I've seen all kinds of things. Even funny.

- Fools! Freaks! Ned got stuck in the conversation! Beasts are stupid - yes, he put you both on one palm, and the other does not even have to slap! You yourself will turn into a wet place, you will go to shit!

Geresard sat down, breathing heavily and wiping his sweat with a napkin:

- They are strong! You're mugs! It's one thing to jerk around in a training room, and another is a real fight! You would do it if you got into situations like Ned!

- What situations? - smirking Hagen asked insinuatingly - did you have a fight over a piece of cake in the soldiers' mess?

- It's none of your business, "the doctor grumbled. He just, last night, killed in a duel a man, a master of the sword - Geresard added unexpectedly - this swordsman would simply chop you into pieces, and he opened him like a fish! Gutted so that they barely collected! So hold your nasty tongues!

- Costa! At the table! - Elsa shook her head reproachfully - what, Ned, exactly? Is it really true?

- Am I lying to you, or what ?! - the doctor was indignant - you ask more! He won the duel of honor! Spear against the sword! You assholes are far from Ned. So shut your tongues in ...

- Costa, please, no army rudeness! - asked Elsa - Ned, could you tell us what kind of duel? I'm interested too. You are welcome...

- If you ask - how can I refuse you - smiled Ned - only is it worth telling? A dirty story.

- Please tell us - Elsa smiled again - after all, I am from an officer's family, questions of honor are not alien to me.

"Okay," Ned shrugged.

The story lasted about twenty minutes, interrupted by the doctor's additions and Elsa's questions. The brothers sat all this time, looking at Ned with wide eyes, and when he finished the story, Hagen said:

- Great! Awesome! I wanted to join the army even more! And what about this very Shentel? Did he commit suicide?

- You can say so - Geresard grinned - he attacked Ned in the morning and tried to kill him. Where was it, Ned?

- In the shower - the guy answered with a frown - he killed the orderly, dragged him into the shower, and there he waited for me to come. And then he attacked me from behind. I accidentally stayed alive ... bent down at the time when the major hit. Otherwise I wouldn't be talking to you now. He aimed his sword at my head.

- And how did you manage ?! - Frightened raising her hand to her mouth, asked Elsa.

- Something like that ... killed him - said Ned - to live for some reason, so he survived.

- Something I do not believe - grumbled Nascar - against the sword ... with your bare hands ... lying? You just invited some kind of demon into the house, not a man. I don't believe in these stories!

- Honestly - I don't care if you believe me or not - Ned chuckled and turned serious - I guess I should go. Thank you for accepting me.

- Sit still! - Geresard was worried - you leave so quickly! And all of you, ohlomons! In which centuries a normal person came to visit, not all of your idiots, friends - so you scared him with your behavior! Idiots!

- Well, he didn't seem to be scared with his bare hands against the sword - laughed Nascar - and then he was scared! He's just tired of our company, and that's all.

- No… company, like company - Ned winked - I've seen worse. But your parents are wonderful. You really are fools that you don't appreciate them.

- But, but! Hold your tongue - Hagen intervened - what we value and what we don't value is our business. Gathered - so walk. Ay!

A piece of pie, started by his father, slammed right into Hagen's face, leaving greasy streaks and bits of filling on it. Elsa got up and looked sternly at her son, said:

- I haven't talked to you for three days. You have crossed all the boundaries. Get out from the table! * * *

Ned walked back to base sad, not at all the same as when he went to visit. It wasn't what he expected. For some reason, he thought that such a good person as a doctor would have such nice children. Alas ... Strange, but he was very annoyed about this. Why? I didn't know myself. As if I got an empty wrapper instead of candy.

And then he remembered the girl-seller. My heart grew warmer, and her face rose in front of her eyes, and also the girl's thoughts that she would not let go of him and grabbed hold of her arms and legs came to mind. Dreams suddenly began to ripen in Ned's brain - what if ...? Maybe?

He dropped these thoughts abruptly, as if he had repulsed an enemy sword - who needs it? Why would some girl, well-bred, clean and homely, a rootless orphan? The lot of such orphans are corrupt women and barracks. Should we hope for family happiness? And I decided - not worth it. And also, I thought - there is free time, can I go to the very women about whom Geresard spoke? By those who live by the temple? Why not? After all, he is a soldier, and not some kind of ... boy!

Ned frowned, stopped in the middle of the road so abruptly that a passerby almost bumped into his back, and, turning over his shoulder as if on a parade ground, walked back to the city center.

Chapter 13

The temples stood side by side like shops in a bazaar. If you want, choose which god to ask for protection. Here you have the goddess of love, here you have the god of war, here you and ... in general - choose gods for every taste.

In the center is the temple of the creator god, the largest, most beautiful, with a gilded dome and a statue at the entrance. She portrayed a hefty peasant, similar to Geresard, with the same beard and wide face. Ned chuckled - how much this chief god looked like a doctor - just amazing.

Ned hesitated - which god should he bow to? I decided - after all, at Kuultuku. The God of War is the best patron for him if the newly made sergeant is going to continue his army career.

The temple of the god of war was reddish brown, like caked blood. On the walls there are drawings depicting the various stages of the warriors' presence in this and the afterlife - here they go on the attack, and here the messengers of the god of war, warlike maidens, carry them to heaven. And the faces of these maidens are so pleased, as if they would now make a stew or porridge with meat from the fallen soldiers. The warriors as one are beautiful, spiritualized and lie in the hands of the virgins as if they were going to bed with them.

However, beautiful girls are an integral part of the afterlife of real warriors. Should someone please the fallen soldier in the next world? A feast, beautiful maidens, battles, songs - this is the warrior's reward for worshiping the god of war and heroic death in battle.

Ned wasn't particularly religious - he didn't have to stand at the altars and pray to the gods for luck and prosperity. He was simply not allowed into the chapels in the village. Rather - a prayer house - it was one for all the gods of the pantheon.

By the way, the god of water and the goddess of love were in the greatest "demand" in the village chapel. The whole life of fishermen and pearl divers was spent at sea, but love. love is eternal. Wherever people live. Kualtuk was not particularly well liked in the Black Ravine.

As for Ned - well, yes, he prayed to the gods, at break - to one, to the other - sitting somewhere under an oak tree and eating a piece of bread. Only there was no good from these prayers. As life was shitty, it remained, although he prayed earnestly and often in childhood. And then he cooled down to religion and began to think - maybe there are no gods at all? Why can't they hear him? He's not a bad boy at all, why do they respond to the same Branko, or the headman, but he doesn't? Finally, I came to the conclusion - the place is not right. Apparently, prayers better reach the gods in specially designated places. For example, in city churches, where they are given money. Like shopkeepers.

Ned walked past the temple attendant, melancholy rubbing the shiny brass doors to the statue of the god of war, standing near the altar and fumigated by streams of fragrant smoke, took out three pieces of silver prepared in advance and put them in the offering bowl. Then he bowed to the statue of Kuultuk, and said quietly:

- Thank you, great Kualthuk, for sending the spirit of Narda to me! If not for her - I would be dead now! Thank you! Help me further on my military path!

Ned blinked, and it seemed to him that the statue of Kuultuk looked at him and smiled slightly. But most likely it was just an optical illusion - the air was distorted, heated by incense burners with coals, on which fragrant resins were laid out. But Ned really wanted the god of war to notice him and give a sign, and therefore, after a minute, he already convinced himself that the statue was indeed smiling.

Bowing to Kuultuk, Ned went to the temple of the goddess of love. Who else if not she should have helped Ned in his future love affairs? Tell someone - they will laugh - a man who has killed more than a dozen opponents is still a virgin, and without a blush on his cheeks he cannot communicate with a woman! May the goddess of love give him masculinity and help him find ... hmmm ... what to find?

This is where Ned was having trouble. Love? Why does he need love? He is not going to tie himself by family ties yet. And what kind of family man is he at seventeen or eighteen years old?

Honestly, Ned himself didn't know how old he was. Seventeen, or eighteen - it will be more accurate. How old was he when they found him? About a year? Maybe less? Maybe more? And for seventeen years he lived in the village. So this age turns out. What's the difference? In body Ned was more mature than many adults, but consciousness ... when how. With regard to love passions - at the child's level.

The goddess of love was dressed rather frivolously - an unknown sculptor depicted her as a young girl, dressed in clothes that were open when walking, exposing slender legs. Her shirt did not reach her navel, and anyone who worshiped could see the deity's seductive tummy, suggestive of motherhood and a conjugal bed.

Girls and women wishing to have a child stroked the belly of the statue during prayer, and that made the stone statue in this place shine, polished by thousands, tens of thousands of female hands during the entire existence of this statue. Who came up with the custom of stroking the belly of the goddess of love when he appeared - no one knew. But the custom existed not only in this small town, but also in other cities, and even in the capital.

Ned did not know about it, he only left an offering - one silversmith (Enough! He does not count on particularly great love!)

Satisfied and hopeful, he left the Selera temple, looked around ... and decided to visit Dinas as well. Who knows what lies ahead - why miss the opportunity to reach out to God the Creator? Moreover, he looks like Geresard. And the doctor is a good person. This means that the creator god is most likely a decent, kind god.

Two more silversmiths. "You will leave all your salary here!" - thought Ned, and hastened to quickly retreat from the square of the gods, until he got the idea to make some other offering.

Ned found the temple of the water god, orientated himself on the terrain, taking the statue of Pryon as a starting point, and walked where Geresard had once pointed him. And sure enough - a few minutes later, Ned was standing in front of a house with green shutters, on which hung a sign with a needle and a roll of cloth painted on it.

The inscription read: "Embroidery and tailoring of women's underwear."

Ned froze in confusion - what has the embroidery to do with it? And in general - how will he take it and go into the shop where they order lingerie? And what if someone thinks that he is a husband? That this linen itself is meant for him?

The thought caught his breath - that was just not enough! Then he calmed down and began to think more sensibly - firstly, who said that he went into the store to order laundry for himself? Maybe he has a mistress who loves beautiful embroidered panties! And secondly ... fuck them all!

Ned gritted his teeth and took a determined step toward the door. He pulled at the polished brass-tipped handle and found himself in a large room hung with lace. In it, by the window, at a large table heaped with pieces of cloth and thread, sat two women - one older, the other very young.

Pretty - not beauties, like Elsa, or her daughter, or like a saleswoman in a candy store, but quite pretty - in the village where Ned grew up, as if they would pass for beauties.

They looked at Ned without surprise, assessing him from top to bottom, and the elder asked amiably:

- What does the young man want? Order lingerie for your girlfriend? We have the best lingerie in the area!

Ned froze - how to say? "I want a woman ?!" What if the doctor was mistaken, and these are ordinary seamstresses? However - well, even if he was mistaken - what will they do to him? Will they kill, or what?

"I... I... from Geresard," he finally managed, and looked expectantly at the women. They looked at each other, then the elder clarified in a deep chest voice:

- Do you want to be with a woman?

Honestly, Ned always wanted this. A young, healthy body demanded its own, and nothing could be done about it. Just say it out loud, and even as calmly as this woman ...

- Eeee ... hmm ... dda! Ned blurted out and blushed deeply.

(Funny boy. I would love to have some fun with him. In which centuries a nice client came, otherwise all are some old freaks. It's a pity that I can't get into bed with him. I wonder if Geresard told him about the price? Money- what does he have?)

- How much do your services cost? Ned choked out.

- Gold in three hours - the woman softly explained - are you able to give such an amount? (Maybe give him a discount? Someone would have paid for free ... and even paid extra, just to get such a guy in bed! Some people need to take a double price at all ... It's a pity that I can't with him ...)

- Yes, I can - swallowing convulsively, Ned nodded and took the prepared gold from his pocket and put it on the table. The woman immediately brushed the coin away so that Ned didn't even notice where it had gone.

- Osara, go with the young man - the woman nodded her head to the girl, who was watching the negotiations with interest, and she readily stood up, going up to the passage inside the house, curtained with a thick curtain - in fact, it is customary for us to make an appointment in advance, we could be busy, but you're in luck. My daughter will serve you as it should, at the highest level. Maybe you wanted to be with us two at once? Sorry, I can't yet ...

"Nothing, nothing…" Ned stammered, crimson as a boiled crab, "one x... x... is enough for me.

- Well, go after her - the woman nodded, and suddenly winked - there are all hers, do not be shy, everything is once for the first time!

(It looks like a virgin! A rare guest in our time!)

Ned followed the girl down the corridor and found himself in a large room with a copper bath in the corner, a large thick carpet in the middle of the room, and a bed in the corner, the size of his bachelor bed five times. There were translucent curtains on the windows overlooking the closed courtyard, so the room was rather gloomy. The girl pulled back the curtains, and it became much brighter.

Turning to Ned, she began to unbutton her dress.

- Take off your clothes, what are you waiting for? Time is running. Now you will take a bath, I will bathe you, and then we will make love. Come on, take off your uniform!

The girl slipped out of her dress, quickly threw off her lace panties, remained completely naked, and without embarrassment went to Ned, straightening her hair on her head, which made her small breasts jumped up. Ned froze, unable to take a step and clutching the button of his uniform as if he was afraid that it would now fall off and fall to the floor.

The girl came very close, smiled in his face, and began unceremoniously unbuttoning his uniform, literally tearing the guy's hands off the lapels, twirling him like a doll. Taking off her uniform and shirt, she pushed Ned to the bed, pushed him backwards and deftly, skillfully pulled off his boots and socks, untied the ties on his trousers and pulled them off the guy in one motion. He tried to grab onto his new, almost worn army pants, but they immediately followed after the pants.

The girl looked appraisingly at Ned, who was trying to hide behind his hands, and nodding her head in satisfaction, said:

- And that, pretty well. I was expecting something like that. Virgin, huh? I feel when you come for the first time. So embarrassed, so all the paws! - she laughed, offensively and merrily, and Ned began to let go a little. He sat up on the bed, reflexively covering his "household", but the girl playfully slapped him on the hand, saying:

- Do not dare to cover! You have something to be proud of, so let's not do this nonsense! You are visiting a woman, so you must take into account her desire. I want to look at you. I feel better this way, this is how I tune in. You want to get as much out of your love session as possible? So - for the future, keep in mind - if a woman feels good, then you will be sweeter. Let's go here. Get in the bath. Aha ... stay like this - now I will redeem you! - the girl went to the wall and turned on the tap on the pipe. Warm water flowed out of it, in stark contrast to the icy water that Ned used to wash at the base. He put his head under the stream, and the girl began to lather his body, cooing something at the same time, without stopping for a second:

- So ... here we will wash, and here ... here ... here ... warm? Yeah ... we have a big tank on the roof, we always have warm water. We can't wash with ice water! It's horror to wash with ice water! We'll waste you ... you will shine like your boots! The main thing is that the birds are not carried away - you will be so brilliant!

If the mother wants, let her continue. Yes, I still agree to Zarsad's proposal.)

- Let me dry you thoroughly - the girl rubbed Ned dry with a terry towel smelling of herbs and incense, and pulled him on the bed ... *
* *

- Don't be embarrassed. Now you will rest, and we will repeat. Did you like it? I suppose I didn't even have time to understand, right? Rest. Come on, while I caress you, I will massage you… what strong muscles you have! Downright steel! You squeezed me so - I thought my ribs would crack. You squeeze more carefully - we women are delicate, fragile creatures ... suddenly crush? Who will love you then? It is necessary to touch it more tenderly ... here ... and here ... yeah ... more ... more ... so, so. Look how it is necessary ... I will teach you - all women will remember you for the rest of their lives! *
* *

Ned walked out from the women as evening began to descend on the dying city. The sun crawled behind the mountain, and shadows rose like black paths, covering houses, streets, warning that their time would soon come.

The guy walked along the pavement, and thought - what has changed? Now he knows what carnal pleasures are. So what? Has he become more courageous? Or stronger? However - he acquired knowledge. They were probably worth gold. Or maybe not worth it? Come on! At least now he can say that he was with a woman and knows what IT looks like.

Osara was gentle with him, very skillful, but ... Ned constantly listened to her thoughts. And the girl was not forgotten for a moment. Outwardly, she portrayed passion, sometimes she really enjoyed it, Ned felt it, mentally she even praised him for his enthusiasm and tirelessness, but ... there was no passion! How did this all differ from self-satisfaction?

No, in general it was different - it took a long time and consumed a gold coin. Is that all?

Ned felt slightly deceived. Well, yes - it should have been done. He needed this, he could not feel like a full-fledged man without trying a woman. But ... Ned expected something more impressive from the process itself, something bright, amazing, to sparkle from his eyes! However - everything is measured, everything is definite, predictable: "Your time is up! Finish! "

No, he did not regret wasted time and wasted gold. Money? What to do with them? He cannot spend even this money - he simply cannot. He does not even remember how much he had left on the account in the treasury of the corps. Time? What to do with it? So he went to visit, was with a woman - now where? To the hateful barracks? Friends are now either on maneuvers, or they are washing themselves, getting ready for dinner and sleep, and he ... he seemed to have fallen out of a pod and can not find a new place for himself in this life. No longer a soldier, but not yet an officer.

Was he good with Osara? Yes it was. At first, it is simply magnificent, then - calm and sweet. At the end, Osara hinted: "If you paid for three hours, this does not mean that you have to use it for all three hours - continuously! You need to take a break, otherwise you will weaken. " And I thought to myself: "I stopped by! Oh Serena! Now for a day I will feel how everything inside me hurts! Strong guy! Just enough, huh? It's a pity the mother is not there, now it would be easier for two. I would have rested, but she would have taken the breath - the mother loves young stallions. "

Ned didn't turn off supersensory perception — he studied. It absorbed everything like a sponge. This whole world, all the sensations, all the thoughts that he heard from others. Like Geresard - when he saw and heard everything that the doctor's children thought about, and could not resist, he expressed it. But why? That won't stop the guys, and it looks like Ned has made enemies now. Does he need it? That's what, and he did not want to make enemies at all.

However - the process of making enemies took place with him easily and naturally. Why did it happen? Ned hadn't thought about it. That is the will of the gods, and that's it! Apparently, this is his fate ...

- Hey, wait! How are you there ?! Ned! Stop, I tell you! Ned turned and saw a group of guys catching up with him, in the front ranks of whom he recognized both of Geresard's sons. And his cheekbones cramped with melancholy - did they really decide to get even for the scandal in which No took part? Here the demon pulled his tongue, made him take, and lay out everything that he spied in the thoughts of the guys! I just remembered about them - and now! And what to do? He won't kill guys or maim, will he? But if they attack him, what will he do?

- Well, here we are ... a hero! - the elder grinned, looming over Ned with all his mass - you say, against the sword with bare hands? Did you beat everyone, won? And weakly beat me?

"I won't fight you," Ned replied calmly, surrounded by guys from all sides.

- Why? Are you scared? Pathetic coward! - Hagen laughed - did you guys see? That's what the army is made of! And dad doesn't want to teach me to be an officer! I would have gotten this trash, I would have taught them how to stand in battle! He came to our house and began to brag about what a great fighter he is! Humiliated us! And if I make you fight, will you do it? If I spit in your face?

- Hug, maybe not, eh? - asked Nascar - he will complain to his father, he will yell. Do we need it? Why should we spoil the mood over some stray puppy? And if you beat him - there will be such a scandal, such - I cannot imagine! Father will kick out of the house!

- I already suffered because of this freak! Mother doesn't talk to me now! What a bastard! Guys, let's beat him up a little, and that's it? Well, for the sake of order, so that he knows who is the boss! Do you hear, puppy, now I ...

- What's going on here? Hagen! Nascar! Efor! Holtz! What are you doing here ?! - a short man in dark loose clothing looked sternly at the guys, and they immediately faded under his gaze - all for one? Did I teach you this? Did I tell you that a mob attack on an unarmed, unprepared person is the highest valor? You disappoint me. I'm already beginning to regret accepting you to school. Why are you sticking to the sergeant? What do you want from him?

- Sorry, master! - Hagen was embarrassed - this guy was our guest today, and humiliated me in front of my parents. He intervened in the family business, ridiculed us, and boasted that he fought today with his bare hands against the sword! And killed the enemy, the master of sword fighting! How is it? We got angry and scared him a little. But they didn't! But you need to punish for lying, for bragging?

"Hmm... it's not good to lie, yes. But he is a young guy, and perhaps he does not understand that lying sometimes leads to a very bad result. You need to punish bad people, but he is not bad, just lost! Right, Sergeant? You didn't want to offend anyone with your lies, you just wanted to raise the prestige of the corps in which you serve, right?

- No. I didn't want to lift anything - Ned shrugged his shoulders - they asked me, I answered. That's all. I don't want to fight these guys. I don't respect them for their idle talk, but I really respect their father. And mother. They are the best people I have ever seen in my life. And it's a shame that the guys didn't grow up like them.

- Again ?! Oh, you creature! ... - Hagen raised his hand to strike, but the man with a sharp shout stopped:

- To stand! Stop immediately! Another movement without my permission, and you will never appear within the walls of the Andug school!

- Excuse me, master - Hagen turned pale and bowed to the man - I will no longer!

The man carefully and sternly looked into the face of the unfamiliar sergeant. He thought: "This is what is happening in life ?! Seemingly quite a decent guy - clean, ironed, correct! And a lie! The lie pervaded the whole being of this man! And what will happen to him next? How will he live? The first big lie - and immediately it led to this result! If it were not for me, they would definitely beat him. Hagen becomes poorly controlled, and his brother follows his lead. And despite the fact that they are leaders, and the best students of my school! Sad, very sad. And which is better - such violent, but honest, or such a quiet, deceitful, dull and calm, like a pack horse? "

But out loud he said:

"I'm ashamed to lie, Sergeant! You dishonor your uniform, the uniform of the glorious Zamar Marine Corps! Shame on you! Let it go, let it go. And so that no one would follow his trail - the man frowned, and looked with disgust at the tall, broad-shouldered guy, who was looking at him with fixed gaze.

The guys parted to give Ned a way, he took two steps along the pavement, and suddenly turned around and asked coldly:

- And where did you get the idea that I'm lying? In general, why did you dare to make incorrect assumptions based on the false words of these people?

The man froze, and even slightly numb from this turn of events. He looked at the guy for a second, then shook his head dismissively.

- How are you mired in lies! Go away! Leave this minute! Otherwise, I'll hit you myself! I hate lie! I hate liars! Go away!

"This is a public street," Ned said, "and you can't get me out of here. And if you hit, you get back. And it will not seem a little to you, I warn you.

Suddenly, the guys began to laugh - loudly, earnestly, turning to hysterical neighing. Hagen clapped his thighs and said:

- Is he! Will answer! Master! I cant! Hold me, I'll die laughing! Oh, I'll just die! Listen - why, really, did we attack him? He's crazy!

The master smiled slightly and raised his hand up, demanding silence:

- So you will give me an answer? It's funny. Sorry, sonny, but ... I think you're exaggerating your powers. (Freak! I devoted my whole life to martial arts! From the cradle! And you say these words to me? Are you really crazy?) Go before you really get into trouble. That's it, the conversation is over.

- No, not finished! - Ned obstinately bowed his head, like a goby that wants to raise his enemy on the horns - you insulted me, insulted my uniform, insulted the corps in which I serve! Sorry! You acted like an unreasonable child, accusing me of what I did, obeying young foolish donkeys (Hey, choose your expressions! - someone shouted from behind) I demand an apology!

Ned himself did not know what had hurt him so. He didn't care about these guys. How few in his life did he meet such ignoramuses who wanted to assert themselves at the expense of other, weaker, from their point of view, people? Yes, I don't care about them - he left, that's all. But the master ... Ned realized it was their martial arts teacher. And after reading his thoughts, I found out that the master was a good person. Straight, as hard as a steel blade. And Ned was terribly sorry that such a person would consider him a liar, insignificant, and not worthy of attention.

And also - Ned was surprised at how easily he began to communicate with people. His vocabulary, once limited by the words that are needed in the village, expanded incredibly, and Ned spoke as if it was not him, but the other - educated, experienced, able to speak and do things for which he would be responsible. Will always answer. So he will answer that no one will bother him.

From within Ned a black, cold rage rose up - he already knew it - so he felt when he was preparing to kill his next enemy. These two feelings - respect and hatred, got in the way of Ned's soul, merging into a contradictory ball, tearing his mind to pieces. And he gave vent to his rage, telling the master everything he thinks - despite the consequences.

"Do you-want-an apology ?! - the master asked coldly, with a disposition and looked attentively into the face of the strange guy - are you ready to answer for your words? Are you claiming that you were able to defeat a swordmaster with your bare hands? Are you ready to prove it?

- Ready - Ned twisted the corners of his mouth, and looked hard into the face of the master - will you apologize if I prove it?

- Yes. I'm sorry. And I will make all my students apologize - the master chuckled contemptuously - I propose to follow to my school, it is located one block away. You and I will go to the training ground ... no! One of my students will come to the training ground, and you will try to resist at least a minute against the swordsman. If you can, I will ask your forgiveness. If not, I'll whip you with a whip like a stupid donkey! I agree?

"No," Ned chuckled, "I disagree."

Behind, the guys began to make noise and laugh, the master turned away with a squeamish grimace, and Ned continued:

- I will only go against you. And if you lose - apologize, and I will lash you three times for acting like an unreasonable child! Do you agree to these terms? If I fail, you will do what you want. Well, is it weak?

- How are you talking to the master ?! - shouted Hagen - shut your mouth, mangy dog!

- Quiet! Okay, so be it! - the master answered coldly - let's follow me. And all of you, if you like. By the way - you will witness that this man himself volunteered to go to battle. So that later there would be no talk that the insidious townspeople attacked him.

A block later, all the honest company was at a long one-story building of red brick. There were no signs or any signs indicating that the building belonged to any kind of activity.

A door unlocked with a large brass key and doorknobs polished with many hands. There is a large hall inside. In the twilight it is not visible - what hangs on the walls, the outlines of various types of weapons are guessed, the pictures depicting fighters in various fighting poses are white, there are benches and battle poles for training.

- Hagen - lanterns. All there is. To the yard. One lantern - here!

The master's speech was abrupt, harsh, like a person accustomed to giving commands. Ned thought that he looked a lot like Sergeant Drankon - just as wise over the years, tough, as if carved from an old tree root, so hard that axes bounced off.

The master went to the wall, lost in the dusk of the evening shadows, took one sword without a scabbard from the wall, nodded his head:

- Come on!

Ned followed, probing the master's thoughts. He thought:

"Strange guy. Either he's crazy, or ... no, it can't be! For a boy his age to have such a skill is impossible! And if it's true? What if I lose? Tyraz, don't make yourself laugh! Who will you lose? This puppy? It's impossible, it's ridiculous! Well, what if? If a?! Then I will fulfill what we agreed on. There are no options. Why did you arrange all this? Why do you need all this? Then - that it is right. If he lies, he will be punished. And the pupils will have a lesson - lies are punishable. If a guy is SUCH a master - which I'm not sure at all - everyone will learn a lesson. Both he and my students. And I. Only that would not cripple him ... a dull sword, of course. This is not a mortal fight. But stupid ones can also be killed. And also - do not humiliate the guy especially strongly. It seems to me that it has a core. Look how he hoisted for the honor of the uniform - that's good, that's right. And also - something is wrong. He is completely confident in his abilities. It's strange. And very, very interesting! "

The wide courtyard, enclosed by the walls of the building, was flooded with light from large lanterns. Apparently the guys stole everything that was in the school here. Ned chuckled - for some reason he had to fight constantly by the lanterns. As if such things require the cover of the night.

- Are you satisfied with the lighting? Do you need something for the fight? Go to the toilet, drink, undress?

- Take off your clothes and take off your shoes - Ned answered immediately - and warm up first. I need some time to get ready.

- Good. You can change in the locker room, or put your things here, on the bench - the foreman pointed to one of the wide benches along the wall of the building - don't worry, no one will touch anything here. All to be silent! Not a sound! And in the meantime, I'll stretch myself ...

Ned calmly unbuttoned his uniform, took it off and folded it neatly, laid it on the bench. From the pockets of his pants he laid out the contents - money, the key to the room, put it next to him. He took off his wallet with coins from his belt - he took with him twenty gold - just in case. Well, he took as much as he could. He left the rest in the room, throwing it on the bed. Although there are already less than twenty gold pieces left - he left one gold with the women, part of the second he spent on gifts.

The guys sitting on the benches watched his actions with interest and thought: "Here is a beast! Look how much money! And sergeants make good money! If such an idiot gets so much - I, with my abilities, will advance far! No - you definitely have to go to the army! "

Ned chuckled under his breath at these boyish thoughts, then turned off his thoughts. It will distract from the battle, and from the preparation for the battle. And he knew for sure that the success of his fight depends on this "warm-up". Master Tiraz is not a stoned Shentel for you! This one is a terrible weapon. Ned knew that for sure. But besides, for all that, he knew that he could and should compete with him. Why - I didn't know yet. But I should.

Ned kicked off his boots, thought for a moment, and pulled off his uniform pants - so that there was not the slightest restraint of movement. The guys rustled in surprise, discussing what had happened, then someone laughed, but immediately fell silent, crushed by the heavy gaze of the master. He approvingly watched the preparations, noting that while the guy was doing everything that was needed. If you want to win, there should be no trifles!

Ned took off his shirt, too, remaining in only linen shorts, which were rather wide and did not interfere with movement. Then he walked out to the area used for classes on days when it didn't rain.

It was a flat stone surface, paved with slabs, through which thin grass sprouted in places, which was mercilessly eradicated by the disciples, but still crawling towards the sun and freedom.

Ned stood on the landing, and forgetting about everyone who was around, began a ritual dance.

He bent low to the ground, poured like mercury, jumped up and froze in unthinkable positions, turning off his consciousness and surrendering to what was stored in his brain. Ned felt the energy called "tsu", the energy of the universe, the energy of strength and joy pouring into him through many invisible pores and channels. It filled with her like a vessel that had not seen this intoxicating drink for a long time, power poured into Ned like a mountain stream, like a sea tide, filling his muscles with power.

The disciples watched Ned open-mouthed, his body glistening in the light of the lanterns, covered in beads of sweat that had protruded from the pores, and the scars, until then invisible, appeared and became visible, like a grid drawn on Ned by a mad artist.

Master Tiraz looked at Ned with wide eyes. He even left his warm-up to watch the stranger and did not regret it. Something strange was going on - the master who knew what he thought was everything about martial arts - DON'T KNOW what Ned was doing! No - he understood that he was taking on the power of tsu, pumped up by special exercises, but this style of connecting with tsu was completely unfamiliar to Tiraz, and he, shocked, watched the guy, already regretting that he had treated him so rudely.

It was evident from everything that this is the Master. No one else could have done all these transitions, dives, punches and kicks with such precision, with such skill. All movements were calibrated to perfection - nothing superfluous, no sweeping characteristic of young students - even promising ones, but practicing not very long ago - no, every movement is verified to its smallest stage, to the very point at which the body once again froze in an unthinkable position ...

Finally, Ned finished his exercises and stood in front of the master, hands down at the seams.

- I'm ready!

The master nodded his head, not approaching Ned, got into a fighting stance, and said:

- The fight will be over if one of the opponents, or both, cannot continue. Or if one of the opponents declares that he is giving up. Let's start!

The master, with short side steps, went forward to the guy who was calmly standing, and suddenly he made a loud hiss, from which several guys on the bench shuddered, and bent low to the ground, took a strange pose that an ordinary person could not repeat. His arms twisted, resembling a tangle of snakes, darted in the air, as if striking blows with poisonous teeth, and his body moved, flowing from pose to pose.

Oh Gods! Where from ?! How? Snake style? Lost and Forgotten! - the master instantly understood - guy, who are you?

But there was no time to think - unless, of course, he wanted to get a whip on the back.

Tyraz entered combat mode, and his sword flashed like a swallow, trying to sting this "snake", wriggling and instantly moving in space. The sword slid between the "heads" of the "snakes", trying to cut them off, but each time they gently moved the blade to the side, and it either clicked on the slabs of the platform, then buried itself in emptiness, finding instead of a living body, whose blood dreamed of drinking, only disappointment and annoyance.

The master accelerated the movement speed to the maximum. His sword merged into a glittering fan-shaped band, and suddenly - raz! - flew out of the hand of a man, frozen motionless, like a statue.

No one, not even himself, had time to notice an instant hit to a point on the forearm and another blow to the neck. These were not even strokes, they were two-finger pinpoints.

"Snake bite" was the name of these touches, through which the force of the tsu poured into the enemy with incredible speed and force, affecting the body and paralyzing his muscles. If Ned wanted, he could kill Master Tyraz. Or cripple him. Or ... in general - to do whatever he needs. And he could not oppose anything. The one who was once Ned was as much superior to Master Tiraz in skill as Master Tiraz towered over his disciples.

The sword that flew out of the master's hand flashed in the air and with such force hit the bench next to the guys who were numb from what they saw that, despite the roundness of the blade, it stuck into a piece of wood and broke off a large chip from it.

Ned walked over to Hagen, looked into his face with black sunken eyes and quietly asked:

- Are you happy? Or do you want some more proof?

- Sorry ... those - said the guy hoarsely, coughing, as if a bag of dust had filled his throat - forgive us! Honestly - I'm sorry!

Ned once again looked searchingly into the guy's eyes, then nodded his head in satisfaction and went up to the motionless master and made a series of point touches in different parts of the body. The latter is in the temple area.

Tyraz settled on the outstretched hands of Ned, he gently grabbed him and carried him to the bench. The master was gasping for air and coughing, moving away from the paralysis - all the time while he was paralyzed, the respiratory system did not work. He gasped, realizing that he was about to die. The muscles brought together by the spasm did not obey, a little more, and Tyraz would have died of suffocation.

The master left in five minutes. His face went from pale to rosy red, his hands stopped shaking, and all his muscles returned to normal.

Tyraz got to his feet and looked at Ned, collecting his things, and wondering how he would rinse - he did not want to put on a clean new uniform over his sweaty body. Then he went into the building, a few seconds later he appeared and with a firm step approached Ned, fell to his knees, burying his forehead in the stones of the site. Then, under the deathly silence of his disciples, he said:

- Master! Forgive me for my arrogance! Forgive me for being unworthily rude to you and did not believe your words! You have the right to whip me with a whip! I deserve it! Take it!

On the outstretched hands of Tiraz lay a black leather whip, woven from thin threads, about a meter long. He sometimes drove her careless students, and now he himself had to be punished.

Ned accepted the whip, turned it over in his hands, then threw it in the direction with a grin.

- Stop it. Stand up please. Better tell me where I can wash myself, otherwise it smells like a goat. Are there showers?

Tiraz got up from his knees, sighed imperceptibly - it's still unpleasant to be beaten with a whip, even if for the cause, then said:

- Come on, I'll show you. I'll give you a towel, soap. And you bastards guard your clothes and money! And don't go anywhere - I'll talk to you.

Taking Ned to the shower room, the master returned, stood in front of the students, silently looked at Hagen, then asked, pushing out the words heavily:

- Have you seen?
- We saw! - the students answered discordantly.
- What did you see?
- Nuuu ... he fought strangely somehow. I have never seen such a style. And I hadn't heard of that - Hagen shrugged his shoulders - it was strange ... and beautiful. He was ... like a snake!
- This is the style of the Snake - the master explained dryly - an ancient, forgotten style. I'm not asking that. What did you saw? Nascar?

"We saw how arrogance was punished. And we learned that no matter how confident a person is in his abilities, there is always something that can defeat him. And that you can't offend a stranger. He may turn out to be a great master. So, Master Tiraz?

- So. Well done, Nascar. And to you - here! - Tyraz several times strongly lashed with a whip on the back and shoulders of Hagen - this is for your rudeness! This is for you rudeness! This is for your arrogance and stupidity! But this - he slapped him crosswise so that Hagen was led in pain - for me! For dragging me into history and I almost died! Do you understand that I was in the balance of death? If the master had not removed my paralysis, I would have suffocated and died before your eyes! And rightly so. I deserve it. You are a young fool, and I ... I am a master. I had to feel, predict. But I could not see a great master in a simple boy! And now - humiliation, shame, shame! Remember this day forever, hammer it into your head - so it will be with everyone who makes such a mistake. And it may not end the way it did today! He could have killed you on the street in seconds, instantly taking the soul out of you! Do you know why he didn't? Say thank you to your father and mother, you fool! For their sake, he did not touch you and endured your mockery. And he refused to beat me with a whip, out of respect for me, which I do not deserve, and I will beat myself! Tyraz slapped himself hard on the back several times. Then he began to whip everyone in a row - to the right, to the left!

- Everything, everything deserved - you, because you did not stop these blockheads, I - because I missed the education of my students. Everyone is to blame! And they were punished. And now remember this forever. Do you remember, Hagen?

- Why don't you remember when your whole back itches, teacher! - he hummed offendedly - I suppose all now in scars!

- That's good, that's right - Tiraz chuckled as he watched Ned leave the shower - get up and greet the Master! It's time to ask for forgiveness, ohlomons!

Chapter 14

- Good. I see - you know - Drankon nodded in satisfaction, looking at Ned, sweating with mental effort. For the last two hours, he chased him on all points of the military regulations, according to the regulations, according to the regulations of the guard service. Ned puffed, but stood to death like Corps.

For four days he sat non-stop at the base, and crammed, crammed, crammed, until finally he came to Drankon and said - I'm ready!

"Listen carefully, Ned... there is one truth you must learn - you are not alone. You are not a lonely fighter! A company behind you, one hundred and fifty lives. And you must make sure that they come out alive from the battle. But the main thing is that they completed the task. It often happens that the second is more important than the first. And then ... then many will not return from the battle. But your task is to make sure that the number of non-returners is as small as possible. You must take this into account. But in general - well done. When did you have time to memorize? During these days? Head! Honestly, it was much more difficult for me. - Drankon got up from his place, went to the window, looking at the parade ground, where soldiers were moving in orderly rows, and added - listen to what I want to tell you ... you are now an officer. You are the one who sends these people to their death. And tell me - how can you send them to die if they are your close friends?

- You mean Oidar and Arnot?

- Yes. They sit in your room every day, you constantly communicate with them. Do you understand that this is not accepted? What are you now an officer, and you should have other friends? Friendship between soldiers and officers is not accepted in the Corps, moreover, it is not welcomed. Consider this.

- I will not stop being friends with the guys! - Ned pressed his lips stubbornly - no matter what regulations require it!

- For some reason, I did not doubt it - Drankon grinned - okay, let's leave this conversation. Friends themselves will remain in the past, over time. Someday you will understand me. Soon you will have no common interests. There will be nothing to talk about ... and the friendship will crumble by itself. Now about the case. You need to learn how to wield a sword. I've seen you work for them - not bad for a recruit, but not bad enough for an officer.

- I am good at fighting with a spear, why do I need a sword?

- You are an officer, and most likely, you will go on this career path and further - or I don't understand anything in life. So - the sword is an integral part of the officer's uniform - in certain circumstances. At parades, at court, in society - where it is supposed to put on a ceremonial uniform. In order for you to carry on your side not a piece of iron, but a Sword, you must be able to wield it. You never know what happens in life - sometimes you need to go into battle right from the parade. Maybe you have to protect your commander. Or even a king. And how can you do this without knowing how to fight with a sword? Hand to hand? Against multiple swords and people in armor? With a sword, you have a chance, hand-to-hand - hardly. And the duel? If you are challenged to a duel? By the way, duels are widespread at court. And they all fight with swords. Nobody will let you swing a spear - as you did here. Here it was all taken for granted, but in the capital it will not work. They will laugh. Break your career. You must wield a sword. Everything. Learn. Look for someone who can teach you.

- How did the other officers study?

- I personally studied with comrades, with other officers. And in battle. How are others? Differently. Some hired a teacher, and some were taught by relatives. You are getting a good salary, so you can afford to hire a teacher. And do it as quickly as possible. In two months we are going to war. The Colonel is trying to take the time to train the recruits as best he can, but ... he is not omnipotent. Soon, soon ... Well, that's it, walk. You have three more days of rest - relax, rest - it is possible that for a long time you will not have such an opportunity. Walk, walk - I also need to rest. Today is my day off, and I'm spending on you. And I have a better use of my free time than looking at your dull face. By the way, Ned, do you ever laugh? You smile - you saw it. And so, barely, as if strained. Have you ever laughed heartily, excitedly? It was so?

- I don't remember - Ned answered seriously - maybe he was laughing. Honestly, life has not taught me to laugh.

- Hmm ... hmm. Me too - admitted Drankon - I hope at least you will learn this.

Leaving the sergeant, Ned went to his room, kicked off his boots and lay down on the bed, throwing his hands behind his head. So Drankon put everything on the shelves, and there is nothing to argue. And about friends - too. Their lives drifted apart like two field roads. They went their own way and Ned went his own. At the last meeting, Ned noticed that he had a hard time keeping up a conversation with the guys - what to talk about? He did not talk about his trip to the city. Why? I didn't know myself. Maybe because he didn't want to cause envy? He already felt that the guys were jealous of him. Especially Oidar, a rather vain and proud person. His thoughts were like an open book to Ned. Because - he now began to be slightly wary of the guy. Very unpleasant shoots can grow from the seeds of envy ...

It occurred to me - now, with his ability to read minds, it will be very difficult to find friends, and maybe a woman he loves. Almost impossible. After all, he hears their thoughts - which means that they will not be able to lie to him. At first it seems - it's good! You know that this person is transparent to you, you hear all his thoughts, you recognize all his thoughts. But then ... then it turns into a curse. Why did he have to hear Oydar think: "Why is he so lucky? What did he deserve, redneck? I'm more worthy! And he does not want to reveal his secrets to me - a friend is called! Maybe not a friend at all? An upstart and a good-for-nothing! " What would have happened if Ned hadn't recognized his thoughts? Nothing. But when I found out - immediately alertness, immediately thinking - today he only envies, and tomorrow?

Ned has been trying to turn off his mind lately. Not to hear what people think. In order not to be disappointed in them. This gift is more suited to some king who has no friends, but only subjects, and who needs to know what they think in order to avoid a conspiracy. Why such a gift to a simple sergeant? Not a gift, but some kind of curse!

Reflections were interrupted by a knock on the door, Ned responded, and heard the voice of Geresard, with whom he had not seen for several days. Didn't happen. Or rather - Ned in every possible way eluded meetings. Why? It seemed to him that Geresard would be unpleasant to be reminded of what had happened in his house. The doctor is a good man, and therefore every time he will suffer, looking at Ned, worry that this has happened. And Ned will see how Geresard is worried, and will also be upset. Why would he?

"Ned, it's me! Need to talk. Let me come in!

Ned sighed, and reluctantly got out of bed, opened the door. Geresard cautiously tumbled into the room, shaking the floor like a cabman's cart, looked around, hummed in satisfaction:

- So I imagined! The austere dwelling of a warrior, nothing superfluous, nothing for the soul - everything for the war. May I sit down?

- Sit down, of course! - Ned nodded - there is nothing to treat, I eat in the dining room.

- Yes, you do not need treats - Geresard sank with a sigh on a piteously creaking chair under him, and sadly said - I'm getting old, I guess! In his youth, he could stand on his feet for days on end - to do operations, heal, or even drink all day and night. And now? Walked a little - you have to sit down. I worked a little - I'm tired! Can you lose some weight? Something fat began to choke me, the belly grew. You think - why bother, huh? Waste my time? I want to talk. No, not about that day - of course, I'm uncomfortable that it happened, but ... I'm even glad that it happened. Funny, huh? Not because I'm glad you were offended. I have already given them for it so that they will not forget. And because you showed me how illusory everything in my house is - order, peace. And how much I missed my guys. Oddly enough - I came to you to consult - what to do with them. They want to join the army, but I don't know What do i do. The funny thing is that my wife doesn't mind, but I, who have served in the Corps all my life, are against it! To whom you tell - they will laugh! I wanted them to do medicine like I did. Or they became merchants. Or ... in general - to everyone except the military. Do you know how many crippled, dying people passed through my hands? Chopped up, shot, crushed? How can I imagine that one of them is my son, and ... hands down. I don't know if you will understand me ... you are very young, but it seems to me that you are much wiser than many adults. I feel like you've been through a lot, right? So, you don't have to answer. And you have to understand both me and my guys. After all, you are the same age with them. By the way, you know, I mentioned you yesterday, they somehow looked at me strangely, and said that they were fools, and very much regret that they treated you so. And that they were wrong. The mother was even surprised. Did you communicate with them after that? However, it doesn't matter. So what about the army?

"You know what…" Ned thought, "I would suggest this: if they see only a beautiful shell in the army, show them the wrong side! Ask the colonel to take them as recruits - two months before we leave for the war. Let them run around in all their harness, march with everyone, dig out the night fortifications, get sticks for their slowness - if they endure all this, and still want to join the army, then let them go. By the way, they will see what life is like for an ordinary soldier. Maybe then they will start to appreciate their subordinates. Yes, and arrogance will come off them. And you will know where they are during the day.

- Exactly - contented Geresard nodded his head - so I will! But how to make sure that no one knows that they are my children, so that without indulgences? But these are already details. This is my business. Thanks. Sorry to interfere with your vacation!

- Nothing. I myself was going to leave now - Ned smiled - I'm going to town. It is foolish not to take advantage of the last days of your vacation by sitting in the barracks. Tell me, is there a shop somewhere that sells books and scrolls? In the city, I mean.

- Yes … there is one shop - Geresard looked at Ned with respect - do you want to educate yourself? Right. It will come in handy. It is in the center, next to the temple square, is the Khurad shop. Everything is there - from treatises on mathematics to romance novels. True - the prices are not sparing enough. But everything is there. Everything, everything - I'm leaving! Thank you.

Geresard stomped to the door and pulled the handle, almost tearing it off by the roots, until he realized that the door was opening outward. He grunted, shaking the room, and went outside, leaning the door as if it were glass.

Ned looked after the doctor, grinned, and began to get ready. In ten minutes he was already approaching the gates of the base.

- Hi Sergeant! - the guard standing at the gate winked - listen, I have one thing to do with you.

- What's the matter? - Ned frowned, looking into the broad innocent face of the soldier.

- Yes, here … you know a certain Sanda?

- What kind of Sandu? - Ned was taken aback - I don't know any Sanda. I hardly know anyone in the city. And who is it?

The girl is alone. He comes every day and tries to enter the base to look for some young sergeant. Of course, no one lets her in. Colonel's order - civilian entrance only by passes. And what sergeant? Who would give her to walk around the base and look in the face of all the sergeants? Maybe some kind of sorceress ... So I thought - isn't it Ned? And the girl is beautiful - uhhh! Ritar tried to roll up to her, he thought she was bargaining with herself, but no - she punched him like that, you could hear from here! Ritar, how did you get it from the girl?

- Got it! - the soldier grinned, looking out of the booth above the gate - a heavy little hand. Like our sergeant. By the way - there she is! It goes! Look, sergeant - you know, no?

Ned looked with interest at the road, intrigued by the story, and saw in the distance a light figure in a white, fluttering dress. From here it was not visible who was walking, but for some reason his heart skipped a beat, beat, fluttered like a leaf in the wind.

Ned nodded to the soldiers and went to meet the girl. When there were a hundred steps left to her, he recognized - the saleswoman! The candy store clerk he kissed!

Ned slowed down a little, looking incredulously at the girl's face, she went faster, faster, faster ... and finally ran! With acceleration, she rushed to Ned, almost knocking him down and grabbing him with both hands, biting into her lips, closing her eyes, and sniffling, trying to do two things at the same time - to catch my breath, and ...

Then she looked up from the stunned guy, and still panting from running, she said:

- Got it! I returned your kiss to you! I've been catching you here for four days, and yet I found you! And now I won't let go!

The girl grabbed Ned, who had fallen into a stupor by the arm, turned to the guards who watched with a grin, waved her hand cheerfully and pulled her companion along the road towards the city.

- Here! And he said - does not know her - the guard shook his head incredulously - that's why it was necessary to lie!

- And the guy is not a miss - the second grinned - I would have gone after her to the ends of the world! Well, what a girl! Just death to the men! It's scary to even approach such a person - it was not made for ordinary people.

- Was that why you drove up to her the day before yesterday? And I was not afraid! Or maybe I did it in my pants out of fear, I should have sniffed you! - the first laughed.

- You fool ... - the second gently brushed aside - I thought she came to earn some money. I was ready to give all the weekly salary for such a beauty! And I would give ... I would give anything, if only she came running like this and threw herself on my neck!

- Yeah ... we do not shine like that - the second guard sighed - as always, who cho, and who nicho! Someone has awards, fame, money, beautiful women. And someone is a checkpoint of a fucking parade ground! Well, where is the justice ?!

"Exactly ... last week the sergeant told me - you have a rust stain on your scabbard!" Can you imagine? This bitch found a spot on me and deducted a silver coin from my salary! What a bastard! And the fact that I stand in the sun all the time, under the open sky, everything is gathering dust - is that nothing? And by the way, they don't pay us enough. I've heard from the sailors ...

And the soldiers, as always, moved on to the standard whining about what kind of bastards bosses are, and what they are, unfortunate servants, and how little they get and how much they work - already completely forgetting about Ned, about his girlfriend, and in general about everything, besides what was the main thing in their life ... * * *

- Where are we going?

- Who cares?! - the girl laughed happily - what is your name?

"Hmm… my name is Ned. Ned the Black.

- Why black? Don't you wash yourself? No?! Clean. You smell like soap. Will. Glaaadeny like that! And I'm Sanda. Sanda Nitul. Where were you going to go? Let's go together?

- Let's go - hesitated a little, Ned said, bewildered, half-turning looking at the top of his new acquaintance, shiny, smelling of herbs. She was just on his shoulder - small, neat.

- Somewhere there is a shop of Khurad - do you know where it is?

- Sure! We buy books there for school! - Sanda beamed - let's go, I'll show you.

- What about your job? Who stayed in the shop?

- Oh! The shop is generally a story. Skaandaaal! I told my mother that I would go to look for my fiancé. They thought I was crazy. Swearing - already horror. Then dad said that let the girl take a walk, maybe she really will meet someone. And then in this shop he does not see anyone, some old women and women, greedy for sweets. Men, they say, do not come here, but she needs to arrange life, and they have grandchildren to nurse. Mom immediately calmed down. If she knew who I was going to!

- And to whom? - Ned smiled slightly, catching the cabby's eyes. One he would have run faster, but having a girl hanging like a weight on his hand, they will drag to the center for a long time.

- Nuuu ... to you!

- And who am I?

- Are you kidding me? Sergeant! Who else?

- I'm not asking about that. Who am i? What do you know about me? Except that I walked into your shop and kissed you on the cheek. What else? Am I a killer? Maybe a sorcerer? Black magician? Maybe ... anything! And you throw yourself on my neck? Why on earth? Maybe I'll drag you into the bushes now and use your innocence!

- Right now? - the girl laughed - maybe you can at least rent a hotel room? It's not very pleasant in the bushes. True, the girls told me that the first time was not pleasant at all, but painful.

- Listen, what are you talking about ?! You're crazy? - Ned stopped, grabbed the girl by the shoulder and turned sharply to him - go away! Leave now! Home, go home! You throw yourself at the first comer and you are ready to lie under it at that very moment! What are you ?! Stunned ?! Leave now!

The girl went out and looked at Ned with lost eyes. Then she turned and walked slowly along the road, bumping into passers-by and not paying attention to the abuse and shocks. Ned was already turning away from her when he noticed how a hefty cart, drawn by two horses, was rolling straight onto Sandu, and the driver, swearing, was pulling the reins - where was it? Several thick logs lying in the cart do not allow the horses to stop immediately. The bityugs wheeze, drop foam, but the cart is slowly approaching the girl, as in a dream.

Ned let out a belly roar and rushed forward as fast as he could to snatch the girl out from under the horses' hooves.

She hung limply in his hands, like a rag doll, and when he began to pull at her, she just silently shook her head, not understanding what they wanted from her.

Suddenly a noise hit Ned's ears - the horses were whinnying, a carter was swearing loudly, a woman was screaming shrilly. Only then did he realize that everything happened in some moments. For him, they passed like minutes ...

The girl looked at him with wide open eyes and was silent, then she stretched and hugged his neck, pressing her cheek and bursting into tears:

- I am not like this! I'm not like that at all! I've been looking for you for four days ... waiting ... looking for ... and you! And you! - she pulled back, swung and punched Ned on the cheek so that his ears rang, and in his head flashed: "Her handle is heavy!" Precisely heavy.

- You need to go home! - Ned lifted Sanda, brushed off the stained hem as best he could, and taking her hand, led him in the direction where her parents' shop was. Sanda dragged limply behind, moving her legs as if they were made of wood, showing with all her appearance how she was against the violence committed by the guy.

Ned stubbornly dragged her along until he got tired of it:

- So what are you portraying? Good. Let's talk! - he moved his head from side to side, noticed something like a tavern, with a white sign depicting a cup and a curling steam above it, and resolutely pulled Sanda there.

In a few minutes they were already sitting on soft chairs at a table in an office that looked like offices in an officer's mess.

- What will you order? Asked a plump, pretty waiter with a white lace apron in front.

"I don't know what you serve..." Ned hesitated. "Something for the girl. A drink, something tastier. Well, me ... something. You know best what they take the most.

- Good! - the girl smiled cheerfully - a funny order, but I understand you. And the wine? Will you order? And yet - we have separate offices with a lockable door and a long couch ... would you like to?

- No. We do not wish - Ned blushed, not looking at the amused Sanda - just bring something better, that's it.

The servant went off to carry out the order, and Ned pulled a finger into his mouth to bite off a piece of a nail. He brought it to his mouth ... and changed his mind. He's an officer now, and an officer shouldn't walk around with bitten nails — Drankon had told him that. Yes, and he himself understood - one must observe decency. Learn manners.

Grimacing in annoyance, he turned to Sanda, wiping her tears with a napkin. I noted for myself - there was no paint on it, which is usually used by girls to seduce men. Sanda herself was so fresh and beautiful that even a tear-stained face with reddened and swollen eyelids did not spoil her.

Ned carefully turned on his supersensible perception, determined to listen to what she was thinking. Weird girl...

"How cute he is, though a bastard! But I love him anyway! Madness ... am I out of my mind? He thought I was a whore! And it was her own fault - why did she start chatting ?! Shame ... she told him everything, even girlish secrets. What's wrong with me ... oh, I can't ... how he looks with his eyes - at least where with him! Into the bushes? Let's go to the bushes! Sweetheart ... sweetheart ... sweetheart ... Is it really love? Is this love ?! I don't want her! She is like a thief, she, like a robber, jumped out of the alley with a knife and thrust it into my heart! What's wrong with me ... sometimes hot, sometimes cold ... but what difference does it make to me who you are, you fool? I can't live without you, that's all! And let the whole world collapse! The main thing is that you are next to me ... look at me, look ... I melt under your gaze ... Fool! And I didn't believe in love? Selera, you punished me! And I am happy..."

Ned shyly turned off his "hearing" and leaned back in his chair, looking around - and the establishment he found it difficult. The hall was almost empty, only two couples were sitting in the corners - well-dressed, well-groomed, women in veils that hid their faces. Some kind of apprehension emanated from them, and Ned, interested, decided to listen - what kind of people are they?

"... If only nobody knew... he will kill me... Orman is so jealous! Well, what if I sit with a friend's husband! We're not making love, are we? By the way - why not? I want him ... I wonder if he will offer? ... "

Ned shyly shut off from the young woman's thoughts — everything was clear. You could have guessed it yourself. A tavern for couples, where you can quietly retire with a girlfriend or boyfriend. And most of all he was embarrassed that it turned out to be the wife of Sergeant Orman from the third company of crossbowmen.

Lost in thought, he did not notice how the waiter came up and began to put on the table what she had brought on the tray. She put everything on the table, promised that she would come up again, and left, looking favorably at the cute couple.

- You are angry at me? - Sanda asked unexpectedly - I really behaved like a fool! I told you everything ... I don't know myself why. Or rather, I know. Love you. And I don't care what you are and who you are. It happens so! Fall in love with the first guy you meet. Do not believe? And rightly so. I don't believe myself. Some kind of glamor. I'll do anything for you. Everything!

- Will you even go home? And won't you come back? Smiled Ned.

"I don't promise you," Sanda chuckled.

- That means not everything. So you're lying! - Ned smiled even wider - why did you rush under the wheels? The cart would crush you, that's all. How is it possible?

- Why did you chase me away? I wanted to die. I would come home and hang myself. And you would be to blame.

- You're crazy! Surely she's crazy - Ned snorted - to commit suicide for the sake of a stranger !? How does your head work, okay?

- And nothing unfamiliar! I know - your name is Ned! - Sanda laughed merrily, loudly, so that a couple sitting at the table looked back at them. The girl covered her mouth with her hand and said in a strangled voice:

- Sorry! Behaving indecent!

"That's for sure," Ned laughed.

He felt good. Sitting in a beautiful tavern, decorated with gilding and stucco molding, on an expensive soft chair, in front of a beautiful girl declaring her love for him, in front of delicious dishes on a polished table - isn't that happiness? Wasn't that what he once dreamed of? Or rather, I never even dreamed of it. I dreamed of a girl. I saw in dreams and in reality how he hugs, undresses Sally, strokes her ...

O demons! - Ned felt himself become aroused, looking at the chirping Sanda and with an effort of will made the erotic pictures go out. What can I say - youth, there is youth. It is impossible not to imagine a beautiful girl in your arms, and even if she did everything she could for this.

For several minutes they ate in silence what they brought them. And it was tasty - some salads with incomprehensible filling, some buns, spicy, salty, sweet. The pies are not clear with what - Ned was surprised, biting off another piece, and Sanda with visible pleasure absorbed everything that stood in front of her, not caring about her waist. Catching Ned's gaze, she explained with a smile:

- I'm not getting fat, don't be afraid. I eat like a cow, not get fat! Mom is always indignant - she just has to look at a piece of pie, and then she is bursting with leaps and bounds, and as I was thin, I remain. All in the father. He's thin too. He was told: "The pastry chef must be fat! If you don't get fat from your cakes, then you don't eat them! So they are tasteless! So everyone will think! " He just laughs and says that he has special cakes for those who don't want to get fat. And that's why all the ladies come to us.

- Some strange pies - said Ned, carefully examining the filling - what do they put here? I don't even understand.

- Didn't you know? - giggled Sanda, holding her mouth with her palm - these are pies with exciting herbs! Well ... for those men who want to but can't. By the way - you are already eating the third pie ...

- Khe-khe ... - Ned with difficulty swallowed what he managed to bite off (Don't spit it out on the table ?! It's ugly!) - where did we even get?

"This is a lovers' tavern. It's called "The Hand of Selera" - Sanda winked - I always wanted to sit here, but there was no one with whom. Thanks for inviting me here. And what, they cook deliciously here. And it's cozy here, isn't it? Can I sit closer to you? - the girl got up, and moving the chair closer to Ned sat down so that her knees touched the boy's thigh. She gently rubbed her thigh with her knee, and Ned felt with displeasure that he was getting aroused again.

He caught a glance at the handler, nodded to her, she came up, smiling radiantly, like the sun after rain:

- Anything else for you? Can you still go to a separate office?

- No - Ned answered a little hoarsely, trying not to notice Sanda's intrigues - I want to pay off. How much do I have to pay?

- Eight pieces of silver - the waiter said slightly disappointedly, and having received the gold piece, she said - now I will bring the change. Can you still think about it? No? Well now ...

She departed like a ship sailing through the hall, and Sanda put her hand on Ned's thigh.

- Maybe we'll sit still, eh? It's so good here! Expensive, of course ... but good! I always imagined this day like this: my fiance, I ... and he invites me to marry him! Right in this tavern! He kneels down, hands me a wedding bracelet, and ...

- Take your hand ... yeah, like that. And sit back. Now I will take you home, you wash, go to bed and rest. And in the morning everything will be the same again - no sergeants, no fairy tales that you have invented for yourself. Where did you get all this? Did you read romantic books for ladies, or what?

- Well, I read it! And what is it ?! - the girl pouted her lips offendedly - love at first sight, so what? You are beautiful, strong, I am beautiful - isn't it beautiful? Here. And why can't there be love between us? Why are you making yourself hard to touch? Actually, I must resist, and you try to paw me and drag me into the office! Listen, maybe you ... love men? Well ... sorry, you don't have to make such a face! Well, she blurted out! Sorry!

"That's the worst offense to a corps officer, you fool. Never say such words again! - Ned managed hard - now let's deal with your feelings. You know me for four days, of which one fleeting kiss and sitting in this cafe are worth attention. And you declare that you are ready for me for anything, that you want me, that I am your fiancé - is that okay? No, tell me, is THIS normal?

- No, not normal - the girl answered easily - so what? Did it make me uglier? Less seductive? Why are you behaving as if I am a freak, and that communicating with me do you hardly bear?

- I feel sorry for you - Ned chuckled - you are young. How much
would you like? Sixteen? Yeah. And you don't know anything about
life. You throw yourself on the neck of the first person you meet,
who, as it seemed to you, is worthy of your love. And also - you
want to show your girlfriends what kind of guy you have! Wipe their
nose! What's wrong? So. Well, yes, you are in love with me. But this
is now. A week or two will pass, and you will think - what did I find
in this guy? Some kind of soldier! Lost at work all day long, and I
miss. What happened next? You must understand - I'll be leaving
soon, in two months. Whether I will return from the campaign or not
is unknown. I may die in battle. And if I come back - most likely, I
will be sent to the capital - to study to be a senior officer. And you
will stay with your parents. Wouldn't it be better to find a groom
here in the city? Someone who won't go anywhere and will not leave
a widow? Therefore, you need to think for a while, cool down and
not make hasty decisions. Yes, I like you. Yes, you turn me on. Yes,
you are very beautiful - one of the most beautiful women that I have
seen. But ... I have no right to ruin your life. I am a country boy who
by chance ended up in the army, I have a five-year contract. And I
have to do it. And I don't belong to myself. Do you understand this?
- I understand everything - Sanda frowned - you didn't like me,
you consider me a whore who can lie under any man, I'm a freak and
a fool! But I don't care! I will prove to you that it is not! I didn't tell
anyone what I told you! And I love you! Fuck them, your reasoning!
Shouldn't a well-bred girl put it that way? Fuck your good manners!
If I want to - I'll leave the house altogether! Tired of everything -
they bring up, educate, educate ... I found myself a man - so he
brings up! Ugh! Here's to all of you! - Sanda folded a neat muzzle
and twisted it in front of Ned - here, here, here! Will not be yours!
You chase me away - I will go to the base to the chief, I will say that
your mistress and wife, I will strive to be allowed to live where you
live! And if they don't let me, I'll catch you at the gate, wait, see you
off, walk behind like a dog! And you won't do anything to me! Only
if you kill! Here!
"Oh Gods! About Selera! What have you done to me! " - Ned
moaned to himself - "I put you only one silver piece, but what have
you done? You worked for the gold purse! Well, I asked for love,
but not the same! Why did you hang THIS on me? "
And it seemed to him that somewhere in the distance, high above,
there was a cheerful girlish laugh ...

They walked to Sanda's house for half an hour. She hung on Ned, kept telling him something, groping around with her eyes, trying to see one of her girlfriends-neighbors - do they see which guy Sanda grabbed?

Already near the door of the shop, Sanda grabbed Ned by the neck right on the street and kissed him hard on the lips. He smelled of fruit, freshness, and not to say that Ned did not like it.

Taking from Ned a firm promise that tomorrow they will see each other and he will come to visit her, Sanda stroked his cheek and flew up the stairs to the porch, blowing a kiss from there. Then she disappeared into the bowels of the pastry shop, under the approving smile of a plump lady, ascending to the shop for another portion of pastries that did not spoil her waist at all.

Ned quickly retreated from the shop, again striding towards the center. From time to time he looked around, as if he suspected that now this hurricane of passion would change his mind, and with a whoop would pounce on him from behind, so as never to let go of his hands. Ned smiled, but for some reason he felt good and calm in his soul - was there really at least one person in the world who was waiting for him and who was not indifferent to what would happen to him? However - he immediately scolded himself - and Geresard? He worries about him. And friends - those, too, probably are not indifferent to his fate. However ... who knows? If something happened to him, what would they do? Well, they will sit down, pour wine into mugs, remember: "He was a good guy. Of course it is sad!" They will drink, and ... they will go to the whores. Everything. There was Ned, and there is no Ned. And a woman ... she is different. After all, she can leave in this world part of Ned ... little "Ned". And then he won't completely die.

Scolding himself for stupid and strange thoughts, Ned continued on his way and forty minutes later again found himself in the Square of the Gods. This time he did not enter the temples, glancing especially disapprovingly at the temple of the goddess of love, proceeded further to where he noticed a huge wooden scroll-sign, fortified above the entrance to an inconspicuous house, painted with white, slightly yellowed lime. Without even asking passers-by, one could guess that this is the shop of the bookseller Khurad. * * *

- Greetings, young man! The bookseller was clean-shaven, dressed in a good suit, and a scarf around his neck, on which was a pin with a gleaming and shimmering jewel.

Ned immediately remembered his treasures - pearls - left on the seashore. I wonder how much they would cost in the city? It is clear that the buyers in the village paid only a fraction of the real price for the pearls. Ned didn't know exactly how much, but that price was enough to keep the families of the trappers relatively comfortable.

- Did you want to buy something? Or see the pictures? For a couple of coppers, I can offer you to look at books with pictures depicting poses for copulation - this is the treatise "The Art of Love, consecrated by the goddess Selera, presented by the royal draftsman Arut Snarsky" There are such pictures - you will see, you will never forget! Again, a young officer definitely needs to know how to please a lady! This promotes a career - the shopkeeper winked conspiratorially and made a dirty face.

Ned looked at the antics of the suspicious shopkeeper (He was suggestive of husbands) and asked coldly:

- What, all your books are devoted only to bed pleasures? Or have you decided that, due to my stupidity, I am not capable of anything else? Don't you feel like you're taking too much on yourself? Is there any other store here where I could buy the books I need without being insulted?

- ABOUT! Forgive me, for God's sake - the shopkeeper was confused, and even, as it seemed to Ned, he was slightly frightened - I didn't mean to offend you! Sorry - again! We are often visited by soldiers and officers, and they ... sorry, sorry! What would you like to purchase? Which of the books are you interested in? Invented stories? Historical treatises? Or maybe something from the sciences?

"You have to be more careful with these soldiers from the corps! Look how he looked! Look like a shark! That and look bite off his head! Really, what does he want? On the face - a boy, and shoulders - like a loader from the port. Handsome, handsome boy ... oh no! Throw out these thoughts! There they have such madness in the building - they kill for love with a man! Offer him - maybe hit, or even kill! No, no and NO. Today I am going to Elor's ... something we haven't seen for a long time. Somehow he will find another lover for himself. The last time something hinted that it was time to change something in his life. There is no acuteness of experience, you see! Scoundrel! I'll have to buy him a gift ... "

Ned, frowning, turned off his extrasensory perception, so as not to listen to all the nonsense that the man was carrying (If you can call him that after the pictures that Ned saw, overhearing his innermost thoughts), and once again scolded himself for listening to other people's revelations ... They did not bring him anything good. Now it was unpleasant for him to communicate with the seller.

However - he didn't like him from the very beginning, with the very first words he lowered Ned to the level of ... who? To whom did you put me down? - Ned chuckled - to the level of a soldier? Too early I got used to the role of an officer ... only a few days ago I was running around the parade ground with a spear at the ready, and now - I am already above the level of a soldier! Hmm ... in fact it is really higher. I myself did not notice how I began to reason differently. Before, I would not have thought to go to a bookstore. I am changing! I am constantly changing. And I would not say that I do not like it. Except ... it's scary. It's like it's not really me anymore. Or even - not me at all.

Ned stayed in the shop for more than an hour, breaking all the shelves, demanding to get more and more books, driving the shopkeeper to the frenzy, after the guy left, he began to look more like a street cleaner than a well-bred bookseller - the suit was covered in dust, and hung on a neckerchief web.

And we must clean up on time! And don't breed spiders! Ned thought gloatingly.

He forced the shopkeeper to get dozens of books and scrolls, rummage through the storerooms, and now Ned's bag, which he received right there, in the store (If only he could get out of here quickly!), Lay more than two dozen books and the same number of scrolls rolled into tight rollers on a wooden tube.

As the trader said, some of these scrolls are very, very ancient, and the sergeant will not be able to read them. However - perhaps he needs them for beauty? Therefore, he will receive them at half price. For ... for ... ten pieces of silver each!

The price was exorbitant - Ned read the thoughts in the merchant's mind of how happy he was to get rid of these scrolls - in the entire existence of the shop, no one had ever bought them. Simply because they cannot be read.

He even wanted to sell them to some scribe so that he would wash the ink off the strong thin skin on which these letters were written, using it again. But - it turned out that it was impossible to wash them off. The ancient ink, made from forgotten recipes, was so stable that it was not taken by any of the tricks used by modern alchemists to wash off paint. The scroll's skin would rather have shattered than the ink soaked into it would have disappeared.

In general - Ned became poorer by fifty gold, and richer by fifty texts, some of which he most likely will not be able to read. All these books and scrolls were about geography, about the origin of the world, about everything that interested Ned.

And also about magic. The shopkeeper, by the way, was very surprised to see Ned's interest in treatises on magic. He shrugged his shoulders in bewilderment when the guy demanded such books and said that the soldier definitely had no benefit from them, however - like everyone else. Not only are these books unsuitable for an ordinary person - if you do not have magical abilities, you will never be able to learn magic - they are also written in such an archaic and strange, allegorical language that it is a big, very difficult work to wade through the text. Especially - a course on demonology and curses - here the demons themselves will break their heads by examining the minds of magicians. But in general - the client is the client, and if Ned pays money, he has the right to get what he wants.

And Ned got it.

The next point of today's trip was the brothel. Ned had not planned to visit him. Moreover, after the last time he had an ambiguous impression of the "miracle" of the transformation from a boy into a man. But what was left for him after he ate pies with exciting herbs? (Demon Servant! Demon Sanda with her love ... with her lovely figure ... her smooth skin ... her adorable slim hips and full sweet-smelling lips ... ahhhh!)

Osara this time was shocked by his enthusiasm, and when the guy left (much earlier than the time required - throwing out all the charge of passion and lust) - she sat for a long time in the bath, exhausted, like a loader after a hard day unloading a five-mast ship, and with sadness I thought that she was jealous of the girl that this guy was thinking about today, lying on her.

It was not difficult to guess that he was making love today not with Osara, but with a woman unknown to her. She hadn't noticed such a violent, growling passion last time. And besides, the client tried not to look his partner in the face. And yet - at the most acute moment he moaned: "Sanda! Oooh ... Sanda! "

And once again Osara sadly thought that it was time for her to complete this labor activity. Maybe then she will come across such a guy, instead of fat, old rich men and pimply youngsters who saved up to visit a woman for a whole year ... However, she understood that such guys just don't walk the streets and they have long been tucked into the hands of nimble rivals. And it saddened her even more * * *

Now Ned was faced with the most important thing, for which he, in fact, went into the city. Everything else was secondary.

The guy on duty at the school door looked curiously at Ned, who was loaded with a heavy bag. When he introduced himself, said who he was, and asked to invite the master, the boy opened his eyes wide, as if he saw the appearance of Kualtuk, instantly disappearing into the bowels of the school, like a drop falling behind a hot stove. Shshshshikh! - and no.

The master came out a minute later. He bowed ceremoniously to Ned, which caused more confusion in the ranks of the boys peeking from behind him and goggling with sparkling excitement eyes. Then he said with a slight smile:

- I knew you would be back. Thank you for honoring us with your visit.

- I have a request for you ... - began Ned, and the master immediately interrupted him:

- Nothing on the street. Let's go to school, sit down at the table with an invigorating drink - by the way, it's time for me to take a break, I've earned something, and we'll talk. All I can do is for you. Let's go, let's go! Hey students - quickly take a bag from the master!

- Heavy - Ned was embarrassed - would not overstrain.

- Nothing - the master laughed - do not look that small - they are strong. Come on, come on, oohlamons, faster! Hurry up!

A crowd of boys, eight or ten years old, rushed to Ned in a stormy stream, snatched the bag from him, and like a dry splinter of spring, dragged her to school.

- They won't break anything? - asked the master anxiously, watching the boys puffing out the bag from each other.

- No - Ned waved his hand - books. Scrolls. I bought it in the shop today.

- Ltd! You are a versatile person - Tiraz nodded respectfully - let's go, have a strengthening drink, let's talk. I really want to talk to you. The last time failed. We were busy ... with something else. Thank you for coming.

Chapter 15

The courtyard, in the middle of which there is a small pool, and in it there are fish - Ned has never seen such. Spotted, beautiful, they poked their heads out of the water, opened their mouths, which made quiet sounds in the air, as if someone was kissing, kissing behind a wall of lush grapes.

The bunches, partly ripe, partly green, with their weight cut off the braiding of the gazebo, and the sun, already leaning to rest, did not break through the green canopy, unable to touch the interlocutors with hot rays.

Tyraz noticed Ned's interest in grapes, stood up, took a short sword lying on the mounts hammered into the wall, cut down a large bunch in one lightning movement, caught it in the air, and put it in front of Ned on a china plate:

- Try it. This is my pride. I brought a vine from the southern continent. I drove through many countries, and it cost me a lot of work. And even greater work was to teach her to live here, to bear fruit on an unfamiliar soil for her. This is my hobby - gardening. I thought of everything in this courtyard myself. And the pool, and plants, and the selection of fish for the pool. Fish are also not easy - they swim in the king's pond. This is an ancient breed - colored sirus. If you only knew what it cost me to get them! But I won't say anything - the master smiled, and his eyes clouded over, as if he were recalling the vicissitudes of this adventure. However - Ned knew how he got them. I overheard. They cost the master a lot of money. It seems that Tiraz was not a poor man ...

Ned nipped off a large berry - to be honest, he never tasted grapes. He did not grow up in the village of Black Ravine. And the firm, slightly crunchy flesh seemed to Ned just delicious. He gladly sent it into his stomach, reached for the next one ... and until he had rid the bunch of half the berries, he could not stop.

The master watched with a slight smile as the guest was saturated with his treat, and when he considered that he had already eaten enough, he finally asked:

"Well, what brings you to me, dear master? And don't hesitate - drink the drink! It is made according to my recipe - it refreshes and restores lost strength. It is advisable to drink without sugar or honey, they beat off the taste, but if you like sweeter, then there is nothing wrong - drink as you like. Here is honey, here is cane sugar ...

The master pushed a pretentious china cup to Ned and poured a fragrant dark liquid from a heavy earthen teapot that smelled of spices and flowers.

Ned nodded gratefully, took the cup in his hands, and inhaled with pleasure a scent that somehow reminded him of Sanda's hair.

The master smiled slightly and said:

- They say that the smell of chia is reminiscent of what the drinker wants to remember most. You remembered something good, right?

- Thank you, yes - smiled Ned, sipping a sip of liquid, washing away the sweetness of the grapes and hot stomach - I came to you with a request. Teach me how to use a sword.

- You ?! With a sword ?! - the master was sincerely amazed - don't you know how to wield a sword? Why? How did it happen?

- Please, do not ask about what I can not tell - asked Ned, lowering his gaze to the table - I do not want, I do not want to lie. But I can't tell the truth either. For what reason? I can't say that either - I'm sorry. I'll pay you for the lessons. I have money. Not much, but there is. And I really need to learn how to master the art of sword fighting. It is assumed that after a while I will go to the capital to study at the officer's school. And I must be able to wield a sword. Do you understand? Now I am in this art below your youngest students.

- I do not need your payment - the master answered calmly - you are interesting to me as a riddle, as a strange person who defies my understanding. In return for the lessons, I will ask you to demonstrate to me everything that you can do. And more than once. And I will teach you what I can. Do you agree?

- I agree! - Ned sighed with relief - how will all this look? When can we start? Where will we train?

The master pondered, sat with his eyes closed, then said:

- Let's do it this way: you will come to me when you have time and when it is convenient for you. Even late in the evening if you wish. I don't sleep much. Three to four hours is enough for me to recuperate, and I can distribute them over the day. Where do you live now?

- In the officer's barracks of the base.

- It is better that you live somewhere nearby. You need to rent a room somewhere nearby, then you can come to me in your free time. Anytime.
- And I ... will not interfere with you? Family?
- I have no family - the master answered dryly - there was once, but ... everyone died. I didn't start a new family. My family - all these boys who come to learn martial arts and girls. There are some, albeit a little. I believe that in some types of martial arts, girls are even stronger. And besides, girls need to be able to stand up for themselves. If my wife at one time owned a sword ... "Gods, gods ... why didn't you put your mind to me then? Why did I think martial arts were not for women? She would be alive now ... and my boys ... I am a fool, a fool. What's the use of finding and shredding the robbers to pieces? I just got dirty - physically and mentally. And love cannot be returned. Vyzhglovsø. Burned out ... "
- Excuse me, I thought - the suddenly silent master raised his eyes - where did we stop? Yep - you need to rent a room as close to the school as possible. You also need an attire for training - loose clothing, light leather sandals, preferably two sets. It is easy to get it in the market - there is Doras's shop, it has everything you need. Also - bathing devices - soap, a towel. Everyone brings it with them. Well, and ... in general, everything. The rest I have - swords of various kinds. Blunt edges. And wooden swords - at first you have to use one. What's your name ... Ned?
- Ned Black is my name. And you can call on "you", you are at least three times older than me.
- How old are you ... are you?
"I don't know," Ned admitted honestly, from seventeen to... I don't know how many years. I am a found, I was found on the seashore. So - how many full years I am, I cannot say. How did I learn martial arts - I can't tell you, I'm sorry.
- I see. I am two and a half times older than you - the master smiled - I had to go through something, because I look older. Anyway. Let's get down to business. So, we agreed with you. I will also clarify - you will show your art in front of me and my students, and I will teach you here in the backyard. I do not want to destroy your image of a great master. Do you understand?

- I understand - Ned nodded - tell me, can you help me with finding an apartment? I don't know anyone here, maybe you have some information - who rents a room, or an entire apartment, or a house.

- I will help. When you leave the school, turn right towards the sea. You walk two hundred steps, you will see a large two-storey house - a woman named Zadara lives there. This is an elderly woman, her children are in the capital, so she lives alone. She has many rooms, and if you want, there is a guest house in the courtyard. At my request, she will host you.

The master took a piece of paper from the table next to the main table, carefully cut off a strip from it, then took out an inkwell, a sharpened wand from the drawer, and carefully and beautifully tracing letters, wrote something. Then he sprinkled the paper with sand from the sandbox, shook it off and handed to Ned:

- Here. Give it to her. She knows my handwriting. Once I lived in her house and was friends with her children. Chia has cooled down, and you never finished it - he chuckled - well, nothing, he is cold and pleasant. Finish your drink, and now we will go with you, choose a weapon and check - what you can do in sword combat. Are you ready? Let's go.

Ned sent the fragrant liquid into his mouth, swallowing as he walked, and hurried after the master as he emerged from the arbor. He suddenly turned around and said:

- In public I will refer to you as "you." So it should be. We are both masters. Alone - "you", because from this moment you are my student. Let's go.

They went to the training yard, where about thirty children diligently brandished wooden swords under the supervision of an older boy. The master approached, made a few remarks, straightened his hands on the "swords" of the three students, then went into the winter hall, beckoning Ned to follow him.

- Look here - see the swords hanging? Now you have to come up and choose the sword that, in your opinion, suits you best. There are fighting swords hanging over there. Take something from them, and then pick up an analog and training swords. How to choose a sword? Hold it on your hand, try to swing, check the balance, is it comfortable. The sword you need will fit in your hand itself, do not hesitate. And I will tell you whether you made the right choice.

Ned went to the wall. Dozens of swords, a whole arsenal. It seems that the master saved them for many years, collected, lovingly kept them - each sword was in its place - fasteners were driven into the wall, in the form of wooden bars with a recess in the middle, into which the sword was laid, like in a cozy bed. The bars are polished and varnished - in themselves almost a work of art.

The swords lay in orderly rows and Ned involuntarily admired the sight of these murder weapons, made with such care and skill that it was impossible to look away. Some were sheathed, so it was impossible to determine what the blade was, but most were flickering with dull blades, on which, like all expensive swords, a sinuous pattern of layers of metal was visible.

Ned already knew that blades like this were made by forging twisted rods from the finest grades of steel, and some grades, he was told, had precious stones added. So this sword could be very expensive.

Suddenly, his attention was attracted by one sword - rather short, straight, with a simple hilt, not decorated with any engravings or figurines. But on the blade, Ned noticed the inscription made by those same unfamiliar runes - like on his spear, like on a sword that the ubiquitous old Pernal dug out of a pile of iron. That sword was now in Ned's armory.

Ned carefully removed the sword from the bed, in awe of the fact that the sword would twitch, and the head of the demon would protrude from it, but nothing happened. This sword, like the one in his room, was silent, lying quietly in his hand. Ned interrogative n looked at the master, he came up, looked, and asked with interest:

- What? This sword is definitely not for your hand, it is too short. This is the second sword, for the left hand. Or right-handed - if you're left-handed. He must have a pair - that is, a long sword, with the same runes. They always go in pairs.

- And what is this sword, I can find out? Where did he come from?

- Ltd! It's a long story. In short, I'll tell you - this is a rather expensive sword, it costs more than the same weight in gold. But that is not all. If he was bewitched - it would cost much more.

- How is it - bewitched? - asked Ned - tell me!

- Listen. Legend has it that the weapons marked with these runes were made in some ancient order of black magicians. Which one? I do not know. There was talk that this order was once destroyed. But only they, these magicians, knew how to enclose a demon in a blade with a special spell, and when the owner of the weapon killed the enemy, he took the life force of the enemy and transferred part of it to its owner. Demons feed on life force, so ...

- And what will happen when the owner of this weapon uses a sword for a long time? Well, this, bewitched?

"Hmm… I don't know anything about that. I also know that it seems like the demon does not sit in the blade forever. Then he disappears somewhere. An example is this sword. There is nothing in it. He's clean.

- How do you know?

- I tested it. Once.

The master's eyes clouded over ... "Yes, I did. This creature screamed and begged for mercy. But I cut off his hands. Those hands with which he killed my family. And then he ripped open his belly. The sword drank blood ... "

- You know, master ... - Ned decided - I have a pair for this sword.

- Where from? - Tiraz was amazed - however, I don't ask ...

- No, nothing so secret - I received an army sword in a warehouse, so the storekeeper gave it to me. He says he found it in old swords, captured and collected from nowhere. He says it is ancient, and is not listed at all in the register. I gave him a silver piece, and he gave it to me. Absolutely.

- What?! For a silver piece? Ha ha ha! What a fool! If he knew ... - the master laughed rollingly, and even shed a tear. Then he wiped his eyes with his wrist, calming down, said:

- It costs a lot, a lot of money. Keep him safe! He does not get dull, does not break. And the fact that there is no demon in him - maybe it's for the better. Well them, these demons. Although ... sometimes it happens that vitality would not hurt. By the way, what does that sword look like?

"Hmm… well… if you take this one, yours, and lengthen it twice, you get that sword. By the way - he really suits me.

- Then there is nothing to invent, to look for a sword - this is the one that is most similar. Is he?

The Master removed a sword from the wall and handed it to Ned. The sword was exactly the same as the one that remained in the barracks, only without runes on the blade, well, it was also decorated with a small ornament on the handle. An ordinary, quite decent sword of a high class.

- Yes, one to one. Only without runes.

- Well - the master nodded with satisfaction - now tell me, what kind of weapon do you own? I do not mean the crossbow and stone throwing machines, you can not mention them ...

- I work well with a spear. Very good. With a knife. Can throw knives - pretty good too. Nuuu ... that's all.

- Pole? Sixth how?

- I haven't tried it. We didn't have poles.

- Must own a pole. The spear is the same pole, only with a tip. Hmmm ... interesting, very interesting. It seems that you were taught in some offshoot of the ancient orders. There, more importance was attached to working with poles and secret weapons - such as knives, throwing knives. Although they also wielded a sword well. But not all. It was believed that the sword is a weapon for stupid warriors, and a real fighter hides his skill in order to get closer to his victim and stick a knife in her back. Or throw a knife. Or hit the victim with a special technique so that she dies in the near future - not immediately, not on the spot, but after a few hours. And yet - they used the "traveler's pole", and mastered them masterly. By the way, many of the poles were equipped with such swords. It was strengthened at the end of the pole, and it turned out to be a cross between a sword and a spear. A killer thing. The most interesting, that outside it was a stick, like a stick, but when the scabbard was pulled off from it, such a sword appeared. And then ... then you will not envy the opponents of this fighter. Especially if he owned the Snake style ... you own the Snake style ... and you saw and held such a spear sword, right, Ned? - the master's eyes narrowed, became hard and prickly, like thorns of thorns.

- Yes ... and I have such a spear. But I do not wish to harm you or anyone else. Unless he himself wants to harm me. You don't have to worry about me.

- Just a couple of questions - did you study with these masters?

- No.

- Is this order still alive?

- I think no. Not sure. I have never met any of them, Ned stated firmly.

- Well ... I believe you - the master lowered his eyes - I believe. Although everything inside me protests - this cannot be! I know that yesterday you could have killed me, for sure. But he didn't. Therefore - I believe you.

- Believe it. I will never harm you. I swear to everything I have. Unless you yourself want to harm me. But I've already said that.

- Said. Okay, to the point. Then we will proceed from your battle tactics. It means that you are used to hitting with a pole, or its like. How did you hold the part that is crowned with the sword? You're right-handed, aren't you?

- Right-handed. I held the spear with the tip on the right, slightly lower than the shaft in my left hand.

- So we will build your battle tactics. You will fight as if it were not a sword, but a spear. There is also such a style of sword fighting. I suspect that he went exactly from this order. That is - in fact, you own a sword. Only you were taught to use it in a completely different way. You're an army sergeant. You were told - a shield in your left hand, a sword in your right. You lean out from behind the shield and stab - rraz! And back. Rrraz! And back. And the individual fight is completely different. We'll need to learn a few styles. One is the one that you will use in individual fights, your main one. The rest are more or less ordinary. And all of them - with the use of a dual sword-dagger, and without it. Now look - take this sword with a grip not as you were taught in the army, but as if you were holding a spear with a sword tip. That is, with the handle up, and with the blade down and to the right. Imagine you have your spear. Well, is it more convenient? Try to strike an invisible enemy. So, yeah, not bad, not bad at all. You need to hone your movements, remind your body that it already knows how to do - and you will be a master of the sword. If you fight like this. And just a decent swordsman - if you fight the way ordinary swordsmen fight.

- I have two months, no more. Soon we will sail to the Isfirskaya border.

- Yes, yes ... I heard. It's sad. They say it's very hot there. People don't want to ... well, nothing. Two months is enough for us. You don't start from scratch. I thought it would be much worse. And you just didn't understand your skills a little. Everything will be good. You will fight as well as me, and maybe even better. Why not? By the way - have you ever fought with this very spear against the sword? Not given?

- It was given - Ned said shortly - I killed the enemy.

- Hmmm ... if not a secret - who was it?

- An officer. It was a duel. They let me take a spear instead of a sword. It was a few days ago at the base. There was a duel of honor. Sorry - I can't say more. This is an internal Corps affair, and the rules prevent us from sharing information with civilians.

- I understand - the master drawled thoughtfully - but you don't understand how lucky you are. If these fools knew what I know - never in my life, even on a crossbow shot, would they let you approach the place of a duel with such a spear! They just didn't have any chance! Arrogant idiots ... They should have insisted that you fight with the sword. And then ... then you would have had a bad time. Your combat instructors have managed to confuse your movements, teaching you to fight with a sword in a different way than you are used to. And now we have to break your habits and teach you again. Well - not the first time, so don't worry. Okay, that's enough for today. Once you get your workout clothes, take the time to work out properly, come. Did Zadare take the paper? Yeah. Let's go get your bag out of captivity. I'm waiting for you, and soon. * * *

Ned looked up at the sky - the sun was still quite high, but it was already setting. He grinned - time flies at a gallop, like a cow from gadflies, its tail lifted and dusty hooves on the ground ... It seems that I just left the base, and here you are - evening is already approaching.

Waving to the boy on duty standing at the door of the school, he went where the master advised, with a sigh, putting a heavy bag of books on his shoulder. To be honest, this accumulation of concentrated wisdom in the form of hefty and not very tomes got him badly. And after all, with this bag, trudge to the base!

The house of a familiar master was indeed not far away. Two-storey, strong, slightly dilapidated - any house requires maintenance, and if there are no hands that take care of it and cherish it, it quickly grows old, turning into a peeling barn. From somewhere, weaving plants are immediately taken, entwining it, like lianas entwining trees in the jungle, trying to suck the life juices out of them. Huge weeds are taking over the garden, nodding spiny heads to their less fortunate colleague in the neighboring garden. Roadside grass crawls through the cracks in the slabs of paths, completing the destruction, and showing that if a person disappears - nothing in this world will change. Flowers will bloom, grass will grow, and only a bird, sitting on the ruins of a house, will sing to him a funeral song ...

It had not yet come to complete destruction, but everything was going to that. The fence had been painted a few years ago, and the gate, once strong and sturdy, cracked slightly and creaked pitifully after Ned tried to open the gate. The gate was locked, so he had to bang his fist into the gate several times, and then, when it had no effect, kick it several times, which caused crumbs, chips, and bird droppings to fall from the gate.

- Iiidu ... I'm coming! Now! - Finally, an old man's voice was heard, cracked like an ancient bell, broken by vandals - and there is no need to knock like that! I'm not riding a horse around the house! I need time to get there. I'm not a girl anymore! Don't you know what ?!

The gate opened with a squeal, but carefully, as if the one who opened it was afraid that it would fall off its hinges. A woman appeared in the doorway - absolutely gray-haired, but dressed as if she were going out - a strict dress, a hat, shoes. Looking closer, Ned saw that everything was quite old, slightly faded, as if these things had been washed many times. However, the woman was very elegant, and it is clear that she was once a beauty. Ned wanted to listen to her thoughts, but changed his mind. What can he hear that he needs? And it was stupid to fill your head with old woman's thoughts about illness and domestic bustle.

The woman's blue eyes were gleeful, and the wrinkled face was benevolent and not at all the same as that of old women who have lost their minds. The woman was old, but clearly not at all stupid. It became clear from her very first words.

- And who's knocking here? Oh Gods! What a young man he has come to me! I hope you haven't come to rob the poor old woman? However - what to take from me, besides this old house ... - the woman grinned, and looked at her guest from top to bottom - what did they want, officer?

- Hmmm ... - Ned was taken aback - actually I didn't come to rob. I am with a note from Master Tiraz.

- Gozar? How is he? Haven't seen him for a long time. Tell him that it is not good to forget old Zarada! However - do not. He has a lot of things to do, he teaches his boys all the time at school. This is how they constantly bring food from him, he never forgets about me. He was brought up with my boys, sons, and then they drove off to the capital, and he went to the army. He returned already gray ... For many, many years he was gone. But I recognized him immediately, yes! I'm not out of my mind yet! What are we talking about, come in! Lock the gate - the neighbors' boys got into the habit of climbing into the garden, they broke off all the branches, you bastards. I have to tell Gozaru to tame it. Well, you are tearing the fruits, but why break the branches? Give me a note, well, well, what is he writing there? Yeah ... see what my vision is? Young people will envy! No, it's too early to write off me as torn boots ... so ... Ned? Yeah, Ned ... well, Ned - if you want - live in the house, but if you want - let's go and show you another place. Do you see the guest house by the well? Yeah, there. Here ... I hid the key here, under the porch. Come in!

The one-story house was a sturdy stone structure, surrounded by a garden overgrown with weeds and self-sown flowers that smelled sweet in the cold evening air. In the garden, a bird was singing, trilling, and Ned involuntarily took a deep breath, absorbing the clean, fresh air.

- Okay, right? - the woman grinned - that's why I didn't go to the capital, to the children, although they called me many times. Sell a house, and come. Where am I going from here? My whole life has passed here. My husband died here. Here we were happy, raised children, loved, suffered and rejoiced. And there? What is there? Who needs me there? Children send me money for living, so I am not in poverty, but keeping the estate in order requires a lot of money. They do not want to hear to restore their father's inheritance. Looks like they are waiting for me to die, and then they will sell the house. Only I do not want to please them in any way, I creak and creak myself. Already survived all her friends. And everything is alive! Once upon a time I was a beauty, and now ... an ancient old woman.

- Yes you look great - said Ned sincerely - you are a beauty now! I would never say about you that you are an old woman.

- Here! At least one real man appeared in this city! - the woman smiled - not counting Gozar, of course. All the other men are just some rude trash. Well, look at the house, look! If you don't like it, I'll show you the rooms in the big house.

Five rooms, a kitchen with a fireplace, a bathroom with a large copper bathtub covered with greenery. Bedroom with a large bed - Ned ran his hand over the bedspread - dust rose and the hostess sneezed loudly.

- Pchhi! Nobody has lived here for a long time. And once upon a time, after all, guests constantly came to us, whole families! And now - everywhere dust, desolation and longing.

- And how much do you want for this house? How much should I pay for a post? Ned inquired cautiously. Talking about financial difficulties slightly alarmed him - maybe the old woman will make so much money now that there will be nothing to talk about. In fact, he had no idea at all about the prices for renting housing in the city, and now he scolded himself, but that he did not find out this information from Tiraz and did not find out somewhere else on the side.

- Hmmm ... to be honest - I am not interested in money much. I have everything. All I need - Zarada said proudly - just for the sake of not being at all stupid - gold a month. Will it suit you?

- Will arrange - Ned sighed with relief - very much even. I will most likely live here no more than two months, then we will be sent to war. And then ... then I don't know what will happen. If everything works out, I will go to the capital to study as a senior officer.

- Do you want to devote your whole life to killing people? - Zarada said sadly - this is how Gozar ... how we argued with him ... I told him - this is a bad profession! Killing people is bad! And he - I'm not going to kill, but to protect people! From enemies! Who is right? I don't know, maybe he is. And the husband is just as he spoke. Okay. It's not about that. In general, so - we will clean up the house, wash all the sheets, put new ones. Something, but this junk - sheets and covers - I have enough. We will do the cleaning, we will clean everything - right tomorrow morning. We'll clean up everything in the kitchen, clean the bathtub to make it shine. Did you see the hearth in the bathroom? The boiler - you fill it from the well, you light up the stove, the water heats up. Coal and firewood behind the house. For a long time we did not heat the stove in this house. By the way - the bathroom is not simple. You lock the doors, and you will have hot air, especially if you splash water on the stones that lie on the stove. Steam is very healthy. All diseases come out. There is a bucket on a rope in the well. The water is clean, tasty, so you can drink safely. I'm embarrassed to ask - what's in your bag? Is this all your stuff?

- No - smiled Ned - I bought books, I will read. I still have a lot to learn about this world. I'm not educated at all.

- Well ... this is a real deal. The main thing is that you are smart and you have a good heart. I'm feeling it. And education ... that's all nonsense. Well - I just graduated from the high school for girls of the highest aristocrats, the one in the capital, "School of noble maidens." By the way - there, in the capital, and picked up her husband! - Zarada giggled - he was a brilliant officer, just fire! All the girls were running after him! And I beat it off. So - well, I graduated from this school, so what? Not very useful for life. Especially in a small town parasitizing on a military base. Well, yes, I know how to behave in society, I have excellent manners - they literally beat me with a stick, through my ass. They flogged everyone mercilessly. So on the women here, my education acted like a red rag on a bull! "Educated! Fu you, well you! ". Officers' wives ... this is a special story. Viper! Here is their exact description. Military City, where the wives of the majors grovel in front of the wives of the colonels, and the wives of the lieutenants in front of the wives of the majors. Its own hierarchy. I insisted that we do not live in a military town. The husband bought a house in the main town. I hate these sycophants. I have a masculine character, as my late Cedar said. He was from an ancient, rather famous family of nobles, close to the former king. Then the clan decayed, and Sedar had to somehow spin. Moreover, he loved to spend his fortune beautifully. When you are a girl, I like it when you are bombarded with roses and bathed in sparkling wine, and then when you become a wife it is already annoying. Moreover, if it is not you who are being bathed in wine ... I have a masculine character, as my late Cedar said. He was from an ancient, rather famous family of nobles, close to the former king. Then the clan decayed, and Sedar had to somehow spin. Moreover, he was very fond of spending his fortune beautifully. When you are a girl, I like it when you are bombarded with roses and bathed in sparkling wine, and then when you become a wife it is already annoying. Moreover, if it is not you who are being bathed in wine ... I have a masculine character, as my late Cedar said. He was from an ancient, rather famous family of nobles, close to the former king. Then the clan decayed, and Sedar had to somehow spin. Moreover, he was very fond of spending his fortune beautifully. When you are a girl, you like it when you are bombarded with roses and bathed in sparkling wine, and then when you become a wife it is already annoying. Moreover, if it is not you who are being bathed in wine ...

- And what, downright wine? A whole bath of wine? - Ned shook his head in disbelief.
- You do not believe me? - the old woman laughed cheerfully. She looked up dreamily, and said quietly:
- If you knew how nice it is to feel the bubbles pinching your skin ... and the smell of good wine! And those hot male lips looking for your horny mouth, and ... in general - you have nothing to listen to! Small yet! - the woman winked slyly - and there is nothing to smile like that! Well, yes, I haven't always had very strict rules! So at least there is something to remember! By the way, if you want, you can bring women here. You are a young man, you need a woman's affection. Otherwise, you can get sick. My husband always said that if he was not with a woman three times a week, he would definitely get sick. I had to close my eyes to some of his pranks. What can you do? Life is like that. Either you are like a smart woman, and close your eyes to the fact that all men are lustful males, or ... But there is no such thing - "or". Fools who do not understand this truth are quickly left alone. In general - if there is a girlfriend, or you bring some whore - it's okay. The walls of the house will not collapse from this, and the world will not turn over. He blushes ... oh gods! At least one man I know blushes at the mention of whores! What kind of boy you are ... although - a man. Blabbed you out right? Is it time for you to go to base?
- In general, yes ... that is, I mean - it's time to go to the base! - Ned thought to himself - and so - I am with you very, very interesting and pleasant. Yes, here's another thing I wanted to ask - you said WE will clean up, and who are we? I'll be busy in the morning, I can't be here. I'll just come to dinner... I need to collect my things, resolve the issue in the office.
- Stupid - but I didn't mean you! Am I going to make a man do women's business? - the woman laughed - I have two slaves ... or rather - no longer slaves. Former slaves. They are both maids and girlfriends. We have been living together for many years. Today I sent them to the shops - I had to buy something. And go to the market. I thought it was they rattling at the gate, and this is you. I opened it - I didn't even ask. In general, we will clean up everything for your arrival. It will be clean and good. By the way, where are you going to eat? When are you here? Will you cook yourself, or do you need a cook?

- I myself can ... but I would not want to waste time on this. If you can, let someone cook for me. I have so little time - I need to study at the Tiraz school, read books, and relax a little. At the base I ate in the officers' mess, but here ... after all, I rent a house to study with Tiraz, here it is two steps to school. Otherwise I would have lived in the barracks. And I also wanted to ask ... I don't even know how to say ... I do not know how to behave at the table. I am a village orphan, and I am very uncomfortable that I don't know how an officer should behave. And I can't dance. And ... I can't do anything. Except how to fight. Can you teach me good manners?

- It's very good that you know how to fight! - Zarada laughed - you will chase the boys out of the garden! As for manners, I will teach you. I still have nothing to do, it's boring. Just don't be offended when you get a pull from me! First of all, stop biting your nails! You just drag to stick your finger in your mouth when you're worried! Firstly, this is a bad form and a sign of a redneck, and secondly, you betray your excitement, and the officer must keep his feelings in check and not show what he feels. Well ... unless he's in bed with a lady. Here it is better to SHOW how he feels. She will be pleased ... As for the cook - we will agree. Will you allocate some money, they will write you fodder instead of food in the canteen? And they should allocate for an apartment - you see, I know military life. Give me - I will take what is necessary for food and the cook for work, nothing more. She will look after you - clean up, cook, wash and wash. An officer should not do all this himself - unless he is on a campaign. There already - does as it turns out. Here - should rest.

- Can I leave the books here? The bag pulled my entire shoulder. So what ... shall I pay you now?

- And as you want - the woman waved her hand - if you want - now. And if you want - later. See for yourself - how convenient it is.

- Here are five gold pieces. Two - for accommodation, and three - for food and servants. How will it end, say. I'll give you some more.

- Well - Zarada easily agreed - go to the barracks, calmly pack your things, we are waiting for dinner tomorrow. If you have any questions - do not hesitate, ask. I'll have to bring you lanterns here, how will you read? And sitting in the dark is unpleasant. I'll give you the key to the gate, let's go ...

They left the house, reached the gate and Zarada pulled out a long patterned key from the keyhole:

- Here you are. It jams a little, so if you twist it a little, it will work. I'll take another key. Walk, it's getting dark already. Waiting for tomorrow! And it will be more fun for all of us ... at least there is someone to care for and what to discuss. Especially if you bring some girl - there will be a conversation - for a week! - Zarada laughed merrily and looked sideways at the windows of the mansion, in which the light flickered - here! They came and did not even ask where I had gone! Well, look, what scoundrels! I'll go give them a hack! Servants are called! Bastards!

The old woman snorted and waved to Ned and slammed the gate. He turned, clinking on the pavement with the horseshoes of his boots and went towards the base. Ned felt good, light and calm in his soul. As if guiltily giving up his debt, fate has recently brought him together with very good people - Tyraz, and now - Zarada. Ned liked the woman very much, and again he regretted, like Geresard, that he did not have such a mother. However - maybe it was, maybe it was even better - he doesn't know that ...

The streets of the city plunged into twilight. Lanterns burned only in the very center, near the temples of the gods, the rest of the streets went under a dark veil for the whole night. The windows of the houses flickered with the dim light of the lanterns, but most of them were dark - people in the city went to bed early to get up early and use less oil from their lanterns.

It was at least an hour's walk to the base, even at a brisk pace, and there was time to think about everything that happened to him today. Especially - about the words that he heard from the master Tiraz.

Ned himself, in his own mind, went as far as what the master had told, to the extent that it concerned the spells of swords. Is it just himself? On reflection, I came to the conclusion - he himself would never have been able to get to the bottom of the truth, no matter how sad it is to admit it. Then how could he? And in general - what happens to him? How did he go from being a simple shepherd to having intelligent conversations with educated people?

Ned was smart enough to understand that a simple shepherd COULD NOT feel so free in the company of these people. For example, today he quite adequately conducted a conversation with an aristocrat brought up in a school for the children of courtiers. How did you manage? Where did he get his vocabulary from? Why does he learn so quickly, as if he doesn't learn everything again, but REMEMBERS? Where are HIS thoughts, and where are thoughts ... NOT his? And who is he now? Person? Yes, man. Is he possessed by a demon? No. The demon would most likely devour him from the inside. Ned saw what happens to those in whom the demon is. Which, by the way, he also launched.

So, we can conclude: the soul of a person who previously belonged to the sect of demonologists somehow ended up in it. Ned learned his skills, part memory, part knowledge ... what else? And here it is already interesting - if he completely assimilates the soul of this demonologist, his memory and knowledge, then who does he become? Certainly not Ned. And someone else. And if Ned fails to keep his own soul in this body, then a foreign soul will dissolve his consciousness, like a hot chia dissolves a sugar cube. And only chia will remain, slightly sweetened with what used to be this very piece. Wasn't that what the soothsayer was talking about?

Ned came to the conclusion that there was a need to read books - was it not for nothing that he had collected so many books on magic? Another interesting thing. Today, Ned suddenly UNDERSTOOD what was written in ancient runes on the blades of swords and spears. And this inscription read: "I conjure you, give me strength, O Winged Horror!"

How did he know the content of the inscription? Moreover, looking at the blade, today he was able to understand the meaning of several runes, as if he remembered what they are called and what they mean. And honestly, it scared Ned. Penetration, fusion of someone else's personality and his soul was happening more and more. A week ago, he had no idea about the meaning of the runes, and he could not even imagine that he would recognize the content of the inscription.

Ned walked past the familiar sign at the inn, grinned, and winked at the heavens - yes, Selera threw a joke today! The revenge of the gods can be so sophisticated that you can't imagine! Why did he give Kualthuk more money than the goddess of love? So I got the goddess's revenge. Asked for love from the goddess? Got a girl's love! Well at least Selera did not hang the love of some fearful people on him. That would be a laugh! Hey, hey - don't! Enough laughter! - Ned shook his finger at the sky - love is enough! By the way, I wonder - will he go to Sanda tomorrow? Maybe we should not? Don't go, and that's it. I was busy! By service. And let her rest. Will think. Maybe during this time the goddess of love will change her mind and aim this beautiful shark at another unfortunate person! And why the unfortunate ... as if he was not glad that a beauty fell in love with him. Don't lie to yourself - you dream so she goes to bed with you. You sleep and see how you stroke her tender body ... thighs ... breasts ...

Ugh! Get out of your head!

Without noticing it himself, Ned had already reached the gate of the base, and was surprised - the base was not sleeping. A reinforced outfit of Security Guards stood at the gate, the passage was blocked by a heavy grille moving along the guides. Torches were burning on the parade ground, people were moving - everyone was running, fussing, commands were heard - and this was almost at night, when everyone had to sleep on their beds.

- What happened? Ned asked as he walked to the barred passage to the base.

- Night maneuvers - the guard turned around, grinning deeply - the authorities have a fit of madness. They wonder, they don't let anyone sleep.

- Hey, be quiet! - grunted another guard, and quietly added - what are you talking about? He's the Colonel's favorite! Will report - you will get sticks. And a deduction from your salary. Do you need it? Come in, Ned, not up to you. We represent the reflection of the attack from the city side. You are on vacation, so rest, do not fuss. Go to your barracks.

- Let me go - and I'll walk! Ned chuckled.

The guards, swearing and groaning, rolled back the heavy grate blocking the entrance. She rolled on metal guides, and was so weighty that six guards could barely roll her back enough for Ned to squeeze through the opening.

- Enough - you will get through! - shouted one of the guys puffing from the strain - we still have to close it back. And I advise - whether you are on vacation or not - dump into your hole and do not show yourself to the authorities. Otherwise, they will definitely be harnessed to run with everyone. And so - you don't seem to know about maneuvers.

Ned, who had already gathered a healthy soldier cynicism, did so. He - sometimes at a trot, and sometimes at a sliding step, made his way to the barracks, quietly like a shadow, slipped past the duty officer who stood at the entrance and watched what was happening on the territory of the base, and carefully turning the key, opened the door to the room.

The attendant turned around only when the unlubricated door hinges creaked, letting the guest in, but not seeing anyone in the corridor, shrugged his shoulders and continued to watch as crowds of people with weapons at the ready with a crash collided to add work to the team of doctors in the morning.

No matter how hard you try not to injure anyone, no matter how hard you use blunt poles instead of sharp war spears, there will still be broken bones, knocked out teeth, eyes, and pools of blood. Often and killed.

The soldiers, furious from lack of sleep, often go into a rage and beat the "enemy" as if he were to blame for not being allowed to sleep. Probably, the whole point of night maneuvers is just to anger the soldier as much as possible to awaken the fighting spirit in him - the soldiers reasoned. Or maybe - and most likely so - the commanders are nasty stuffy goats who like to shit on people. In any case, everyone knew that they would not be able to sleep until the next night. Of course - no one will allow you to sleep during the day. Well ... except during the day's rest, of course.

Chapter 16

"The demon is a spawn of Darkness. It feeds on the life force of people and serves destruction. But not only destruction. Like any other object, a demon can be used both for the benefit of a person and in order to harm people. Everyone owns a knife. But this knife can be used to kill a neighbor, and to protect your life and the lives of loved ones from the enemy. And here you have to understand - the same knife is an unreasonable object that does not have its own will. The demon, on the other hand, is soulless, but intelligent. And woe to the magician who tries to cope with the demon and cannot do it! The demon will consume his soul, kill his body. And in the worst case, he will seize him, subjugate him, and then a person will become his slave, he will begin to do cruel deeds, he himself will become a demon in the flesh. "

Ned put his book down, drummed his fingers on the table, and got up from his chair and walked around the kitchen. The second day he tried to fish out something useful from books, something that would help him understand the essence of demons and learn something new. Alas - I could not find out anything except what I already knew - there are certain entities called demons. They can be controlled, but if you don't control them, they get out of control and kill their master. Or enslave him. And nothing about what demons are, what these are living beings, or not, why they can be controlled and HOW they can be controlled. In those books that Ned got in the bookstore, everything was said in allegories, some kind of hints, half hints and no specifics. None at all.

The last book that Ned read was called "Treatise of Yusarra Tinagra on the Origin of Demons", and there was nothing in it either - the author filled the treatise with magnificent, eloquent phrases, moralizing and stories about what scoundrels these same black magicians are who let their demons in. And that one should beware of them - both magicians and demons. Long stories about how demons eat people from the inside, with all the details and even drawings. Descriptions of perversions and mischiefs committed by demonologists. And nothing more.

One got the impression that the author enjoys describing various dirty tricks perpetrated by demons and demonic masters. There was no information about the nature of the demons, or about the spells that are used to protect against the effects of these creatures.

Very little and vaguely were said about those who can control demons: "Magicians who control demons have been very rare for some time now, and this knowledge is prohibited" Who is it imposed by? What is the ban? Nothing concrete was said, not a single word. There was only one way left - to look for knowledge in the very scrolls that no one can read.

Ned walked over to the shelf on which he had put the purchased scrolls, and carefully looked at the ends of these "books." The scrolls were yellowed, spots were visible in places, as if the skin had been scorched by fire. Yes, the scrolls were leather, made of very thin, soft leather, only slightly hardened from time to time.

Ned had not yet skimmed the contents of these rolls, primarily trying to find what he was looking for in books printed in common language. He meticulously leafed through all the books on magic in which at least something mentioned about demons, spending all his free time from training on this. Killed time but didn't get what I wanted.

Two ago he moved to Zadara's house, and all this time he was either in training, or sat and lay, looking through books about magic. He devoted four to five hours a day to training with the sword, the master said that it was no longer necessary. Moreover, Ned grew incredibly quickly in skill.

As Tiraz said, the feeling is as if his new student is not learning again, but is recalling the past, lost after a long and serious illness. He instantly grasps everything that the master teaches him, all that remains is to hone the movements to the perfection that distinguishes the masters. And now, after only two sessions, Ned was approaching the level of a senior student, almost a master.

The Master did not ask Ned how this was possible, although the thoughts in his head wandered differently - from the version that Ned hides his abilities for a reason unknown to Tyraz, to the assumption based on the possible loss of the student's memory. Ned did not dispel all these assumptions. He was just silent. The master, on the other hand, took everything as it is, especially since during each training Ned showed him everything that he knew in martial arts, and Tyraz carefully watched, memorized, sketched the racks, punches, throws, movements of his student.

For a master, whose life was completely connected with military affairs, the restoration of an ancient, forgotten style of combat is incredibly important and interesting. Much more interesting than the fate of Ned himself.

Ned took off one of the scrolls, dark, as if it had been smoked over a fire, carried it to the table, to the lantern, and, making the lantern's flame brighter, began to gaze intently at the lines of runes that covered the scroll as if a crowd of cockroaches were running over it. The slightly faded ink was lost in the yellowish skin, and for a long time Ned tried to make out what had been written, sorting out, remembering the writing of the runes, until his eyes hurt and he vexedly put the scroll away. It seems that reading the ancient scrolls is not for a dull evening ...

Approaching the dining table in the dining room, he grinned at the memory, pouring himself an apple broth from a tall earthen jug. Three old women touchingly looked after him for two days all the time while Ned was in the house - they constantly came, offered some goodies, decoctions, demanded clothes for washing, and only calmed down when Ned openly asked them to leave him alone. saying that he wants to work out, and they are now interfering with him. This killer argument immediately swept the women out of the house, although he heard their footsteps near the window - sneaked in and watched Ned read books.

When Ned moved in, the house that had been prepared for him was really sparkling and glittering. Zadara's two maid-girlfriends, gray-haired like her, but a little younger, rubbed, cleaned, washed the house, and finished just in time for noon when Ned moved the things.

The hostess proudly demonstrated the cleanliness and from that moment on Ned fell under the hard pressure of the love of three women who were suitable for him as grandmothers.

It was rather difficult for him, an orphan who never received the slightest parental affection, to fall under the wheel of love of grandmothers. And strange. It was not in vain that Tyraz visited the old ladies quite often, and now Ned understood why.

Goraz grinned cheerfully as Ned complained about the pressure of the old ladies, and shrugged his shoulders: "Children are far, grandchildren are far away - do you need to babysit? Nothing, you will be stronger. But now you know what boundless parental love is - when they strive to take you to the toilet almost in their arms! "

With slight indignation, Ned read in the master's mind that he had deliberately sent him to Zadar, having achieved two goals at once - Ned received a cheap, comfortable housing, and the old woman - a big toy with which you can play the fun game "Grandma and Granddaughter". And everyone is good. And the fact that Ned is indignant about unnecessary care is the result of the guy's orphanhood - after all, the guy does not know any parental love, so he thinks the care of old women is unnecessary. Never mind, he will soon go to war, he will live in tents - then he will remember this hospitable house and regret leaving it. Until he comes back here again ...

So that's how Ned's last two days of vacation passed. Tomorrow he will begin his duties as a sergeant.

At the base, they took his move quite simply - he received "apartment", "rations", ordered a cart for himself to take things, left his current address, and at noon the cart, which was driven by one of the base's carriers, already stopped at the gate of Zadara's house. So his life began in a new place.

Ned went back to the books he had put aside. He reads the scrolls during the day, and now at least learn something about magic, at least understand a little what it is.

"Fundamentals of Magic" - read the title, and opened the book. The first thing I saw was: "If you intend to study magic on your own, without teachers properly trained in agar - leave this business! You can incur the wrath of the gods, you can harm yourself and others! Think about it! Contact the nearest agar, and you will receive proper help! "

Ned chuckled - no, he certainly wouldn't get into the agar. Why did they forbid even talking about demonology? And what will they do with the ready demonologist, the black magician? Maybe they'll send you to the fire? Somehow I don't want to ... you will interrupt!

"The Nature of Magic" - he read the first section and went deep into reading. Half an hour was enough for him to understand that he did not understand anything. Well, nothing at all. It seems to be written in understandable words, in ordinary letters, but when he starts reading, he falls into a stupor.

Well, how to understand, for example, the sentence: "The essence of magic is in magic itself. Gods give strength to those who can accept this strength and do not give the weak "? He understood it this way: there is magic, and those who have abilities can magic. Why not write like that - simply, without any frills?

Ned remembered what the shopkeeper had said when he was selling books, and shook his head in annoyance - indeed, getting through the textbooks would be very difficult. Probably the text of the textbooks is drawn up so floridly precisely because teaching should take place in magic schools, and not independently. If someone tries to learn on his own, he will face big problems with reading comprehension. More precisely, he simply cannot understand the text.

Abandoning his attempts to understand the origins of magic, Ned leafed through the book and found a section called "The Simplest Spells to Develop Abilities." He chuckled contentedly - that's what you need!

So:

"A spell called the Spark of Shadra. Used to ignite flammable substances and release a fireball.

Execution: the right hand makes the gesture "negation" in the lower plane, the left hand "throw Goursat" vertically down.

Pronounced: "Heler tunar arsss" in two heights - the first word in the lower tone, the other two - in the middle. During the pronunciation, the student must imagine a magical space from which he draws the required amount of energy.

Warning - when capturing more than enough energy, the effect after casting the spell can be unpredictable - from the appearance of ball lightning to a burst of flame.

Both gestures are made simultaneously with the pronunciation of magic words, the difference between the actions of words is no more than a second or a half. "

"Wow - the simplest!" - Ned was indignant - "And what is Goursat's throw? And what is the gesture of denial? "

I looked through the list of sections and found: "The gestures needed to make spells work", opened it. Found: "Throwing Goursat. Imagine that you are grabbing something invisible from the air with three fingers of your left hand and throwing it in the right direction. This direction is different for each spell. A deviation from the angle of the throw by more than a third can lead to unpredictable results. "

"A gesture of denial. The right hand with an open palm is located in a plane above the horizontal surface. You move your hand from left to right, as if in denial. The movement must be precise, deviations are not tolerated.

The gesture "negation" is carried out in three planes, for each type of spell - in the lower, middle and upper levels. The lower level is the level of the magician's lower abdomen, the middle is two fingers above the navel, and the upper is the level of the nipple. The movement is carried out with the hand, the forearm is relaxed and remains motionless. Warning! If the forearm moves from its place during the execution of the denial gesture, the result may be unpredictable! "

Ned swore - intimidated! "Unpredictable" - what is it? Foggy threats - well, it would not be clear - what will happen if you make a mistake, and they ?! Scoundrels ...

He went to the middle of the kitchen, relaxed, closed his eyes, imagining a kind of magical space from which he would take energy for the spell ... or rather, tried to imagine. Then he made gestures, simultaneously saying: "Heler tunar arsss."

Eee... nothing happened. No - not really nothing - the air smelled of burnt rags. And that's all. Ned swore again and remembered forgot to change the key. The first word is in a low voice, the second and third are of medium pitch.

He stood in the middle again, performed the passes, shouted out the words ... empty. Nothing. If the first time it smelled like a burn, the second time - absolutely nothing.

I repeated it again ... and again ... and again ... exhausted myself, and sat down at the table, reread the textbook again and think - what I did wrong.

After half an hour of reading, I realized that he does not know how to draw energy. Can't connect to magic source, if any. It was necessary to start from the very first pages, where it should be described how to do all this. You cannot skip over all those sections that are devoted to the training of student magicians.

For some reason, Ned thought that, as with the martial art, which he got a gift, he would just take it, say the spell, and ... now he is already a magician! After all, he has already sent demons, why then cannot conjure?

And then he answered himself: who said that the one who penetrated his brain knew how to do magic like that? Maybe he had a completely different direction of magic? Maybe demonology and ordinary magic hardly intersect? In addition - he still did not know how to deliberately release demons. On all the occasions he did so, Ned acted in a time of mental confusion. That is, it seems that he was doing magic, Ned, but it seems that he was not ...

Ned slammed his fist on the table in annoyance - no way! Well, yes, he knew it would be difficult, but not to the same extent! However - why not this? Here in martial arts - the master shows how to hold a sword, how to move, how best to take a blow, how to parry. Why did you decide that it would be so easy with magic? Because he wanted it so much?

Going into the bedroom, Ned sat down on the bed, threw off his shirt and pants, remaining in only his underpants, and froze, pondering what to do next. If he continues his studies in magic, then ... hmm ... but it is not known what "that". Two days of independent study was enough to understand that he was completely unprepared to use magic. And that you can't take it from a swoop. All he can do is memorize a few "simple" spells, trying to play them every day, hoping that it will work out. It is almost impossible to understand witchcraft without a teacher. And this is very, very annoying.

Ned got up, vigorously did a few exercises, warming up after several hours of motionless sitting in place - don't say so, but still, martial arts are the most important for him now. He also reads about magic. Will study literature. But these books, alas, will not protect him from an enemy spear or sword (unless, of course, they are folded with thick feet and tied around the body in the form of armor). So you have to work hard ...

By the way - about "sweating" - Ned was really sweating, so he decided to go outside and rinse himself with ice water from the well. You could, of course, heat the water in the boiler, pour it into the bath ... in the middle of the night? It is easier to pour a bucket on yourself, dry yourself with a towel - so you have washed yourself. I didn't want to go to a clean bed sweating. He pushed back the bolt. Closed just in case. And from old women who want to catch attention, and from adversaries who can encroach on Ned's treasures. What treasures? Yes, at least a spear or a sword. Or books. And Ned has some money. Why lead people into temptation?

The red moon has already come into its own. The crimson light, reminiscent of the light of a torch, filled the garden with an unreal, magical radiance. In a minute, Ned's eyes got used to the darkness, and he was happy to stand on the porch, inhaling the smell of night flowers and looking at the moths twinkling in the air like living stars. They hummed, moving from flower to flower, and glowing rings were visible on the backs. According to legend, these moths, called moon butterflies, belonged to the goddess of the red moon. She marked them with rings that resemble the disk of this night star.

Ned looked into another sector of the sky and noticed a black moon - it could be seen only when it covered the stars with its disk. The black moon was rising two hours after sunset, from which Ned concluded that it was more than midnight, and he needed to hurry up to wash and go to bed to rest for at least four hours.

Approaching the well, he opened the lid, rotating the gate, lowered the wooden tub down until the rope loosened, waited, and began to lift the heavy bucket. I put the bucket on the edge of the well, tried it on ... and stopped - not sleeping in wet shorts? Stripped naked, took the bucket, walked to the side, onto the grass, and cringing with anticipation, lifted the bucket and poured it over his head and shoulders.

It seemed to Ned - he was scalded! The water was so icy, in contrast to the hot body, that the body perceived this shake, as if boiling water had been poured on it. Ned almost yelled - he jumped on the spot, snorting like a horse after a watering hole and waving his hands, splashing on all sides. Then he did some exercises to disperse the blood. When he finished, he put the tub on the lid of the well, and, picking up his panties, went home, putting his feet in sandals.

Suddenly there was a rustle and a bright figure slid around the corner to meet Ned. He noticed her with a peripheral vision, and immediately taking a fighting stance, stepped towards the enemy, preparing for a fatal blow. The body sang from the received energy, because the adversary will receive everything he deserves.

The stranger rushed to Ned, he intercepted him in the air, holding him with a stranglehold, raised his hand for a crushing blow ... and then the stranger's face fell under the light of the moon, which came out from behind an accidental cloud.

Sanda! It was her!

Ned froze, stunned by the "meeting" - it was just incredible! All the days that he broke up with the girl, Ned did not maintain any contact with her. The next day she was not at the gate, and how she found out his new address, how she ended up in the garden, is unknown.

- What are you doing? - He asked hoarsely, letting go of the shocked girl from the capture - is that really what they do ?! I could have killed you!

- I didn't kill you! She snorted happily - I watched you swim and gallop across the lawn. That was funny! And you look good naked ... I've never seen naked men. Babies don't count.

Then Ned remembered that he was standing in front of the girl completely naked. And the light of the red moon does not allow us to hope that any details of his anatomy will be hidden from inquisitive girls' eyes, carefully examining him from head to toe.

Ned wanted to immediately retreat into the house, then decided that it would be more correct to hide his nakedness under a piece of cloth, which he held in his hand, and during the attack he threw on the grass. He lifted his panties and pulled them on wet hips under the girl's mocking gaze.

"What a beautiful! Well, how handsome he is! And a strong ... scoundrel! How dare you deceive me ?! Darling ... And what is his ... is that, everyone has such? "

- How did you get here? - Grimly asked Ned, hastily shutting off the perception of the girl's thoughts, driving him into paint.

- Can you let me into the house? I was chilled something - Sanda said plaintively.

- Come in - Ned nodded and turned and entered the porch.

His head was in complete confusion - what to do with it in the middle of the night? No - he knew exactly what to do with girls in the middle of the night, but that was not the case! Should I take her home? And what will it look like? He brings the girl in in the middle of the night, and who would believe that they had nothing? Only an idiot would believe. And as Ned had already figured out, Sanda's parents weren't idiots.

Kick her out of the gate? It is the same as if he gave the girl to be torn apart by night robbers, rapists and slave traders. By the way, they could actually steal and send them into slavery. And it's not surprising - such cases were quite common - his colleagues told him this. Decent girls living in a prosperous family will not wander at night, and there is no one to intercede for the orphan. So the girls went on a long journey, including to other continents - in the south, they say, white slave girls are appreciated. Local leaders pay for them with pure gold and precious stones, or give many of their own, dark-skinned slaves. Therefore, wandering at night was categorically not recommended for all beautiful and not so girls. However - and guys too, if they don't have a good blade on their side, and he doesn't know how to wield it.

Ned closed the door on Sandoy, trying not to look at the girl, pulled on his pants and shirt. Then he pushed an unoccupied chair to the table and sat down, watching the girl quickly devour the pies baked by the cook, washing them down with apple broth.

"So you'll tell me what you're doing in this garden and where did it come from?" - Ned began coldly - what demon brought you here, and even late at night? Do you have no mind at all? What are you doing?

- Sorry - I'm so hungry! - Sanda smiled apologetically, chewing on the last piece - I am now, now!

She swallowed, happily washed down food from an earthen mug, leaned back in her chair and shrugged her shoulders, said:

- So I found you! I told you - you're not going anywhere from me. Why did you deceive me? Who said he would come to my house?

- Well - I said! So what? I already told you - it's useless, we won't succeed. So what demon were you looking for me? How did you find it? How did you end up in the garden?

- Found here. At first I waited. You did not come. In the morning I went to the base. Began to ask to call you. She said that I am your bride, pregnant, whom you have villainously abandoned. They chased me away, but I cried and sobbed. They took pity, and when the inspector came, they told him about me. The inspector went to look for you, found out that you rented an apartment and left. And also - he gave the address where you went - if only I did not hang out at the gate and did not interfere with the guards. I went, found a house, found a hole in the fence - there, in the corner, one board moves away. You can get through. Big ones won't fit there, but I'm thin, so I got in. But it was already dusk. I decided to wait for you to leave - I saw your silhouette in the window. And also - wait until it gets dark. After all, you do not have the conscience to drive me out at night looking. You went out ... and now I am with you. Everything.

Ned froze, not knowing what to say. Then he looked at the girl, pleased with himself, and asked sharply:

- And if I now take the belt and whip you?

- It won't be good. But I will endure. Just don't chase it away and let me live with you. Anyway, you are now officially my fiancé and I'm pregnant with you! - Sanda giggled happily - and I found you great, right?

- No - well, how dare you accuse me of seducing you, an innocent girl ?! And now everyone will say that I am a villain? Do you yourself understand what you've done? Stop! And parents?! How will they react ?! Oh Gods! Now wait for the delegation to the base commander! Blamed for all sins! Seduced and kidnapped the girl! Or kidnapped - then seduced?

- In general - so: the fact has already happened. I'm in your house, you seduced me, so you have nothing to lose. Let's go to bed, huh?

- That's what - you will sleep over there on the floor. I'll put you something in bed and sleep. And I'm on the bed. And yet - because of you now I will sleep less than I should. Than hoping to sleep. In the morning I will take you to your house, and we will settle this misunderstanding.

- How will we settle it? - Sanda asked with interest - will you marry me?

- Khe-khe! - Ned coughed - we will settle it, it means - you will go to your home, and I to my home! And nothing else! Everything! Finished!

- And we haven't finished anything. We haven't started yet - the girl stubbornly shook her head - okay, we'll talk tomorrow. Where can I wash my face? Is there a bath?

- There is a bath! Not for you! - Ned got angry - why did you come here? Take a bath? You will wash yourself at home. That's it, I'm going to make the bed, and you quickly go to the toilet and sleep. Over there, in the guest room, I'll make a bed. There is a couch there, so you won't have to sleep on the floor. Ladies blanket. Home in the morning. The conversation is over!

Ned got up from the table, grabbed the lantern and went into the bedroom. I looked for extra sheets, found it, went to the guest room and made a bed for Sanda. Then he returned to his bedroom, undressed and lay down in bed, listening to the girl making noise with water, humming something, sometimes oohing when she overturned another ladle.

Although water was previously poured into the boiler of the bathroom, and did not burn with cold, like well, it was difficult to call it warm. You have to light the stove to warm it up, but neither Ned nor Sanda did.

Listening to what was happening in the bathroom, Ned painfully imagined Sanda standing in a copper container and pouring water on herself under the light of the red moon falling through the window. He wanted to be with the girl, and to be honest, he was glad that she appeared in the house, despite the fact that this demon glorified him in front of the whole base. But ... a lot of "but". And most importantly, he loved her. And if now what should happen - to leave her in an interesting position, did he have a moral right? This is not to mention the scandal that Sanda's parents will throw - in the end, they will figure out the place where the dissolute daughter is. They will go to her friends - and she has already boasted to them that she has found a groom - they will inform about Ned, the parents will go to the base ... and he will have to take the rap in front of the Colonel, explaining that Ned did not kidnap anyone, that everything was by mutual consent, and ...

Ned's thoughts were interrupted by a slender figure that slipped under his blanket. The girl pressed her whole body to him, hugged him, and trembling said:

- I'm so cold! I will freeze there alone! You're not the kind of animal to make me freeze? Look how cold your hand is! - Sanda put her hand to Ned's stomach — the hand was really icy.

Ned, not expecting this from himself, gently hugged Sanda, resting her head on his chest. He imagined it so many times in his dreams that he was not even surprised when his hands did it by themselves, as if without his participation. The firm, cool chest of Sanda with hardened nipples rested against his side, and the top of his head, with wet, herbal-smelling hair, was right in front of his lips, which he did not fail to use, kissing her with a light kiss. Ned's hand lightly stroked Sanda between the shoulder blades, which made her shudder, and with a quiet giggle, said:

- It tickles ... but so good! Since I saw you, I dreamed of how we would end up in the same bed. True, I imagined all this a little differently, but ... after all, everything is never the way you imagine, right? Let's forget who we are. Let's just stay in love, huh? Well, at least for one night! I understand that we may not have a future. But we have two months, isn't that enough? Many people didn't even have that. Goddess gave us love, why should we refuse? Why do you resist the will of the gods? They can get angry ...

Sanda turned over on her stomach, crawled onto the silent Ned, and began slowly and tenderly at first, then more and more quickly kissing him on the lips, cheeks, eyes, dropping lower and lower ... Then she threw back the blanket and resolutely pulled off the last remnants of Ned's clothes. The bastion in the form of army cowards surrendered without a fight at the mercy of the winner. * * *

- Tired?

- What am I tired - Ned chuckled, looking relaxed at the ceiling - you did everything. If I didn't know, I wouldn't believe it ...

- Don't you think that there are too many conventions in our life? - a girl shouldn't want her boyfriend ... shouldn't run after him ... shouldn't ... what else shouldn't she? Many things. And why? Am I not the same person as you?

- Hmm ... not quite like that, of course ...

- How are you different? Is that all?

- Oh! No need to pull! It hurts! Careful ... it will come in handy again.

- Sorry. I was worried about something. All my life they have been hammered into my head - you are a girl, don't do this and that, you shouldn't be ... you are not supposed to ... you ... but a lot of things "for you!" But I wanted you, and took it! Here!

- What took, then took ... let's sleep, huh? I'll go to work tomorrow. However - I would not mind one more time ...

- Enough for now. To be honest ... while I am aching. Will you wait a couple of days?

- I'll wait. Sleep ...

The lovers hugged, and a minute later Sanda was already asleep, throwing her leg over Ned and hugging him across his chest. Ned, on the other hand, could not sleep, excited by the girl's closeness, remembering what had happened shortly before.

Still deciding to fall asleep, he took the girl's hand and leg off him, carefully tucked the blanket under her, and getting out of bed went to the guest room. There he took another blanket, went back and lay down, turned away from Sanda and closed his eyes, listening to her even breathing. He felt very good. Like never before in my life. She is right - come what may, but this night belongs to them two, and there are still many days and nights ahead. And there - come what may. What the gods have mixed in this mug called "peace", so it will be, whether you make a guess, or rely on the will of providence.

Five minutes later he was asleep and he, calmly, like a child in a cradle next to his favorite toy. * * *

- Well, get down to your duties! - Drankon chuckled - today according to the plan physical training - running in full combat weapons, then practicing combat, after lunch rest - working out the battle in groups of two or three people and one on one. End at six o'clock in the evening. The workload has now been reduced by order of Colonel Heverad, so that after six you can safely walk towards your pregnant bride.

- What, everyone already knows? Ned grimaced.

- How do you want? The whole base knows. The performance was outstanding. Wait, the colonel will also call. Did you really fix the baby to her and leave? Look - the townspeople really don't like this kind of thing. You can get punishment from the command.

- What is the penalty for? Isn't it my own business, which girl to sleep with?

- On the one hand - yes, when it comes to corrupt girls. But when this is the daughter of respectable townspeople, and you seduced her, and God forbid raped her - hang on here. Each case will be dealt with separately. So, if you did not drag the girl into the bushes and rape, no one will give you up to the city authorities, however - if you raped - too. They'll hang you here. Or they will beat you with sticks. But ... the colonel does not need a scandal - the townspeople will write to the king, a commission will be sent from the capital, they will begin to investigate. They will gnaw the colonel's head, and he will gnaw us. Do we need it? In general - think, think. I don't know what you're doing with the girl, but it's better that the city authorities don't get in here. Everything, with your business finished, now to the service. So, you have a company under your command. She is included in a full company - these are two companies, one hundred and fifty soldiers each. A full company is commanded by a lieutenant, yours is Lieutenant Shusard. He was sent the other day - right after school. The guy is young, a little older than you, proud, from the nobility of the first class. That is, the lowest class. There is a lot of ambition, but little land and respect at the court. He strives to assert himself all the time, to show that he is not such a fool as one might think.

- Can you think about it? Ned chuckled.

- You can - Drankon nodded seriously - Shusard is a young fool. Only he shouldn't talk about it.

- Tell me - how many classes of nobles are there?

- Don't you know? Oh gods, what hole did you come from? Twelve classes. The highest is the twelfth. This is the king and his blood relatives - princes and princesses, brothers and sisters. Most likely, you will only see them from afar, unless, of course, you get into the bodyguards or the king's personal guard - they see the twelfth grade every day. However - without much joy, as far as I know. Sometimes it is better to face the enemy in a direct battle than to look at ... Hmm ... but you don't need it - Drankon frowned - let's go introduce the new commander to his company. By the way - do you have a whistle? Yeah. Whistle to build. Do you remember the signal?

- Rota, stand up! - Ned stood next to Dracon, peering into the faces of those with whom he would have to stand in battle. However, these same faces were not visible behind the protruding cheeks of the helmets.

- Come on, command, sergeant - whispered Drankon - I do not interfere. I'm leaving. This is your company now.

"Upstart! Colonel's favorite! Look how they make a career! " - Ned heard the thoughts of his former comrades, and remembered Dracon's words that now he will not have friends.

Cutting off other people's thoughts, Ned scanned the line of soldiers, and said loudly:

- Guys, now I'm your commander. Whether you like it or not. And it depends on us how we will fight. We will go to war soon, so let's try to make sure we don't get killed for as long as possible. Don't forget - you have a five-year contract. And these five years must be lived. I warn you - I will mercilessly punish those who do not want to stay alive. To die is his own business. But he is in the ranks, and the life of the rest depends on him. Without it, the formation will weaken. So now he will run - thirty laps. Then we divide the company in half - into the first and second numbers, and we begin to practice the battle in small groups. After lunch, one-on-one fights and hand-to-hand combat without weapons. So, build, napraaavo! On command, follow me, run ... march!

Ned ran ahead of the line, and all a hundred and fifty men stomped behind him. They rattled with armor, weapons - everything that could be rattled. The sound of clanking metal had already eaten into their blood and flesh. Long after they finish serving in the army, they will hear the rumble and clanging, and also - the whistle of the unmerciful sergeant ... if they live to be fired, of course.

Ned, too, donned armor, donned a sword, a dagger - everything that was due to a sergeant. The morning sun was already beginning to warm up, and soon thick salty drops of sweat were pouring out from under the helmet ... and there are still thirty long, very long circles ahead.

In the morning he did not wake Sanda, leaving her to sleep in bed. Ned woke up as if someone had pushed him in the shoulder - somehow right away - he was asleep now, and no longer sleeping. Habit. The army habit of waking up a few minutes before getting up.

The head is heavy, cloudy, but a bucket of icy water knocked sleep and lethargy out of him. The old women in the big house were apparently sleeping too. Why should they go up this early? It's Ned who needs to be at base until morning wake up, not them.

The time here was counted either by a sundial or by a huge sand-glass, but some very rich people had a mechanical watch made by piece on a special order. They cost more than the same weight in gold. At the base, however, special people assigned to the hourglass turned them over as soon as the last grain of sand fell down. The "course" of this watch was enough for four hours. They were constantly checked by the sundial. At the base, the time was fairly accurately determined, and each turn of the clock was marked by the striking of a bell - many townspeople followed the time by the bell of the case, which was heard from all parts of the city.

Gathering himself, Ned grabbed a couple of pies from the table, quickly chewed them, glancing at the girl scattering in her sleep and shook his head in distress - how did he allow himself to be seduced? He knows there will be problems. No, but what was he supposed to do when a naked beautiful girl with whom he is in love climbed into bed?

That he was in love, Ned realized even when they were sitting with her in the tavern. She at the same time repulsed him with overly eccentric manners, but also attracted - with beauty, cheerfulness, and ... but who knows what attracts you to an object of the opposite sex, if you love him? They love not for something, they love because they love. So Selera wished to play such a joke, to pierce hearts with love - and she did. And who can resist the goddess? Not Ned ...

Covering Sanda with a sheet and fighting the urge to kiss her goodbye, Ned walked out into the yard, shutting the door tightly behind him.

He was caught already at the gate, when Ned was struggling with a cunning bolt - you had to first pull the bolt on yourself, and only then he moved to the side.

- How did you sleep? - he heard a slightly mocking voice of Zadara.

The woman stood fully clothed, as if on the way out to the city. It seems as if she never went to bed.

"Slept well," Ned replied, squinting at the old lady's sly eyes.

- And her? - Zadara winked.

- Who is she to? - allegedly did not understand Ned - sorry, I already have to run! Wake up soon!

- Don't act innocent. I hate it when they lie - Zadara lightly slapped Ned on the head with a folded fan. That it was a fan, he realized when she unfolded it and began to wave it languidly, as if it were not the morning chill, but the heat of the day.

- You can't hide anything from us! - the woman shook her head reproachfully - quickly tell me who she is and where she came from. I have a vague suspicion that you are in trouble.

- Did they look out the windows , or what? - Ned chuckled - how did you know?

- What business is it to you! Maybe they spied. Tell me! The girl is definitely not a whore, you can see it at first glance. The clothes are not the same. And it is clear from her that she is not a corrupt girl, they can usually be immediately identified. So the daughter of one of the respectable townspeople. And they really do not like when their daughters sleep with warriors. Unless, of course, they are not married to the soldier. So - wait for the guests. Wait?

- Wait ... - Ned sighed, and briefly told the woman everything he saw fit about their relationship with Sanda.

- A virgin? Here are the things ... - the woman folded her lips with a tube and blew, as if blowing off the dust - it means that soon her dad will be here, and a crowd of all kinds of relatives. What will you do? In general, what are you going to do with her, with this ... Sanda? I do not mean bed pleasures and your poses - the old woman calmly added - I am talking about your joint future.

- And what is our joint future? Ned sighed with a shrug - none. They will either kill me or send me to the capital, and she will remain here. That's all.

- Hmm ... we must count on the best - Zadara objected calmly - maybe they won't kill. Let's think about what to do when a crowd of people comes here along with the city guards. Apparently - they will accuse you of kidnapping and seducing their daughter. They'll make a complaint to the colonel, or maybe to the king. Well, well ... we need to think about how to get out.

- Why get out? She is more than fourteen years old, and I read in a book that from fourteen girls can legally marry. And no parental consent is required. She came here herself. I didn't drag her. What can I be accused of?

- The fact that you have bewitched her, that she is stupid, that you have seduced and will leave. And if they manage to make the girl say that you raped her, then it's quite a disaster. You can thunder on trial. Okay. Until we take any hasty steps - I need to talk to the girl - find out what she wants. And understand what to expect from her. Tell me, if you have to go to Selera's temple and you and her declare yourself husband and wife, will you go for it?

- What's the point? - Ned asked stunned - I have nothing, I'm a beggar! They will kill him in the war, and what kind of husband is me ?! I can't even imagine myself as a family man - what if suddenly a child ?! Whereas?

- And you had to think before you poke your ... hmm ... in general - I'll talk to her. And you get ready to put on a wedding wreath if you don't want trouble. Get ready to meet your bride's parents. Fool! If you hadn't touched her, her virginity would have remained intact - she could have been examined and said — all the accusations are lies, no one touched her, as she was a girl, and remained. Now what? Everything, run to your stupid base, and Aunt Zadar will think about how to get you out of the hole into which you drove yourself. By the way - you wouldn't have kissed her then, and nothing would have happened! Why gave the girl hope ?! Eh, where are my seventeen years ... - the old woman winked sadly - I envy her. Get out of here! Go shake your pieces of iron! * * *

- So you are the sergeant of the first company? - the young lieutenant carefully examined Ned, and gestured to sit down at his table - why were you absent from the base?

- I was on vacation. On the occasion of being awarded the rank of sergeant, Ned explained dryly.

- I heard that you are the colonel's henchman. So - I don't give a damn about it! - the lieutenant's face became haughty and contemptuous - I know that you are a peasant who does not understand anything in military affairs. It's sad that you were entrusted with a company. I would not trust. And in general, so that you know - I am opposed to the villagers occupying officer positions. You commoners simply don't have the intelligence for that. You will listen to what I am telling you, okay? If you do not fulfill the order, you will go to court.

The lieutenant tossed a piece of cake into his mouth and turned away from Ned, as if making it clear that the conversation was over. Ned got up:

- I can go?

- Go, sergeant. And remember what I said!

Ned turned around and walked between the tables and left the officers' mess. His soul was heavy. It seems that the future service will not seem syrupy to him.

Stepping back into the shade of a tree, Ned sat down on a bench by the fence, and closed his eyes, considering what lay ahead. And I saw nothing good. The mere thought of having to go to an officer's school with such fools as Shusard was depressing. Ned wanted to go talk to Oydar and Arnot, but they were with the company soldiers, and he didn't want to talk to them in front of his colleagues. And they themselves did not approach him. Maybe they were tired, or maybe they harbored some resentment - in any case, he sat alone, as Drankon had once predicted.

- Sergeant Ned Black! - I heard the voice of the colonel's adjutant - urgently to Colonel Heverad! Calls! Now, run!

Ned looked at the lieutenant, sighed, and got up from the bench and trailed behind the aide-de-camp, staring at his back.

The lieutenant was clean, well-groomed, he didn't have to run thirty laps around the base in full combat gear today. Ned smelled sweat a mile away, all mail, trousers, shirt - everything was soaked in acrid sweat. Ned did not take off his armor during dinner, and walked around as brilliant as an iron man. And smelly like a stray dog.

There was no time to undress - first Ned had lunch, then the new commander called him to tell him what a shit Ned was, then ... he just didn't have time. And for the best - it would be inconvenient and stupid to drag all this harness in the hands of the colonel, and it would be even more stupid to go and leave it to the storekeeper.

I thought - we need to have our own closet here for storing office things. At least for lunch time. Other sergeants had such, you just need to go to the office and get a paper for the allocation of personal storage in a common warehouse.

With these gloomy and mundane thoughts, Ned dragged himself to the corps headquarters and walked down the echoing corridor to the colonel's office. The lieutenant signaled him to wait, and Ned remained standing in front of the oak doors, under the quick shots of the curious eyes of the clerical rats.

As soon as he was about to probe the thoughts of the clerks, to find out why he was called, when the door opened and the lieutenant, looking out from there, ordered:

- Come in, sergeant!

Ned crossed the threshold of his office, and froze - there, besides Colonel Heverad, there were five other people - a middle-aged man and woman, soundly dressed, in new, good clothes, a stout man of about forty-five in a strict suit with a large civil servant's badge on his chest, and two men of about thirty-five or forty, with the signs of the city watch on their chests. Looks like detectives, or investigators - Ned didn't really know who was who.

- Sergeant Ned Black has arrived! - Ned saluted, stretching out at the seams - waiting for your orders, Colonel!

There was a silence in the office, such that one could hear a fly, sadly and persistently beating against the glass of the office, hoping to free itself and fly away. In this, Ned's wishes were akin to those of a fly. He already knew what he was about to hear.

- Here he is, the rapist! - the woman said angrily and stood up, shouted from her place - where are you going to our daughter, scoundrel ?! Speak! Arrest him!

- No one will be arrested on the territory of the corps without my permission - the colonel said coldly, glancing at the detectives who had risen from their seats - we will understand, then we will make a decision. No need to get excited. I know Sergeant Ned Black as one of our best officers, an honest and decent guy. What you have said here is most likely not true. Ned, please explain what you have with their daughter and what do you have to do with her disappearance? Do you know where she is now?

"At my house," Ned said in a low voice.

- Here! Here! He seduced the girl, took her away, probably raped her, and now he keeps her in his house! Arrest him! - the woman was beside herself with rage.

The man, probably her husband and Sanda's father, tried to stop his wife, but she continued to shout, threatening that she would write to the king himself that she had a cousin at court, that she was a noble family, ancient, older than the colonel, and that she was so this business will not leave. Finally, she finally calmed down, and sank down on the spot, panting, looking at Ned like a nasty rat trying to eat the master's cheese.

The colonel looked at the pale Ned, grimaced slightly, and drummed his fingers on the table top, said:

- Let's start the interrogation now according to all the rules. Lieutenant, take the minutes. We will write everything down so that later there will be no allegories. The accusation of kidnapping, rape is too serious to be ignored so easily. If our sergeant is to blame, Mr. Burgomaster, he will be held accountable according to the laws of the kingdom. If he was slandered, the one who defamed his honor will be punished.

- And how do we know that he is telling the truth?

- And who prevents us from checking his words? - the colonel - lieutenant shrugged his shoulders, invite the chief of security too. Let it be present. This is his business. We are waiting, gentlemen. As soon as Major Sert arrives, let's start.

Chapter 17

A line of three carts solemnly rolled down the street, scaring away with a roar of iron-bound wheels bystanders who did not have time to hide from the midday sun under the roof of stone houses. Ahead were Ned and two Security Guards, led by a rather angry Major Sert, whose head was filled with thoughts of how good it would be to whip this demon sergeant, or even better, hang the bastard that made him trudge to no one knows where no one knows why! Here the villain was impatient to shove his demons' scion not into an ordinary whore, a soldier, but into the daughter of an eminent citizen of the city! And on top of that, a citizen married to a harmful woman who has high-ranking connections in the capital!

Ned turned off his mental perception - listening to those evil thoughts was pretty hard. Moreover, the Major's dreams of punishing the wicked could soon come true.

For a moment, Ned wondered - what if he was really sentenced to punishment, or even to death? Will he humbly wait for this to happen? And I decided - no. Nobody else will ever bully him. Enough. I ate enough of this "pleasure".

The second carriage was carried by the burgomaster and Sanda's parents. They were silent and gloomy, like at a funeral. After Ned told them the truth, Sanda's mother screamed for a long time, saying that Ned was a vile villain, a liar and a scoundrel, and that their well-bred daughter could not do that. And that they will expose his lies when they go to his house, where the bastard is holding the unfortunate girl.

The colonel, delighted that he could get rid of the proceedings on this issue, immediately clung to her words, and twenty minutes later the whole crowd was rushing through the streets of the city.

On the third cart rode the guards from the city order service, seemingly dull types with sharp, noticing eyes.

The carriage ride to Zadara's house did not take long. Fifteen minutes - and they are at home. It was as if they were expected - the gate swung open, and Zadara appeared in it, looking menacingly at those who had driven up from a height of her small stature so that it seemed that she had grown at least four spans.

- What is this procession ?! - she asked in a menacing, ringing, metallic commanding voice - take the trouble to explain what you need at my house!

- Here! She is hiding her guest's crimes! - Immediately yelled Sanda's mother, rushing to the gate and trying to push aside the old woman with her shoulder, who stood like an iron pillar in her path.

- Back! This is a private residence! And until I let you in myself, you have no right to enter! I will defend myself! Asana!

Zadara stepped aside, and was replaced by a dark-skinned woman, towering like a tower over the head of her mistress. In her hands was a hefty battle ax, and on her head was an old horned helmet that belonged to some big man, to see the mistress's husband, and taken from the northern pirates. It was polished to a shine - you see, it was polished with sand, and all this - a helmet, an ax, and the hands of a cook, as thick as the leg of an ordinary person, said that the adversaries would now have a very bad time.

And also - a thin, wiry woman of about fifty, holding a loaded army crossbow in her hands, peeped over the shoulder of a black battering machine. She squinted angrily over the stock of the crossbow, and a steel bolt was aimed at the chest of the pale Major Serta.

A small dagger appeared from somewhere in Zadara's hands, and the way she held it indicated the mistress's ability to handle a sharp blade. Still, being married to a desperate warrior and not learning even a little martial arts is out of the question.

There were agonizing seconds of silence, interrupted only by the hoarse breathing of the sides, then Ned, with a wry smile, cleared his throat and said:

- Aunt Zadar, it's me.

- You? And I didn't even notice you! - said the woman serenely, shining slyly with the eyes of the old fox - and what are these people doing here? Did you invite them? I thought it was an attack on my house.

- What do you think, you old fool? - Angrily shouted one of the city guards and immediately pinched his nose, from which streams of blood splashed. Zadara, without a swing, deftly punched him into the face with her left hand, clenching her fingers into a fist that turned out to be truly steel.

- I may be old, but not a fool! - she said coldly - and I will file a complaint with the burgomaster about your behavior!

- Here I ... - said the burgomaster bored, stepping forward - sorry, Mrs. Zadar of this idiot. There was a misunderstanding.

- And you are here, Mr. Burgomaster ?! - With an expression of immeasurable surprise the woman asked - what is actually happening? Why is this group of people trying to break into my house, and the burgomaster not only does not stop this act, but is also part of the criminals ?!

- We have information that there is a kidnapped daughter of these gentlemen in your house - the burgomaster pointed to a couple who walked aside just in case and looked with apprehension at the ax in the hands of a black warrior - tell me, it is true that there is a certain Sanda, whom this young man has kidnapped and is holding in captivity?

- Sanda is. But nobody kidnapped anyone. Since yesterday, this pleasant young lady, the bride of a young man, my guest, has lived in his house, is engaged in his housekeeping, and in the morning she applied to the Selera temple to perform a marriage ritual. The ritual is scheduled for the day after tomorrow, if the young man agrees to the marriage. And as far as I understand, he will agree. Really, Ned?

"True," Ned said a little dejectedly, and sighed lightly — true.

- So what's the matter then, gentlemen? Did you hear what he said? - Zadar asked again, bewilderedly - or do you still insist on breaking into my house?

- We heard! - Sanda's mother declared belligerently - only all this is a lie and nonsense! Until I hear what my daughter has to say about this, I won't believe you! All of you are criminals and liars! Rogues!

- What ?! How dare you say such words to me ?! - Zadara came out of the gate, demonstratively playing with a dagger, and the woman screamed, hiding behind her husband's back:

- Take her away! This old woman is crazy! Burgomaster, why are you standing and doing nothing ?! Let her be tied, she is mad!

- I'll cut off your ears now, you stupid creature! - said Zadara coldly, slowly moving in the direction of the adversary - so that she wiser and does not talk her long tongue!

- Quiet! Everyone calmed down! - commanded the gloomy burgomaster - if the situation is as Mrs. Zadara said, then the matter completely changes. Be quiet, I said! You've already got me into history! It was necessary to keep an eye on my daughter better, so as not to run around the sergeants!

- How dare you ?! - began Mrs. Nitul, but the burgomaster interrupted her:

- I dare! Mrs. Zadar is a famous, honorary resident ... or rather a resident of the city, her husband was a colonel, a famous person ... with connections in the capital. And she's not the last person in the kingdom either! By putting forward groundless accusations, you run the risk of getting the opposite effect - if she files a complaint for libel, you will be fined one hundred-gold, and also serve a week in a city jail! Clear? Like this. Madam Zadar, could you please take us to the bride of this young man to put an end to this strange and stupid story. I ask you to.

- Well ... since you are asking ... only for you, - Zadar said gruffly, heading for the open gate, where the defenders of the bastion - girls - were standing, let them in. I would not want, gentlemen, to disturb my guests. They are like my own children to me. But since the burgomaster asks, I cannot refuse him. Let's go!

The women lowered their weapons and parted to the sides. Ned could hardly restrain his laughter, and even bit his lips so as not to laugh - the cook and Zadara's servants looked as menacing as they were amusing with their formidable weapon. However, I noted for myself that both handled weapons quite confidently, like old warriors. And Zadara did not look like a helpless old woman. Incidentally, the dagger disappeared just as instantly as it appeared - somewhere in a secret place, not visible from the outside. The colonel's widow knew how to stand up for herself, that's for sure.

The whole company proceeded solemnly to the guest house in the garden. Ahead of Zadar, on the sides, a convoy of two warrior cooks, followed by the burgomaster, gloomy as a cloud, then a couple of parents, and the rest, including a city detective with a swollen nose, glaring angrily around.

Ned was walking next to the mistress of the house, when they came to the door, he stopped behind her.

- Sanda, darling, come out to us! - the old woman shouted loudly, and the door immediately opened, as if the girl was just waiting for a signal.

Sanda appeared on the porch, looking in bewilderment at the crowd of people:

- What happened, Aunt Zadar? ABOUT! Mom, dad, where are you from here? It's good that you came - meet my future husband Ned. The day after tomorrow morning, he and I will be married in Selera's temple. I applied today. You can congratulate me!

Deathly silence. Then the burgomaster turned to Zadar and asked loudly:

- Mistress Cedar! Will you file a libel complaint? Your business is winning. The minimum fine is one hundred gold, plus compensation for non-pecuniary damage by court order. By the way, Sergeant Black can also count on compensation. Sergeant, will you file a complaint?

- On your future relatives? - Ned smiled - you never know what happens in a family, right? It was not enough to interfere with the authorities here. No, I will not. And you, Auntie Zadar?

- No. Although I really want to - the old woman smiled - to call me, a respectable lady, the colonel's widow, a robber! What a horror!

- And who will compensate me for a broken nose? - The detective cried angrily - am I not a man at all, or what? May she compensate me for the damage incurred in the performance of my duties!

- Let the kualtuk compensate you! Spear in the ass! - Zadara answered maliciously - say thank you that I didn't sue you for your heinous accusations! Get out of my garden! Gentlemen, if there are no more questions for me - leave my garden, and give a rest to the weak old women in their last abode ...

- How - the weak! - he muttered the detective, cautiously looking at hefty cook - take a look at the nigger, but she bare fist deer kill! My thigh is thinner than her hand!

- Get out of here, my dear! - a deep voice said "nigger", and spun the ax, raising the wind stirred up a strand of hair from arbaletchitsy - and now as the embedding, so completely thighs will not you! Woooh!

The guards burst out to the gate, looking back at the ax, the burgomaster cautiously backed away, muttering to himself something like: "You managed to get me into a mess!" place, looking reproachfully at her daughter and disdaining the threat of reprisals.

- Daughter, how is that? The mother asked plaintively, shaking her head - sergeant, some kind of rogue? Do you have a head? We offered you good games, didn't you? Well, if you had the urge to marry, you would marry the son of a merchant, he has the title of an aristocrat of the first rank, albeit not yet inherited, but this one? From the Corps? There is one rabble, robbers and thieves!

- I ask you not to talk about my fiancé! - Sanda said sharply, walked up to Ned, standing on tiptoe grabbed him by the neck and kissed him on the lips - I don't need another! And your son of the merchant is a complete idiot! And by the way - what, the folder was rich, or what? He worked as a pie boy!

- You said something there about two hundred years as confectioners ... - Ned whispered softly, looking into the mocking eyes of his future wife - she lied, you useless!

- Well, you lied, and why? - she was not embarrassed - are sweets and cakes bad? The folder can do them. And my mother is an aristocrat - she fell in love with him, and that's it. Left home.

- So, this is your family? - Ned chuckled - well, I'm in trouble ...

- Vlip. Shut up. Now I'll deal with them. Mom, dad, why don't you congratulate me?

- Congratulations, daughter! - Sanda's father smiled broadly - there was a misunderstanding, but thank Gods - everything was resolved. Will you invite us to the ceremony?

- How can it be without you? - Sanda laughed, and ran away from the porch hugged her parents - the day after tomorrow, at ten in the morning. We won't invite anyone else. And we will not do the feast.

- How can we not? - Zadara was indignant - we will! First time getting married - and without a wedding ?! We'll have a feast here. The house is big, why not? And we have more fun. By the way, parents, what about the dowry?

"There will be a dowry," said Sanda's extinct mother sadly. Not a trace remained of her belligerence.

- That's great! - Zadar shone - let's go and talk to you, let's leave the young to deal with their problems. And we will discuss - how everything goes for us - about the wedding, of course. Let's go, let's go to the house! Girls, follow me! Asana, take off this pot! I have circles floating in his eyes, so shining! What did you clean him with?

- Crushed bricks. And what, shines great, right? I found him in the basement. Strong! Do not break! Pegra, try to knock ... Oops! Where did you hit? You fool! I said on the helmet, but why are you kicking in the ass ?! Now I will hit you kaaak!

- Girls, be quiet! Stop immediately! Let's go into the house and discuss the wedding feast. Enough, she said! Let her go, strangle her! What a demonic woman! Do not pay attention, they will tinker now and will come. So they are good, that's just a little foolish. So, I propose to arrange guests .... by the way, how many guests will there be? Did you decide?* * *

- Well, glad? - Ned with a sad smile looked into the face of Sanda, who was sitting across from him at the table - married to herself, and are you happy?

- I'm glad. Why should I cry, or what? - Sanda laughed - by the way, it turned out funny. It was about the same with my mother. She wanted to marry her father - and left. True, I had to leave the capital, but still married the folder. That's it, my dear! This is our family.

- Hmm... somehow everything started spinning fast... so fast that it's unthinkable to imagine. I was single, and suddenly ...

- But you're still single, yes. The day after tomorrow you will be married. My parents constantly shoved suitors on me. And all such freaks - stupid, terrible ... and rich. Mom tried everything. She said - you need to get me out of this hole, out of this town. Then they spat and told me to look for a groom myself. And how I found it - what a performance they had. Are you on fire because of me?

- No. The Colonel for me - Ned said thoughtfully - thinks that if I did something to you, I need to cover me somehow. And he does not believe that I am capable of nasty things.

- How do you know what he thinks? - Sanda grinned - however, you are smart, perceptive. Look how you guessed then what I dream about. About love. And I got it.

Sanda got up from her chair, walked over to Ned and climbed onto his lap, hugging her neck:

- Will you stay? Don't go, huh? Let's say that you are shocked by events and you need to rest. Let's lie on the bed ... and then we will rest, huh?

- Hmm ... so - then I do not mind lying with you ... and rest, but I have to go to work. But I don't want to leave like that, to be honest!

Ned hugged Sanda to him, found warm, firm lips with a kiss, stroked her back, which made the girl almost purr and shivered slightly from tickling, pressing against her beloved. Then she laid her head on his chest, and so they sat for about five minutes - in silence, without saying anything.

"Dear, darling, darling ... oh Selera, how good I am! How nice it turned out ... I'm sorry, Ned, I couldn't let you go! Never mind, I'll make a real officer out of you, you will be a colonel! No - a general! Let everyone be jealous! We will live in the capital, we will have a beautiful white house with two floors and a garden. And also two children. Boy and girl. No - three! No - four! Two boys and two girls. You will go hunting with the boys, and I will be with the girls ... by the way, why are these privileges for men ?! I will go hunting too! That's it, we'll ride in a crowd! "

- Darling, do you like hunting?

"No," Ned chuckled, shutting off his thought perception — or rather, I never hunted.

- By the way - you never told me about yourself! - Sanda deliberately furrowed her eyebrows - who are you, where are you from? Who is your family?

- And before you were going to marry me, could not ask? Ned chuckled.

- What for? I don't care who you are or where you are from. Just wondering. Should I know with whom I will spend my whole life and from whom I will give birth to children? Don't frown - not right away the kids, not right away! For your information, Zadara took me to a magician healer, and he cast a pregnancy spell. So I'm not as irresponsible as you think. As soon as we decide together with you that we need to have a child, we will immediately remove the spell.

- And after that night ... you have not suffered? - Ned inquired cautiously - what's the point in the spell if ...

- No. The magician eliminated everything. Such a funny guy! He looked at me all the time, and asked if I had communicated with some magician these days! Did this magician deprive me of my virginity? And what took it into his head? Barely lagged behind.

Ned was doused with cold water - wow! And how did the healer know that Sanda was sleeping with the magician? Maybe there are some ways to see the traces of the aura on the one with whom you slept? He knows nothing about magic - almost nothing. Maybe they somehow see these very traces of the aura? After all, the doctor in the village immediately saw his aura. Maybe the local one can? Most likely - he can. Why can't Ned be able to see her? Or maybe he can, but does not know how to do it? Most likely it is.

And again he was seized with annoyance from his inability and ignorance. If only he had a teacher! If only he could study properly!

- Why are you frowning? - asked Sanda - will you tell me where you came from? Or will you hide from your wife?

Ned thought for a moment, then answered:

- An orphan. From ards. Found on the seashore. He worked as a shepherd, in the position of a slave. Escaped. Enlisted in the army. Everything. There is no family.

- Poor! - Sanda stroked Ned's cheek - now you have a family! A little crazy, yes, but family.

The girl giggled and pressed closer to the guy, he gently but firmly pushed her aside:

- It's time for service. I'm leaving. I'll come in the evening.

Sanda silently nodded her head, with a sigh slid off the lap of her future husband and sat down on a chair. Then she followed him onto the porch and looked after him for a long time, smiling slightly, content and calm. Everything worked out as it should. Then she looked at the parents leaving the house of Zadara and hastened to find out - how will go what she dreamed of all recent years - her wedding with her beloved. * * *

The next few days passed for Ned as in a kind of fog. The wedding is not very magnificent by city standards, but for him, who has not seen another, it is simply amazing.

He sat next to his young wife, looked at her, at those around him and seemed not to understand what was happening to him. Stormy events captured him, carried him like a leaf that fell from a tree is carried away by a stormy rain stream. Ned seemed to be looking at himself from the sidelines, as if everything that was happening was not with him. Guests, kisses with his wife to the screams of guests, new faces that he had to remember and new names that he tried to remember and could not.

Then trips to girlfriends began - Ned was introduced, shown how a new toy and he mechanically bowed, smiled on duty, readily hugged his young wife - did everything that was required of him.

People reacted differently to the arrival of Sanda's new husband. Some were sincerely happy for Sandu and her young husband, others outwardly smiled, congratulated, and thoughts of envy, anger and even hatred, similar to disgusting poisonous snails, slid in their heads.

And there were many of them. Which, however, did not surprise Ned. During the time that he heard people's thoughts, such duplicity was not a revelation for him. Sanda enjoyed the attention, and also the love games. They spent the nights in each other's arms, and the girl was inexhaustible in bed inventions. When Ned once asked her how she knew all these things, Sanda replied that a woman in bed should be a whore, even if outwardly a strict and respectable matron. This was told to her by Zadara, who slipped books about IT to Sanda, saying that every woman should be able to please her man, otherwise he will actively look to the side. However, she added, he will still look to the side, but at least he will go back, comparing and coming to one single conclusion - his wife is the best.

This is how Ned's new life passed - at night Sanda's love hugs, in the afternoon - service, after it a mixture of training (he did not give up sword training) and hiking to Sanda's relatives, Zadara's lessons - she taught them both good manners, reading books, and much more, much more ... time was sorely lacking.

For the wedding, Ned was given two days off, the colonel himself offered to provide time off, having learned about the incident.

Sanda's parents paid for the wedding feast. They also brought to the house of Zadara, where the young people lived, a whole cart of dowry - sheets, blankets and a bunch of all the little things the newlyweds needed.

Sanda's mother shed tears and said that she had been preparing for her daughter's marriage for many years. And that he wishes the young only happiness. Alas, she understood happiness in her own way. And this happiness consisted in the fact that when Ned went to war, they would beat him there, and then Sanda would be free again. Of course, she is no longer a virgin, but still there is someone who wants to marry her. With such a beauty of the girl, there was no doubt about it.

Ned listened to the thoughts of "mom" and frowned - he personally was not going to part with his life in order to please this worthy woman.

Sanda's father was sincerely happy with the choice of his daughter - he liked Ned, who looked like himself in his youth. At the wedding, daddy had a good drink of wine, and for a long time declared his love for his son-in-law, glancing sideways at his feisty wife and winking at his beloved daughter. There was no evil in him, and as often happens - he went through life in the wake of his energetic wife, sincerely loving her, although often not approving what she did. But love is love, people forgive their loved ones that they would never, for anything, forgive anyone, even if he were the most wonderful person in the world.

Sanda ... it was more complicated here. The girl was not mean, bad, or mean. As a child who wanted a toy, she did everything to get it. Smart, calculating, with all her extravagance and eccentricity, Sanda clearly understood what she wanted. And she wanted Ned. And also - to become an adult. Rather, and at any cost. Fly away from home, lead an independent life, your own home, sleep with a man, catch on yourself the envious glances of friends and disappointed - familiar guys. She got all this. And she enjoyed it.

Ned sometimes thought about their future together and understood - if everything continues as it goes, then their family will face the fate of the family of Sanda's parents - a strong, self-confident, aggressive woman and a kind henpecked who does everything she orders.

Ned was not going to play the role of henpecked, and therefore, two weeks after he and Sanda lived together, he said that he was in charge of the house, and he would do as he saw fit. And if he doesn't want to go to Sanda's cousin, then he won't. If he does not want to come to Sunday lunch at Sanda's mother, then his feet will not be there.

Sanda was not offended, smiled slyly, and thought to herself: "Nothing! The folder also rebelled at the beginning. And then he calmed down. Without women, you men are nothing, but with us you are everything! I will still lead you to the people! "

Ned nearly revealed his abilities, barely refraining from responding to his wife's unspoken thoughts. Ned didn't like these thoughts.

Everything went well during the service. His company was no worse than others, there were no particular complaints about the soldiers, and they soon got used to being commanded by a former colleague. Ned was not familiar with his subordinates, but he did not indulge in arrogance, unlike his immediate commander, Lieutenant Shusard. He showed with his whole appearance what kind of cattle he was commanding, and that this cattle was not worth his nail.

Ned talked about Shusard with Drancon, who shrugged and said:

- You are still young. No commanders are chosen. Wait, you will go to war, everything will be clear there who is who. And here - but what is he to you? Well, he does not like us, a cattle rootless, so what? What can he do? Take away your salary? Punish for no reason? Don't give him a reason, that's all. And so - let him go and make faces. Don't give a damn about him. Most likely - he will soon dump somewhere in a warm place in the headquarters, and this will end the whole thing. Forget about him. Prepare your soldiers - it depends on them whether you survive the war or not. Soon, soon on the road ... I have a bad feeling. How would this local conflict develop into a full-scale war. This is where things go. I heard that Isfir's army advanced eighty more deep into our territory? Here. So wait for the commission soon and go to the front. I feel that we will miss many. Recruitment has been announced again - to replace you.

And Ned calmed down. The demon is with him, with this lieutenant. He will die himself. Or an enemy bolt will shoot through the head. Why wring your nerves?

And the commission that Drankon was talking about did not take long ... * * *

- Gentlemen officers! A commission from the capital has arrived to us. Tomorrow there will be a general review! After the show - the competition. Look, they find violations - I'll drink your blood from you! Check your equipment, check your weapons - no specks! Sharpen weapons, grease, chain mail to shine! Is there any sand in the mailbox cleaning boxes? Believe it! The screening will begin at ten in the morning, with a competition in honor of the high commission at noon. Running, wrestling, hand-to-hand combat, crossbow shooting. Sword Fighting among officers for the Corps Champion Prize. Sign up - which of you officers will perform among the swordsmen. By the way - please do not shirk, we must accept a commission on the highest level, show our combat skills! Any questions?

- Mr. Colonel! - one of the captains rose, a forty-year-old veteran with a crippled left ear, of which only half remained - can we show our skill on the battlefield? Why are we going to jump before the commission like comedians? For nothing ...

- Exactly - one of the majors supported him, as far as Ned knew - the commander of the battalion of crossbowmen - every time the same thing! Get drunk and will watch as we jump here for them! They would have gone....! They won't be sent further than the front anyway!

"You will not be sent," Heverad thought angrily. Of course not. But me - for sure. Why don't you shut up your stupid throats ?! As if I am pleased to placate the commission! I am the one who has to buy them a crowd of whores, pour wine over their throats and put on performances! And it's up to you to shake your backside a little! "

- In general, so, gentlemen - said Colonel Heverad coldly, not betraying the rage that raged in his soul - my order: there must be at least a dozen officers for the swordsmanship competition. And at least a dozen soldiers and officers for each type of competition. If you do not find it, you will be subject to penalties, with entry into a personal file, plus monetary deductions in the amount of a monthly salary! And I'll start with the commanders of the regiments, and they will already screw up the commanders of the battalions! So that in two hours the lists of those who will take part in the competitions are in the office! Do you understand everything ?! Or repeat again? I see it on your faces - understand. Now I'll sweeten you the powder. Everyone who wins the competition will receive a prize. The officer who won the sword competition - three hundred gold. A soldier or officer who wins a hand-to-hand combat, running, wrestling or shooting competition - one hundred gold. This is a lot of money, gentlemen. So do not make such sour faces, as if you were dragged from your mistress in the middle of the night and forced to march with your bare bottom!

- Well - it sounds better with prizes - the captain of the swordsmen grinned.

- Well, of course! You will receive this prize! Normally! The captain of the crossbowmen, a thin, long man with a rough-faced carter, shouted sarcastically.

- Well, you get for shooting, so what? - retorted the swordsman - what's wrong? Moreover, it is not a fact that I will get it. Over there - young shoots have appeared - Do you remember how Black fought in a duel? And its commander, Lieutenant Shusard, is the "silver sword" of the officers' school. Do not hide your abilities, gentlemen, do not - here are the first two participants in the competition. So it remains to be seen who will win.

- Ned fought with a spear. No one in the competition will allow him a spear - the crossbowman parried - besides, why is it a hundred gold for crossbowmen, and three hundred for swordsmen? What is this humiliation of the shooters?

- And because even a market trader can use a crossbow - the swordsman grinned - directed it at the target, pressed the bracket - bam! And past ... Heh heh ... But people learn the art of using a sword for years. One must have a penchant for this, among other things. So it's only natural that swordsmen will get more. Like this. So, gentlemen, we are looking for craftsmen, well, and ... preparing pockets for gold!

- That's great - Heverad intervened, watching the skirmish with a smile. "As always happens, money decided everything. A good prize always acts like an armful of hay in front of the donkey's muzzle, makes it run forward. "Lord! On the day of the competition, the gates will be open for everyone who wants to support their husbands, fathers or children. In addition, there will be a tent selling beer, pies, we will put tables and benches for the audience! You can invite whoever you want! Free admission!

- Then half of the city will be dragged! - Major Sert shouted gloomily - and how can I ensure safety in this case? Someone has a holiday, but someone, as always, weekdays!

"It always happens, Major Sert! - Heverad chuckled - and if you are not satisfied with the position of Chief of Security, you can always apply for a transfer, and I will gladly put you in command of the spearmen battalion. You will be given the opportunity to breastfeed the enemy on the battlefield! Don't you want to? Then serve, and don't make that face. Everyone has their own service. All, gentlemen, have dispersed! Getting ready for the show and for the competition! Colonels - I'll ask you!

The officers' meeting slowly dispersed from the hall in the headquarters, cheerfully discussing tomorrow's event. Sergeant Drankon was gloomy and unhappy. Noticing Ned's gaze, he whispered softly:

- A sure sign that the war is coming soon. The commission did not come in vain.

- And why on earth suddenly this holiday? Competitions? - Ned shrugged in bewilderment.

- The usual thing. We must entertain the general, the crowd of his hangers-on. The financing of the Corps depends on what report they write, and how they will treat the commander. They come about once every six months. Get drunk, get drunk, get drunk with the women, and back to the capital ... until next time. So the colonel is trying. Disgusting, of course, but where to go? It has always been and will be. From time to time, scandals arise with the loafers accompanying the general. They break loose when they come to our city. They get drunk and fight. And then we are surprised that the townspeople have such a bad opinion of the military. Here's what ... pick up someone there for the competition. By the way - here's a reason to knock down arrogance from Shusard. Did you hear what Captain Aston said? Well, the one, the captain of the swordsmen? Shusard "silver sword" of the officer's school. It means, that he is the second most skilled in swordsmanship in the officer's school. Will you participate? The prize is excellent, the colonel was not stingy. However - and on hand-to-hand combat the prize is very good. But according to the rules, you can only participate in one competition. Well, so how?

- Hmm ... I would like to try myself in the sword competition - admitted Ned - I have been training all this time, so I think there are chances. Will the fight be with sharp swords?

- Are you crazy? - Drankon chuckled - so we will be left without officers! There are heaps of dull training swords in the warehouse, why do we need combat ones? So on swords ... interesting. And how do you assess your chances? Bet on you?

"I don't know... I haven't seen the same Shusard or Aston fencing. As I understand it, this same Eston is a local celebrity, an eternal winner?

- Exactly. He always wins. The slayer is still the same. Animal strength, tremendous speed, endurance like a mule, and all this together multiply by ruthlessness, like a forest beast. So you get Eston. So he's a good guy, reliable, he will always cover his back. But it is better not to stand against him - he will trample him like a bug. See how long his arms are? It is far away. A real swordsman. Think before you go for a sword fight. Maybe it's better for melee? One hundred gold is great money! And faithful, you can put anyone here in hand-to-hand combat like a child. Or I don't understand anything about people. By the way, did you notice that Aston mentioned you? Do you know why?

- Why?

"He wants you to oppose him. After that duel, he announced that he would have won this fight against you. That you're not that good. You just got lucky. Came out against the fool. But if he was ... they even made a bet with Captain Gears that he would beat you. Fifty gold pieces. So that's it.

- Why then was he against the competition? I can not understand anything. He got up and began to speak, that he did not need any competitions and all that jazz. Why?

- I squeezed money from the colonel - Drankon grinned - but as he squeezed out, he immediately gave up. Everything is played. Aston loves performances like this. Moreover, he always wins. Okay. Will you invite someone to the competition? Wife?

- I'll ask. I invite you - maybe it will. Is there anyone else I can invite? Or just close relatives?

- Who else would you like to invite? So everyone is free to invite whoever he wants. If, of course, this corresponds to the status of the Corps. Slaves, for example, are not allowed to enter the base. Or some rogue from the street. The ragamuffins.

- I want to invite the hostess from whom I rent the house, Zadara Ivarron.

- Ivarron? ABOUT! Sure! Are you ... Colonel Ivarron is a legendary figure. He served in the corps for a long time, commanded one of the regiments. A desperate grunt was. And his wife ... the beauty was so few. I already thought she was dead. Because of her, there were several duels, five killed. The Colonel did not like to be shown signs of attention ... too persistently. She knew how to turn her head. I was still a young man when I saw her for the first time. Zadara was not young then ... wait ... how old was she then? Ugh! Just over forty ... but I thought she was a sort of middle-aged matron. And now I understand - a woman is just death to men. She was a real beauty even at forty. It would be interesting to see her. The colonel died by accident. Or maybe not by chance ... it was said that not everything is so simple. It seems like someone avenged the officer killed in a duel, who hit his wife. It was rumored that Zadara did not always have very strict rules ... However, the colonel also allowed himself to relax. Not one of his illegitimate offspring runs somewhere around the world.

- How did the colonel die?

- The horse carried and fell off the mountain path into the abyss. They say that someone shot a stallion in the balls from a sling. The colonel was later found on the seashore. Broken. Here's a story. All evil is from beautiful women! However, from the ugly - too. Women are generally evil. How did you get married?

- Entangled - Ned chuckled - I didn't understand, just! And married. And it all started with one innocent kiss.

- Exactly! First, kisses, and then you wake up - bam! And you are already in their networks. Married! No ... an honest whore is better - he gave her money, the girl worked, and went home. No concern, no trouble ... unless, of course, picked up something - Drankon laughed sharply, surprising those around him. Seeing Dracon laughing was as amazing as seeing ... laughing Ned. On this, both sergeants agreed.

- Claim me for a sword contest, okay? And for melee ... I have a man. I'll go check the company's equipment and appoint those who will take part in the competition. I'm going home soon, I don't want to spend too much time here.

- Are you in a hurry to see your young wife? - Drankon chuckled - well, yes, well, yes ... bye, I suppose, you like everything. Every day a bed, kisses ... and then it starts ... it will nag about money, don't go there, don't go here. Well, yes, I was married. And nothing good came of it. I'd rather sit in my barracks room. Well them, it's a woman. Okay, I will declare you a sword, but ... look, you risk. However, it's your business. * * *

"Ned, don't sip so loudly — this's not good! See how Sanda gently takes small sips? Don't frown - you're already making progress. Incidentally, I expected you to be a much bigger redneck. And you are quite at the level of city guys. Only ill-mannered. No, don't wipe your mouth with a tissue! Get your mouth wet! So, neatly ... Knife in right hand, fork in left. By the way - in different states in different ways, oddly enough. With us, he cut off a piece and put it in his mouth. And in the malicious Isfira - he cut the whole piece of meat into small pieces, put the fork in his right hand, and swallow them as you want. Ill-bred people.

- Aunt Zadar! Tomorrow there will be a show and competitions. Would you like to visit the base? Sanda will go. And I will perform in fights of swordsmen.

- The base ... I haven't been there for a long time ... - the woman smiled sadly - as my husband died, since then I haven't appeared at the base. Of course I will. Can I take my girls with me?

"Well ... they are ..." Ned began embarrassedly.

- Slaves? - interrupted Zadar - no. They don't even have a slave earring, as you can see. I let them go a long time ago. I know about the stupid ban on slaves visiting the base. By the way, I don't know who invented it and why. Some kind of stupidity. Take the girls?

- Let them go - Ned shrugged his shoulders - it will be more fun. I never asked you ... tell me, how did your husband die?

- What, already told you? - Zadara grinned, looking into Ned's eyes - and I'm a whore, right? And that my husband was a real duelist, who killed people in batches in fights? Yes? Did they tell?

- Well ... not so, of course ... but ... they told - Ned confused.

- So - it's all true! - suddenly declared Zadara, and glancing at the dumbfounded Ned, she rolled into a cheerful laugh - come on, I'm joking. So, I had some flirtations - nothing more. I was just such a beauty that many men were drying up for me. And my husband was jealous, hot - a real man! And in bed, and in battle! Uhhh! The fire! For that, she forgave him all sorts of pranks. It seems that they brought him to death. He seduced a beauty, most likely married, they were afraid to touch him openly, so they secretly killed him. Yes, yes, killed ... I know that. Who killed? How do I know. We went for a walk with him, rode horses. Mountain trail over the sea. I fell slightly behind, but I heard his horse whinnying and carry it. And she saw a ball of lead lying around - either from a sling, or from a slingshot. Then they looked for the ball - they did not find it. Someone picked it up. That's how it ended up. I have already raised the children myself. But let's not talk about sad things. Better about tomorrow - what will happen there?

- Competitions, festivities, guests, tables and sales of drinks, pies and buns. Should be fun.

- Oh, Heverad! I recognize him! - smiled Zadara - he always knew how to benefit from everything. Here I will put a hundred gold pieces against the copper, that all the tents will belong to his merchants, from each colonel will have a bribe. What difference does it make to us? The main thing is to be comfortable and fun. Well, all right, you have dinner, and I will go and tell the girls - let them get together by tomorrow.

Zadara quickly jumped up, disappearing into the bowels of the house, and Ned and Sanda exchanged glances, smiling and winking at each other.

- And our hostess took a walk in due time - Sanda grunted.

- I hope you will not follow her example - raised eyebrows Ned - when I come back from the war, I learn something bad about you - I will kill you!

- Hmm ... yes, maybe you will kill - Sanda looked appraisingly, narrowing her eyes slyly - but I don't need anyone but you. They are all fools, and freaks. You yourself were there, in the war, especially ... not being naughty. No, I understand - buying a whore is a soldier's business, but ... try not to abuse it, okay? And choose cleaner girls. It was not enough to bring the infection into the house.

- Actually, I was not going to go to the whores - Ned was confused - where did you get that?

- All of you men are like that. Okay, don't be angry. I just told you in advance so that you understand - I'm not a fool. Are you gorged? Maybe put some more? Try this salad - our family dish. Mom brought him from somewhere in the capital. By the way, it contains one herb that increases the bedding ability of men ... You are going to hike soon, so I want to take everything I can from you. When will you and I see you again ... - Sanda sighed sadly, then flashed her eyes - well, let's go home? I heated the water there ... now we will swim ... together. Then we'll get into bed ... I hope you're not going to read your stupid scrolls before bed? By the way - how do you manage to read them? What language is that? How did you recognize him? What is it written about in these scrolls?

- Just old scrolls - Ned tried to twist - it is written about different things - about magic, about demons - as the ancients understood them. I like. You won't be interested.

- You did not say - how do you know the ancient rune language? - Sanda narrowed her eyes - again secrets from his wife? What are you hiding?

- I? Hide it? I think I'm open, like this plate! And just as simple!

"You're not easy at all, my dear," sighed Sanda. "Okay, if you don't want to, don't answer. Let's go home. Aunt Zadar! Let Asana put some salads with him, okay? Refresh in the evening.

- Now it will! Go, kids, go! - Zadara responded, from somewhere in the depths of the house, where she talked with her hangers-on - your business is young, you need to strengthen your strength, yes! A man needs to be fed, otherwise he will ride like a thin stallion!

Sanda smiled and got up from the table. Ned jumped up, politely pushed aside his wife's chair - as Zadara had taught him, and taking her arm, walked gravely towards the exit. Then he could not resist, smiled, grabbed the girl in his arms and ran with her to the entrance, looking into her shining loving eyes.

Chapter 18

- Become! Soldiers, thank you for your service! - the colonel was more solemn and serious than ever.

- Ahhh! Ahhh! Aaaaa! - three times shouted the soldiers of the corps, which caused the birds, perched on the garbage dump behind the building of the utility block, screamed frantically, and flew away, furiously flapping their wings. Apparently they decided that their last hour of life had come. Several thousand sips, shouting out "Glory!" roared so terribly, menacingly and merged, as if a many-legged and many-armed beast, somehow miraculously wandered into a military parade ground.

Heverad examined the Corps, lined up in squares, and his heart warmed - his brainchild. His Corps. Whatever happens in the world - the Corps is the most combat-ready unit of the kingdom. And all this is the result of his activities too. To be able to put the right people in key positions - for this you need to have such an intelligent head like his. To notice the necessary, efficient person, to elevate him and not to be mistaken - isn't this art?

Here, for example, is the latest find - Ned the Black. The boy was a village idiot, uneducated, naive and dark, like the last carter in a seaside town - and look at him now - an eagle! The helmet is shining, the chain mail is burning with fire, a picture, not a soldier! And his company - shines, shines, and not a single comment on the show! And this despite the fact that in his company there is one rabble, due to an oversight not caught by city guards of different cities, criminal types, vagabonds, and just stupid guys. I could! Didn't shame the commander's trust!

Heverad glanced sideways at General Burtos, who was standing next to him, turning clearly so that his heels clicked, raised his hand in a military salute, reporting:

- Mr. General! The Marine Corps is built! Ready to receive comments! Corps Commander Colonel Heverad reporting!

- Congratulations, Colonel - The corps is great. You, as always, are on top, and I will report this to our king - the general's face, flushed from the sun and from the wine he had drunk the day before, expressed complete satisfaction with what he saw.

The general spent an excellent night with two young whores, and in the morning got drunk so that he was barely raised to the formation. He would have been glad to finish with the official part as soon as possible, and therefore - he had no time to inspect the lined up regiments.

Heverad noted with a smile the presence of black bags under the general's eyes, and quietly, barely audible, suggested:

- Eras, maybe you should send a doctor? How are you feeling?
- To be honest, not very good. I went through something tonight. Nulan, please order a light wine, better than a white one. And colder. And well water, ice cold, diluted. Is there a place to sit? Are you going to host competitions now?
- Of course, Eras - a place is already ready for you, over there, under the awning. Everything you love is there - cold light wine, snacks, everything you need. The competition will begin now. Will you be placing bets?
"Hmm... rates? You know, I missed a little ...
- Do not worry! A loan of one thousand gold will be opened for you, so don't worry about money. If you win, then you win. And if you lose, no one will demand a return from you.
- Perfectly! - the general sighed with relief - you are at your best in this. I love coming to you - always order, always kindness and clear organization of the case! It's not for nothing that His Majesty the King values you so much. By the way - he recently asked - isn't it time for you to go to serve in the ministry, won't you be enough to meet enemy arrows with your chest? Think about it - the position of Deputy Minister of the Ground Forces will soon be vacated, so ...
- I think, Mr. General - Heverad closed his eyes for a moment gratefully. The offer was really very good - it is one thing to keep a hand on the cash flows that fill the treasury of the corps, and another to keep the land forces numbering tens of thousands of people. And everyone needs to eat, drink, put on shoes, dress - this opened up wonderful prospects.
- Just about, think - the general nodded - in our department there are not so many combat, efficient and intelligent officers. It is necessary to raise people like you, giving them the opportunity to prove themselves already at the state level, and not in individual units. All the more so - at the present, sad time ...

"Goats!" - the colonel thought with a fierce grin - "We shit at the front, and now you are pulling out those who can actually fight? But what about your relatives who have flooded the military department? What, they pull the shit out of their pants? Stupid creatures! The only thing you can do is get drunk and chase women at balls! How many of you did my whore wife get fucked? The whole headquarters? They giggled, I suppose, they say, a military colonel, and your wife ... Isfir pressed you? Well - it's stupid for me not to take advantage of this situation. It's time to go to the capital ... it's just a pity to leave the building. Very sorry. But you can control it from the capital ... "

- What, things are so bad? What's at the front?

- Bad - the general answered quietly, glancing sideways at the officers of the corps, who were standing a little further away and diligently not listening to the conversation of senior commanders - worse than many think. The Isfirians have advanced a hundred and fifty li deeper into the territory of Zamar. They leave garrisons in cities and fortify themselves. This is not a border skirmish, this is a full-scale war. And things got worse and worse. Think, think strongly about my proposal. Otherwise ... there will be no time and no one to think. I hope you don't want Sholokar to rule the kingdom? That's the same ...

- Let's return to this conversation after the competition. And you need to rest after the review, and I will assess the situation. Of course, I will not leave my king without help, after all - I am a loyal subject to the crown. By the way, how is his royal majesty feeling?

- Not really. Shortness of breath, doctors do not crawl out of his chambers, use his majesty - worries about the fate of the country, does not sleep, worries. All in business.

"You need to eat less! And smack the wine! And your deeds, ragged bitches, are known - get drunk and somersault with women! And let someone put their butt for you at the front! Nights, you see, he does not sleep! What kind of mistress does she sleep with? He's fucked up the whole yard, a fat hog, "thought the colonel, outwardly without giving out his feelings.

- Very sorry. I wish His Majesty to get well soon, and I will not leave him in my support. I assure you with full responsibility.

- Nice. We knew that we could rely on you - the general nodded contentedly - will you accompany me?

- Sure. Now I will order Zayd to give orders, and we will settle down under a canopy. By the way, was it convenient for you last night? Is it hot? Did everything suit you?

- That's it - the general grinned - thank you. Let's go.

- Colonel Zayd - command by the end of the show and the start of the competition. Let the commanders see that the equipment is stacked neatly. And post posts to the armory rooms at the barracks - today there are many outsiders, you never know what ... * * *

- At last! And we are already tired of waiting! - Zadara, sitting on the bench, was lively, her eyes were shining, and her cheeks were flushed, like a young woman - did you have time to take a shower? OK. After your piece of iron-armor from you, the warrior, bears like from goats. Sometimes the husband would come from maneuvers - the smell of sweat from him - already shivered from his feet! I didn't let him near me until he washed. Tyraz, what are you not eating? Eat, eat more - you are completely emaciated. And he was such a plump boy! When my husband brought him in the saddle, I went out, I looked - such a rosy boy, a little chubby! And where did that go? There - poke in the side - knock off your fist! How iron all!

Zadara gently patted the imperturbable Tiraz on the cheek, and he quietly made a sweet face to Ned and Sanda until the old woman saw.

- I see, I see how you make faces there! Here is a restless boy! He always ran with mine, came with bruises! They roamed the city and fought with street boys. It was there that bad thoughts got into his head - to go to the soldier. He was so smart! So restless! He always got into fights. But we must pay tribute - never lost and never gave up. It's a pity, my husband does not see how you grew up, Gozarchik ... what a pity.

- Yes, sorry for my father - Tiraz nodded his head, and, catching himself, glanced at the surprised Ned and Sandu. Then he turned away and pretended to be busy examining the soldiers setting up the rails of the competition area.

- Yes, yes ... do not be surprised He is the son of my late husband - smiled Zadar - from his mistress. Cedar brought it to me and said: "Do what you want - beat me, cut me, kill me - but I will not leave him. This is my son. She died, and he has no relatives. I'm sorry if you can. But if you can't - go to the demons! " Well, I ... punched him in the face, he then walked with bruises for more than a week. I told everyone that I came across a branch in the forest. And she took the child and brought up with her children. Brother is theirs. And he is a good boy, I love him like my child. Come here, Gozarchik, let me kiss you ... Here, good boy! Asana, pour him a drink, you see, the boy's throat is dry! And cut off the fresh ham! He is very thin!

- Yes, he still has, he did not eat it! - the black "tower" in a colorful bright dress, from which rippled to the eyes, boomed.

- Nothing that is! Put something fresh! What, hands will dry up, or what ?! What a lazy woman, huh ?! Guys, you too, eat, eat! Ned also needs to eat properly, he has to ride there with the pieces of iron now! You need to gain strength.

- Now you understand why I don't often go to mommy? - Tiraz whispered conspiratorially - she will suffocate with motherly love! How are you there, have not yet howled from such attention?

- Aunt Zadar is great - Ned answered evasively, winked at Sanda - yes, I only see her in the evening, besides - we lock ourselves ... she will scratch herself, scream near the window, and leave. Only you can't go out, otherwise she immediately rushes in, and begins to command. And the doors must be locked - in the middle of the night, at the most intimate moment, she can burst in and shout: "Baby, how are you lying down, the boy is uncomfortable!"

- Really? - the master laughed, looking at the grinning Ned and the giggling, blushing Sandu - was it really so?

- It's true! - laughing, the girl nodded - she almost began to correct her leg! I almost burned out with shame! Horror!

- Hey, what are you whispering? - the old woman shouted suspiciously - are you discussing me? What rascals! Take advantage of the fact that I have become a little deaf! There is nothing to discuss me! Look better at the guests - over there, see the man? Once he whipped me. Cedar broke his nose. But this Hagar was such a handsome man ... an officer, one word! They fought in a duel because of me. By the way, I got a gossip that Cedar was playing with his wife. I interrogated Cedar, but he never confessed. And what kind of officer is hugging her?

"Hmm… that's actually my immediate commander," Ned frowned. "Didn't know he was from here.

"Her son, it looks like that…" Zadara said slowly, with an arrangement, gazing intently at the stranger with faded senile eyes.

The old woman darkened and pointedly turned away, thrusting a sugar-coated nut into her mouth. She somehow immediately fell silent and went into her thoughts, and the interlocutors looked at each other, shrugging their shoulders. Apparently I remembered something from the past.

- Today we will see how you prepared in a sword fight - Tiraz chuckled - do not shame your teacher. And here's another thing - don't spare your opponents. Hit it as best you can. It may not be a duel, but it will not be weak here.

- And how will everything go? I've never been to a competition.

- Now they will break everyone in pairs, start yelling, and you will go out onto the site, choosing a sword from that heap of pieces of iron. Sword and dagger. Well, fight until the colonel stops the fight. Either until one of the opponents refuses, or cannot continue it. That's all. Just.

- Are kicks, punches, other body parts allowed? Ned asked, just in case.

- Hmm ... that is not prohibited, but ... it will look ugly - smiled the master - this is a fencing tournament, not hand-to-hand combat. By the way, who did you put on hand-to-hand there?

- Oidara, corporal from my company. My friend. We enlisted together with him, in the barracks we slept on neighboring bunks. And then fate scattered a little - I became a sergeant, and he was my subordinate. So we are on good terms, but ... I am an officer, and he is a corporal.

- Yes, I know that - the master nodded his head - when you have to send today's friend to death tomorrow - the thought naturally suggests itself that it is better ... not to be a friend. Then everything is easier. Better to be friends outside the service. With those who are not related to the army.

- With me, for example, - Sanda smiled, and with a seductive smile, she kissed Ned on the cheek.

The girl looked just charming. The fine silk dress her mother had given her on account of her dowry wrapped around her hips, outlining their beautiful shape.

The fabric, brought from somewhere from the southern mainland, shimmered either golden or bluish-white, and was slightly transparent, outlining the beautiful breasts on which Sanda had never put on a bodice - that even without a bodice stuck out forward, as if made of hard wood.

Ned, when he first saw Sanda in a candy store, paid attention to her breasts, and only then he considered everything else. However, in this he was not at all original, this would have been confirmed by thousands of men at all times.

The girl's feet were shod in woven leather sandals, which no longer served as shoes, but as an ornament for her slender, smooth legs. When Sanda walked, it seemed that she was dancing, and not just walking along the road.

Wet eyes of a deer, velvet clean skin, shiny hair - the girl breathed with freshness, beauty, and such passion that the officers and even more the "hungry" soldiers of the corps turned their necks, surreptitiously and openly looking at the girl's charms sticking out from under the dress. Fortunately, his neckline was quite bold - at the suggestion of Zadara, it was lowered ... a little. Just three sa. Or four ...

The breeze from the mountains was fresh and slightly cool, so that Sanda's nipples almost pierced the thin fabric. "Death to men!" - this would describe her outfit.

Zadara, when she examined her ward from head to toe at home, was satisfied with the result, and said that if she were a man, she would go after her and to the end of the world. And Ned would be a fool if he didn't appreciate his wife's attire as it should be.

Ned appreciated. At first he raised his eyebrows, then frowned and said that Sanda looked like a dear whore. To which he received a stern reprimand from Zadara, and an inflated face from Sanda. Then he shrugged his shoulders and said that if she liked to walk around in such an outfit, he would not mind. The main thing is that she is not naked, and okay. Although ... better naked. It wouldn't look so challenging.

By the way, no underwear was found on the girl when felt. Zadara explained that no panties are worn with dresses like his wife. It's too thin for that. But don't worry - the dress is still opaque ... almost opaque. And who knows - did she wear something there, or not? She will not allow anyone to check it.

To which Ned said he was very hopeful. I would not want to chop off anyone's ears, and publicly strangle my wife.

To which Zadara replied that he was a dork, an egoist and a redneck, who did not understand anything about fashion and how a real woman should present herself. And if he wants the woman to sit in the barn and not go out, then he had to marry a cow - and the skin is thick, and no one will pay attention to the udder, which means that there is no need to be jealous. Then Ned was exhausted.

This is how Sanda became the queen of the current gathering. Men whistled enviously, and women snorted frontily, burning with the desire to rip off "this bitch" her shameful dress and take out the reptile in the mud so that their faithful would not show off his stupid jaw, devouring this whore with shameless eyes.

Ned pulled back slightly from his wife, patting her hand affectionately, and said:

- I'll go to Oydara, check how he is there.

- Can I go with you? - offered Tyraz, glancing sideways at Zadara, just at that moment, distracted by another rebuke to her second hanger, who gave her the wrong pie.

- Of course - smiled Ned - let's go.

- And I?! - squeaked Sanda - will you leave me here?

- Watch out for Aunt Zadar - Ned said seriously - or her birds will take away. See the shiny hat she's wearing? And birds love shiny things!

- Iehhh! Rogue! - Zvdara chuckled and laughed - everything is joking at the grandmother! Go, you scoundrels! Sandochka, leave them - they are either going to the toilet, or discussing us women. However - they usually combine these two pleasant activities. Men are such gossips! Listen, I'll tell you a story ...

- Come on, let's go soon! - the master grabbed Ned by the hand and dragged him away - Zadar's mother is a wonderful woman, but in large doses it can be unbearable. Better to accept her love in portions, as well as chatter. Forgive me for putting you in to live with her. However - everything turned out pretty well, didn't it? And he rented a house inexpensively, and even a beautiful wife was formed. By the way, keep an eye on her. Later everyone will get drunk - as if there were no problems ... She is such a bright girl that everyone stares at her. Maybe it would be worth dressing somehow more modestly? Forgive me for not getting into my business ...

- It's all Zadar! - Ned winced in annoyance, passing by a group of soldiers, heatedly discussing future fights - her job. I just gave up on everything. Let them dress as they want.

- Zadara ... you should have seen her when she was in her prime! That was a beauty! As the father died, it somehow immediately went out ... They were always fighting, swearing, feathers were flying! Mom is a sharp, strong woman, don't look that fragile! So it will embed - it will not seem a little!

- I know already - Ned chuckled - she snapped the detective's nose, he didn't even have time to blink an eye.

- In-in. So, she is on her own, young, and dresses Sandu. And by the way - because of Zadara's mother, it seems that my father died. Who killed him - no one knows. But ... many wanted to remove him from their path, later marrying a widow. Or at least by putting her in your bed. After his death, she did not get along with anyone. She locked herself in the house and sat until they forgot everything about her ...

- And what did your own mother die of? Sorry if I poked a sore spot ...

"No... no big deal. I hardly remember her ... they say - she fell ill and died. I tried to find her grave, find out who she was, how everything happened, but my father was no longer alive, and there was no one else to ask. If only mom Zadar. But she is silent. He is just silent and that's it. She never said anything to me. She really treated me like a family, especially when my father died. After all, I am very much like him, very much. Especially this crooked nose and hair and this chin hole. Her own sons for some reason are not so much like him, more like her, but I am a spitting image of a father.

Ned nodded his head and wondered - where else did he see this nose, this hole ... where did he see a man so similar to Tiraz?

I never remembered, then shook his head to drive away the obsession and slightly increased his pace, seeing Oidar with a group of colleagues.

Oidar warmed up, doing the exercises and absorbing the Force. He didn't see Ned until he came up and stood on the side, and when he did, he smiled happily.

- Hello! Thank you for putting me in the competition! One hundred gold pieces are not superfluous for me!

- Master, this is Oidar - smiled Ned - he is a master of uatsu, he has a tark.

- Hmm ... a promising young man - Tiraz nodded his head, carefully following the movements of Oidar - to get a tark at this age ... and who examined you for tark? Can you name the masters?

- I ... this ... - Oidar blushed deeply - in general, I did not pass the exam. Did not have time. But my teacher said that I was exactly at the tarka level.

- I see - Tiraz nodded - you are not bad. But after a long absence of training, a kind of laxity, fuzziness appeared in your movements. However, it is easily removable. I could study with you and take you as a senior student if you wanted to. When you finish your contract service, of course. "And if you live to see it," the master finished mentally.

"Are you ... a master?" - Oidar asked dumbfounded, and respectfully bowed his head, putting his right hand to his heart.

- Yes. I have my own school in this city - Tiraz nodded his head - so - I invite you when you are free. Now, look - this exercise needs to be done a little bit differently. Here! - she smoothly sat down, moving her arms forward and to the sides - repeat! Look - your kankers open up more fully, and the power flows more freely into your body ... like this, so ... you grasp quickly, boy. You have a great future. I'll wait for you. The main thing is not to let yourself be killed.

The master winked and stepped aside, watching Oidar continue to warm up. Ned glanced over and whispered softly, trying not to distract Oidar:

- I `ll leave for a while. I need to check something.

Casting a glance at his fellow training friends, Ned turned and walked over to where Lieutenant Shusard stood with his loved ones. They talked, glancing around, and did not notice Ned.

Ned slowly walked to the group, and stood a step away from them, looking at the elderly man, whose bearing remained the officer's - a little flabby, gray-haired, he haughtily looked at the preparation of the competition grounds and frowned, as if remembering his departed youth. Then he noticed Ned, his eyebrows raised, and the man said in disgust:

- Anton, is this sergeant to you?

Shusard looked around in bewilderment, saw Ned and exasperatedly said:

- What do you want, redneck? Looking for me?

- No, not you - Ned said calmly and with a nod of his head pointed at the elderly man - him!

- What relation do you have to my father? - the lieutenant frowned - get out of here! Not only do you stick out in front of me on the parade ground all day, but you also get it here!

- Wait, Anton - the old man stopped, and asked warily - what do you want, sergeant?

- Why did you kill him? - suddenly asked Ned, peering into the blue eyes of the man. Once he was really handsome. Even now he was handsome, as well-groomed, self-conscious, "thoroughbred" old men are.

- Whom ?! - slightly shuddered the old man, casting a glance into Ned's face - I have killed a lot of people in my life. Both in battle and in duels.

- Colonel Cedar Ivarron. You killed him, I know!

"Where from ?! What does he know ?! Where did he come from ?! No, it can not be. Nobody knows. And I cut Jasson's throat, so that the ends are in the water. I suppose the old bitch sent, she suspects, but she can't prove it. Creature! I would cut your throat without thinking! Anton? What are the children, if they cannot cut the throat of your abuser? Even if these children are not yours ... "

- Anton, what the hell is this sergeant? Is he crazy? Or just decided to offend me? And you look at it calmly?

- Get out, Black! I already told you! - hissed Shusard Jr. - or give you a kick ?! How dare you pester my father ?! Creature!

"He's not your father," Ned said coldly. "Your real father is Cedar Ivarron. Your mother was the colonel's mistress and carried away from him. And your alleged father molested Ivarron's wife - Zadara. And he hired a man named Jasson to kill the colonel. And he killed Ivarron. And then Shusard cut Jasson's throat and lowered his body into the sea. He achieved two goals at once - to avenge the fact that Ivarron slept with his wife, and to get Zadara, the first beauty of the corps, and even the city, into his bed. He succeeded in the first task, but with the second ... it did not work, right, Major? The colonel's widow refused to sleep with you anymore? Despite the fact that she always suspected you of the death of her husband, she just could not prove it.

- Ahhh! - a woman standing nearby, the lieutenant's mother, grabbed her head, staggered and fell into the arms of a retired major - she lost consciousness. The lieutenant, numb with amazement and stiff as a pillar, suddenly struck Ned in the face with all his might.
- The creature! You dare to insult my father ?! Duel! To death!
- Kill him, son! - the former major glared at Ned's face with hatred, and could not stand it, croaked in a choked voice - yes, yes! I killed that upstart! But you will never prove it for anything! Kill him, son! Damned Ivarrons! They ruined our whole life! He took my place as regiment commander! Because of him, I did not receive what I should have received according to my origin, my position! And I fucked his wife! Yes! And more than once! She was a whore! And now she is the same whore, only now an old, decrepit whore! And it is she who is to blame for the death of her husband! If Zadara hadn't given me hope ... What are you looking at, Anton? Well, yes, I have not always been faithful to your mother, so what? Wake up, this is life! Kill this villain, and we will close this topic!
- Shusard, you know I told the truth - Ned touched his cheek, burning from the blow - apologize, and we will end on this.
- In front of you? Apologize? You keep lying! Hit you again, or do you still dare challenge me to a duel? The lieutenant answered calmly, frowning and obviously pondering something.
- Good. Duel. I do not insist that she be dead. Until the first blood.
- No. I accept the duel, but it will be to death. On swords. Here or elsewhere. Better here during the match competition. The rules allow, at the request of the fighters, the replacement of training swords with combat ones. Only death will stop us!
- Why, Shusard? - Ned shrugged in bewilderment - why would you die for a lie, for a criminal, not even your father? He lied to you all his life, killed your real father - he is a scoundrel! You are not a fool not to understand this!
- I hate you. I hate people like you - upstarts, rootless creatures! And your words mean nothing. You, rootless cattle, are ready for anything, just to belittle the noblemen to your level. And you need to be taught. And you won't be the first person I teach good manners. Rather, I will forever wean from bad manners. You will die. Get ready.
- That's right, son. Well done! - Shusard Sr. nodded in satisfaction - kill this creature. The peasants must know their place.

- I will declare a duel to Hevarad - nodded Shusard - and you, Black, prepare to die. Go say goodbye to your whore. After you die, the whole body will fuck her. Tell them to take no less gold for services, and not let the soldiers near her, otherwise the price will go down ...

Ned hit the lieutenant in the face, briefly, without a move, breaking his lip. He wiped himself off, licking the red drops, and nodded his head:

- It's good. You will die. Now you definitely have to die.

Ned turned around, and ignoring the lieutenant, walked over to where his wife and Zadar were sitting. He did not see how the people around were whispering and pointing at him and the lieutenant - the incident between the two officers could not be hidden from the eyes of those around him. Few did not notice the skirmish, and the last episode, when Ned hit his commander, was seen by almost everyone. Including Sanda.

The girl jumped up from her seat, ran to Ned, whose face resembled a mask carved out of stone, and asked in dismay:

- What?! What was it? Did you hit the lieutenant? For what? What happened? What will happen now?

- There will be a duel - Zadara nodded in satisfaction, screwing up her eyes, as if she had taken Ned's opponent at the sight of a crossbow - your husband will kill the insolent today. Ned, why did you go to them?

- Informed that killing colonels is not good - muttered through his teeth Ned, inside of whom rage was seething, looking for a way out - you know who killed her husband, right?

- I know. What can I do? - the extinct Zadara sighed wearily - I myself am to blame for this. There was no need to mess with Hagar. But Cedar is also to blame - why slept with Shusard's wife? When I found out, I was completely furious ... and took revenge. Yes, I slept with Hagar. But she broke up with him as soon as he did IT. How did you guess? Lieutenant? Yes, he is the spitting image of Cedar. Like Goraz. Notice how similar they are? Yes, you're smart. Few people would have guessed, but you could. What did Hagar tell you?

- That you and your husband ruined his life.

- He broke himself. He just dragged himself after other people's wives, and did not want to be engaged in official business at all. That's why my husband stalled his promotion.

- Hmm ... how it all got mixed up - Sanda stretched out thoughtfully - what are you doing, everyone slept with everyone, or what? And that was considered normal?

- There was such a time, the girl - Zadar shrugged her shoulders - then it was considered in the order of things for a woman to have one or two lovers, except for a legitimate husband. Well, men - so they were not limited in connections at all. Especially in such small towns, where the majority of the military. There is boredom, there is nothing to do, only entertainment - intrigue in the service, but flirting. Treason was encouraged - the then king, the father of the current one, was an adherent of the sect at the temple of the goddess Selera. They preached the rejection of the usual family values, numerous connections on the side and all kinds of exotic entertainment, in a group and without her. I did not approve of this, my husband too, but we could not be free from fashion. Those who adhered to old family values were ridiculed. When everyone around them says that it's okay to have a lover, that those who remain faithful are hopelessly behind, that they are rednecks and dark villagers - do you think this can leave its mark? Willy-nilly, he will impose. Here is the result ... cross-pollination, so to speak - the old woman smiled - now everything is stricter, the current king cannot stand the priests of Selera and does not allow sectarians to visit him. However, this does not prevent him from sleeping with all his court ladies. They say - I will not save from him, drags everyone to bed. What to say? He's his father's son ... that's all. What to say? He's his father's son ... that's all. What to say? He's his father's son ... that's all.

- Ned, what happened? - the voice of an alarmed Tiraz was heard behind - everyone talks about a duel between you and the lieutenant!

- Duel. To death, Ned explained shortly.

- The reason?

- He insulted my wife. And also ... I told his father that I knew he was the killer of Cedar Ivarron.

- Are you sure? - Tiraz's voice is suddenly hoarse - perhaps this is just speculation? We always suspected that the murder was his doing, but it's one thing to guess, and another to know for sure.

- Exactly. I told him on purpose that I knew he was a murderer. And Shusard could not resist. He began to accuse the late colonel of having stalled his service. And also - that the colonel slept with his wife.

- What, he said? In front of everyone?
- Of course not. The lieutenant heard, and his wife. Well, me, of course. Nobody else. And it looks like the younger Shusard knows. He knew that his father had killed the colonel by hiring an assassin. And not at all against it. I don't understand - after all, Ivarron is his real father! How can that be?
- Not always the one who conceived is the father. And the one who brought up, who raised, who put the mind. I don't remember my mother, and Zadar's mother became my mother. And in my mind she is the mother, and not the one who gave birth. Do you understand? Moreover, who knows how he raised him and what he told him about my father. To death, so ... hmm ... funny. As I knew. Here, take it— Tyraz handed Ned a small oblong package, which he took from the bench — he wanted to give it to you after the competition, I was sure that you would win it. But now ... let it be right away. Look what's in there!

Ned unwrapped the package - he already knew what was in there. The sight of the precious "sword for the left hand" delighted him - the black lacquered scabbard, with a quiet rustle, released the matte blade covered with patterns, and golden runes flickered in the middle: "I conjure you, give me strength, O Winged Horror!"

- I give. In memory of me. You already have one, and this is a pair for him. From the master to the master. Secretly - I believe that you have already reached the level of a sword master. There is nothing more I can teach you. It is possible that you have already outgrown me. I do not know the reasons for your rapid growth, but fact is fact. It was as if you were recalling what you passed earlier, and now you remember everything. Owl.

Tiraz took the sword with both hands and gave it to Ned with a slight bow. Ned, just as ceremoniously bowed, coughed embarrassedly and asked in a low voice:

"Such an expensive gift ... can I repay it with something?" No, no - don't think bad, I'm not offering money. If something unexpected happens in your life, you just have to contact me, and I will always help. I swear.

- Thank you - the master replied seriously - I know that I can always count on you. Now get ready. Colonel Heverad literally runs here. It will begin now ...

- Ned! Explain to me what kind of duel it was during the commission's work? - the colonel was not a little angry - what happened? Why is Lieutenant Shusard claiming to be cutting off your head and nailing it over the doors of the estate? What happened?

"I found out who killed Colonel Ivarron," Ned said firmly, "and Shusard is protecting his... father. The pause between Ned's words was barely perceptible, but the colonel still twitched an eyebrow - he understood.

- There is no evidence - Heverad said in an undertone, and glancing to the left, grunted in surprise - Goraz ?! You're here?! Haven't seen you for a long time ... How did you end up here?

- Here, I came to see the fight of my student. And besides, my mother is here, I wanted to accompany her. Isn't it possible?

"Hmm... no, please. Do you know what Ned said?

- I know. As far as I know, the Major himself confessed to him of the murder, right, Ned?

- Yes. The reason for the murder is love passions, and office plots. That's all.

- That's all ... - the colonel repeated thoughtfully - that's all. Why did you bring up this story? So many years have passed ... everything was so quiet, calm.

- You are quiet and calm, right, Nulan? - said Zadara sharply, and got up from her place, clenching her fingers into fists - you all knew that it was his fault! So what?! What have you done to punish the murderer? Thanks to Ned - made a fuss. For me. Let everyone know who the killer is. Let be! Let him sit in his estate for the last years of his life, being afraid of people's views! And let him experience the pain of loss! Ned, kill his son! Let Hagar learn how hard it is to lose loved ones!

- You are cruel, Zadara - the colonel said quietly, shaking his head - once you were kinder.

- Taught! Well taught! - the old woman narrowed her eyes angrily - how many tears I cried in a lonely bed! Did this creature live? How many times have I wanted to kill him! And then she hardly stopped herself - and the children? You would have sent me to the gallows for the murder of this cattle! Now ... now let her cry. Well done Ned!

"Are you sure Ned will win?" - the colonel chuckled - how would you not have to cry again ...

- No. He will win! Goraz taught him. And Goraz will put your fighters in packs, if necessary! Announce the beginning! Let Ned gut this puppy!

- As you say, Zadara - the colonel grinned, and slightly softened his voice - and you look good. Everything is as beautiful as before. By the way, what is the beauty next to you? Daughter? All in you. You were the same. I remember looking at you as a boy ...

- You know how to make compliments, Nulan! - smiled the old woman - that's what women have always loved you. However - not only for this. They say you would always be very good in bed ...

- Come on ... lie. I would always be just great! - the colonel laughed - so what kind of beauty is there, won't you introduce me?

- Let the husband introduce you - Zadar winked - this is Ned's wife. Do you remember that story with the attack on us by the Nitul couple, with the support of the burgomaster? So this is it, that girl.

- Oh Gods! Now I understand how she managed to lock our rock-hard Ned! - Heverad smacked his lips - where were you hiding, beauty? I would leave my wife for you and take me to the end of the world! Congratulations, Ned is a great choice.

- Quiet, quiet, Nulan - giggled Zadara - girl, don't listen to him. He's a famous ladies' man! Always trying to fool the women! Come on, he jokes ...

- "Not so ... what a joke. With such a beauty, to have some fun - anyone would give ... a lot "- thought the colonel -" really, Ned had to grab such a beauty! Look, what legs, chest, face ... if it weren't for Ned, I would ... What good head off - a serious guy. And the girl shoots with her eyes ... loves men, worship. You will cry with her, boy. My wife was like that too - young, beautiful, she shot with her eyes ... and now she shoots, bitch! Be careful, kid. "

- Back to our sorrowful business - Heverad shook his head, chasing away the obsession - so you, Ned, confirm the challenge to Lieutenant Shusard?

- I confirm.

- The reason for the duel?

- He insulted my wife and hit me in the face.

- Is reconciliation possible? Revision of the terms of the duel?

- Now it is not possible. Until he touched Sandu. Conditions? He insisted on lethal.

- Clear, clear ... - the colonel thought - in general, this is how we conduct the tournament as it should be - with a blunt weapon. If you meet him at a tournament, take a combat one. If any of you kicks out of the tournament earlier, you will meet immediately after the tournament, in the presence of witnesses. You have enough of them - how many! - the colonel nodded his head at the parade ground - you have to write a will, which will be transferred to the office of the Corps - just in case. Shusard will leave the same. This is necessary in any case. You didn't write to whom to transfer your salary in case of your death in the war or as a result of an accident? Well, and so - you will write. Go to Major Stirt, he will take the paper and seal it. By the way - how do you assess your chances?

"The boy is not easy ... just remember his previous duels. And Goraz is really good. His school is the best in the kingdom's seaside area. If Tiraz prepared the guy properly, there is a chance to get a good jackpot. I'll bet a thousand on Ned. And on Shusard there are three hundred. No - two hundred. Two hundred is enough. Or maybe a hundred?

Oh, the girl is good. and her outfit ... my blood rushed already ... even uncomfortable. Like a boy! That's why all the officers turned their necks at her. Zadarov school. That's for sure. She also always walked like the incarnate goddess of love! It was because of her that there were always duels. And it started again! All evil is from women ... but where can we go without them ?! "* * *

- First pair! Sergeant Black and Captain Aston! Training weapon. I ask you to go to the site - the voice of the steward, Major Stirt was cold and impersonal, and the whole crowd of spectators gasped: "At once to Eston ?! Gotcha, guy ... that's bad luck! "

Chapter 19

- Sorry, boy. But I can't lose to you! Captain Aston was complacent and clearly sympathetic to Ned. Which, however, will not prevent him from whipping the young sergeant according to all the rules of the tournament.

- Understand, I need these three hundred coins - to be honest, I have run out of money. Because - I have to clean you up. By the way - as you get away from the bruises - hit this impudent Shusard. This young insolent person is too arrogant, boasts of his origin. Well, how are you - ready?

- Gentlemen! Enough talk! We will never start this! - shouted Major Sert - time is ticking, start!

- Ready - Ned smiled slightly and froze in a strange stance that surprised the captain of the swordsmen. He held the swords with the blade towards him, with a reverse grip, which was not accepted by the officers of the corps. Moreover - none of them have ever seen such a fighting style.

The conversations subsided, people fell silent and peered intently at what was happening on the site, forgetting about their glasses, mugs and pieces of meat fried on coals. All the attention to the fighters slowly converging in the center of the site.

Aston was very fast and strong. His attacks, like the blows of two hammers, rained down on Ned so that the other person, if he had not missed the attack, would have already dropped the sword from his hand - the blows simply dried his hands. But Ned did not meet swords like an ordinary man trained in the army. His sliding oblique signals, reminiscent of the movements of a praying mantis, knocked the blades to the side so that each time the captain almost lost his balance.

Alas, this did not mean anything - Aston was as fresh and strong as at the beginning of the fight, despite the fact that the fight had already lasted ten minutes at the highest speed inaccessible to most of those present at the trunir. The blows did not weaken, the blade stung just as skillfully, looking for flaws in the enemy's defense. Unfortunately for the captain, there were no flaws. Ned glided easily over the platform, gently deflecting blows as if the blades were an extension of his arms.

Finally, the captain began to get angry, blushed, and no matter how impossible it seemed, he increased the pace even more.

Now the training steel blades merged into one whirlwind that swept over Ned, like water after a tropical downpour floods a roadside ditch. scan:

- Es-ton! Es-ton! Yes, wai! Yes, wai! Yes, wai!

The screams of the spectators seemed to have poured new strength into the captain, he gave his best, showing incredible skill in the fight ... and suddenly everything was over, under the deathly silence of the crowd.

The steel whirlwind crumbled, and Aston slowly bent down and fell forward on his face - the left hand remained under the body, the right one froze in the attack and was now lying on the ground, pointing towards the enemy. Ned stood a little to the side, carefully examining the fallen. Then he went up to him, felt his neck and nodded to the jury of senior officers:

- Alive. Request to send a doctor.

And then the audience exploded with a roar of applause, shouts and cries:

- Ned! Ned! Hail! Glory to the sergeant!

Geresard immediately approached the captain, slightly panting from walking, made a sign to his assistants, and the captain was taken to the medicine. Geresard went up to Ned and said, smiling:

- Strong! No one has been able to defeat him with swords in five years! That's disgusting - I didn't have time to start! I had to go to the city on business, I could not. But still arrived in time for the most interesting! Let's go! Free up space for the next couple.

He grabbed Ned by the shoulders and, like a heavy draft horse, dragged him to the bench where Sanda, Tyraz, and everyone else sat. Sanda immediately threw herself on her husband's neck, gripping his lips, hung on him like a pear for about five seconds, then, breaking away, took a breath and said in his ear:

"You were so ... courageous! I want you so much! You are a real man!

- Hey, hey, you namilis at night! - Zadar shouted and pushing Sanda aside, she also hugged Ned, leaving traces of powder smelling of flowers on his cheek - well done, boy! Goraz, clever girl, is that how you taught him ?! I'll clip you too! Come here ... oooh! Who is this with us ?! Costa, darling! Go quickly to Aunt Zadara! Haven't seen you in ages! Oh, you heard ... well, a real bear! How does Elsa stand you? You'll crush her!

- Normally endures - Geresard boomed, hugging the old woman - and you, auntie, are energetic and just as beautiful as always!

- Here is a ladies' man! Believe me - once he was such a handsome man, all the girls used to dry on this doctor! True, he was big then. Many girls were afraid - how they would squeeze ... Elsa was not afraid, and she was not mistaken - she turned out to be a great family man. Beautiful healthy kids, a great family - just the envy of everyone. My daughter is beautiful - you should have seen, no worse than your Sanda!

- He saw - Geresard winked embarrassedly - and saw the kids. He even taught me a little wisdom. By the way - they are sitting there, watching! - the doctor waved his hand, and from the edge of the site two smiling young men answered him - Ned, did you seriously injure Eston there? Where did you put it?

- He stabbed the captain in the groin with his right sword, and hit the back of the head with his left - Tiraz chuckled - a clear victory. In a real fight, he would castrate the guy, and then blow off half his head. Well done.

"Fffuuu… castrating is so cruel! - Zadar frowned - to deprive a man of the most precious thing, what he thinks!

- Hmmm ... I wonder then, what do you think women think? - said Geresard thoughtfully.

- I will not say - Zadara grunted grumpily, and burst into a ringing laugh. The cooks, Sanda, Ned, and everyone else began to laugh at her. They rolled with laughter so that the spectators, watching the course of the second fight, began to look back at them.

However - that ended very quickly. In a matter of moments, Shusard broke the jaw of the swordsmen lieutenant with his sword, which made Geresar winced and said that now he would have to use the services of the magicians, go to them.

- Why aren't they here today? Ned asked, bewildered.

- Well, of course - they are above all! The show is not for them, and they never took part in public festivities. Well, of course - these are magicians! They can't!

- And why are magicians so disliked in the Corps? Ned asked with interest.

- Why? - Geresard frowned his forehead - why ... but who knows? Well ... we don't like them, that's all. They are always separate, always clean and important with their secrets and arrogance. Maybe we envy - he honestly admitted with a crooked grin - but we will never say about it. Magicians are always with money, always in a special position, even their food is separate, like colonels or generals. And we used to gnaw crackers. And also - people do not like something unknown, strange, not amenable to understanding. Therefore, we are not the only ones who dislike them. All residents of the city. Mages live separately, even in a military town they do not crawl out of the agar. So ... You are called! Good luck!

The next fight ended quickly. The lieutenant of the crossbowmen was openly afraid of Ned, and he dealt with him in an instant - knocking out a long sword and putting a second, short one, to the enemy's neck. The crossbowman sighed with relief, saluting Ned, ran to pump himself up with beer - and at the tournament he lit up under the admiring gaze of the ladies, and was not injured. Is it worth celebrating with a beer?

Shusard dealt with his opponent just as quickly. It has long been clear that the two duelists will meet at the tournament site. Everyone knew about the duel. There was not a single person left who did not know that Shusard promised to nail Ned's head over the gate of the estate, and also that Ned accused the lieutenant's father, retired Major Shusard, of killing Colonel Ivarron.

The news, having bypassed the entire parade ground, was overgrown with new details and now one half of the audience said that the major was definitely a killer, and where is the guard looking?

The second claimed that Ned and the lieutenant were fighting over Ned's wife, whom he allegedly caught with Lieutenant Shusard in bed after returning from duty. The sergeant forgave his wife, as it usually happens (how not to forgive such a beauty ?!), but the lieutenant decided to castrate and nail his "household" over the gates of his house.

At the same time, no one was interested in the fact that Ned did not have any home of his own, and therefore he could not find his wife in the arms of the lieutenant. But everyone was confident that Ned would try to fulfill his intentions, since he had already conducted training on Eston, punching the unfortunate captain in the groin.

The subsequent fights were quiet, rather routine and even boring. Ned and Shusard were busily destroying the swordsmen's hopes for a big jackpot, and it was clear that the tournament leadership was setting the participants for fights so that the lieutenant and sergeant would not meet among themselves until the very last, final battle.

There were about twenty of all the participants. Among them were those who came with the general. Either they seriously expected to take a big prize, or they just wanted to light up in front of the audience, but in any case, their hopes were not destined to come true - Shusard and Ned cut them down the way a mower chops down fresh meadow grass - with rustling and whistling.

If anyone could compete with these two fighters, it was Aston, but he sat on a bench by the table gloomy, hunched over as if he had diarrhea and filled his sadness with a mug of strong, strongest beer that the merchant had, Neda with the last words. Today he was to visit a high-ranking and very pretty lady who adored dashing grunts, and his genitals turned into a continuous bruise and swollen to the size of an udder - why should he love Ned? In addition, my head ached terribly, in the back of the head of which the sergeant's merciless sword fell.

Aston remembered with slight annoyance and shame how he boasted to Ned, discussing how he would deal with him, and cursed the day this unsmiling guy appeared on the Corps parade ground.

Ned sat on the bench next to his loved ones, and he felt good - a beautiful, loving wife, friends, a healthy body - what else does he need to be happy? Perhaps Ned was happy.

However - he had nothing to compare with. From a completely vile, cruel reality, he was suddenly thrown into another world, in which he found himself at the top. And Ned could not believe that he was not dreaming, and that all this would not disappear one fine moment. Life had taught him that short pleasant moments are usually followed by long periods of trouble, and Ned subconsciously expected this deterioration and did not relax.

Several times he wondered why he went to the Shusards and declared the major a criminal, a murderer? At first, he himself did not know what prompted him to do this. He suddenly understood - it SHOULD be done. And now, sitting on the bench while resting between fights, he reasoned - so why, what happened to him? The fact that he was pushed to this step by the second - I sitting in his brain - is understandable. But why did he do that?

And after a while I came to the conclusion - it was necessary, yes. Help Zadar? Why help her? She already knew who the killer was. I would like to punish him - I would have punished him long ago. She felt more guilty than pinned it on Hagar. If Zadara had behaved more modestly and had not slept with Shusard, then most likely her husband would have been alive. At least Hagar wouldn't have killed him. She was the prize over which the men grappled. And being a smart woman, Zadara understood this perfectly.

What then? A personal relationship between a lieutenant and a sergeant? Oddly enough - yes. They are sent to the front, where the same lieutenant will own the life and death of Ned. And if he sends a sergeant to hell, to certain death, he will have to go. And Ned read in the lieutenant's mind a certain desire to settle scores with Ned. In any way. Or kill, or bring him to the officer's court, accusing him of unwillingness to carry out his orders. If Ned refuses to carry out even the notoriously stupid, murderous order of the lieutenant is a serious military crime.

Why did Shusard hate commoners so much? Education, of course. You never know the nobles contemptuously treat ordinary people, consider them half-animals, unworthy of human treatment? And even among them Shusard was distinguished by extreme extremism, carefully nurtured and cherished by his "father". However - and as a mother, too - she came from an old clan of the tenth rank, almost a royal family, therefore she contemptuously treated everyone who was below her origin. An exception was left by Colonel Ivarron - a real male, even if he was from a noble family of only the fifth rank. But he was handsome, and in bed beyond praise, unlike Shusard, a listless and loose type.

So it was definitely beneficial for Ned to get the lieutenant out of his way, if only in order to preserve his life and health. Reading the thoughts of others is sometimes absolutely necessary in order to save your life ...

Of course, it is unpleasant to constantly hear other people's thoughts, especially evil and cruel ones, from people unpleasant to you, but if this can save your life ... where to go?

Ned tried not to listen to other people's thoughts, but from time to time purposefully listened to those on whom his fate depended. And as it turned out - not in vain.

In fact, Ned conspired to assassinate his commander using the laws of the kingdom. He did everything for the lieutenant to give him a reason to challenge him to a duel. Or for him to call him himself. And one more thing - Ned knew that he needed to move up the career ladder, which means that the image of a desperate grunt, a duelist would come in handy.

Ned made decisions intuitively, just knowing what he needed to do. And so far his second-self has not failed.

Sometimes he felt annoyed - where is he thinking, and where are the thoughts of his second nature? How do you know where Ned is thinking and where is his double? But after agonizing thought on this topic, having acquired a headache, a spoiled mood, Ned stopped trying to distinguish between thoughts. So far, everything was fine, so was it worth it to strain your brain ?.

- Sergeant Ned Black and Lieutenant Anton Shusard are summoned to the main battle of the tournament! Gentlemen! Due to the fact that an agreement has been concluded between the opponents to duel to death, the battle will be fought with military weapons. Both are invited to provide weapons for inspection. Seconds, deliver the weapon to the master!

Tiraz nodded his head to Ned, took both swords and, slowly, under the gaze of the audience, went to the table of the senior officers. Everyone was watching him intently, and someone, apparently, recognized, because a whisper went through the rows.

The lieutenant's second was his father, who sullenly, ignoring those around him, walked quickly in front of the rows and laid his swords on the steward's table.

Ten minutes later, the inspection of the weapon was completed, and the seconds returned to their places. Now they were responsible for the weapons with their honor and even their lives. After the battle, they will inspect the weapon again, making sure that there were no additives on it like a film of poison, and that this is the very weapon that they examined. But if the listed mischiefs are discovered, the second will answer in all the severity of the law. Up to the deprivation of his life.

This was followed very strictly. Duels were part of the life of high society, and it, this very society, did not want to be a fool. Especially if there were bets on the duel. And this was almost always - after bed entertainments, bets on fights, on horse races, on anything else - were the main entertainment for the king's subjects. And for the king himself, too.

- Opponents - come together! - commanded the steward, and Ned, taking in his hands both blades, already freed from their black patent clothes, slowly walked to the center of the platform, where Shusard was waiting for him - tense, predatory, like a wild animal preparing to jump.

One step ... another step ... and another ... eye to eye ... movements are slow, insinuating. The noise around has died down, and only the wind rustles in the ears, and somewhere in the height a bird is whistling for a long time, hunting for insects.

Who will strike first? It's always harder to be the first. Any mistake you make can lead to an unpredictable, and even sad result. Going with the flow is always easier, but choosing your own path, your own path ...

The right hand is extended far to the side, the left is extended towards the opponent. He is as tense, as alert as you are. His foot in soft boots moved slightly from side to side, as if pressing closer to the ground of the parade ground, looking for support ... for what? For an attack? Yes!!! Let's start!

Biting, and at the same time soft criss-cross blows, leg sweeping, lunge - past. Precious blades with subtle singing take the blow of the enemy on themselves, trembling, and wanting to drink his blood. Now, now, dear ones, you will taste this beautiful, thick, salty liquid, the basis of everything!

Whistle of the Right, a short rustle of the Left - there is! A red line swollen with blood on the enemy's hand, and the parade ground was decorated with red stars marking the enemy's steps.

Just a scratch, yes, but it has a psychological meaning - the enemy is already slightly shaken. A thought rushes through his brain: "It can't be!" Prior to that, he almost never received wounds, damage in duels. Natural speed and acquired skills allowed him to sneer at opponents the way he wanted. And so - what is it ?! He realizes that he can actually die, and this thought chills his hands, binds his feet with a grave cold. But the enemy is too experienced. By an effort of will, he overcomes the chilling fear of the soul and comes into a battle rage, increasing strength, speed, allowing him to ignore wounds, pain and fatigue.

Yes, there is a way to win, which is available to a few of the masters, but this way is vicious. It washes away the strength of the body. After such a fight, the master will lie down in bed for a day and will lose several zusans of weight. But it will win. Or he will fall on the site without strength, putting his head under the enemy's sword. But the enemy still needs to live up to this moment.

Ned bends, twirls, meets the enemy blades with his runes, passes the enemy swords so close to his body that one of them cut off a piece of the collar of his shirt, as if it was not a silk cloth, but a spider web. Blades are the sharpest, cutting light female hair on the fly. One mistake and you're dead.

There are no thoughts in the lieutenant's head. He seemed to have become an extension of the blades - a ruthless war machine.

Ned knew that Shusard had been practicing fencing almost from his infancy, that then he continued his studies at the best school in the capital. It was not for nothing that the lieutenant won the Silver Sword. In fact, he was the strongest in the school, but ... the first place was taken by the director's son, also a strong master. He should have won, and he won, that guy. He's the son of a lyricist. Unfair, yes.

This guy did not understand who killed him when the winner was leaving the inn on a dark night. Neither the reaction of the master nor the skill saved them - what can you do against the sword falling on your head from around the corner? The director was in grief, the whole school was worried - but the killer was never found.

Ned knew a lot, a lot about this man who had become his commander. How ambitious he was, how far his plans extended, and how promiscuous the lieutenant was about the means to achieve these goals. And how strong he is.

Ned had no illusions - Shusard was almost equal to him in the ability to wield a sword. Almost ... but that was almost everything. What is almost? Almost won? Almost dead? There is no "almost" in battle. Either he died or he survived. And if your skill, under equal conditions, is higher than that of the enemy, you are the winner.

From the side it seemed that Shusard was winning - incessant blows, the ringing from which spreads throughout the hushed field. Ned steps back, twisting like a snake and with obvious difficulty parrying the blows of a distraught opponent. But why only the lieutenant is bleeding? Why is Ned unharmed, and, as if reluctantly, beats off Shusard's blades, not wanting to lie down and die, as a rootless upstart should be?

One mistake - and the sword for the left hand flies off along with this very hand, or rather with its hand. Blood splashes in a fountain, pouring over the face, turning it into a terrible, demonic mask.

Several women gasped and fainted, seeing such a terrible picture, the men began to hum, discussing what had happened - but the battle did not stop. The enemy, not feeling pain, practically losing control of his mind, continued the fight with one hand, laughingly directing a gushing stump into Ned's face, flooding his eyes and preventing him from blinking.

Ned took a couple of steps back, as if trying to escape, the lieutenant rushed forward with a roar and ... the sword with a crunch cut his ribs, entering half of his body.

Turnover! The tip dug into the solar plexus, coming out of the back. Ned's opponent strung himself on the blade, stepping forward in another swing.

Ned took his sword to the Left one, tore the Right one out of the dead, but not yet aware of his death, body, and with an oblique movement from bottom to top, from right to left, cleanly took off Shusard's head. Then he stepped aside so that the decapitated corpse would not fall on him, and froze, lowering both swords.

Silence. Silence again. Only a sobbing on the bench - the elder Shusard was crying. Not out of pity for my son. He never had much paternal love for the offspring of the one he killed. No. Shusard cried out of rage, from the impossibility of doing what he wanted. And he wanted to kill, tear to pieces, destroy this impudent boy, who destroyed everything that he had created for many years - status, position, respect of people. Now he is a retired major, a murderer whose guilt has not been proven, but who is known to everyone. A person who is ashamed to accept in your home is indecent. Even shaking hands is indecent, much less dealing with such a bastard. In such a tight enclave parasitizing the Infantry Corps, it was very, very unpleasant. A cramped world in which you can't hide, the same people, the same faces. Now - just leave. Leave the city. Or maybe the country.

The people on the benches are noisy, clapping, screaming! Even well-mannered ladies scream as if they were not noble mothers of families, but simple street vendors, accustomed to express their opinions with fierce shouts. Today Ned is the idol of the crowd. He gave them an unforgettable pleasure, an adventure that they had never seen before. And for that they loved him with all their hearts. In their closed world, devoid of events, he gave them the Spectacle. Hail Ned! * * *

- You were magnificent - Tyraz was solemn and laconic - you are the Master!

- I am delighted! - Zadara happily tugged at Ned's sleeve, while Sanda carefully wiped the blood off her husband's face - you need to drink for it!

"I don't drink..." Ned tried to resist, but the old woman had already handed him a large mug of wine, and Ned, wincing, slowly pulled out the red, tart liquid. There was a noise in my head at once, the world became bright, noisy, colorful ... it started spinning, spinning ...

He was congratulated - familiar and unfamiliar, clapped on the shoulders, hugged, kissed. Some women, young and not very hung around their necks, Sanda shoved them away and almost got into a fight with one girl who stuck on Ned's lips.

He was presented with an award, presented to the general, who for a long time muttered something about real young officers, the hope of the kingdom, boo-boo-boo ...

Ned seemed to pass out, becoming a puppet, taking everything as if it was not happening to him. He smiled, said something, answered someone, but all this passed by my consciousness. Then, he was left alone, no small merit in what was Sandy and Zadara. They, like klushki attacked anyone who tried to disturb Ned's peace, and then - they simply dragged him home, putting him on a cab, which had accumulated at the gates of the base of a dozen and a half - they all found out about the holiday, and after all, people would leave him, so they got together all the whip and reins sharks at the greasy feeder.

Ned was brought to their house with Sanda, after which Zadar left, leaving him in the care of his wife. She gently took the precious swords from her husband, placing them next to the bed, then undressed and sat in the bath, washing off the remnants of someone else's blood and slowly combing his hair. After washing it properly, she took him to bed and climbed into the bath herself. Soon they were fast asleep, embracing, as beloved should be.

Ned woke up late at night, even before the first roosters. They say that at this time, demons prowl the earth, looking for lost souls in order to take them to their underworld. The world sleeps, the sky sleeps, and only distant stars, torn off by the mighty winds, sweep across the black sky to fall and drown in the endless sea.

Sanda quietly slept beside her, holding up her strong breasts with brown nipples hardened from the night's coolness, her swollen lips were slightly parted, her neat little nose brought out quiet roulades, singing the anthem of the night.

Ned smiled, admiring the sight of his sleeping wife, and carefully covered her with a sheet, keeping her out of the cold. At night it really became cool, the peak of the heat had already passed, and the world was moving towards autumn.

His head was cracking, and Ned thought with annoyance that he shouldn't have agreed to drink this demon wine. After all, he knew that wine drinking was not his skill. That nothing good will come of it - and here's to you! I got drunk from one mug! I didn't even watch the rest of the competition. It's a shame!

Then Ned wondered - what woke him up now? Something was bothering him, spinning in his head.

Ned quietly got out of bed, tucking the sheet under his wife's bare thigh, and walked over to the bucket of water. He picked up a ladle and began to drink greedily, spilling water on his chest.

Suddenly, with a peripheral vision, he saw a shadow flicker outside the window. Ned put the ladle down and quietly tiptoed to the window. Exactly! Outside the window, people ran across, rustles and whispers were heard. Ned remorsefully thought that he had left his spear in the base's weapons room, and rushed to the swords on the floor by the bed. There was no time to look for clothes, and he grabbed swords, then pushed the sleeping Sanda:

- Wake up! Hurry!

The girl opened her eyes, saw Ned and held out her hands to him:

- Nice! Come to me! I just dreamed of you ... so handsome, so courageous ... I want you so much! Go quickly!

- Get up! - Ned said sharply, in a low voice - the house is surrounded. It looks like they are going to attack us now. Put on some clothes and go to bed! Do not get up under any circumstances, and do not come out - until I call!

Sanda jumped out of bed, like a madman rushed around the room, seized with horror and completely lost orientation in space. Ned silently grabbed the dress he had thrown off the evening off the floor, threw it over her shoulder and pushed her against the wall. The girl sank to the floor and began to dress feverishly, pulling on her clothes and squealing softly at the same time:

- Mama! Mommy! Aaaaaa ....

- Shut up - Ned said heavily, saw, at last, his pants, boots, in a few seconds put them on, took swords and sat down on the bed, pondering what was happening. But he was not allowed to think it over.

The door fell off its hinges, knocked out by a mighty blow - the attackers dragged a log from somewhere, rocked it, and with this ram they demolished a not very strong barrier.

In the doorway silently ran people, dressed in dark clothes, with their faces wrapped up and with swords in their hands. Ned was already standing in front of the door, in the middle of the room, relaxed, filled with the Force and ready to fight. Swords sang, steel rang. The first two attackers died almost simultaneously, at intervals of a split second. The other two died on the doorstep, pierced through.

Ned jumped out into the garden, and immediately found himself in the midst of enemies. There were at least three dozen of them - professionals in their field, they did not interfere with each other, did not crowd, did not climb forward. When the attempt to take Ned sleepy failed, they changed tactics.

A short man, whose dark eyes were hidden in the shadow of a hood, quietly ordered:

- Networks!

Several people immediately appeared, who began to prepare thin nets for catching people for throwing - they were slave traders who traded in human goods. Then Ned knew - it's time!

He stuck his swords into the ground, and in front of the astonished slavers, he began to cast a spell.

Unfamiliar words fell in silence like cast-iron weights, and after a few seconds half of the robbers lay on the ground, twitching with pain, pressing their legs against the pain-torn stomach.

One of those who remained on his feet screamed heart-rendingly, breaking the darkness of the night:

- Let's run! Save yourself! This is a black magician! What fool said that it was a simple sergeant ?! Freaks!

About ten robbers rushed to the gate, and some ran to the fence, hoping to escape in the dark.

No.

Two squads of demons, launched by a black magician, rushed after both groups and knocked them down, devouring from the inside, turning the entrails into bloody mince.

Ned moved his hands, uttered a short phrase, and a ball of white flame shone over the garden, small, dim, but enough to see what was happening — he still learned how to use this spell.

Then Ned took out his Right Sword, walked over to the groaning bandit and lightly slashed him across the neck, releasing the blood that fountained towards the blade and washed the sharp blade with a warm, soaring jet. Ned's mouth opened, and words poured out - terrible, hissing, like the roar of a beast and the hiss of a snake. The blood boiled, and before my eyes it began to be absorbed into the metal, as if it were porous, like a sponge. The blade flickered, the runes glowed, a demon escaped from the body of the slain and was immediately drawn into the sword, sucked like rainwater into a sewer hatch. The sword shuddered in his hands, accepting the guest, and calmed down, becoming warm as blood.

Approaching the next person, Ned did the same for the Left Sword. It didn't take long.

Then - Ned walked through the garden, killing everyone who was still alive. He tried to strike as if these people had died in a sword fight. The demons that ate the bandits, upon contact with the cursed swords, immediately left the body and returned to where they came from. Where to? Probably to Hell, where they belong.

Ned went around all the bodies and pierced each with a sword, driving out the demons. Finally, there were only corpses in the garden, and a luminous ball, which Ned extinguished with two words.

- What was it? - Suddenly heard behind the voice of Sanda - Ned, you are a magician ?! So it's true - what you said ?! Are you a black magician ?!

Ned walked up to Sanda, who was looking around in horror, and looking into her eyes, said quietly:

- You didn't see anything. You know nothing. Remember this!

His eyes were as dark as two wells, terrible, and it seemed to Sanda that in them she saw an underground fire. The girl shuddered, and involuntarily recoiled from Ned's hand, with which he touched his wife's cheek. She nodded shallowly, frightened so much that she almost wet herself with fear.

Emitting a vague muffled sound, Sanda ran to the corner of the house, and she vomited for a long time, tearing her insides, painfully and scary.

Ned waited for the seizure to end, went up to his wife and took her inside the house, put her to bed and covered her with a blanket. Sandu was shaking, she shuddered, curled up into a ball, and did not pay attention to either Ned or what was happening around.

He sat next to her, waited for the girl to fall asleep, and began to "clean up". Four corpses, which covered the entire floor in the house with blood, he took one by one out into the garden and threw them on the ground. Then he lifted the door and tried to somehow fit it into place. None of this, of course, worked, and Ned abandoned the idea.

And then a terrible thought struck him. Grabbing his swords, Ned rushed to the two-story house of Zadara, where he was horrified to find that the door was also knocked out. Having carefully penetrated into the room, Ned went up to the second floor and immediately came across Asana's body.

A huge dark-skinned woman was lying in the hallway, holding her heavy ax in her hands. Near her are four corpses, cut almost in half. The woman has several deep sword wounds, under her is a pool of blood.

Further, at the door of Zadara's bedroom is Pegra's corpse, a crossbow lies nearby, and a bolt sticks out in the wall. She missed.

Zadara lay next to her broken neck, staring at the ceiling with calm, bright eyes. On it lay the corpse of the murderer, from its back protruded the tip of a dagger Ned knew, with which Zadara never parted.

Ned's eyes burned, but he did not cry. I didn't know how.

After standing by the body of the old woman, who almost became his mother, Ned looked into her eyes for the last time, bent down, and closed them - forever. Then he went out into the corridor, went down the stairs and went to his house. Having searched the surroundings with his mind-hearing, he was convinced that there were no hiding robbers anywhere. Then he dressed to the end, put on swords, and went to the gate - it was necessary to notify the authorities about the incident and demand punishment of the one who sent these people. But, most likely, Shusard was no longer at the estate.

Epilogue.

The old women were buried together, in the family tomb of the Ivarrons, next to Colonel Cedar Ivarron.

There were voices in favor not to bury the two cooks next to Zadara, but her papers revealed a will, according to which she demanded that they be buried next to her. There they were put to rest, especially since Tyraz, the funeral director, sharply insisted on fulfilling the will of the deceased. Women have not been slaves for a long time, and died like soldiers, defending their mistress, therefore they deserve a good rest. In recent years, they were the only friends of Zadara, as she wrote in her will.

According to the same will, she signed the house with all the property to her adopted son Tiraz, who had been helping her all these years.

Oddly enough - the old woman did not forget Ned either - she included him in her will, giving him the house in which he lived all these days.

The most interesting thing is that the will was written in the evening of the same day when all the events took place on the parade ground. Zadara seemed to know what was coming soon. And perhaps she knew - because the women slept with weapons in their hands and were ready for battle. Like no one else, Zadara knew her former lover Hagar well ...

Shusard was not found in the estate. He urgently sailed on his ship in an unknown direction, taking from the house everything that he could hastily collect. And what he could not - domestic animals, livestock - he destroyed everything. Animals were mercilessly killed, and furniture, walls, dishes were chopped up and destroyed. He did not burn the house, apparently because it would attract the attention of neighbors.

Sanda did not endure the events of the night well. She shuddered when she saw Ned, got scared, and asked to stay with her parents in order to calm down and forget about what happened. Ned didn't protest - he heard her thoughts. She was afraid of her husband, a black magician who controlled demons. She was afraid to such an extent that even his touch was unpleasant to her.

Ned sadly thought that all good things must come to an end - and this white streak seems to be over. However, they still remained husband and wife. At least for now. Officially.

Ned had a long military campaign ahead of him, so perhaps the old relationship with time will return - everything is once forgotten, dragged out by the mud of time ...

The guards and commanders were satisfied with Ned's story that he single-handedly killed thirty people. He justified this by the fact that he ran around the garden in the dark and killed them one by one, knowing well the territory of the neglected garden.

They did not call the mages for investigation - the death of the robbers from the blade was obvious. If anyone had any questions about the nature of the wounds, they kept quiet. Everyone needed this story to calm down sooner. Who needs this noise, investigation, squabbling? The perpetrator is known - he was put on the wanted list. The henchmen were punished by the heroic sergeant, who was awarded the "Star of Courage" for steadfastness in the fight against the enemy, and ... that's all. Closed the question.

Five days after the commission headed by the red-faced general left the corps, an order came to send the Corps to the front, and the running, bustle, economic squabbles began, in which the latest events drowned. The main thing remained - the war, which was getting closer and closer to the capital of Zamar.

Six days after the events described, Ned stood on the prow of a huge landing craft, one of the three that transported the Corps to the landing site, breathing in the fresh sea air with delight, peering into the horizon and thinking about what lay ahead. With him he had only his weapons, ancient scrolls and memories of friends and love, which, perhaps, he had already lost. Or maybe she wasn't there? Who knows ... End of the first book.

CPSIA information can be obtained
at www.ICGtesting.com
Printed in the USA
LVHW021637140721
692677LV00012B/928

9 798562 325747